MURDERS & ROMANCE

LASHELL COLLINS

This book is a work of fiction. Names, characters, places, and incidents are either a product of the author's imagination or are used fictitiously. Any resemblance to actual events, locales, or people — living, dead, or undead — is entirely coincidental and not intended by the author. This book contains content that may not be suitable for young readers (under age 18).

1

The little girl's high-pitched scream felt like a needle piercing his temple, and Detective Isaac Taylor woke with a start.

Panting.

Sweating.

His heart was running a marathon.

Damn dream. It wasn't the first time he'd had it. It wasn't even the first time he'd woken up in a cold sweat because of it. The case was over. The Lullaby Killer was dead. Hell, Isaac had killed the bastard himself. Well... sort of.

Death by telekinesis.

Had that really happened?

He sat up and shook his head as if to clear it of the ghosts, then he looked over at Sidney. She was sleeping peacefully. Finally. A sense of immense relief spread throughout his chest, and he reached out and gently moved a stray curl from her lovely face.

He hoped she was having a sweet dream.

Sliding out of bed, he intended to go pee. But his ringing cell-phone had him reaching for it with lightning speed so that it didn't wake Sidney.

"Taylor."

He could hear both the sleep and the aggravation in his own voice.

"Morning, Detective Sergeant."

The dispatcher's tone was clipped and efficient, and much too perky for this time of night.

"There's a dead body down on University Circle, near the Case Western campus. Officer on scene says it's pretty gruesome, sir."

Isaac sighed and glanced at the digital clock. 3:45 am.

"All right. Call Detective Vega. I'll be there as soon as I can."

He ended the call and looked back at Sidney. She was still sleeping soundly, thank goodness. As long as it had taken her to fall asleep, the last thing he wanted was for it to be cut short.

He headed for the bathroom to shower and get ready. Fifteen minutes later, he was out the door.

He climbed behind the wheel of his metallic blue Mustang GT thinking about how he and his partner, Pete Vega, had been pulling a whole lot of overtime these last two weeks, covering not one fallen detective team, but two. He'd been a detective for over nine years, and he couldn't ever remember a time when they'd been stretched this thin.

He pulled up at the location and looked around. University Circle was a busy hub of one square mile. Sort of a converging point for Case Western Reserve University, several hospital facilities, and many different cultural destinations — like museums, music halls, botanical gardens, college bars, and restaurants. In fact, one of his favorite ramen noodle joints was part of the busy University Circle hub.

Isaac got out of his car just as Pete pulled up. They acknowledged each other with the standard silent 'what's up' lift-of-the-chin guys always did, and made their way over to where the pair of uniforms stood with a body. And Isaac did a double take at that body.

"Jesus."

The horrified whisper dropped from his lips as Isaac studied the crime scene.

The body was completely naked and tied, spread-eagled, to a large tree trunk. The victim was male. Or at least, he had been before he was thoroughly and completely castrated.

Blood.

Everywhere he looked there was blood. And the victim's, uh... appendage was lying on the ground at the body's feet.

"Holy Mother of God," Pete said.

Isaac's gaze darted all around, weeding out the CSU members and taking in the important details. There were no discarded clothes anywhere. That meant whoever had done this heinous deed wanted their victim to be publicly humiliated in death. This staging had been carefully deliberate.

Isaac quietly cleared his throat and turned to the nearest uniform.

"Who found the body?"

"Those two there." The female officer pointed a few yards away to where her partner stood with two college-aged women, and then consulted her notes. "Kim Barns and Leslie Rowan. They were returning to the university about an hour ago."

"Thanks." Isaac motioned to Pete and they walked over to the women. "Detective Sgt. Ike Taylor. Detective Pete Vega. Can you tell us what you two were doing out here so late? Or early?"

The one to his right flipped her green hair over her shoulder. "We both work at one of the bars in the circle. So, we walk back to campus together. Safety in numbers, right?"

"Do either of you know the victim?"

"I think I've seen him around campus, but I don't really know him," the other one spoke up.

"And you are?"

"I'm Kim Barns."

"And you mean you've seen the victim around the Case Western campus?"

"Yes, sir. Leslie and I are both undergrads."

"And what about him? You know?"

The girl shook her head. "No. I'm sorry."

Isaac looked around and pointed to the path they were on.

"This trail. Is it normally a popular place?"

"Yes," green-hair spoke up again. "I walk this way all the time. It's normally full of people in the daytime."

"And when does it typically slow down? About what time?"

"Usually when it gets dark. This time of year around 8 or 9 at night."

"And did you see anyone else near the body? Did you pass anyone else on the path?"

"No." Both girls shook their heads and answered in unison.

"Okay." Isaac sighed. "Thank you both. Don't leave town. We may have more questions later."

He motioned to Pete, and his partner handed out a couple of cards to the girls, saving Ike from the dreaded skin-on-skin contact. Then they walked back over to the body.

"What do you think?" Pete nodded back toward the girls.

"I think it would definitely take the both of them to string a guy his size up like this. But with the amount of blood here, they'd both be covered in it after it was done."

"Agreed. Not to mention that whoever did this had to be very pissed at this man. You do not cut off a guy's junk for the fun of it."

Isaac shook his head in agreement.

"No, you don't. But without a positive ID on him, we've got nowhere to start. Let's leave CSU to do their thing and see what Hiroshi has to say. Meantime, you and I will go through Case Western's student roster. Maybe we'll get an ID that way."

He dug his cellphone from his pocket and took a picture of the victim's face.

"Or... you could give him a touch," Pete said. "See what you see."

Isaac glared at him. "Or not."

Pete held up his hands in surrender.

Isaac looked back at the body and briefly entertained the idea. Since his ordeal with the Lullaby Murders a few weeks ago, and what he'd been through after touching each of those poor little girls, he was less than eager to touch another murder victim. At least so soon. He knew it would be the fastest way to glean useful information, but he simply couldn't bring himself to do it.

"I'll meet you back at the station, Pete."

"Yep."

Pete's response was distracted, and Isaac understood perfectly. The scene was grisly. Isaac would even call it macabre.

"Come on," he said in an effort to get his partner moving.

They headed to their respective cars and, once behind the wheel of his, Isaac's thoughts drifted from the horrific crime scene to his Sidney.

He thought about how peacefully she was sleeping when he'd left, and for some reason the thought warmed him.

A ghost of a smile crossed his lips when he remembered the joy he'd felt at learning she was pregnant. That he was going to be a father. The idea of it blew his mind even now.

He pulled into the back lot of the police station and parked behind a row of marked black and white cruisers. Then he yawned as he headed inside the building. He was tired, but the nearly 4 am call-out was only part of the reason.

There wasn't really much he and Pete could do at this hour besides begin the preliminary paperwork and make notes for when the university offices opened later in the morning and they could speak to someone. After seeing to those things, and beginning a case board with the victim's picture and a big question mark for the name, Isaac turned to Pete.

"Go home, partner. Get a couple more hours sleep or eat

some food. Meet me back here at eight o'clock sharp and we'll head to the university."

"Sounds good."

They both dragged themselves up from their desks and headed out of the detective's pit.

2

"Tell me the truth, Ike. How is she really doing?"

Simon's voice was full of concern, and Isaac was grateful that he had such a good relationship with his future brother-in-law. He took a deep breath and thought about the question, and about how quiet Sidney had been at breakfast just a few minutes ago.

"I don't know, Simon. She's not good. I mean... physically she's fine. Emotionally she's just not her usual bubbly self. But it's only been a couple of days though."

"Do you think I need to come?"

"No, no." Isaac shook his head as though Simon were in the room with him and could see the gesture. "I don't think you need to take leave and miss work and all that. She'll be okay. It's just gonna take some time to get over, that's all."

He hoped he sounded more confident than he felt about the situation. Simon sighed, and Isaac could feel the weight of it even over the phone.

"Okay, I'm going to trust your judgment on this, Ike. But please call me if things change. I can be there in less than 4 hours."

"You know I'll keep you posted, Simon."

"Yeah. Hey, maybe she'll feel better once you two set a date, huh?"

His tone was lighter, and Isaac appreciated the attempt at levity.

"Yeah, maybe so. I'll catch you later, man."

"Yep. See you."

Isaac ended the call and glanced around the sunroom. Then he tucked his phone into his pocket and went in search of the woman in question. When he'd taken the call from her brother, Sidney had been in the kitchen cleaning up their breakfast dishes. Now the kitchen was empty.

He walked through the living room and wandered down the hall. He found her in their bedroom.

"Hey."

The sound of his voice made her jump, and Isaac watched her drop something into an open drawer and quickly close it.

"Hey," she replied quietly, running a hand over the back of her neck. Then her whole body sagged on a sigh. "I'm sorry."

Isaac moved closer and pulled her into his arms from behind, and looked at her face in the mirror.

"Darlin', you don't have to apologize. And you don't have to hide that little t-shirt from me either."

She leaned back against him. "It was silly of me to buy it in the first place."

"No, it wasn't. Sidney, you were happy. You were excited about being pregnant. About becoming a mom. About the new life we made together. There is nothing wrong with any of that."

Keeping one arm snugly around her, he reached out and opened the drawer. Then he pulled out the tiny t-shirt that was covered in teddy bears.

"And there's nothing wrong with hanging onto this as a way to remember that life. Even though it was fleeting. And someday real soon, there will be another baby. One that will actually get the chance to wear this itty-bitty thing."

She took the t-shirt from him and looked up into his eyes in the mirror.

"You really believe that?"

Isaac slowly turned her around to face him, and looked down into her eyes.

"Didn't the doctor tell us there was likely no medical reason why you can't conceive and carry a healthy baby in the future?"

Sidney nodded, but her eyes held so much hesitancy.

"Yes."

"Okay, then." Isaac caressed her face.

"So... we try again? Sometime?"

Her question was asked with a full load of uncertainty, almost as if she were afraid to hear his answer, and Isaac wondered why.

"If that's what you want, yes."

"But is that what you want?"

Was she for real? Did she actually need reassurance from him? Isaac gently took her face in both of his hands.

"Oh, Sidney. I want *everything* with you, darlin'. Don't you know that by now?"

She smiled at him, and his heart constricted. It was the first genuine smile he'd seen from her in two whole days.

"Hey. Just imagine my blond hair with your crazy curls on top of a chubby little face. How cute and funny would that be?"

The smallest of giggles spilled out of her, and Isaac's heart swelled with something akin to relief. He kissed her sweet lips.

"There's my girl. I've missed that laughter."

"I'm sorry."

"Um mmm. Don't be sorry, darlin'. You don't ever have to apologize for your pain. Just don't try to pretend it isn't happening either, okay? You don't have to hide it from me."

"You're sad too. I can see that."

"I am. I admit that I'm terrified of parenthood. But I was actually looking forward to taking that adventure with you."

He watched the tears well up in her eyes, then she leaned her head into his chest, and Isaac wrapped his arms around her again and kissed the top of her head.

"We will take that adventure together, Sid. We'll get our shot eventually. Grandad told me so."

"What?"

Sidney looked up at him, wiping silent tears, and Isaac caught one on his thumb.

"He wouldn't give me any details. Just implied that there would be a little one."

"Really? When did he tell you that?"

"When we met him in Tennessee. Remember the little blue teddy bear he gave me?"

"Yeah, the one that had been yours when you were little."

"Yeah. Well, he said he thought I might want to pass it down to my child in the near future."

"He saw something?" She sounded so hopeful. "With his superpowers?"

Isaac nodded, and Sidney's tears fell anew. But he was fairly certain they were tears of a different sort this time. She smiled at him, and Isaac was so happy to have made her feel at least a little bit better. He kissed her forehead.

"Well, I have to get going, I'm afraid. I have a very gruesome new case to get back to this morning." He stepped away and grabbed his gun, clipping the holster to his side. "You going to be okay?"

"Yes, I'm fine." She took a deep breath and squared her shoulders. "I'm going to go on into work too, so I also need to get moving."

Isaac wasn't sure he liked the sound of that.

"You sure you want to go back to work already?"

"I'm sure. I don't want to keep moping around here. I want to work. I followed the doctor's orders to get plenty of rest for the first 24 hours, and then some. Plus, I'm all cried out. Now, I just want to get back to my normal routine."

Isaac heard the determination in her voice, but he also felt the turmoil in her heart. He understood it. You couldn't simply turn off the sadness by flipping a switch, no matter how hard you might want to. Still, he wished he could change her mind about going back to work so soon.

"Well, you just take it easy on yourself today, okay Maybe just a half day?"

"I'm fine, Ike. Really."

He smiled at her and then kissed her lips. "Call me if you need me."

"Back at you."

He grinned at her spark of sass and kissed her once more.

"Love you."

"I love you back."

3

At the station, Isaac stood by in the briefing room and listened while Lieutenant Gavin Hayes conducted the morning briefing. He glanced around and took note of the detectives present, and those that were absent.

Gerri Miller still hadn't surfaced since her partner, Curt Dorn, had been shot during the apprehension of the Schiffer family in connection with the lullaby murders three weeks ago. Isaac silently swore, knowing that the mega-overtime hours were most likely going to continue for a while.

It wasn't just the loss of the Miller and Dorn detective team at the heart of their manpower crisis. Detectives Barker and Wheeler were both out for medical reasons. So, Hayes had wisely put their partners together to form a new team. But on a shift with only four detective teams, they were down two, and unfortunately homicide didn't take a vacation.

When the morning briefing was over, Isaac followed Gavin Hayes to his office and walked in uninvited.

"Still no Gerri?"

Gavin sighed very loudly, giving Isaac the impression that he really didn't care to talk about it.

"Something I can do for you, Sergeant?"

His tone solidified that first impression. But Isaac pressed on.

"I'm sorry, sir. But I'm just curious. I know it's only been two weeks since Dorn's funeral, but with Gary Barker's stomach troubles and Mark Wheeler's hernia, we seem to have lost the equivalent of two detective teams in one fell swoop here. The homicide unit's day shift is getting a little taxed. Pete and I were called out at quarter to four this morning."

Gavin put his hands on his hips and stared at Isaac.

"You don't think I know how shorthanded we are, Ike? It's my job to know these things. Now, I can't do much about Barker's bleeding ulcer, or Wheeler's recovery time from his hernia surgery. But I am diligently looking through the list of candidates to fill Dorn's position on this team."

"Yes, sir. I didn't mean to imply that you weren't." Isaac stepped further into the room. "I was just wondering about Gerri Miller. Have you heard from her? Has anyone?"

Gavin sighed once more and looked away.

"Have a seat, Sergeant."

Isaac walked over to the chair in front of his boss' desk and sat down. Gavin handed him a piece of paper and then took his own seat. Isaac studied the paper and then looked up at Gavin. Was this for real?

"She transferred out?"

The amount of shock and disappointment in his own voice was no surprise. Gerri was one of the best detectives in their unit, and Isaac hated to lose her.

"She gave me that form about a week before we closed the lullaby case and Dorn was shot. I never processed it."

Isaac handed the paper back to him and shook his head.

"I don't understand."

"I never authorized her request, and I didn't push the paperwork through because I was hoping to change her mind. Then

Dorn was killed, and per protocol, as his partner she was ordered to take a week off to get herself together."

"She's been off since he was shot. So, it's been *three* weeks now," Isaac stated the obvious with growing disgust at the situation.

"I know that."

"And? Has she called or reported in at all?"

"She has. And she's not doing well. She requested a leave of absence. Barker's stomach issues hadn't flared up yet at the time, so I granted the leave. On the condition that she see Dr. Clark Newman for a while."

Isaac sighed and sat back in the chair. He'd had his own run-in with the department's shrink, and he didn't envy her the intrusive conversation.

"So, do you think she'll be coming back here after her leave, or moving on to another precinct?"

Gavin spread his hands wide in an I-have-no-clue gesture before clasping them together, elbows on the desk, and rested his chin on them.

"Unfortunately, I don't know. But I do plan to go see her personally to check in. See how she's doing."

"She was a wreck at Dorn's funeral."

They were both silent for a moment, remembering the way their colleague had broken down at the service.

"Yeah," Gavin said quietly. His voice was stronger a second later. "Well, I'm reluctant to make this a search for two new detectives without first trying to hold on to Gerri. She's good at what she does, and I'd hate to lose her."

"I agree wholeheartedly. She's a damn fine detective, and this unit is better with her." Isaac just couldn't figure out her motives for requesting the transfer, and he shook his head again, puzzled. "Did she say why she wants to transfer to another precinct? I didn't realize she was unhappy here."

Gavin hesitated, and Isaac's overdeveloped sense of empathy

could suddenly feel his boss' unease at that question. It was palpable. And strong.

"She had personal reasons."

Isaac waited for more, but Gavin wasn't giving anything else away. The look on his face told Isaac that there was more to the story. A lot more. He refused to pry though.

"So... what do you need from me, sir? How can I help?"

"I'm glad you asked." Gavin reached for a small stack of manila file folders on the edge of his desk, and handed them to him. "These are files on the prospective candidates for Dorn's position. Look through them and bring me your recommendations."

Isaac took the pile of files, but he was surprised.

"You want *my* opinion on the new hire?"

"Well, the final choice will be mine, and the Chief's, of course. But I wouldn't mind your input. You know I like your instincts."

"Okay. Can I take these home with me and let you know my thoughts tomorrow?"

"Absolutely. In the meantime, tell me about this case you and Vega caught this morning. I heard it was... interesting."

"Yeah, that's one word for it." Isaac rolled his eyes. "Vic was spread eagled around the largest tree trunk I've ever seen, naked as the day he was born, and all his junk was cut clean off."

"All of it?"

"All. Of. It. We're waiting to hear back from Hiroshi on the cause of death, but my money would be on the genitalia excision."

"Damn."

Gavin visibly winched and moved his knees together. Isaac understood the impulse.

"Yeah. Pete and I are headed out to the University now to see if we can get a copy of a student roster or something similar. Try to ID our guy."

"Keep me posted."

"You do the same after you speak with Gerri."

Gavin nodded, and Isaac got up and left the office.

Once Isaac left for work, Sidney headed for the shower. She was getting a late start, having only just decided to put on her big girl pants and go back to work, so she tucked her mountain of curls under a satin-lined plastic shower cap. She didn't have time to blow them dry this morning.

She stood beneath the hot stream for a little longer than she'd planned. It was a big mistake. Lingering in the steam only gave her more time to think about what she'd lost.

She'd been so scared when the pink lines appeared on the stick. So worried about how Isaac would react to the news. So worried about his reaction that she hadn't even considered her own.

She hadn't been prepared for the overwhelming sense of joy. And when Isaac's eyes lit up, she knew that he was just as happy. They'd made a baby.

They'd basked in that joy for exactly eleven and a half days before it was ripped away.

Eleven and a half days.

Just long enough to fall in love with the idea.

Sorrow reached in and ripped out her heart all over again.

The tears streamed down her face, and the water washed over her.

One last cry.

That's what she told herself. She'd have this one last cry here in the shower, and then she would carry on with her life.

Ten minutes later she got out and dressed in a nice pair of brown slacks and a cream blouse with brown polka stars. She put on a matching pair of brown slingback pumps, wrangled her copious curls into a bun on top of her head, and added a pair of tiny pearl earrings to complete the look.

She stood in the mirror for a long time, staring at the chosen outfit and wondering why making herself pretty wasn't giving her the usual boost-my-mood feels.

"Because you're still sad, Sid," she mumbled at her reflection. "That's why."

She grabbed her purse, her car keys, and her I-can-do-this attitude, gave the cat a loving scratch, and then left.

She was grateful they'd only chosen to tell three people about the pregnancy. The three people they trusted most in life — her brother, Simon, and Ike's brother and sister-in-law, Adam and Bree.

In her car on the drive to Hope House, the women's shelter where she worked, she forced herself to think only of the day ahead.

"We're not going to wallow, Sidney. We're going to move forward."

The pep talk to herself wasn't completely working, but she decided she would just repeat it throughout the day, however many times she needed to hear it. She would focus on the work, not on her sorrows.

It wouldn't be a hardship. She enjoyed her work. In fact, she'd been loving it the past couple of weeks. Zoe Ridley, the shelter's owner and director, had been off recovering from minor brain surgery — an emergency procedure after being whacked in the head with the butt of Tom Billings' gun during a domestic disturbance when one of the residents' husbands had held them all hostage for several hours.

Thank God Isaac had been there to get them all out safely. But while Zoe recovered, Sidney had been in charge at the shelter, making sure things ran smoothly in Zoe's absence.

It was perfect timing that Zoe had come back to work when she did, just in time for Sidney to miss two days due to...

"But we're not going to dwell on that, Sid. We're not going to wallow; we're going to move forward."

She pressed on, navigating the morning traffic, and pulled up outside Hope House only fifteen minutes late.

She walked into the shelter and spotted a chubby-cheeked four-year-old with a syrup smile and a milk mustache standing in the kitchen doorway.

"Hi, Miss Sidney."

"Hi, Laney. Did you just have pancakes and milk for breakfast?"

The little girl nodded, and Sidney smiled at her.

"Laney, let me clean your face." The girl's mother, one of the residents, came to her wielding damp paper towels. "Oh, hi Sidney!"

"Good morning, Ann."

Sidney waved at the little girl and headed for the back office. Zoe looked up from her desk with a bright surprised smile.

"Sidney! You're back."

"I am."

"How are you feeling? I hear there's a summer flu bug going around. I only hope no one carries it into the house. That's all we'd need, right?"

Sidney smiled and locked her small purse in the bottom drawer of her desk, and took her seat. "Well, it won't be me. I didn't have the flu. I was just a little under the weather."

She had no intention of sharing the details of her absence with her boss or anyone else. It was no one's business as far as she was concerned.

"So, how are you doing, Zoe?"

"Oh, I'm fine. The doctors said my bleed was very minor. Whether it was caused by the blow from the gun or when my head hit the floor, they aren't completely certain. But they've given me a clean bill of health, and that's all that matters."

"Still... you should probably take it easy."

"Well, I'm not sure what your ailment was, but right back at you."

Her smile was coaxing, but Sidney simply grinned and let the subject drop.

"Any word on Diane and Tom Billings?"

Zoe looked disappointed at the change of topic, but she thankfully followed Sidney's lead.

"Yes, actually. Tom will be staying in police custody until his court date in three months."

"That's great to hear." Sidney nodded, and opened up her work files.

"Unfortunately, we'll all probably be called to testify. So, keep that in mind."

Sidney softly groaned at that idea.

"Diane has filed for divorce and is making plans to move to Palm Beach to be near her parents."

"Wonderful. A fresh start will be good for her."

She got to work on Dress For Success — the program where they took in donations of gently used business attire to help those residents who needed something nice to wear to a job interview, or to court. But she looked up to see Zoe watching her.

"What?"

"Hmm. What about your fresh start?"

Sidney felt her brow crinkle. "Excuse me?"

"Well, I know I got hit on the head pretty hard, but I seem to recall something about a spontaneous marriage proposal. It's been over three weeks now, yet I still don't see a ring on your finger. And you seem extremely distracted and a little blue. Is everything all right with you and your beau?"

The look she gave her bordered on pity, and Sidney huffed out a small breath.

"My beau and I are doing very well, thank you. I'm just... not a hundred percent yet, I guess."

She looked away, wondering why she felt so annoyed by Zoe's gentle probing. The woman was only trying to show concern. She glanced back at her and saw Zoe gearing up to respond, but someone caught her eye.

"Oh!"

Sidney turned to see Dr. Lance Tobey standing in the doorway. He stepped inside the office with a sheepish grin.

"Good morning, ladies. Hope I'm not interrupting."

"Of course not!" Zoe smiled at him. "Come on in. I have that paperwork you needed right here."

She grabbed a form from her desk and handed it to him.

"Oh, Sidney, I almost forgot to mention... We got a note from Carla Day yesterday. She and her children have settled down in Cincinnati. She begins her new job next week, and the boy... Kevin was his name, right? He was a student of yours?"

"Yes, that's right."

If it hadn't been for her helping Kevin when he was being bullied at the school Sidney was substitute teaching in, she never would have found the Hope House or her new job here.

"Well, Kevin will be starting school there in the fall," Zoe continued. "It sounds like they're really doing well. Here's the card if you'd like to read it."

Sidney moved to get up.

"Oh, I've got it."

Lance beat her to it, taking the card from Zoe and walking it over to Sidney's desk.

"Thank you."

Sidney reached for the card, but Lance purposely hung onto it, causing her to look up at him. When she did, he smiled at her and let go.

Sidney gave him a polite smile and then busied herself reading Carla's note. She took her time just to have an excuse to ignore him, but she could feel his eyes on her. She always felt his eyes on her whenever he was there volunteering.

It made her skin crawl with imaginary spiders.

"Well, I have to get to the hospital. Thanks for getting this together so quickly, Zoe."

"Oh, you're welcome."

"It was good seeing you both."

"Thanks, Lance!" Zoe called out. "We'll see you later."

"Sidney."

Even the sound of his voice made her uneasy.

She looked up at him, purposely distracted.

"Yes. Have a good day."

She turned quickly back to the pressing matters on her desk, and he left the office. She exhaled once he was gone.

"You're bad." Zoe's tone was amused, and Sidney glanced up to see her smirk.

"What?"

"He looks at you like a love-starved puppy, and you just ignore him."

"What would you have me do, Zoe? Flirt with him and lead him on? I'm practically a married woman. Besides..." She glanced at the door to make sure he was really gone. "He gives me the creeps."

"What?" Zoe's tone implied that she couldn't believe what she was hearing. "He's so handsome!"

"So was Ted Bundy. I can't stand the way he's always staring and lurking."

"Well, he stares because he's interested in you! And he doesn't lurk."

"He lurks! How long had he been standing there in the doorway listening to you ask me if there was trouble in paradise, huh?"

"Oh," Zoe gave her a dismissive wave of the hand. "He wasn't lurking."

"He lurks. *That* was lurking."

A soft knock on the open door got their attention and they both turned to see a young woman standing there.

"Knocking." Sidney gestured to the woman in the doorway. "Making yourself known. That's not lurking." She smiled at Zoe. "See the difference?"

"Oh, stop it." Zoe turned back to the woman at the door. "Beth. Come on in."

The woman stepped into the office, and Sidney noticed she was severely bruised on the left side of her face, and clearly afraid of her own shadow. Her demeanor made Sidney's heart ache with sorrow and unhappy memories of herself in similar circumstances.

"Beth, I'd like to introduce you to Sidney Fairchild." Zoe gestured Sidney's way. "She's the Assistant Director, and my right hand around here."

Sidney stood and stretched out her hand. "Hello, Beth."

"Hello."

Beth barely looked her in the eyes, and Sidney just wanted to hug her.

"Beth and her daughter came to us yesterday. They're still getting settled in." Zoe smiled at her. "What can we do for you?"

The woman hesitated for a second, unsure what to do with her hands.

"Um... I was just wondering... well, I-I mean..."

"It's all right, Beth," Sidney spoke up, hoping her voice was soothing. "Whatever it is. If we can help, we will."

"Well, it's just that... I can't send Kylee to school because my husband... well, we're not really married, but... well, Hank could get to her there. He keeps threatening to take her and leave town."

Sidney closed her eyes for a split second.

"I'm sorry you're going through that."

"Yeah, well... anyway... I was just wondering if you had any schooling she could do while we're here? Any textbooks or home schooling?"

"No, I'm sorry. We don't." Zoe's expression was as apologetic as her voice, and she and Sidney shared a look.

"How old is your daughter, Beth?" Sidney asked.

"She's eight."

"So, she'd be in the third grade, right?"

Beth nodded.

"You know, I'm actually a teacher by trade. I'd be happy to tutor your daughter in a few subjects while you're a resident here."

"I-I can't pay you..."

"Of course not. I wouldn't dream of charging you."

Beth finally sent her a timid glance.

"Really? You wouldn't mind?"

"Not at all." Sidney smiled at her. "What subjects does Kylee need help with?"

"Well, mostly math. She's a really good speller, and she loves to read." Beth perked up when she talked about her daughter's skills. "But numbers give her a hard time, and I want her to do better at them. Maybe that way she can grow up to be a banker or an accountant or something, and she won't allow herself to end up like me."

Sidney and Zoe exchanged another look.

"Seeing her mom fight to break free of an abusive situation will help keep Kylee from ending up in one herself someday," Sidney said. "Your strength and courage. Those are two of the best things you can teach her."

Beth finally met her gaze head on, and smiled.

"That said, it would be my pleasure to help Kylee with her math."

"Thank you so much!"

"You're welcome. I'll bring in some materials and we'll get started tomorrow, okay?"

"Okay."

Beth thanked her again and left the office.

"That was very kind of you." Zoe grinned at her.

Sidney shrugged a shoulder. "It's not a big deal." She sat back down at her desk. "So, what's her story? Beth?"

Zoe sighed and sat back in her chair. "I got a call from Sgt. Malone at CPD yesterday afternoon."

"Malone?"

Zoe nodded. "He works in the domestic violence unit. He asked if we had room for two more. I guess her neighbors called and reported the fight. He said they do that a lot."

"Is the husband, boyfriend, baby-daddy in custody?"

"Actually, no. Sgt. Malone said when they showed up at the house he wasn't there. They found the daughter huddled next to Beth in the kitchen, crying and afraid her mother was dead."

"Jesus," Sidney whispered.

"Right? So, here they are."

"What's her plan?"

"Well, I know she's filed a restraining order, and the cops are actively looking for him... Whatever his name is."

"I think she called him Hank."

"Mmm. Other than that, I'm not really sure she's made any big decisions."

They were quiet for a moment, and something flitted through Sidney's thoughts.

"Hey, Zoe?"

"Hmm?"

"Have you ever thought about hiring security for Hope House?"

"I have. But the idea of big burley men hanging out around here might not be the best thing for our residents, you know? Some of them get quite spooked around strange men after what they've been through."

Sidney nodded, still turning it over in her mind.

"Yes, I totally get that. But we could hire female security." She perked up as the idea took shape. "I mean, we could request female security guards from whatever agency we hire."

"Female security?"

Zoe sounded as though the idea had never occurred to her before, and Sidney smiled.

"To any irate spouse or boyfriend who comes charging in, they'd just think she was one more battered woman. Until she flattened him on his ass."

Zoe looked intrigued for a moment, but that was replaced by skepticism.

"I don't know, Sidney. Where would we find a security agency that employed women?"

Sidney shrugged a shoulder. "I don't know, but I bet they're out there. I'll ask Ike about it. Maybe he knows of a place."

Zoe lifted an eyebrow at the mention of his name.

"So, about Ike. Everything's really okay with you two? He's not the reason you're so gloomy?"

"I am *not* gloomy!"

"Yes, you are."

Sidney sighed, her shoulders slumping.

"Fine. I'm gloomy. But it has nothing to do with my relationship with my fiancé. And yes... he is still my fiancé, and we are still very much in love."

"Okay. I'll stop prying then. As long as I know you're all right."

Sidney smiled, resigning herself to Zoe's mother hen routine.

"I'm all right."

Zoe nodded and left the office. And Sidney let out another long exhale.

4

On the university campus, Isaac and Pete entered the admissions building and went straight for the office. Flashing his badge at the young lady at the front desk, Isaac stared at her.

"Detective Sergeant Ike Taylor. Detective Pete Vega," he said, motioning to his partner. "We need..."

"Oh, my God!"

The young woman looked at him with unbridled glee.

"You're here about the body, aren't you? I heard the crime scene was totes gross!"

Isaac and Pete shot each other an is-she-for-real exasperated glance before Isaac turned back to her.

"And where'd you hear that?"

He gave her his patented intensive intimidation glare, and it didn't let him down. The young woman faltered, suddenly unable to look him in the eyes.

"Huh?"

"Who told you the crime scene was gross?"

"Oh. Well, the whole campus is buzzing about it, that's all. I'm not sure who specifically mentioned it to me."

"Right." His flat tone was evidence he didn't believe her explanation, but Isaac didn't press the issue. "My partner and I were hoping to get our hands on some kind of list. A student roster, or something similar. Can you provide us with one?"

The young woman suddenly became intrigued again.

"Oh! Well, I guess that's a matter of public record, so you wouldn't need a warrant for that kind of thing."

Isaac's patience was running thin, and he slapped an I'm-one-second-away-from-putting-you-in-handcuffs smile on his lips.

"I know we don't need a warrant. What we do need is access to your current student roster. Can. You. Provide me with one?"

A confused expression lodged on the young woman's face, and Isaac wanted to scream.

"Yes, of course we can, Detective."

The voice was efficient and clearly in charge, and Isaac looked from the girl at the desk to the older woman now standing behind her.

"I'll see to it right away."

"Thank you, miss...?"

"Ivan," the woman offered. "Mrs. Sylvie Ivan. I'm head of the Admissions Office."

"Thank you, Mrs. Ivan." Isaac gave her a slight nod as something suddenly occurred to him. "Any chance that the gossip mill around here may have already identified our victim?"

When the two women looked at each other, he knew his hunch was correct.

"Well, there have been whispers," Mrs. Ivan replied. "One of the girls who found the body... Kimberly something, I believe..."

"Kim Barns?" Pete asked.

"Yes. That's right. She mentioned to someone that the victim was Bobby Cook, so that's the name that's been floating around this morning. But again, that's only a rumor."

"Thank you," Isaac said. "We'll still be needing that student roster, ma'am."

"Right away."

She walked off to another office, and Isaac turned to Pete.

"Seems like we need to have another talk with Miss Kim Barns."

"Sounds that way, doesn't it?" Pete nodded. "You want to do it nice or not so nice?"

"Well, she did withhold information the first time we met, so I'd say she's earned a little not so nice."

"Agreed."

"You want to give patrol a call?"

"I'm on it." Pete stepped away pulling out his cellphone. A minute later, Isaac heard him asking patrol to pick the girl up and bring her in for questioning, just as Mrs. Ivan reappeared.

She handed him a colored copy of the student roster.

"Thank you, ma'am."

When he and Pete left the building to head for the car, they noticed several news trucks setting up around the campus.

"The vultures are circling."

"Yep. I wonder if they've gotten wind of the possible ID of the victim." Pete opened the passenger side door of the car.

"For the family's sake, I sincerely hope not." But as he slid behind the wheel, a sinking feeling began to swirl in Isaac's gut.

As they drove back to the station, Pete flipped through the student roster.

"Robert John Cook. I think the rumor mill is right. That definitely looks like our vic to me."

He held up the booklet so that Isaac could see, and pointed to a photo near the bottom of the page. Isaac glanced at it and shook his head.

"Why lie about whether or not you know the victim's name?"

"I don't know. All that does is make her look guilty to me," Pete replied.

"Exactly."

They drove on in silence.

By the time they got back to the station, up to the detectives pit, and over to their desks, Isaac's work phone was ringing.

"Your witness is in interrogation one."

"Thanks."

"Thank you."

They answered the passing patrolman in unison, and Isaac grabbed his ringing extension.

"Detective Sgt. Taylor."

The voice on other end of the line was male and frantic.

"Hello? Y-yes, my name is John Cook. My son is Bobby Cook; he's a senior at Case Western Reserve University. I just heard on the morning news that he's dead! S-so, I called the police, and someone transferred me to you. Please, God, tell me that news wasn't right!"

Isaac sighed and flopped down into his desk chair. He hated this shit storm of a day.

"Sir, I am very sorry you heard this news on the TV. The truth is that we have not officially identified the victim we found earlier this morning, and whoever is reporting that we have is being grossly irresponsible."

"But it's not my son?"

The man was desperate for it not to be true, but Isaac couldn't tell him what he wanted to hear.

"Honestly, sir... I don't know that for certain yet. If you would like to come in and possibly identify the body, that would be the best thing at this point. Again, I am very sorry."

Once he finally got the distraught man off the phone, Isaac looked at Pete.

"That was uncalled for. Come on."

He got up and headed for the interrogation room. The instant they stepped inside, Kim Barns stared at them with frightened eyes.

"Why am I here?"

Isaac ignored the question and sat down across from her. He

nodded for Pete to start the recorder and state the date and the parties present.

"Please, why am I here? What's going on?" Kim asked again.

"You're here because you lied, Miss Barns."

Isaac could hear the disgusted and annoyed tones in his own voice, but he made zero effort to hide it. As far as he was concerned, this woman deserved his attitude.

Kim vehemently shook her head.

"I didn't!"

"Okay, maybe *lie* is too harsh a word. You withheld information. Information that could have saved us valuable time in identifying the victim. And that naturally makes us wonder what other information you're currently withholding."

"But I didn't withhold anything. I swear!"

"That's not what we hear, Kim," Pete said. "In fact, we could arrest you for impeding an investigation. Obstruction of justice."

"What? No!"

"Word around the campus is that you identified the victim as Bobby Cook." Isaac glared at her. "And that news has spread far and wide. Now if you'd told us that information last night at the crime scene, we could've gotten a jump on our investigation. Maybe held the news media off a little bit. Most importantly here, is that we could have gotten to Mr. Cook's family before they heard about his death on the TV!"

Isaac was practically yelling now, but he couldn't help it.

"How do you think it might feel to learn about a loved one's tragic death on the news over your morning coffee, Miss Barns?"

The girl looked stricken. Her face blanched, eyes wide.

"Oh, God!" It was a horrified whisper, but it did nothing to sooth Isaac's ire. "I'm so sorry!"

"How do you know the victim?" Isaac ignored her apologies and pressed on.

"I don't. I don't know him. I just know who he is. We had a class together once, I think. Economics. Or maybe it was Ethics?"

She shook her head. "Anyway... we had to work on the final project in groups, and Bobby was part of my group. That's all! That's how I know him."

"And why didn't you mention any of that last night?"

"I don't know! I... I don't know." Her voice broke on a small sob.

"You weren't friends?

"No, sir."

"You didn't date?"

"No."

"You weren't enemies?"

"No. Nothing. We had nothing in common except that one class. I swear."

"Who did he hang with? Who were his friends?"

"I'm not sure."

"You know more than you think you do! Who did he hang with?"

Isaac slammed a hand down on the table, causing Kim to jump.

"Craig Wentworth! He's tight with Craig Wentworth. That's who I saw him with all the time."

"And who's Craig Wentworth?"

'He's an engineering student. They both are."

"And what's your relationship with this Craig Wentworth?"

Kim faltered again. Just for a split second.

"I... I don't have a relationship with him."

Her cheeks got pinker. Her voice lowered in pitch.

"But you wanted one," Isaac said with certainty.

Her pink cheeks became red, and she looked him in the eyes.

"H-how did you...um, I... I like him, yes. But he doesn't know I'm alive. Not really."

Isaac sat back in his chair, studying her. Now they were getting somewhere.

"What else can you tell me, Miss Barns?"

Kim swallowed. "I don't know."

"Were Bobby and Craig on the outs? Did they have a fight?"

"Not that I'm aware of."

"When's the last time you saw them together?"

"Um... earlier that day. They'd come into the student union together. Laughing and talking. They seemed tight as ever."

"No arguments over girls, or grades, or anything that you know of?"

"No." Her tone was emphatic, and she shook her head.

"And who were Bobby's other friends? Anyone you know?"

Kim took a breath and appeared to think about that.

"Honestly, I... I'm not sure he had other friends. I mean, I paid more attention to Craig, obviously. But now that I think about Bobby... I don't recall ever seeing him hang out with anyone but Craig. Bobby's sort of a loner. Keeps to himself. Sometimes a little nervous acting. Weird even."

Isaac watched her for a long moment. Then he looked over at Pete, who raised his eyebrows in silent response.

"Thank you, Miss Barns. We're done here. Don't leave town, as we may have more questions."

They stood up to leave.

"I can go?" Kim sounded shocked. "I'm not under arrest?"

"Should you be?" Isaac gave her a pointed glare.

"No! Thank you."

They left the room, and Isaac looked at the uniformed officer outside the door.

"She can go back to campus.

"Thank you, Detective."

They headed back to their desks.

"You came on a little strong in there, Ike." Pete sat down and looked at him. "I don't think I've ever seen you that pissed at a witness before."

Isaac rocked back in his chair and shook his head.

"The vic's father found out his son was mutilated and killed on the morning news, Pete. Shit like that should never happen."

Pete nodded. "No, it shouldn't. So, what do you think?"

"Well, unfortunately, I don't think she had anything to do with stringing our vic up and cutting off his junk. But I did find what she said about him being a loner interesting."

"Yeah, me too."

"Okay. Let's get into this guy. You take his social media, and I'll start looking into his financials. See what we come up with."

"On it."

Gavin stepped off the elevator and walked slowly down the stylishly decorated hallway, searching for apartment 10B. He'd never been to Gerri's place before, and he hated the circumstances that brought him here now.

Outside the door, he took a couple of deep breaths and wondered what he'd say to her.

The last time he'd seen her was at the funeral, and she'd been in no condition to talk then. He should've come to check on her sooner; he knew that. But he simply had no clue what to say. Not with all the feelings and the tension hanging between them.

"Suck it up, Gavin."

He raised his fist and softly knocked.

To his right, a door opened at the next apartment, and an older Asian gentleman stepped out. He smiled and bowed a greeting Gavin's way.

"Hello." Gavin nodded, and waited for the man to step into the elevator. Then he knocked a second time, slightly harder.

Finally, he heard movement on the other side of the door. It was a few more moments before the door slowly opened.

The first thing he noticed was that her dark eyes — normally bright and soulful — were red and puffy, and lacked the spark of fire that he usually saw there. But even so, she was beautiful.

"Lieutenant?"

Her voice was meek and hollow, almost as though she were drugged, and Gavin instantly regretted not coming sooner.

"I came to check in on you. May I come in?"

Gerri looked behind her, seeming to consider his request. Then she stepped aside, opening the door wider.

"Don't mind the mess. I wasn't expecting anyone."

He stepped inside and glanced around.

The place wasn't what he'd call a mess, exactly. But there were used tissues scattered around the space like forgotten un-melted snowballs. Half-empty bottles of water and juice dotted the coffee table in front of the couch, and the shades were drawn, keeping out the sunlight. The air in the place was stale, like she hadn't been out in days.

Gavin turned toward her. "How are you?"

She wore a pair of pajama pants and a matching t-shirt, and Gavin suspected she'd been wallowing this way for three whole weeks.

"Me? Oh, I'm just peachy." She wandered over to the couch and flopped down. "How are you, boss?"

Gavin took note of her sarcasm, and her obvious sorrow, and he sighed.

"I spoke with Dr. Newman today. He said that he's only seen you one time since the shooting. And that you've rescheduled your next appointment with him multiple times."

"Ratted me out, did he?"

"He's worried about you. Like we all are."

Gerri swayed her long slender legs back and forth.

"Yeah, well. I just couldn't get myself together to go in."

Gavin finally sat down at the other end of the couch.

"Seeing Dr. Newman was a condition of your leave of absence, Detective."

He watched Gerri's gaze roll over the ceiling.

"I know, Lieu. I just..." She paused and shook her head. "I don't think that it's for me."

"Everybody feels that way about therapy, Miller. It's normal."

"No, sir. I don't mean therapy." She hesitated and fidgeted with her fingers. "I mean the job. I don't need to see Dr. Newman because I don't think I'll be staying with the department. I'm not sure police work is for me anymore."

All the air left Gavin's lungs.

He took a deep breath to steady himself. Her knee-jerk decisions were giving him whiplash.

"First you want out of my unit, and now you want out of the job altogether?"

Gerri sighed and sank further into the couch, saying nothing.

Gavin angled his body so he could look directly at her.

"Detective..."

He paused and looked down at the couch for a second. Then he licked his lips and tried again.

"Gerri... I know Curt's death has been hard on you. Your partner practically bled out in your hands."

Just the mention of it brought back the memories of that day. When Curt was shot in the apprehension of the Lullaby Killer, Gerri had tried her damnedest to stop the bleeding.

"And there was nothing you could do to stop it. That kind of thing would trip anybody up. I've seen it happen to hard, macho men who thought they had it all together."

"Yeah, well seeing it happen doesn't mean shit. No offense."

Her tone held a lot of bitterness, and Gavin couldn't blame her.

"No offense taken. Because you're absolutely right. Seeing it, and experiencing it are two very different things. I know."

"Oh, stop trying to pretend you know how I feel. You don't know!"

The sight of her tears gripped his heart.

"Actually, I do."

Gerri wiped at her tears and looked at him.

"You do?"

"I was still in uniform at the time. I'd been on the job for four years to the day. My partner, Tony Deacon, and I were on a routine traffic stop. The car had blown a red light, and we pulled it over. It came up completely clean when we ran the plates. But it turned out the passenger inside the car had multiple warrants for assault and armed robbery."

Gavin paused and gave himself a moment. Reliving one of the worst days of his life always made it difficult to breathe.

"I approached the driver's side to get license and registration while Deke approached the opposite side. Passenger got spooked. He shot at Deke three times and bolted from the car. I didn't know what to do. Should I go help my partner, who's bleeding out on the ground from a bullet to the face, or should I run after the asshole who'd just shot him?"

He saw it all so clearly in his mind, felt it all so deeply. Still.

"What did you do?"

Gerri's voice was soft and intense, hanging on his every word.

"I took the car keys, and cuffed the driver to the steering wheel. Then I stayed by my partner's side and called for a bus. He had two wounds. One in the gut, one in the face. I didn't know which one to concentrate on. Officer Tony Deacon died in my arms that day, and there was nothing I could do to stop it from happening. All I could think as I held him was that two minutes before we stopped that car, he'd been singing a B.B. King song."

They sat in silence for a long time, and Gavin revisited the laughter and joy of those two minutes.

"He loved B.B. King."

"Afterwards..." Gerri stared at him with big questioning eyes. "Did you dream about it? Did you have nightmares?"

She sounded like such a little girl in that moment, like she didn't really want to know the monsters she asked about. But Gavin had to be honest.

"Sometimes I still do."

He looked over at her, and was gutted by the emotion on her beautiful face.

"You need to talk to Dr. Newman, Gerri. He can help."

She burst into tears, and Gavin scooted closer and wrapped his arms around her. He held her for a long time while she cried, cooing softly and whispering words of encouragement.

He truly did know what she was going through, he'd lived it. He knew the guilt she couldn't help but feel, no matter how misguided. He tightened his arms around her, wanting only to take her pain away.

Gerri looked up into his eyes, and Gavin was lost in her hypnotic beauty — so lost he had no idea what was happening until he felt her lips on his.

"Gerri..."

He tried to pull away, but she clung to him.

"Please."

She kissed him again, this time with clear intent.

Gavin was powerless.

He gently took her face in both of his hands, and kissed her deeply, his hands sinking into her silky black hair.

He felt her hands at his waist, pulling at his shirt and lifting it up as their kiss became something fevered and urgent.

Clothes fell away, along with all of his reasons for not getting romantically involved with her.

"I need a condom," he mumbled.

"I don't care."

"I do. Don't move." He left her to fish a condom from the pocket of his pants, thanking his lucky stars he'd never tossed them aside after the divorce.

He rolled it on in total disbelief that this was actually happening. Then he reached for her.

Her body was everything he'd been fantasizing about ever since she'd let her feelings for him be known — full, perky breasts, a tiny waist, rounded hips and a tight, firm ass.

His hands didn't know where to begin, so he led with his mouth, exploring every inch of her with his lips and his tongue, bringing her to vibrating completion before he'd even entered her.

When he finally did, she wrapped her long shapely legs around him and hung on for the ride.

He pounded into her with an abandon he hadn't expected. Hearing his name drop from her lips, first in moans and then in screams, triggered emotions inside him he'd thought were long gone.

They sailed over the edge of ecstasy together, and Gavin knew with every fiber of his being that he never wanted to be without this woman again.

5

Back at the station, Isaac and Pete spent the afternoon looking into Bobby Cook's background and his friendship with Craig Wentworth.

"Listen to this."

Pete's tone said he'd just stumbled on something interesting, and Isaac looked up from his computer.

"What you got?"

"It seems Kim Barns was right about our vic being a loner. Even in high school he was kind of an awkward duck with very few friends."

"Okay." Isaac drew the word out as he tried to piece this kid together.

"But he was always tight with Craig Wentworth. They go as far back as fourth grade from what I can tell."

"Hmm. Long time."

"Yeah," Pete continued. "His social media didn't raise any flags. He's got a presence on Facebook, Instagram, and Snap Chat, but not much of one. He doesn't post often, and when he does there's not much engagement. Nothing that would make you think someone was pissed enough at him to string him up and cut him. No girlfriends. No enemies. Just nothing."

"Huh. Well, I'm not finding anything unusual in Bobby Cook's financials," Isaac stated. "His parents pay his tuition in full, and keep a small amount of spending money in his account. He doesn't seem to have a part time job. No unexplained big purchases. Nothing."

He sat back and thought again about touching the victim. He knew it would be the easiest way to get a lead they could follow, but he simply couldn't bring himself to do it. He couldn't open himself up to that kind of torment right now.

He was about to say as much to Pete when a presence suddenly loomed over his desk. He looked up to see Dr. Clark Newman standing there.

"You've been avoiding me for two weeks, Sergeant. I've let it go for as long as I can."

Isaac sat back in his chair with a sigh.

"You can't be serious, Doc."

Newman smiled at him. "You know the rules, Detective. I don't make them up; I only help enforce them. With your lieutenant's help, of course. In fact, the only reason I've let it slide this long is because I'm aware of how shorthanded the homicide unit is right now. But we've got to get it over with sometime."

Isaac rolled his eyes. "Fine. I'll be in your office in ten minutes."

Dr. Newman cocked an eyebrow at him.

"I give you my word, Doc."

"All right."

He turned and walked away, and Isaac looked at Pete, who smirked at him.

"Stop killing people and you won't have to see him anymore." Pete chuckled at his own joke.

"Just wait. Your turn is coming."

Isaac stood and walked straight for the break room. If he had to go head-to-head with Doc Newman again, he was going to make sure to be on his toes. He grabbed one of the paper cups and poured himself a full measure of the strong black coffee they always kept freshly brewed there.

He savored a sip. Then he turned to leave just as Sgt. Natalie Bains entered the break room wearing that perpetual smirk on her lips.

If he were playing into Sidney's assertions that he was some kind of psychic superhero, then Natalie Bains would be his number one archenemy. The woman was toxic. She hated the fact that Isaac repeatedly turned her down. She'd even gone out of her way to try and make trouble for him because of it. And she couldn't hide her jealousy over his relationship with Sidney.

She'd recently reported him to Internal Affairs for inappropriate behavior with a female witness — that female witness being Sidney. When that move failed to make things difficult for them, Natalie actually made a thinly veiled threat *against* Sidney. And Isaac was not having that.

Oh, yeah. Archenemy. Number. One.

Natalie tossed her blond hair over her shoulder and struck a pose.

"You look like shit, Ike. What's the matter? Little woman keeping you up too late?"

"That's right." Isaac never missed a beat as he headed for the door. "She wears me out every night. Sexiest woman on the planet."

He enjoyed the look of envy on her face as he walked past her and out the door.

He headed for the stairwell and went down two flights to the second floor. He walked past the dispatch area and made his way to Dr. Newman's office at the end of the hall. He stepped through the open doorway, and Dr. Newman looked up.

"Sgt. Taylor! Come in, please."

He motioned to the chair in front of his desk, and Isaac closed the door behind him before he stepped further in.

"Why do you sound surprised, Doc?"

"Well, to be quite honest... I thought you'd stand me up."

Isaac sat down, taking a sip of his coffee.

"What would be the point? You'd just track me down again."

"True." Newman grinned. "Shall we?"

Isaac gestured as if to say, 'go ahead.'

"So... how are you?"

Isaac sighed.

"Tired. Pete and I were called out at quarter to four this morning."

"Hence the coffee." Newman jutted his chin in the direction of Ike's coffee cup.

"Oh, I'm sorry. Should I not drink during our session?"

Newman shrugged. "As long as it's just coffee, I have no objections."

Isaac stared at him for a second.

"If that was a jab at my alcoholism, Doc, you shouldn't worry. It's been going on eight years since my last drink."

"Congratulations."

"Thanks."

"So, how long has it been since you *wanted* to take a drink?"

Isaac froze, cup halfway to his lips.

His stomach seized.

His heart sliced open by a memory.

"Two days ago when my fiancée had a miscarriage."

His voice seemed hollow in the starkly quiet room, and Isaac silently cursed Newman's stealthy ability to go straight for the jugular.

He took his sip of coffee, hoping it would soothe him going down.

"I'm sorry for your loss," Newman quietly said.

Isaac hesitated in his thanks.

"We found out she was pregnant the same day we laid Curt Dorn to rest. The same day we finally closed the book on Jeffery Schiffer and that whole legacy of death and destruction. It was like... my reward for finally catching the Lullaby Killer. That's how it felt. Like a prize. I was the happiest I'd ever been."

Isaac paused and thought about that.

"And then, two days ago I watched the woman I love double over in pain. The look on her face was so hard to watch. She knew. Right then, she knew something was wrong. We both did. And there was nothing I could do to stop what was happening. The blood running down her inner thigh..."

He paused again, seeing it all in his mind.

"It was bright red. And I remember thinking, 'maybe if I can just get her to the hospital fast enough.' But..."

He took a deep breath in hopes of steadying his voice.

"I scooped her up into my arms and got her out to the car. Even flipped on my lights and siren, but by the time we got to the ER, it was all over. And I wanted a drink so bad in that moment I would've done almost anything."

He took a sip of coffee and wondered why the heck he'd just spilled his guts about the most important, most gut-wrenching moment in his life to a man he didn't want to be talking to in the first place.

"Aside from traumatic events like that, how often are you feeling those urges to drink?"

Isaac shrugged a shoulder, but he didn't verbally respond. It wasn't a topic he liked to discuss.

"Are you going to meetings regularly?"

Finally, Isaac sighed. "I go once a week without fail. I talk to my sponsor. If I need more in between, I go."

"Good." Newman nodded. "Let's talk about Jeffery Schiffer."

"What about him?"

"You killed him."

"Yes, I did."

"How does that make you feel?"

Isaac looked him in the eyes. "What kind of question is that?"

"It's an important one," Newman asserted. "You've just killed another man, Isaac. Your second, by my count. You must have some feelings about that."

Actually, it was his third if you counted Sidney's former husband — the abusive, murderous pig — but that one hadn't been attributed to Isaac since the 'official' story was that he'd fallen backward into a shelf, bringing the cement blocks stored there down onto his head. The actual story was the first appearance of Isaac's telekinesis, but Newman didn't need to hear about that shit.

"It gets easier the second time."

Isaac's tone was flippant, but Newman was not amused. He stared at him in that way that made Isaac nervous.

"Okay," Isaac sighed. "Bad jokes aside, I get it, Doc. There are cops all over the country who go their entire careers never even firing their weapon once, and here I've killed two men in the same year."

The first was Nacio Rivas-Solis, the drug lord who wanted Sidney dead after she'd witnessed a gangland shooting that he'd ordered.

"And how do you feel about that?" Newman asked again.

"The first man — Rivas-Solis — was trying to kill my fiancée at the time. The second — Schiffer — was a serial killing dirtbag who kidnapped, raped, and murdered 16 little girls that we know of. Honestly? I feel pretty damn good about that."

Newman studied him for a few tense moments.

"And how are you sleeping?"

"I sleep fine."

"No nightmares?"

"Not about the Lullaby Killer."

It wasn't a lie, but it wasn't the whole truth either. Nightmares of the last moments of the last four lullaby victims — the ones he'd touched — had plagued him a lot over the last couple of weeks. But he refused to mention it to Doc Newman because he knew there was nothing the man could do, short of prescribing something Isaac didn't want to get dependent on.

Newman stared into his eyes for the longest of moments, and Isaac knew he was evaluating every word, gesture, and nuance.

"If you'd like to talk some more about the loss you and your fiancée have suffered, come see me."

Isaac narrowed his eyes. "That's it?"

"That's it."

"I'm clear to keep working?"

"You're short-handed, remember?"

Isaac stared at him, twisting his lips.

Newman grinned. "You're fine, Sergeant. I'll be sure to let your lieutenant know."

Isaac stood and moved toward the door.

"Thanks, Doc."

He turned to leave, but stopped and took a breath. Then he turned to face him again.

"This helped. With the personal stuff, I mean. Thanks."

Dr. Newman smiled. "That's what I'm here for. Door's always open."

Isaac nodded and left.

The curtains were drawn, and the bedroom was dark. Just like the rest of the apartment. Gavin looked over at Gerri, who was sleeping peacefully, and he suddenly wondered when was the last time she'd actually slept.

When he'd arrived at her apartment a couple of hours ago, her eyes had been puffy and red, no doubt from crying. But he'd also seen evidence of fatigue — small bags beneath her eyes, and slightly sunken cheeks. She hadn't been taking care of herself during her grief.

He carefully slid out of her bed and left the room in search of his underwear. Out in the living area, he pulled on his briefs and took note of the pervasive darkness. Well, that sure as hell wasn't conducive to Gerri's healing.

He walked over to the windows and opened up the blinds, flooding the space with the bright afternoon sun. Then he picked up the mountain of tissues and discarded water and juice bottles that were scattered around. At least she'd been keeping hydrated while she hid out in the darkness.

As he picked up around her place, Gavin thought about the pain of losing a partner. He remembered it well. And he remembered how difficult it had been to get over. It had taken him a long time, and he knew that it would take Gerri a long time too. But he worried that she was in danger of allowing her grief to take over her life. The way she talked so casually about walking away from a career he knew she loved and had so worked hard for. That was the grief talking. It had to be.

Back when he'd first recruited her for his homicide unit, one of the reasons he'd chosen her was because he'd read about how hard she had worked to prove that she could be just as good a police officer as any man. How her struggle had been even more difficult because of the color of her skin, and the fact that most of the 'boys club' only saw a pretty face and a nice rack when they looked at her.

She'd actually had the audacity to write those exact words in her letter of intent when she put in for the position of detective. Gavin had wanted to give her a chance to prove herself.

Just like he'd wanted to give Ike Taylor a chance when everyone laughed and shunned him over the whole trippy psychic thing.

Isaac hadn't disappointed him. And neither had Gerri. She was an excellent homicide detective, and he was prepared to fight to keep her on the job.

He wandered into her kitchen to throw away all the trash, and then it occurred to him that Gerri probably hadn't been eating well either.

He opened up her fridge and took inventory. Then he opened up her cabinets and did the same. There wasn't much, but he spotted a can of chicken and wild rice soup, and pulled it out.

Opening other cabinets in search of cookware, he found a small pot and set it on the stove. Then he dumped the contents of the soup can into it.

He moved about her kitchen with ease, finding spices and slicing fresh mushrooms, and adding them to the canned soup. As he worked his cellphone chimed, and he rushed to the sofa, where his pants still lay, to grab it.

"Trey?"

He smiled as he took the call from his son.

"Hey, Dad. Bad time? I know you're at work."

Gavin glanced around Gerri's apartment and guilt creeped in.

Yes. He should've been back at his desk at the PD by now. Instead, he was standing half naked in his grieving subordinate's living room.

Oh, this would look so bad to Internal Affairs.

"Uh... no. It's fine. You know I'm never too busy for you."

He walked back to the kitchen and stirred the soup, turning down the heat.

"What's up? Everything okay?"

He had a habit of being slightly overprotective when it came to Trey's emotional well being ever since the divorce. He just wanted to be sure his son was handling things okay after Gavin and his ex-wife split. And with Trey down in Columbus at Ohio State, keeping tabs on his state of mind wasn't always easy.

"Everything's cool," Trey said. "I was just calling before I hit the road. I'll be home in a few hours."

"Okay. You pay attention and drive safe."

"I will, Dad."

Gavin could hear the eye roll in Trey's voice.

"Don't give me that exasperated tone. People are crazy. You pay attention to the other drivers."

"Yes, Officer," Trey joked.

"Yeah, and you remember that response too. If you ever get pulled over, you keep your hands in plain view, and *be polite.* 'Yes, Officer. No, Officer. My father is a Police Lieutenant, Officer.' Don't give them any reason to shoot you!"

"Dad!" Trey drew the word out on a long sigh. "I know. You've told me this a million times. I'm a Black man, and I have to remember that if I'm ever pulled over by the police, even though my dad is a cop."

Trey recited the things Gavin had been drilling into him since he was a pre-teen, and Gavin nodded. He hated that it was even an issue, and Lord knew sometimes it was hard to admit he was associated with the police in any way. But the fact was, he loved his profession. Yes, the institution as a whole had its issues to overcome, but at its core, it was still a noble and necessary job, and he was proud of the career he'd built.

"All right, Trey. I'll see you soon."

"Okay. Cheeseburgers for dinner?"

Gavin laughed. The cheeseburgers were an inside joke between the two of them.

"Sure. Drive safe, kid."

"I will."

"I love you."

"Love you too, Dad."

Gavin set the cellphone aside.

"Is Trey all right?"

Her voice held a soft, dreamy quality, like she hadn't fully awakened yet, and Gavin glanced up to see Gerri standing there in a t-shirt and panties, looking as tasty as the soup he was stirring.

"Yeah. He's fine. He's driving home from Columbus today. He'll be staying with me for the rest of the summer."

Gerri walked over to the island that separated her kitchen from the living room and sat on one of the stools, facing the kitchen.

"Are you cooking in my kitchen, Lieutenant?"

Gavin grinned at the amusement in her tone.

"Yes, I am, Detective. It doesn't look like you've been eating much lately."

"I haven't exactly had an appetite."

All amusement floated away, and so did Gerri. She got up and moved over to the couch, flinching at the brightness streaming in through the windows.

Gavin poured the soup into a bowl. Then he found a spoon and a small box of saltine crackers. He grabbed a bottle of water from the fridge, and carried it all over to the couch.

"Here. You need to eat."

She started to protest, but he wasn't having it.

"Hey. I will tie you down and forcibly feed you if I have to."

His tone told her that he wasn't playing, and she carefully took the bowl. He put the water on the table and sat down beside her, watching as she blew over a spoonful and took a tentative bite. Then she took another spoonful, and another.

"Mmm. This is really good. You made this?"

She took another hearty spoonful, and Gavin was glad she was eating.

"Well, not completely. It's just a can of soup I found in your cupboard. I added a few spices to it... some rosemary and thyme. A little seasoned salt. Some sliced mushrooms you had in the fridge."

She smiled at him. "I had no idea you were such a gourmet chef."

Gavin chuckled. "I opened a can of soup and doctored it up. Not a big deal."

She dipped a cracker into the soup and took a bite, watching him as she chewed.

"You want to talk about the actual big deal? The one we're trying so politely to avoid right now?"

Her eyes were bright as she asked the question. Her lips holding just the wisp of a smile, and Gavin wanted to kiss her. Instead, he sighed and looked at the table in front of them.

"What's there to talk about? You were hurting and I gave you comfort."

He looked back at her. Gerri took another bite and nodded, chewing slowly. Finally, she met his gaze.

"Is that all it was, Gavin? Just offering me comfort?"

"Look, Gerri... right now, you're in a bad place, okay? You're not making the best decisions. And me? I was irresponsible. I never should've let things go as far as they did. We've been all over the reasons why this..."

"...is such a bad idea." She cut him off, throwing his words back at him. "Yeah. I remember the conversation."

There was sadness in her voice, and turmoil in Gavin's gut. He wanted her. He wanted her in ways he'd never wanted any other woman before. But he had to be sensible, didn't he? He had to do the right thing.

What was the right thing?

"But see, the thing is," Gerri continued, "when you held me earlier? When you kissed me and made love to me? That didn't feel like a bad idea. It didn't feel like a mistake, and it certainly didn't feel like it was just comfort. It's a whole lot more than that, and we both know it. Please stop trying to tell me it's not. You are never going to convince me that you don't want this every bit as much as I do. You're lying to both of us, Gavin."

He stared at her for a long moment, not trying to think up a rebuttal, not looking for a stronger argument. He just stared at her — at her beautiful face with the dark soulful eyes and the full kissable lips. God, she was sexy as sin.

"Okay. No more lies."

He took the near empty bowl of soup from her hands and put it on the table. Then he pulled her into his arms and into a passionate kiss. He stood, lifting her easily, and carried her back into the bedroom.

The day dragged on for Isaac, and the wheels of justice went nowhere on their new case. But he and Pete were able to make an arrest on another case they'd been working on. He'd just finished up the paperwork on it and got up to take the report to Lieutenant Hayes' office.

Near the door, someone slapped his left arm, causing him to flinch.

He spun to see Gavin Hayes breeze past him into the office.

"Got something for me, Sergeant?"

His tone was light, and Isaac noticed that his step was almost peppy. He frowned and glanced back toward the pit before looking at his boss again.

"Yeah. Paperwork on the Meyers case. Pete and I finally located the brother. He confessed to shooting the bar owner, but he insists it wasn't over the money. Says he did it because the man insulted him and disrespected his woman. He and his morals are down in booking now."

He handed the file to him.

"Ah. Good work!" Gavin smiled and plopped the file in the basket on his desk.

Isaac grinned, but he couldn't help wondering who this pod person was, and he feared his facial expression gave him away.

"Um... sir? Is everything all right? You seem to be in a noticeably better mood than you were this morning."

Come to think of it, Isaac couldn't recall seeing his boss in the last few hours. Had he been gone all afternoon?

Gavin rolled up his sleeves and a momentary look of embarrassment passed over his eyes before his game face settled on.

"Everything's fine."

Then he cleared his throat, and his voice came down a few octaves to normal.

"I just spoke to my son. He's on his way home from college. He's going to be spending the rest of the summer with his old man."

Isaac got the feeling there was more to the story, but he smiled. His boss was entitled to his secrets, after all.

"Oh. Well, that's nice. I imagine it's been a little strange being an empty nester of sorts."

"Yes, it has," Gavin confirmed. "Especially so on top of the divorce, you know? It's like my whole life changed overnight. Suddenly I'm single again, and my kid's out of the house. Then the house is gone and I'm in a whole new place. It's been a hell of a year, that's for sure."

Gavin's voice sounded wistful, and a wave of sadness and regret engulfed Isaac. The swell of it was so strong it nearly knocked him over. He took a deep breath in preparation of trying to mentally push his boss' emotions away, when they suddenly lifted. Replaced by what felt like lightheartedness. The sensation both surprised and puzzled him.

"Well, uh..." Isaac paused to clear the confusion. "What kind of trouble are you and Trey headed for tonight?"

Gavin grinned at him.

"He's obsessed with the cheeseburgers at this little all-night diner we found a few years back. The place is the very definition of greasy spoon, but the burgers are great. He's already put in a request to have dinner there tonight."

Isaac smiled. "And I'll bet he can put three of them away in one sitting too."

Gavin laughed out loud. "Sometimes, yeah!"

Isaac laughed, but he wondered if everything was okay with Gavin. He'd never seen his boss in such a weird head space before. His emotions were all over the place. But at least he was able to laugh.

"Hey, Ike. You ever think about having kids?"

The question caught him completely off guard, snapping thoughts of Sidney's miscarriage squarely to the forefront of his mind like a rubber band. It took him a minute to recover.

"I didn't. Not until I met Sidney. But, uh... yeah. I think about it now."

"You should marry that girl, you know? There's probably not many women out there who can put up with the likes of you."

Isaac laughed again.

"You two set a date yet?" Gavin asked.

"Nope. Not yet."

"Well, don't wait too long."

"And give her a chance to change her mind? My mama didn't raise no dummies!"

Gavin chuckled, and Isaac headed for the door. He stopped and turned toward Gavin again.

"Oh. Were you able to speak to Gerri Miller?"

Gavin looked slightly startled by the question, but he recovered quickly.

"Uh, yeah. I did."

"And? Did she say anything about coming back, or transferring precincts?"

Gavin sighed. "Actually, she said she's questioning whether she's staying on the job at all."

"Well, shit. That ain't good. I mean, if her heart's not in it anymore, then she probably shouldn't come back. But that leaves us in a bind."

"Yeah, well. I'm not sure that's the case. That her heart's not in it, I mean. I think that's the grief talking. And I think she's got a lot on her mind on top of the grief."

"Like what?"

Gavin clammed up and changed directions.

"Just some... personal stuff."

"Personal stuff. Yeah, you mentioned that before."

An awkward silence encroached, and they stared at each other.

"She gonna let you know her plans at least?"

"I've asked her to see Dr. Newman one more time before she calls it quits. I'm hoping he can convince her not to make any hasty decisions while she's grieving. I'll keep you posted. In the meantime, I want you to look over those files I gave you this morning and give Dorn's replacement some serious thought. I want your input."

"You'll have it."

He left the office then and went back to his desk. Listening to Gavin talk about his son inevitably made him think about the baby he'd just lost. Could he really picture himself a father? Would he be a good one?

One thing he knew for certain... Sidney would be an incredible mother someday.

He picked up his cellphone and sent her a text.

Isaac:
I love you

Her response was immediate.

Sidney:

I love you back

Isaac smiled at the familiar words. But he wondered how she was doing at work. It had only been two days, after all.

Sidney:
I'm ok
I promise

He chuckled to himself. It was like that woman could read his mind sometimes. Or maybe it was just the incredible bond they shared.

Isaac:
Ok

6

Adam slow danced around the posh living room of his house with baby Isla in his arms, quietly rapping Tupac's "Ghetto Gospel" to her. It was a dinnertime routine they'd fallen into since bringing Isla home from the hospital, and truth be told, it had quickly become Adam's favorite time of day.

He stared down into her light blue eyes, so much like his own, and marveled at how she watched him so intently. She was brilliant. He already knew that his little girl was going to be absolutely brilliant.

As he rapped and danced her around the room, her fervent gaze began to wane, and he watched her beautiful blue eyes flutter closed.

"Is it working?"

Bree was laid back on the chaise lounge, watching the show.

"Of course, it is. 'Cause Daddy's got the magic touch, and she loves it when he raps for her."

He crossed the room and slowly lowered the baby down into the bassinet situated next to the chaise lounge, and covered her up. Then he carefully slid onto the chaise next to his gorgeous wife.

"Did you ever think that maybe she goes to sleep when you start rapping just so that she can get away from it?"

Adam shot her a look that he hoped was a blend of surprise and hurt. He poured it on thick.

Bree giggled.

"Wow," Adam said. "That was harsh, babe."

All amusement left Bree's face, replaced by shock and regret.

He had her.

"No, I'm just kidding. That was a really bad joke, honey. Isla loves it when her daddy raps to her."

"She really does!" Adam insisted. "She loves it."

"I know she does." Bree grinned and patted his leg. "She loves her daddy."

Adam smirked at her.

"Yeah, you better be nice to me. Otherwise, I might decide not to give you this."

He pulled a small, square, Tiffany's box from his pocket and Bree gasped.

"Adam! What is this?"

He handed it to her, and shrugged a shoulder as if it were no big deal.

"Just something I wanted the mother of my child to have."

Bree looked at him with a wry grin.

"A push present? Really?" She made a face and said, "Are we those people?"

"Not so much a push present. More like a 'you-are-the-most-amazing-woman-in-the-world-and-I'm-so-damn-lucky-you-love-me' present."

He watched tears spring to her eyes, and it startled him.

"Oh, Adam."

"Those are good tears I hope."

He wiped an escaped one from her cheek with his thumb.

She smiled at him. "Yes!"

"Good. Open it."

She opened the box and softly gasped once more. The platinum and diamond bangle bracelet twinkled right on cue. Adam took the box from her and lifted the bracelet out.

"Are those charms?"

She reached out and studied them — a platinum heart, and a single perfect pearl.

Adam fastened the bracelet around her wrist.

"Yes. The heart is engraved with Isla's name on the front and her birthdate on the back. See? And the other one, the pearl? Well, that's her birthstone. I figure we can add more charms as Isla's siblings come along."

Bree laughed through her tears.

"Whoa. Slow down there, cowboy! Let my body recover from this one first, okay?"

"No pressure. Just sharing the plan, that's all."

Bree held out her arm, admiring the bracelet from all angles. Then she brought it to her chest, hugging it.

"Adam, it's so beautiful! I love it; and I love you."

"Woman, you got no idea how much I love you."

He leaned in and kissed her. What was meant to be a sweet expression of his affection quickly became a blistering inferno as the kiss deepened and morphed into something near X-rated.

"How much longer are we supposed to wait?" he asked against her lips before kissing her again.

"You know the answer to that, doctor. Four more weeks."

Her voice was throaty and sexy as hell, and Adam groaned.

"I'm not going to make it."

"Well, maybe I can make things a little easier on you."

He felt Bree's hand run over the bulge in his pants, and he shuddered.

"Oh, my God. Don't tease me."

"Would I do that to you?"

She kissed his chin and unlatched the button of his jeans, reaching into his pants.

His cellphone rang just as she took hold of him.

"Aw, shit!"

Bree giggled, and then she pushed him away.

"Oh, make it stop before it wakes her!"

Adam grabbed his cellphone and silenced it. Then he looked at the screen and wanted to throttle the caller. He hit the answer button.

"You are seriously messing with my game, mutant! This better be good."

"Well, hello to you too."

Isaac couldn't help the testy pitch in his tone, but that greeting hadn't exactly been friendly.

"I'm sorry, but you have really lousy timing, bro," Adam said.

"I can call back at a better time if that'd be more convenient for you."

He knew his voice was dripping with annoyance, but he couldn't help it. Then he sighed and backed down.

"Never mind. Just... I'm sorry. And sorry for interrupting. Go back to what you were doing."

"No. Ike, wait!"

Now Adam sounded annoyed. And a little worried.

"What's going on, man? You and Sidney okay?"

"Yeah, we're fine."

That sounded convincing, didn't it? He took a breath and tried again.

"I just... you know what, it wasn't important. Really."

"Ike. Talk to me. You sound... I don't know. Troubled. Where are you?"

Isaac huffed out a soft breath, and grinned.

"Don't worry. I'm not planted on a bar stool, Adam. I'm sitting in my car in the PD's parking lot, getting ready to head home."

"And? How's Sid doing?"

Isaac heard the concern in his big brother's voice, and he appreciated it.

"She went back to work today."

"Yeah?"

"Yeah."

"Well, it's probably good for her to jump back into her routine, you know?"

"Yeah, that's what she said too. But the sadness clings to her like a bad stench, and I don't know what to do about it."

He could hear Adam's deep sigh over the phone.

"It's only been a couple of days, Ike. Just give her some time. Bree and I haven't been through it, but I've heard enough about miscarriage — both from the medical side and the civilian side — to know that it just takes time to get over. She'll bounce back. You'll see."

"I know she will, Adam. It's just hard to see her so down. I want to do something to put a smile back on her face. Only I've got no clue what that should be. And I guess I was just calling to ask for your advice is all."

A long silence hung over the phone line between them.

"I'm honored you want my advice, bro."

Adam sounded touched, and Isaac wondered why.

"Well, what the hell do I know about making a woman happy?"

Isaac rolled his eyes at that sad truth. Because of his huge freakdom — the hypersensitive psychic thing that plagued him with major touch issues — Sidney was the one and only woman he'd ever had in his life.

"Of course, I want your advice. She means everything to me, Adam. I don't want to screw this up."

"That woman loves you, Ike. You can't mess this up. Just let her know that you're there, and that she can come to you."

Isaac's gaze rolled up and over the header of his car. "She already knows that."

"Of course, she does. But tell her again. Tell her every day. *Show* her."

"Show her?"

"Yes."

"How?"

"By being there. By doing what you're already doing, man. Making her feel special. Letting her know that you love her, and that she means the world to you. It's like I already said, Ike. Sidney loves you. You've got this."

Isaac sighed, but he didn't respond. He didn't think Adam was fully understanding his plight.

"You've got this," Adam repeated, more forcefully.

"Yeah. Thanks for the pep talk, man."

"You're welcome."

"Kiss my niece for me, will ya?"

"I'll do that."

Isaac ended the call and sighed. Again. Adam didn't get it.

His Sidney was light and sunshine. Only now that light inside her had gone out, and Isaac was desperate to get it back.

He started up the car and slowly pulled out of the parking lot, thinking about his conversation with Adam. His big brother hadn't really given him any advice he could use. Nothing helpful anyway.

"Show her!" Adam's voice seemed to scream at him.

Hmm. Show her.

Show her what? Show her how?

His brain rolled those questions over and over in his mind.

Maybe Adam's advice hadn't been completely useless.

He drove home thinking up all the different ways that he could show Sidney how special she was to him.

By the time he got home, Isaac had a solid plan of attack.

Or, at least, he had sort of a plan. Do things to make her smile and show her how much she means to him.

Would that cheer her up? Maybe. Maybe not. But at least she would know how much he loved her.

He let himself into the house and was surprised when no kitten came to greet him at the door. In fact, the house was quiet.

"Sidney?"

"In here."

He headed down the hall and found her in the home office at the computer, where the growing kitten sat on her lap pawing at the keyboard.

"Hey, darlin'."

"Hi, baby."

He bent down and kissed the top of her head.

"How was your day?"

"It was okay. Uneventful."

"Yeah? I see you got some help at the keyboard there."

Sidney grinned and scratched the kitten's head.

"Yeah, I think he's having fun."

Isaac glanced at the screen and saw what looked like elementary level math problems.

"Whatcha doing?"

"One of the new residents at Hope House has a third-grader who needs some extra help with her math. So, I'm just looking for appropriate worksheets I can download to tutor her."

"Oh. I didn't realize tutoring the residents' kids was part of your job description."

"Well, it's not really. I just offered to help. Might be fun." She looked up at him. "What about you? How was your day?"

Isaac grunted. "A little disjointed. That 4 am call out had me yawning all day long."

"I didn't realize you'd gone that early. I didn't even hear your phone ring. Guess I finally wore myself out crying."

Her voice was soft, and she turned back to the computer.

Isaac ran the back of his finger down her cheek.

"Yeah, you did."

Sidney clicked the mouse and the printer started up. When she stood, Alfred Hitchcock jumped from her lap and trotted away. She stepped closer to Isaac.

"Thank you."

"For?"

"For holding me and letting me cry."

Isaac wrapped his arms around her and pulled her close. "You're welcome." He planted a soft kiss on her lips.

"Dinner is in the oven. Should be just a few more minutes."

"Okay."

He kissed her forehead and then left the room. He put away his gun and changed out of his work clothes and into a pair of old sweats and a ratty old Cleveland Indians t-shirt that had definitely seen better days. Then he joined her in the kitchen.

"Want to set the table while I throw together a salad?"

"Sure."

He carried plates and flatware to the dining table, and when they finally sat down to eat Isaac looked at the dish she'd placed in the center of the table.

"I don't know what that is, but it smells delicious."

Sidney grinned at him.

"It's a homemade chicken pot pie. Well, semi-homemade. I didn't have time to make my own crust. Don't tell Bree! It's her recipe."

Isaac chuckled. He and Adam loved how close the two women had gotten.

"Well, it looks good to me, so I won't tell her a thing."

He dished up his plate with an overly generous portion and took a bite.

"Mm, mmm. Wow. That's really good."

Sidney smiled and took a bite.

They ate in silence for a few minutes, and Isaac wondered how to set his plan in motion.

"So, how's Zoe doing?"

"Good," Sidney nodded. "She seems to have made a full recovery. No lasting ill-effects of her run-in with the butt of that maniac's gun."

"Good. I'm glad to hear that."

"She leaned pretty heavy on me today about the reason for my two-day absence."

"Oh, yeah?"

Sidney nodded.

"Did you tell her?"

She looked down at her plate and silently shook her head.

"I just didn't want to get into it. It feels so personal right now. Like a piece of my soul. I don't want to hand that out to just anyone."

Her voice was soft and so full of pain, and Isaac just wanted to hold her. He reached out and placed his hand over hers.

"Hey. You don't have to tell anyone ever if you don't want to. If you feel like you need to protect it, and hide it in your heart forever, then you do that. You don't owe anybody an explanation. Okay?"

Sidney looked up and met his gaze.

"I love you."

Isaac brought her hand to his lips and kissed it.

"Right back atcha, darlin'."

They turned back to their dinner, although he noticed that Sidney did more pushing food around her plate than actual eating.

"Did you tell anyone at work?"

Her question surprised him, but part of him was glad that she wanted to talk about it. He nodded and looked at her.

"I had a session with Dr. Newman today over the Lullaby Killer shooting. I mentioned it to him."

"He's the department psychotherapist, right?"

"That's right. I had to meet with him since shooting Jeffery Schiffer in that take down a few weeks ago."

"Did it help?" Sidney asked, after a small pause. "Talking about the miscarriage?"

Isaac looked into her eyes.

"Actually, I think it did."

She nodded and looked down at her plate again.

"Darlin', I'm not suggesting you need to seek out a therapist, or even a grief counselor. But maybe just talking about it with a friend might help. Bree, or Jada. Maybe even talking to your brother, Simon."

She closed her eyes, saying nothing.

"Just something to consider, okay?" Isaac said softly.

Sidney nodded and took a deep breath. Then she took a sip of her water, and Isaac knew he had to do something to steer this conversation in another direction. A better direction.

"Hey, I've been wondering..."

Isaac paused and repositioned in his chair. Why did asking this question make him unreasonably nervous?

"I mean... I don't want to rush you or anything, but I just thought maybe we could um... well, if you wanted to, I mean..."

"Isaac?" Sidney's tone was cautious, and she placed a hand on his wrist, making his skin tingle. "Whatever it is, just spit it out."

Isaac took a breath, buoyed by her touch.

"Well, I was thinking maybe we could, you know, talk about... dates."

"Dates?"

The confusion in her voice was mirrored in her eyes, and Isaac licked his lips before trying again.

"Yeah. Wedding dates."

Her eyes lit up, and his nerves throttled back from danger mode.

"Oh! *Dates.*"

Isaac grinned. "Yeah. Dates."

"Hmm. Well, you know, I have been thinking about that."

She ran a single finger over the back of his hand and up his forearm, and that tingle zipped through his body and connected with his dick. He repositioned on his chair once more, for an entirely different reason.

"Really?" It was the only word he could get out.

"Um hmm," Sidney hummed in response.

Isaac quietly cleared his throat.

"Feel like sharing any of those thoughts with me?"

The question was met with a slender probing foot sliding up his leg beneath the table in a sexy caress. His mind clouded, like fog rolling in off Lake Erie.

Was she purposely trying to get him worked up? Deliberately teasing him when she knew he couldn't do anything about it?

Her foot rose higher, drifting up his inner thigh. Isaac pushed his empty plate away and leaned in closer, putting his elbows on the table and watching Sidney's luscious lips as she spoke.

"Well, I was thinking that I don't really want to wait a long time. I'd rather do it sooner than later."

"Oh, I like that idea a whole lot."

"Do you?"

"Hell yes. In fact, I'm all for flying to Vegas this weekend."

Sidney laughed, and the timbre of it lit up the night for Isaac. He smiled hard, bathing in the richness of the sound.

"That's a little sooner than I was thinking," Sidney said with a smile.

"Ah. Can't blame a man for trying." Isaac reached out and touched her bouncy curls. "So, when were you thinking?"

"Well, ideally I'd like to say Spring. That would give us enough time to plan. But that's nearly a year away and I don't want to wait that long. On the other hand, I don't need some elaborately planned church wedding with all the trimmings either. I had that the last time, and look how that turned out. There's a lot to think about. I just don't know."

"Hmm." Isaac could sense her uncertainty and he needed to resume his mission to put a smile on her face and chase away her sadness. He stood and walked over to the radio. "Well, just keep Vegas in mind while you're deciding, okay?"

He turned on the radio, which was always tuned to their favorite R&B oldies station, and turned up the volume.

"What are you doing?"

Playful suspicion crinkled the corners of her eyes, and Isaac held out his hand to her.

"Asking you to dance."

She smiled up at him.

"You're volunteering to dance?"

Isaac grinned and nodded.

"But you don't like to dance, Ike."

"I like dancing with you."

She took his hand just as Martha and the Vandellas began to sing about dancing in the streets, and Isaac led her to the middle of the room and began moving his body to the rhythm.

Dancing was something he'd only recently discovered he truly enjoyed doing. Normally, the very thought of flailing his body around to the music made him sick with worry. The chance of accidentally touching someone nearby was simply too great a risk. A fool's folly.

But when it was just him and Sidney — just him and the one woman whose touch never caused him an ounce of pain — he could be as free with his body as he wanted to.

He spun around and shook his shoulders, making a funny face at her.

Sidney laughed and finally began to dance with him.

Fast songs and slow. From the Supremes to the Temptations, the O-Jays, and more, they boogied around the dining room for over half an hour. When Marvin Gaye started to belt out "Let's Get it On," Isaac pulled her into his arms and held her tight against his body as they swayed.

He stared down into her light champagne gem-colored eyes and saw so much — love, longing, his future. He loved this woman more than life. She was his world.

Slowly, his hand ran from the small of her back down over the curve of her ass. He leaned in and inhaled the spiced honeysuckle scent of her. His lips moved to the rim of her ear.

"I really want to make love to you right now."

Something close to a whimper escaped her, and he looked down into her eyes once more.

"I want that too. But we can't."

"I know. Two weeks."

He said the words with a hint of dread. How the hell he was going to make it two whole weeks he had no clue.

Sidney pulled back, and he could see her mind working.

"You know? Technically, the doctor's instructions were not to insert anything into my kitty-kat during that time."

Isaac silently chuckled at her colorful euphemism.

"No tampons. No fingers." She ran her hand over the front of his sweatpants, shamelessly caressing the blatant bulge there. "No pythons," she whispered.

Isaac flinched at the contact, unable to hold in the needy groan.

"Well, that doesn't leave much room, does it?"

"No."

Her teasing tone mirrored the sweet torture of her hand, and Isaac nearly buckled under her ministrations.

"But there is another place where you can insert something."

Before her meaning took shape in his mind, Sidney was already on her knees in front of him, slowly pulling his sweatpants down. His eyes closed, and all conscious thought stopped when she took him into her mouth.

He gripped the back of a chair to keep himself steady while she worked. Opening his eyes, he looked down to watch her lips move up and down his thick dick, feeling the caress of her tongue around him.

Something snapped.

Some unknown control-switch inside him flipped.

His free hand delved into her mass of curls and fisted.

He held her head still while his hips bucked, thrusting himself deeper into her mouth, hitting the back of her throat again and again.

He felt her hand on his balls, gently fondling and squeezing.

The move was his undoing.

"Shit. Sid, I'm coming!"

He attempted to withdraw himself, but her hands suddenly grasped hold of his ass cheeks, keeping him in place.

He emptied himself down her throat with a shuddering groan.

He had no clue how long it took him to surface from the depths of ecstasy, but he felt Sidney kiss his lips. He opened his eyes just in time to see her cocky smile. She stepped around him and began to clear the table.

Isaac pulled up his sweatpants and turned toward her. He took the plates from her and set them back on the table. Then he took her into his arms and gave her a searing, sensual kiss.

"You are a fucking goddess," he whispered against her lips. "You know that, right?"

"I'm not a goddess. I'm just a woman in love with an incredible man."

Isaac shook his head.

"You can't fool me. You're a goddess sent to Earth just for me."

He kissed her again, slower this time, molding his lips to hers and caressing her tongue with his own and leaving them both breathless.

"Why don't you let me clean up here?" He gestured to the dining table. "You go relax."

She smiled at him, and Isaac couldn't decide if it was more sarcastic or amused.

"And do what? Lay around and eat bonbons?"

Sarcastic. Definitely.

He shrugged a shoulder. "Or whatever it is that you celestial types do in your spare time."

She giggled at him. "I think all that dancing has made you crazy."

"Maybe. But it was fun. And it had a very happy ending."

He wiggled his eyebrows at her.

"Mmm. For you."

Isaac put on his best playfully shocked face.

"Ooh! I see how it is. Well, now let me take this opportunity to make you a promise, darlin'. The minute our medically induced abstinence is over, I will more than make it up to you."

"I'm going to hold you to that, Detective."

She kissed his chin and then walked away.

Isaac watched her go and felt immense satisfaction that he'd put a smile on her face and gotten her to laugh. His plan was working.

Pete pulled his car into the driveway at home and turned off the engine. Then he took his cellphone out of the holder on the dash, took it off speaker, and brought it to his ear.

"I'm just really sorry I won't get to see you tonight."

"Me, too. But I promised my mom that I'd be there weeks ago. I can't get out of it now. Besides... I've been told that I'm spending way too much time with you as it is."

Pete felt his eyebrows shoot for the moon.

"Oh, really? And who told you that?"

"A certain just-turned-eleven-year-old that I know."

Pete laughed. "Wait a minute. I thought Charlie liked me!"

"Oh, he does. He's just used to having my undivided attention all the time. It's an adjustment."

Pete thought about that for a second and realized she was right. It had been just Charlie and his mom for as long as the kid could remember, after all.

"Okay, I get that. Well, have a good evening with your parents, baby. I'll call you tomorrow."

"Okay. And Pete?"

"Yep?"

"Don't call me baby."

She hung up before he had a chance to respond to her sass, and Pete chuckled to himself. He got out of the car and headed for the house. When he walked in the door, he heard his mom and his nephew, Mateo, laughing in the kitchen.

"What's so funny in here?" he asked, stepping into the room.

Julieta smiled at him.

"Mateo was telling me about a funny thing he saw on the computer."

"Oh, yeah? What's that?"

He smiled at Mateo, but the boy gathered up his sketchbook and his colored pencils and stood.

"It wasn't that funny."

He left the kitchen without another word, and Pete watched him go, feeling the definite frost in the air. He looked at his mom.

"What is eating him? That kid has been giving me the cold shoulder for days now. I swear, if he starts going back to his old ways, I will strangle him. I don't have time for his attitude."

He opened up the oven and took out the plate he knew Julieta would be keeping warm for him. Then he grabbed a fork and dug into his dinner before he'd even sat down. He was mid-chew when he looked up and found his mother staring at him.

"What?"

"Pedro."

She gave him one of those looks that told him he was missing something. Something big.

"What, *mamá?*"

Julieta sighed. "Don't you see, *mijo*? Mateo has an attitude with you because he misses you. He's feeling neglected."

"What? How can he possibly feel neglected, *mamá*? He sees me all the time!"

"Yes. After he got in trouble for being in the stolen car, he saw you all the time. You'd take him to his community service locations, and then take him for a soda afterwards. And on his free days, you'd show him how to do things, like clean the gutters, or make him help with yard work, and cleaning the garage. And then it all just stopped."

Pete stared at her.

"Oh, you still drop him off at his community service, but the rest of your free time isn't spent here anymore."

Pete opened his mouth to protest, when Jada's words about Charlie came back to him. Okay, so maybe he and Jada had been a little wrapped up in each other lately.

"For nearly two months, Mateo had your undivided attention. Now you spend all of your free time with Jada."

Pete moved the food around on his plate as his mind worked.

"He asked me the other day if I thought you liked her son," Julieta continued. "I told him you said Jada's son is a nice boy."

She shrugged her shoulders, and an unpleasant idea suddenly occurred to him.

"Mateo is jealous of Charlie?"

"I don't think he's truly jealous *of Charlie*. Only of the time Charlie gets to spend with you. I just think he needs to know that his place in your life is permanent."

Pete sat back and sighed, staring at his plate of uneaten food and wondering how he hadn't seen this sooner. He looked at his mom.

"I'm not doing this very well, am I?"

Julieta propped her chin on her hand.

"Well, these aren't normal circumstances. Legally, Mateo is my responsibility, not yours. You help us both so much, but I suppose it's only natural that you wouldn't feel the burden of guardianship. Of parenthood."

Something about that statement kicked him in the gut.

"But I do feel responsible for Mateo, *mamá*. And I don't like that word, *burden*. Mateo is not a burden. I love him just like I love you!"

"We love you too *mijo*."

Pete let out a heavy sigh and shook his head. He had to fix this. He had to fix it for all of them.

"I'll tell you what. I think you're right about how I've been spending my free time lately. Maybe it's time I brought Jada over for dinner. What do you think? I mean, I've been wanting to introduce you to her anyway. And Mateo could meet Charlie in a relaxed setting. We could all get to know each other."

Julieta smiled. *"Me encantaría conocer a la mujer que tiene tu corazón."*

She'd love to meet the woman who has his heart. Pete couldn't argue with that description. Jada did have his heart, and he hoped she wanted to keep it for a good long while.

"Haré algo especial," Julieta said. I'll make something special.

"No, you won't." Pete stopped her with a raised hand. "I'll do the cooking!"

"Oh. *Una noche verdaderamente especial."* A truly special night.

Pete rolled his eyes at her sarcasm, and they laughed.

7

The next morning, Isaac stood in the galley-style kitchen sipping a cup of black coffee. He'd had another one of those dreams where the sound of a little girl screaming had him bolting awake in a cold sweat.

Memories of it lingered now, alongside thoughts of his encounter with Jeffery Schiffer — the Lullaby Killer.

He remembered the physical pain of struggling over the gun with that bastard. The images of horror that had bombarded his mind when his bare hands touched Schiffer's; the agony of it. And he remembered the rush of relief when he let go of the gun with his hands, but took hold of it with his mind.

Those few moments still seemed so unreal.

He'd gone to see Geneviève Leroux about it the next day — to talk it through with the woman who'd become his psychic mentor. Her words about the incident still haunted him.

"Whether you like it or not, Isaac, your telekinetic powers seem to be growing. They took over instinctually when your physical body could no longer stand the pain."

He leaned against the kitchen counter and Geneviève's words rattled around in his head. Was she right? Had the telekinesis taken over all on its own, like she speculated? And more importantly... would it happen again?

He took another sip of the piping hot coffee and his gaze landed on the salt and pepper shakers on the opposite counter. Why did this aspect of his psychic abilities scare him so damn much?

"You will always fear this side of yourself unless you learn to master it, Isaac. Embrace it. Learn how to properly use it and control it, and it will become a source of strength."

When she'd told him that, he'd thought she was nuts. Embrace it?

He wanted no part of it.

When it had first happened — the day he'd somehow made those cement blocks fly through the air and connect with Damien Jarvis' head, killing him instantly — Isaac thought it had been some kind of fluke. Some kind of mistake. Some kind of hallucination.

Telekinesis was not real.

Then it happened again, with Jeffery Schiffer, and he had no choice but to accept the fact that it wasn't a hallucination at all.

He zeroed in on the salt shaker, concentrating on it with a single-minded focus. Placing the mug of coffee in his left hand, he extended his right hand out toward the salt shaker.

"The left hand is used to glean information, Isaac. The right hand is used to impart affirmations, or to expel power."

Another nugget of Geneviève's wisdom rolled through his mind as he focused on the salt shaker.

The salt slid, ever so slightly, to the left.

Isaac's heart skidded to a stop.

He pushed a breath through his lips and narrowed his eyes, concentrating harder.

The shaker wobbled and jerked.

It hopped to the left.

The toast he'd forgotten he'd started, shot up with a pop.

Isaac jumped.

Sidney breezed into the kitchen.

"Mmm. Thanks for pouring the coffee and fixing the toast this morning. I'm sorry we ran out of time for a proper breakfast."

Isaac choked on his embarrassment and coughed it away. He grinned at her hoping she hadn't noticed.

"I'm not."

Sidney gave him an almost bashful smile that he adored.

She sidestepped him and went to the fridge to put some cream into her coffee, and Isaac stepped over to the other counter. He moved the salt shaker back to its spot, and then went about spreading the mashed avocado onto a slice of toast, and took a bite.

"You know, darlin', I don't expect you to service me while we endure our two-week medical abstinence."

Sidney smiled at him and dumped a packet of sugar into her coffee. "Are you complaining?"

"Hell no. You can wrap your luscious lips around any part of me you want to. I just don't want you to think I expect it." He placed a finger at her chin and looked into her eyes. "You're still recovering from what your body's just gone through, Sid. I know that sex, in any form, must be the last thing on your mind right now. And that's okay."

He leaned down and placed a sweet kiss on her lips.

Sidney smiled and took his slice of avocado toast and walked away, heading to the table. Isaac grinned and spread the remainder of the mashed avocado on the other slice of toast and took a bite just as his cellphone rang.

"Taylor," he mumbled around a mouthful.

"Good morning, Detective Sergeant. You're needed at Wade Park. There's a dead body in the grass."

Isaac swallowed. "Wade Park? You mean the Lagoon?"

"Yes, sir. Patrol is already on scene."

"Okay. Have Detective Vega meet me there."

"Will do."

He ended the call and took another bite of his toast.

"I gotta go," he said, walking into the other room. "Another day, another dead body. I'll see you tonight."

"Okay. Be safe. I love you."

He clipped his gun to his side and leaned down to kiss her.

"I love you."

Then he headed for the door, stuffing the last of his toast into his mouth.

On the ride to the crime scene, his mind worked over the whole salt shaker ordeal, and Isaac tried to convince himself that he hadn't actually seen it trying to move. That didn't really happen.

Except that it did.

He'd seen it with his own eyes. He'd made that salt shaker move across the counter, just by thinking about it.

Okay, so it hadn't moved far. Only a couple of inches. But it did move. And maybe Geneviève was right and it was time for him to stop fearing this side of himself and just try to embrace it.

Or at least try to figure out how to control it.

He took a deep breath and shook his head. His life was so over the top lately. What the hell was that about?

He pulled up behind a marked police cruiser and got out of the car glancing around to get his bearings. Wade Lagoon Park was fairly close to the university, and that alone made him wonder what the odds were that this murder would somehow be related to the one from yesterday that they still had zero leads on.

He walked across the grass where the Crime Scene Unit was already hard at work, taking pictures and gathering evidence, and Isaac glanced at the horrors around him.

"Holy shit."

The victim was a Caucasian male, wrists and ankles bound by duct tape, naked and castrated, just like yesterday's victim. Only this one's genitals had been stuffed into his mouth, balls first. The grass beneath him was saturated with blood, and a small pile of what could only be vomit sat near the foot of the body.

A strong sense of revenge crashed over Isaac while he took in every detail.

"Morning, partner," Pete called out. "What we got?"

Isaac opened his mouth to respond as Pete drew nearer, but only shook his head instead.

Pete looked at the scene as he came closer.

"Holy mother of God."

Isaac nodded.

"What the hell is going on around here, Ike?"

"I don't know. But there's no question that this body is tied to the one from yesterday."

"Do we have an ID?"

"We don't have anything yet."

Pete gestured to the pile of bile. "Do you think the killer lost his dinner after viewing his own handy work?"

Isaac could only shake his head again in response. Then he turned to the nearest uniform.

"Who found the body?"

"Jogger. He's pretty shaken up."

The officer pointed a few yards away where another uniformed officer stood near an older African American man who sat on a bench, hunched over.

"Thanks."

Isaac motioned for Pete to follow, and they walked over to the bench. Isaac flashed the man his badge.

"Detective Sgt. Ike Taylor. This is Detective Pete Vega. What's your name, sir?"

"Roger." The man took a breath and tried again. "Um, I'm Roger Meaux."

"Do you jog this park often, Mr. Meaux?"

"Y-yes. Most days I do. It's so pretty here. It's a nice way to start the day, you know? Well... normally."

Isaac studied him closely.

"Did you happen to see anyone else around the body?"

Roger shook his head. "No. No I was just jogging with my earbuds in. And I saw something on the ground at a distance. I was angry that someone would toss trash in such a beautiful place. So, I jogged over to pick it up and find a trashcan." Roger paused and got emotional. "I thought it was a bag of trash!"

Isaac took note of how genuinely shaken the man seemed.

"Then I got closer and I couldn't believe what I was seeing. I-I'm afraid I lost my breakfast over there."

The words were spoken softly, and loaded with embarrassment.

Isaac nodded.

"Well, that explains the vomit," Pete mumbled.

"I don't suppose you can ID the victim?" Isaac asked Roger.

Roger shook his head once more. "No, I've never seen him before."

"Okay. If you think of anything else, please give us a call." He gestured to Pete, who handed the man a card.

They walked back over to the body, and Isaac scanned the scene once more.

"We've got everything we need here, Sarge." One of the CSU techs said.

"Thanks." Isaac raised a hand and motioned to where the medical examiner and his staff were waiting to transport the body. Then he turned to Pete.

"Until we get a positive ID, we need to assume vic number 2 is also affiliated with the university."

Pete nodded. "We can maybe find a match in that student roster we obtained yesterday."

"Might be tricky with the um... obstruction in his mouth, but yeah. That was my thoughts too. Meet you at the house."

"Right."

Isaac pulled out his cellphone and took a picture of the victim's face. Then he headed back to his car.

Back at the station, Isaac pulled a small stack of files from his car, then he and Pete entered the building together.

"Taylor. Vega." Lt. Gavin Hayes approached them as soon as they entered the detectives pit.

"Yes, sir?"

"You both missed roll call. How was the crime scene?"

"It was a bloody, pukey mess." The look on Pete's face said he was still grossed out over it, and Gavin looked to Isaac for confirmation.

Isaac cocked his head. "Pretty much."

"You think it's connected to the case you caught yesterday?"

"No doubt in my mind, sir. Vic was castrated in the same way."

"Yikes. Okay. Keep me posted."

Isaac nodded.

"In the meantime, can I see you in my office, please."

Isaac frowned, but he followed Gavin into his office and closed the door behind him.

"What's up, Lieu?"

"I was just wondering if you'd had a chance to look over those employee files I gave you yesterday?" Gavin took a seat behind his desk.

Isaac held up the stack of files.

"Got 'em right here. And yes, I did look through them last night."

He took a seat in front of the desk.

"And?" Gavin asked. "What are your thoughts?"

Isaac flipped through them and looked up.

"Well, there are two that I think might make great additions to our team. I like this one."

He handed a file to his boss, and Gavin glanced at the name on the file.

"Jack Runyan. I liked him too. He's experienced; got a good record."

Isaac nodded. "On the surface, he's the easy choice since he's already a detective with the Violent Crimes division at the 5th precinct. He probably wouldn't need a whole lot of training or hand-holding."

"Right."

"But... I also really like this one." He handed over another file.

"Lonnie Spencer. Really? Why this one?"

Isaac shrugged a shoulder. "Impressive record. Both his sergeant and his lieutenant mentioned his quick mind, his natural instincts, and his deductive reasoning skills. Sounds like the building blocks of a good detective to me."

Gavin nodded. "Okay. Thank you for your input."

"Sure. Thanks for asking for it." Isaac handed over the rest of the files. "Any idea when you and the chief might make a decision?"

"Hopefully by the end of the week. I'll let you know."

Isaac nodded and stood. "Well, I have an investigation to get to."

He left the office and went back out to his desk to dive into this new case that was getting more gruesome by the minute. He pulled out the student roster they'd obtained the day before and went through it page-by-page.

"Huh. Didn't see that coming."

"See what?" Pete looked up at him.

Isaac handed over the roster to him. "Check out the lower left corner. Does that look like our second victim to you?"

Pete stared at the small image and then read the name beneath it out loud.

"Craig Wentworth." He looked up and met Isaac's gaze. "That's victim number one's supposed best friend from high school."

Isaac nodded. "Yep. I think we need to dig deeper than social media and financials. Pick them both apart. You take Bobby; I'll take Craig."

"I'm on it."

They got to work then, looking into every aspect of each of the victim's lives. They'd been at it for well over an hour when Pete suddenly spread his arms wide, a look of surprise on his face.

"Whoa."

Isaac looked up at him. "Rape charges when they were seniors?"

Pete's arms fell to his thighs with a sad *flop* sound, and he stared at Isaac.

"Okay, how the hell did you know that? Did your psychic powers tell you that?"

"Nope. The computer did. Apparently, Bobby Cook, Craig Wentworth, and another boy... a Michael Rivers, were all accused of rape by a female classmate when they were high school seniors."

Pete nodded. "Yeah. Just stumbled on that myself. And because one of the boys was 18, and the other two were nearing that age, they were all charged as adults."

"So, our two victims, who we've already established go back as far as 4th grade, were both accused of raping a classmate in high school. Now both of them are dead."

"Dead with their junk cut off," Pete pointed out. "You thinking maybe we should look into the whereabouts of the other boy? This Michael Rivers?"

"I think that's an excellent idea." Isaac rocked back in his chair. "He could be our killer, or he could be next on the killer's list. I also think we need to take a closer look at that old rape case. Obviously, the boys were never convicted. We need to find out the details because it's starting to look like our case has everything to do with that one. I'll start there if you want to track down bachelor number three. If we can locate him, we need to bring him in for questioning."

"Okay." Pete nodded and turned toward his computer.

Isaac got to work looking into the old rape case.

"Hey, Ike?"

He looked up to see Pete staring at him in a squirrelly fashion. Then a wave of nervousness hit him, and Isaac swallowed down the dread and wondered what fresh hell his partner was about to unleash on him.

"Yes?"

"I, uh..." Pete glanced around and licked his lips. "Well, it's been brought to my attention that Jada and I have maybe been spending all of our free time together. Maybe to the detriment of some other important relationships."

Isaac lifted an eyebrow. "Meaning?"

"Meaning that both Mateo and Charlie have been feeling a little neglected lately."

"Ah." Isaac nodded, relieved that this dilemma had nothing to do with him in any way. "Well, that's understandable. But why are you telling me this?"

"Well... see, to counteract things, I was thinking that maybe it's time Jada and I got the boys together to meet and hang out, right? But then I thought it probably wouldn't be good to just throw them in a room together and hope for the best. I thought, maybe we should... I don't know... ease into it a little. Like with a dinner."

"A dinner?"

"Yeah. At my place. Day after tomorrow. And I thought that maybe you and Sid might want to come. 'Cause... you know... it might help to, sort of, break up the tension."

Isaac's relief plummeted to the floor of his stomach.

"You expecting tension? Between the boys?"

"No. Well... a little. But not just the boys. I mean, it's the first time Jada will be meeting my mom too. And I just thought with you and Sid there, it might help. Sidney would be there for Jada, and it would give my mom more new people to concentrate on instead of it being just Jada. You'd both be like a buffer! I mean... if you wouldn't mind."

Isaac sighed. He didn't want to go to Pete's for dinner with new people who might accidentally touch him. But he knew that if Jada mentioned it to Sidney, he'd wind up going anyway.

He slowly grinned. And he hoped it was genuine.

"I'll have to run it by Sid, but I'm sure she'd love to."

Pete smiled at him. "Thank you! Seriously, man, I mean it."

"Yeah, yeah."

Isaac turned back to his computer, but he couldn't help making an observation.

"Things seem to be getting serious with you two."

"Well, technically we're just friends." Pete's tone was uncertain.

"Uh huh. Friends with benefits."

"Actually, no. We put a stop to the sex so that we could slow down and get to know each other. It's been great. I leave here most nights and go to her place. We eat sometimes. We talk for hours. We make out... fool around a little."

"But no sex?"

"Nope. No sex." Pete took a deep breath. "But lately, it feels like we're heading back that way, you know?"

Isaac didn't respond to that. He didn't really want to discuss Pete's sex life. He looked back at his computer.

"Anyway... thanks for agreeing to do this. I really appreciate it. And you won't be sorry. You'll get a fantastic, authentic Puerto Rican meal out of it!"

"I'd better."

Pete chuckled.

"Listen, before I get to work on that high school rape case, I'm going to head over to the morgue and talk to Hiroshi about the bodies. Maybe he can give us something we can use."

"Okay."

Pete got to work trying to locate the third boy, and Isaac left the pit on his errand.

In the morgue, he found his friend in the lab hunched over the midsection of a body.

"Hey, Hiroshi."

"Ike. Just the guy I wanted to see."

"Oh? I hope that's because your examinations of the two castrated bodies uncovered something I need to know."

Hiroshi grinned. "Well, as a matter of fact, I do have some information for you in that regard. But that's not what I wanted to talk to you about."

"It's not?" For the second time in less than an hour, Isaac was put on guard by a friend acting weird. He took a wary breath. "So what's up?"

"Well, first... both of your victims were whacked in the head by a blunt object."

"So they were dead before they were castrated?"

"No. But they were incapacitated first. Most likely so that the killer could tie them up, or transport them, or whatever."

Isaac looked over the body of victim number two, wincing at the gaping hole where the genitals should be.

"So, the cause of death?"

"Cause of death was definitely the castration. They both bled out in mere minutes. And my guess is that they were awake at the time."

Isaac shook his head, closing his eyes for a moment as he pieced the sequence of events together.

"Okay, wait."

He opened his eyes and looked at Hiroshi, but he wasn't actually seeing his friend. His mind's eye was focused on the crime scenes. On how the victims' last few minutes must have played out.

"So you're telling me they were hit in the head with some blunt object. Then they were tied up and transported to the crime scenes, where they were woken up so that they could watch their killer chop off their manhoods."

"Yep."

"That's downright medieval."

"That's one word for it."

"Can you tell me what kind of instrument was used to cut off their um... stuff."

"Something with a long, broad blade."

"Like a machete, or a kukri, or something like that?"

"Exactly."

"Wow. Okay."

His mind was reeling over the possible motives in the case, and now he was eager to get back to his desk and begin his deep dive into the old rape case that he believed was at the heart of it.

"Thanks, Hiroshi. I'll see you later."

He spun and headed for the door.

"But wait. Ike!"

Isaac stopped and turned to look at his friend.

"I wanted to talk to you about something. Remember?"

"Oh, yeah. Sorry. What's up?"

"Well. Now it seems really unimportant after talking about your case, but... well, I was wondering what you could tell me about, um..."

Hiroshi hesitated, tapping on the edge of the metal table holding the dead body.

"About what?"

"About Miku. Miku Barlow."

Isaac frowned. "The Realtor?"

"Yes! That's her."

Isaac stared at him for a second wondering if his friend was moving, or just looking for a hookup.

"Well, she's an excellent Realtor. Sidney and I enjoyed working with her. Sid gave her a list of things she was looking for in a place, and Miku worked hard to find us exactly what we were after. She knows her stuff."

"Yeah. That's great. Um, what do you know about her status?"

"Her status?"

"Yeah. You know, her relationship status?"

Isaac's gaze traveled up and over the ceiling. What was it today? Was he wearing a sign that said, *'Please talk to me about your love life?'* Had he done something to elicit this highly uncomfortable behavior from his friends?

"I have no knowledge of Miku Barlow's relationship status. She was our Realtor, not our friend."

"But she was at your housewarming party a few months back."

"Yes. We did invite her to our housewarming party. Because she was our *Realtor*. It was a nice gesture. A thank you, if you will."

"So, you don't have a clue if she's seeing anyone?"

"Nope. No clue."

"Is she married?"

"No. I do remember Sidney asking her that question, and I'm pretty sure the response was no."

"So you know more than you think you do! Did she ever mention a significant other when she was showing you houses?"

Isaac quietly cleared his throat and reached for his wallet.

"I believe I still have one of her cards."

"Oh, I have her card. She gave it to me at your housewarming party."

"Well, then by all means, please use it and ask her these uncomfortable questions yourself."

"You are not being very helpful, Ike."

"I do apologize."

"No, you don't. Get out of my lab."

Isaac stifled a laugh and looked down at the floor for a second. Then he looked Hiroshi in the eyes, trying hard to hide any amusement.

"I'm sorry. Truly. I don't know much about Miku, except that she's great at her job, and I would recommend her services to anyone looking to buy or sell a home. I know that she's smart and kind and funny in regard to her profession. I know literally nothing else."

"You know that she's cute."

Isaac grinned. "I stand corrected. You're absolutely right. That is one more thing I do know about her. She's quite attractive. I also know that I wish you luck."

Hiroshi narrowed his eyes.

"Seriously," Isaac offered. "I think the two of you might just click. She's got a great sense of humor and so do you. I think you should go for it."

Hiroshi smiled at him. "Thanks! I think I will."

"May I go now, please."

"Get out of here. I've got work to do."

Isaac turned for the door, still hearing Hiroshi laughing as he entered the hallway.

Back at his desk, Isaac got to work, pulling up the old case files on the computer and going through whatever he could find. He looked through the police report of the rape itself, and was dismayed to find that the actual rape kit — the body of evidence collected off the victim that night in the ER — had been booked into evidence, but had never been tested.

It was the dirty little secret behind all rape cases. The backlog of untested rape kits collecting dust on a shelf in every police evidence room across the country.

That knowledge went a long way to understanding how the boys accused were never convicted. The untested rape kit, coupled with the boys' high-dollar attorneys — provided by their rich parents — told the sad story.

Isaac was willing to bet that if he were to request that rape kit be submitted for DNA testing, their two castrated victims would be guilty as sin.

He raised up and stretched out his back, glancing at the clock across the room. He was shocked to realize several hours had passed. It was getting close to shift change.

He balled up a piece of scratch paper he'd been making notes on, and reached to toss it into the small waste basket beside his desk.

At the same time, a janitor reached for the waste basket, his bare forearm connecting with the back of Isaac's hand.

Razor-sharp claws tore at Isaac from the inside, and the flash that came with it showed the janitor shove a man backward out of a doorway. Then he stepped inside the house and proceeded to beat the other man with an old fashioned billy club.

"Ahh!"

Isaac doubled over in his seat, clutching the edge of his desk.

"Ike! You okay, man?"

Pete sounded worried.

"Sorry, dude. I didn't mean to hit you there."

"What? You *touched* him?"

The worry in Pete's voice morphed into pissed in zero point two seconds, and Isaac fought to regain his composure.

"It's okay. I'm fine."

He held up a hand to back Pete up. But he did appreciate the way his partner had become something of a watchdog for his personal space.

"You sure?"

"I'm really sorry. I was just reaching for the trash can here."

Isaac looked up at the guy. He knew that the janitors who cleaned the station rotated on trash duty, but he thought he knew all of the ones on staff. This guy he didn't recognize at all. Must be new.

"It's all right. Do your job."

The man emptied their can and moved on to the next set of desks. Isaac took a good look at the man's face, still slightly panting. Then he took a deep breath and tried to shake off what he'd just seen.

"You sure you're okay, man?" Pete asked again.

Isaac glanced at Pete and thought about telling him, but then decided against it.

"Yeah."

He turned back to his paperwork, but he couldn't get the images out of his mind. And he wondered if that flash had been from the past or from the future. Either way, it had freaked him out. Such brutality and cruelty.

The real question was how the hell a man like that had gotten hired by a janitorial service that frequently went into police stations and courthouses. Isaac knew for a fact that all employees of the service were required to go through a stringent background check, so how had this guy slipped through the cracks?

At any rate, he knew that he had to find out more, because that flash had been more than disturbing.

He glanced around the detectives pit and spotted the man across the room, emptying more trash cans. His gaze zoomed in on the man's uniform, and he took note of the name embroidered there. Savage.

Fitting.

"Did Hiroshi have any news?"

Pete's question brought him back from the rabbit hole's edge.

"Uh, yeah." He tried again to shake it off. "He said both our vics were hit in the head with a blunt object. A means of subduing them for transport to the crime scenes, where they were then woken up and made to watch while they were unmanned with something like a machete or a kukri."

"Damn!"

Pete visibly flinched and repositioned in his seat, and Isaac couldn't blame him.

"What about you? Any luck locating our third alleged rapist?"

"Yes and no."

"Explain."

"Well, apparently he's a senior at Cleveland State University. At least, he's enrolled there. But no one's seen him for a couple of weeks."

"What do you mean?"

"I mean no one's seen him."

"Well, it is technically summer. Maybe he left campus to go home for a few weeks."

"Home is a dwelling in Fairfax where he lives with his older sister. Seems their mother, a single parent, moved to Akron for her job a year ago, allowing Michael to stay with his sister so that he could continue to go to Cleveland state. I've reached out to the sister, who says that Michael actually lives on campus in a dorm and is rarely at the house. I've tried contacting his roommate, but I can't locate him either."

"Huh. That can't be good."

"I'll keep at it."

"That's all we can do, I guess."

Isaac locked eyes with the strange janitor as the man passed by his desk once more on his way out.

8

At Hope House, Sidney stood up from her desk and began to gather her things. Zoe was already gone for the day, and Julie, a social work graduate student that Zoe employed to stay with the residents in the evenings, was getting settled at her desk in the office.

"Okay, Julie. I'm out. If you need anything during the night you know where to find us."

Julie looked at her and smiled.

"You say that every evening, Sidney, but calling you or Zoe during the night is always my very last resort."

"I know. But we're there if you need us."

Julie laughed, and Sidney headed out of the office. She stopped by the kitchen, where the residents were having dinner, and popped her head in the door. She smiled as she watched them. There were only three adults right now — Ann, and her two children, Laney and Ben. Beth, and her daughter, Kylee. And Tyneesha, a soft-spoken librarian in her second trimester of pregnancy — and Sidney marveled at how willing the women always were to help one another through what had to be the darkest time in their lives.

"I'm leaving, gang. Julie's in the office if you need anything."

They all smiled or waved their goodbyes to her, and Sidney headed for the door to leave.

When she opened it, a man stood on the other side.

He was disheveled, with bloodshot eyes and reeking of alcohol, and Sidney's heart clawed its way to her throat.

"I want to talk to my wife."

The heart in her throat dropped to the depths of her stomach.

Flashbacks of the incident from a few weeks ago flew through her mind like a shock reel. She blinked and pulled herself together.

"You're not supposed to be here."

"I don't want any trouble. I just want to see my wife. I need to talk to her."

How would Zoe handle this?

She formed a barrier with her body, one hand on the door frame and the other firmly on the door itself. Then she looked the man in his eyes.

"I don't know who your wife is, sir. And If you..."

"Donald?"

From behind her, Sidney heard Ann's voice, and the woman sounded terrified.

Sidney's stomach sank even lower.

"Annie!"

The man lurched forward, his beer belly nearly knocking Sidney over. But she refused to budge.

"Honey come here! Let me talk to you for a minute."

"No!" Ann yelled. "Donald, you're not supposed to be here."

"Annie, I just want to see my kids! Where are they?"

"No. Donald, go away!"

"Sir, I'm calling the police if you don't leave this property immediately!" Sidney hoped her voice sounded more forceful than it had to her own ears.

Donald ignored her and the barrier she created, and pushed his way into the foyer of the house.

"Dammit, Annie, I want to see my kids! You can't keep them from me."

A surge of frustration and pent up rage ran through Sidney.

Perfectly executing a hold Pete Vega had taught her in the self-defense class, she grabbed Donald, twisted his arm behind his back, and shoved him into the nearest wall.

"You're trespassing!" she growled.

Donald was momentarily shocked.

So was Sidney.

But his drunken confusion didn't last long. He pushed off the wall and backhanded her across the face, knocking her backward into the door.

Ann screamed.

Julie and Tyneesha came running from different directions.

Sidney was hurting, and pissed.

She had no clue where the rage and determination came from, but she was damn sure going to use it to her advantage.

She launched herself at him, punching him three times in the face before she landed a kick square in his chest with her stiletto.

The kick knocked him into the banister of the stairs, and then he flopped to the floor on his ass.

His stunned expression gave her just enough time to pull her .380 Ruger out of her purse and level it at him.

"You're trespassing. And you're violating Ann's restraining order. Julie, call the police!"

"Dialing now!" Julie called out.

"All right, I'm leaving! I'm leaving!"

Donald scrambled to his feet and ran out of the door and down the porch steps.

Adrenaline crashed into Sidney's chest. She could feel the collective rush of relief that everyone else seemed to expel, but she was shaken.

She'd never pulled her new gun on anyone before, and she noted the shaking of her hands when she lowered it and put it away in her purse.

"Oh, my God. Thank you so much, Sidney! Thank you."

She tried to accept Ann's gratitude, but she couldn't do much more than nod.

Ann's kids suddenly ran from the kitchen and into their mother's arms. Sidney watched the woman shoot a grateful smile to Beth.

"Thank you for keeping them in the kitchen with you."

"Of course," Beth said.

"The cops are on their way," Julie announced.

Sidney nodded, still unable to speak. She placed a hand on her chest, silently begging her heart to calm down.

She pulled out her cellphone and sent a text to Ike.

Sidney:
Not an emergency
All ok now
But just pulled my gun on resident's husband

She put her phone down just as the door opened again, and Dr. Lance Tobey stepped inside. He seemed slightly amused and surprised to find them all congregated at the front door. He glanced around with a smile.

"Hi, everyone. Why are we all standing in the entryway?"

His smile suddenly faded.

"What happened?"

Julie launched into an animated retelling of the events, and Lance stared at Sidney.

"He hit you?"

He stepped closer and reached out to touch her face.

Sidney jerked away, glaring at him.

"Your face is beginning to bruise and swell, Sidney. Let me do my job and check you out. Okay?"

"You really should let him look at you, Sidney." Ann's voice was full of misplaced remorse. "Donald is very heavy-handed. I know. He broke my jaw once slapping me that way."

Ann turned her embarrassed gaze to the floor. Then she ushered her kids back into the kitchen.

"I'll wait for the cops out front," Julie said, pointing to the door.

Sidney nodded and then, abandoning her purse and cellphone, walked into the living room and sat down on the couch.

Her hands were still shaking.

Lance followed with his black medical bag and sat down beside her.

He gently moved a curl from her face. Then he lightly touched a spot near the corner of her right eyebrow.

Sidney flinched at the contact, surprised at the pain. It was the first she'd felt, and she knew that meant the adrenaline was wearing off. The whole right side of her face began to throb, and it burned like it was on fire.

"Ah!"

"Sorry. You've got a small cut there that's beginning to swell. He must've got you with a ring."

He opened up his bag and got to work holding a cotton ball there, applying pressure to stop the bleeding she hadn't realized she was doing. Then he added a dab of ointment on the cut, and placed a small bandage there.

"It won't need stitches. Probably won't even leave a scar, okay?"

Sidney nodded, and met his gaze. She allowed herself a moment to study his face. He was actually a very attractive man when he wasn't being creepy.

"Looks like he really did a number on you."

Something about that comment irked her, and she cocked her head, giving him an 'oh really' glare.

"Actually, he did this damage with just one backhanded punch."

Lance moved on to the bruise at her cheek.

"Good thing he didn't have time for more. A little ice should help the swelling, okay?"

His tone was condescending, and Sidney side-eyed him.

"That one punch was all I *let* him have before I knocked him on his ass and pulled my gun on him."

Lance's eyebrows shot up, and then he grinned.

"Well, I bet that surprised him."

"I guess."

"Then you saved the day."

Sidney shook her head.

"No, I didn't. I should've insisted that he stay put until the cops got here. I mean, I was the one with the gun. I shouldn't have let him get away."

"I think Ann would say that you saved the day. You're being too hard on yourself." He put his things away in his bag. "But I get it though. I tend to do that too when I'm feeling down or depressed."

He stared into her eyes, and Sidney wondered what he was talking about. What did he know about the way she was feeling?

He stared so long and so intently that Sidney suddenly felt uncomfortable sitting this close to him. She turned away, and Lance reached out and touched her chin, turning her face back toward him.

She thought he wanted to look at her wounds again. Instead, he leaned in and planted a kiss on her lips.

Sidney pulled back instantly, then she physically scooted away from him.

"What the hell are you doing?"

He smiled, oozing charm.

"Well, it's called a kiss, but if you have to ask, then I guess I did it wrong."

"You shouldn't have done it at all."

"My bad," he grinned. "I just thought we were sharing a moment here."

"Then you read the moment very wrong. We've just had a troubling domestic incident in this house, and I'm not in the proper headspace for your moves right now. Not to mention the fact that I'm engaged to be married, and you know that."

"Whoa." Lance held up his hands. "First of all, I was under the impression things weren't going so well in your relationship."

"Well, you got your facts wrong too! I'm sure that happens a lot when you creep into doorways and eavesdrop on private conversations. But since we're on the subject... even if things were bad in my relationship — which they're not — that still wouldn't give you the right to force an uninvited kiss on me."

She stood and walked away from him.

"Okay. Calm down." Lance stood too. "It was obviously just a misunderstanding."

"Misunderstanding? Do you misunderstand your patients at the hospital and lay kisses on them?"

"No, of course not. But I thought we were kind of feeling each other here. Don't you think you're overreacting just a little? I mean... maybe you're upset with yourself because you *wanted* me to kiss you. Did you ever think of that?"

Sidney turned on him.

"Are you listening to yourself, doctor? We're standing in a women's shelter right now. A safe place for women who've seen all types of abuse from their domestic partners. A place that works diligently to empower those women to stand up for themselves, and you're trying to tell me that I don't know my own mind?"

The smile slowly slid off Lance's face.

"Next are you going to tell me that I'm being hysterical? Or that I was asking for your advances? Maybe my clothing was too suggestive, or I somehow *made* you act like an ass?"

"Sidney, I didn't mean to..."

"I think you should go do whatever it is you came here to do, and leave me alone now."

She glared at him, and Julie ushered two uniformed police officers into the room.

"Sidney, these officers need to speak with you and Ann."

Sidney heard her, but her focus remained on Lance. Until she heard Isaac's voice in the entryway.

"Sidney!"

"Isaac?"

She started for the door when he burst into the room with Pete behind him.

Sidney rushed into his arms.

"God, baby, I texted you back, and I called, but you wouldn't answer." Isaac squeezed her tight. "I was going insane."

"I'm sorry. I seem to have lost track of my phone."

Sidney looked up at him, and Isaac let go of her and gently lifted her chin, turning it so that he could study her face. His light grey eyes darkened like storm clouds. She could see the anger come down like a torrent of rain.

"Who the fuck put their hands on you?"

"Calm down." She placed her hands on his chest. "It's all over now, and he's gone."

"What happened, Sid?"

"Excuse me, Detective," one of the officers interrupted them. "We still need a statement from Ms. Fairchild, and from the wife of the intruder."

Isaac nodded, and then led Sidney over to the couch. She sat down in the exact spot she'd been in before. And she watched Isaac zero in on Lance, who now stood behind the couch.

"Who are you?"

"Oh. I'm Dr. Lance Tobey." He held out his hand, which Isaac ignored.

"Lance works at Cleveland Clinic," Sidney said, her tone flat. "He volunteers here a few hours each week. He bandaged my cut." She motioned to the tiny bandage near her right eyebrow.

"And where were you when some asshole was threatening the women and slapping Sidney around?" Isaac asked.

"Driving," Lance responded. "I arrived just after the asshole left, apparently."

Isaac grunted and sat down next to Sidney and wrapped his arm around her, holding her hand while she gave the cops her statement.

"So, you punched him twice and then kicked him in the chest?" the officer asked.

"Three times. I punched him three times, and then kicked him."

Pete smiled at her. "All those self-defense and kickboxing classes are paying off, Rocky. My prized pupil."

He punched the air like a prize fighter, and Sidney grinned at him.

"What happened then?" the officer asked.

"Then I grabbed my gun from my purse and pointed it at him, and he stopped fighting. That's when I told Julie to call you guys."

"You pulled a gun on him?"

"Yes."

"And that gun is registered to you?"

"Yes."

"Of course, it is, Hamilton." Ike sounded irritated, and Sidney lightly squeezed his hand. "I taught her to shoot myself. Hell, I bought her the gun. She got her Concealed Weapons Permit a month ago. Working here, I figured she needed it."

"You know I have to check, Detective. What happened next?"

Sidney sighed. "He got scared when I pulled my gun and we called the police. He got up and ran out. That's everything."

"And when we find him, do you wish to press charges for assault?"

Ike answered before she could.

"Yes, she does."

The officer looked at Sidney to confirm, and she nodded her agreement.

"Okay." He put his notepad and pen away. "I'm going to go see if my partner's done with the other witness."

"Is Sid free to go?" Ike asked.

"Sure."

The officer nodded and left the room, and Sidney slumped against Isaac.

"I'm so glad you're here."

He pulled her closer to him. "How you doing, slugger?"

"I feel drained. And my face hurts."

"I'll bet it does. I swear, if I ever get my hands on the bastard that hit you, I'll kill him myself." He gently kissed her forehead. "Come on. Let's go home and put some ice on that beautiful face."

"Okay."

They stood, and he took her hand. As they left the room, Sidney could see Lance watching them from the corner of her eye, but she refused to turn and acknowledge him. She grabbed her purse and her cellphone from the table in the entryway on the way out the door.

Outside, the fresh air made her throbbing face tingle. She winced and watched Isaac toss his keys to Pete.

"Pick me up in the morning."

Pete shot a mischievous grin at him. "The keys to the Stang? Sweet! I'm going joyriding tonight."

"My car better be in one piece tomorrow, or I will make work a living hell for you."

"I might have her back from Tijuana by then."

"Pete."

"Calm down. Like I could drive all the way to Mexico in one night. Now, Atlantic City... "

"You're not funny, Vega."

"Opposite direction," Pete said, ignoring the warning in Ike's tone. "But I got a better chance of making it."

"Better chance of catching my foot up your ass too."

Isaac opened the passenger side door of her car, and Sidney smiled at their banter as she slid in.

"Ooh."

Her hand flew to her cheek and she regretted the smiling.

When Isaac got behind the wheel of her car, he adjusted the seat for his 6 foot 4 inch frame, and Sidney leaned her head back and watched him.

He glanced over at her as he drove.

"You okay over there?"

"Yeah."

"You sure? You don't sound okay, darlin'."

Sidney hesitated, thinking back over the events of the last hour and a half. And she wiped the silent tears from her cheeks, hoping that he wouldn't notice them as he drove.

"When that drunk jerk backhanded me..."

She paused, still trying to understand her own emotions.

"I wasn't afraid anymore. All I felt was... rage. Burning anger. In the moment, I didn't know where it had come from. But now I think I do."

"And where's that?"

"Grief. I'm angry that our baby is gone. And I'm angry at myself for being so damn angry."

She burst into tears and lowered her face to her hands. Sobs wracked her body and the tears just kept coming.

She felt Isaac unlatch her seatbelt and pull her closer, and she grabbed hold of his shirt and buried her face in his chest. The scent of leather and sage, with just a hint of citrus filled her senses and eased her sorrow like a balm.

It was the scent of Isaac.

The scent of home.

His arms held her tight for what seemed like the longest time, and she listened to his soothing voice whispering out words of encouragement and love.

He didn't offer any advice. He didn't try to push any kind of counseling, or therapy. He simply held her and let her cry. Like he'd done for days now. He held her and allowed her to slowly pull herself back together.

When she finally looked up and glanced around, she frowned.

"Where are we?"

"Dave's Market parking lot."

Sidney looked at him and smiled. Then they both started to laugh.

"Why are we here?"

"Well, I had to pull in somewhere so that I could properly comfort you."

He reached out and wiped a stray tear from her cheek with his thumb.

"I'm sorry for falling apart on you."

"Hey. What'd I tell you before, hmm? You don't ever need to apologize for your pain. And you don't need to hide it from me either."

"I didn't even know I wanted a baby until I lost ours. How fucked up is that?"

"It's not. Not at all. 'Cause the same thing happened to me."

Sidney wiped her nose and stared at him.

"What?"

Ike reached into his pocket and pulled out a fading light purple bandana-style handkerchief and handed it to her.

"I didn't know I wanted to be a father before the miscarriage, darlin'. Yet here I am, wishing it were so."

Sidney felt the tears sting her eyes again.

"Really?"

Ike nodded. "Really."

Sidney stifled another sob, then she wiped her eyes and blew her nose.

Somehow, the knowledge that they were in this — the sorrow, and the heartbreak and the love — together made her feel like maybe everything would be okay.

She clutched the handkerchief to her chest as she maneuvered back into her seat and strapped on her seatbelt.

Isaac took hold of her hand and held it tight all the way home.

Once they got home, Sidney headed straight for the shower.

While she busied herself in there, Isaac went into the home office and fired up the desktop computer. Seated in front of the screen he glanced at the door. He could hear the water running in the bathroom, so he knew he had a few minutes. He placed a video call to his grandfather, Sterling Taylor.

"Isaac!"

The smile on the older man's face seemed to radiate light, and Isaac wondered if his grandfather ever got truly good and angry at anyone. Somehow, he couldn't imagine it.

"It's so good to hear from you."

"Hey, Grandad. How you doing?"

"Well, I'm doing just fine. How's everything up there in Ohio?"

Isaac grinned when his thick Tennessee accent made the state sound like Ohi-ya.

"Things here are okay." He hoped his voice sounded more convincing than he felt, but he had his doubts.

"And that beautiful future granddaughter-in-law of mine? I trust she's okay after the loss?"

Isaac stared at his grandfather, mouth hanging wide open.

"Grandad, how..."

His voice trailed off and he let that question dangle in the wind because he already knew the answer.

"You saw that? But when?"

Sterling smiled. "Oh, I saw it a while back. Back before you ever came to visit me. In fact, I imagine that I saw Sidney long before you ever did."

Isaac was dumbfounded.

There were suddenly so many questions he wanted to ask. So many that had nothing to do with the reason he'd reached out.

"I don't understand. How could you see something about Sidney before you'd even met her?"

"Well, actually, what I saw was more about you than it was about her."

Isaac sat with that for a moment, trying to work it out. But he'd come to his grandfather for a specific reason, and he had to stay focused.

But first...

"That first visit. You implied that, um...well, that there would be an actual baby at some point."

Isaac's voice was loaded with trepidation and uncertainty, and he took a tentative glance at his grandfather's face on the screen.

"Did I?" Sterling sounded amused.

Isaac gave him a look. The kind that came with begging.

"Come on, Grandad. Don't play games. Not about this. Not now."

The amusement in Sterling's eyes softened to genuine love and concern.

"Is that why you're calling, son? For assurances?"

Isaac's shoulders slumped on a sigh, and he looked down for a second. Sidney's tearful confession on their drive home had rattled him. And yeah... he supposed he needed a little reassuring.

"I don't know. Maybe."

"Very well, then." Sterling's voice was steady and matter-of-fact. "You and your delightful fiancée will have a beautiful family, Isaac. All in due time."

The sudden and unmanly knot in his throat surprised him, and Isaac turned away from the screen to try and get his emotions under control.

"Sidney will be all right," Sterling continued. "And so will you. And the babies will be beautiful. Trust me. I've already seen them."

Isaac wiped his face and sniffed before he dared look at the screen again. When he finally did, he shook his head.

"I wish to God that I'd had you in my life while I was growing up."

Sterling's sad smile nearly did him in.

"I know. But we can't go back and change it. All we can do now is move forward. And I'm here whenever you need me."

Isaac nodded. "I was actually planning to call to get your help on something work related. I didn't even know I needed to talk to you about personal stuff. Not tonight anyway."

"Oh, well, I'll be happy to try my hand at police work if you want me to!" Sterling grinned. "Lay it on me."

Isaac laughed. "I think I've got the police work under control."

"Oh, shoot." Sterling snapped his fingers.

"My question is about touching someone. You know how you said that I can choose whether to see the past or the future when I touch someone?"

"Oh, yeah."

"Can you teach me how?"

"Why, it would be my absolute pleasure."

They stayed on their call for another thirty minutes. By the time Isaac finished up his conversation and lesson with his grandfather, Sidney was out of the shower and curled up on top of the covers. He joined her in their bedroom, holding two Ibuprofen and a bottle of water in one hand, and a fully loaded ice pack for her face in the other. He handed her the pills and water.

She sat up and swallowed them down, and then softly whimpered when she placed the ice pack against her face.

Isaac sat on the edge of the bed, facing her and fuming.

"Pisses me off. I swear, when they pick this guy up, I'm going to..."

"Do nothing!" Sidney cut him off.

"Like hell! Once they've got him in a jail cell, I'm going to go down there and..."

"Isaac, please. I don't want you getting in trouble over this jerk. He's not worth it. And my face is going to be fine. The swelling will go down, the bruises will fade, and I'll be good as new. But if you jeopardize your job just to beat this guy down in revenge..."

"The only one in jeopardy is going to be him. Trust me!"

Sidney sighed, and he could hear the mounting aggravation behind it. So he let it drop and changed the subject.

"How about I put a frozen pizza in the oven? Maybe toss some more lettuce into the leftover salad from yesterday? That way you don't have to worry about cooking."

"Throw in a few cookies for dessert, and some extra cuddle time, and you've got a deal."

"Done."

He stood and leaned down to kiss her lips. Then he headed for the kitchen.

She screamed his name, and Gavin had never felt more like a man in his life.

Her body moved above him, vibrating from her orgasm and still riding him like he was a wild stallion she was determined to break.

His hands moved, groping her shapely thighs, her tiny waist, her full breasts.

Gerri Miller was the most gorgeous woman he'd ever seen — deep ebony skin, bright and soulful dark brown eyes, high cheekbones and full, perfect lips. And not an ounce of fat to be found on her toned body.

Her black hair was soft and straight, and hung just past her shoulders. At the station, Gavin had only seen it pulled back into a severe ponytail that left her model-like features on full display. Now, he sat up — ripping another scream from her lips and sending her into a second orgasm — and ran both his hands through her hair, drawing her in to lock his mouth onto hers.

Their fiery kiss robbed the breath from his lungs, making his own release that much more intense.

"Ahh!"

Gavin let out a loud cry and then flopped back onto the pillows in slow motion.

Gerri climbed off of him and rolled over.

Panting and heavy breathing were the only sounds in the room for the longest time, and Gavin stared at the ceiling. He didn't remember sex with his ex-wife being this energetic.

Or this good.

Or this spontaneous and adventurous, for that matter.

When he'd walked through the door of her apartment an hour ago, Gerri had surprised the shit out of him by stripping off her clothes and demanding he treat her body like a popsicle. Right there on the kitchen island.

So he had.

But that wasn't what he'd come back here for. He removed the spent condom and tied it off, dropping it to the floor. Then he turned his head and looked at her.

"How are you?"

"What?"

Her tone told him she thought it was an odd question to ask.

"I came here after work to check in on you. Not to fuck you. Not that I'm complaining, mind you. But... how are you?"

Gerri chuckled, and Gavin thought he could hear the roll of her eyes in the sound.

"It's okay, Lieutenant. I'd much rather have the genuine fuck than the obligatory concern."

Her words were like a slap to his face, and he stared at her.

"Is that what you think this is? That I'm showing concern because I'm obligated to as your boss?"

Gerri glanced at him and shrugged a shoulder before turning her gaze back to the ceiling.

"Partly. I know you're here for the sex, but I mean... I'm pretty sure you think I'm a mess since Curt died. And you're right. I am. My partner bled out on the street like a dog, and there was nothing I could do to stop it."

"But you did stop it," Gavin insisted. "You heard the doctor that night in the ER. He said that your applying pressure to Curt's wound kept him alive for as long as it possibly could have. You kept him alive until the paramedics got him to the hospital."

"Yeah, for all the good it did."

Gavin propped himself up on his elbow and looked at her.

"But you made the effort, Gerri. You tried your damnedest to save his life. No one can fault you for that. Curt knows what you tried to do. He knows that his partner never left his side."

She wiped a tear from her cheek and leaned up and kissed him. Then she raised her leg, attempting to mount him again. Gavin took hold of her shoulders and gently pushed her back.

"Gerri, stop."

"What? This is why you're here, remember? For the sex."

She tried to kiss him again, but Gavin moved, rolling them

over so that he pinned her to the mattress. He stared down into her beautiful, troubled eyes.

"I am not here for the sex. I'm here for you. Because I can't stop thinking about you. And because no matter how hard I fight it... I can't stay away from you. Not when I know you're hurting. I'm here because I care about you, Gerri. Much more than I know I should."

She stared back at him, seeming to search his eyes for the truth.

"Do you mean that?"

Her voice was small and shaky, and he could hear the hope hiding there. The sound of it squeezed his heart.

"I don't say it if I don't mean it. I spent 20 years being lied to by the woman I loved. The woman I thought loved me." Gavin shook his head. "The one thing I will not do is lie to you."

"But you did lie. For months, you lied every time you pushed me away."

"No. That is simply not true. I never said that I wasn't interested, or that I didn't want you. I said it wasn't a good idea."

"So why now? What's changed?"

Gavin sighed, and swallowed down all of his reservations. She deserved the truth.

"What's changed is that I finally got a taste of you. I finally held you in my arms and made love to you." He trailed his thumb down her cheek in a sweet caress. "There's no way I'd walk away now."

She took a breath and studied his eyes, and Gavin watched *her* eyes swell with tears.

Oh, God.

"Are you sure? Because I love you, Gavin. And I know it's way too soon in this relationship for me to say that. But what you don't understand is that I have loved you for so long. And now that you're here in my arms, I don't want to waste a single minute playing games. We have dangerous jobs, no matter what precautions we take; and I don't want to miss my opportunity to tell you how I feel about you."

The tears were flowing freely now, and her words had him speechless.

"But I know you have some kind of hang ups about our ages and our positions at the PD. So if you don't think you can do this and really be with me, then I need to know that before my heart gets in any deeper. Please."

Gavin stared into her tear-filled eyes, reeling from her rawness.

"Gerri, I..."

He paused, unsure of what to say. He'd screwed this up once because he'd said the wrong thing. Now, that the stakes were so much higher, he didn't want to say something stupid and sabotage something great and wonderful before it had a chance to become great and wonderful.

"I think there's a lot we should talk about."

Gerri wiped another tear, and a tortured sour laugh escaped her.

"I guess I just got my answer."

"No!" His voice was firm, and he stared into her eyes, willing her to hear him out and believe him. "No, that was not an answer. Gerri... you have to acknowledge that our relationship has its issues. Issues that have the power to affect both of our livelihoods."

"Our jobs again." She rolled her eyes.

"Yes, our jobs. Do you realize that if the wrong people found out about us, I could be demoted? I could lose my rank, and my position over the homicide unit. All for taking advantage of a subordinate."

"But you're not taking advantage of me!"

"I know that! And you know that. But that is not how it will look to IAB. I am your direct supervisor."

Gerri looked stricken, and more tears hit her cheeks.

"So then, it's hopeless? That's what you're saying?"

Gavin sighed and closed his eyes for a moment. Then he met her gaze again. He'd vowed not to lie to her.

"While you serve under my command? Yeah."

Gerri wiped her cheek.

"Then that's all the more reason for me to transfer out and go to another precinct."

Gavin rolled over and sat up in the middle of the bed.

"I would never ask you to do that."

Gerri sat up beside him, pulling the sheet over her breasts.

"But you're not asking. Gavin, I love working at the 3rd precinct. Do you know why?"

"Because it's close to your apartment?"

"Because you're there! But if I could have you, and we both still have our jobs, I wouldn't care which precinct I worked at."

Gavin sighed and glanced around the room.

"Well, at least you're not still talking about quitting altogether."

Gerri ran a hand through her hair.

"When I said that yesterday I was just upset. And I was trying to get out of talking to the shrink."

Gavin looked at her. "Well, you do know that you can't come back to any precinct until you're cleared by him. You will have to talk to him again."

"I know."

Gavin took her hand, and they sat in silence for a long moment.

"So, let's talk about your other issue," she said.

Gavin looked up at her and laced his fingers with hers.

"What other issue?"

"The age thing."

He groaned. "Well, let's face it. I'm old enough to be your..."

He hesitated. They both knew the word he was going for. And

it was entirely possible, if he'd had her when he was 16. But somehow, he simply couldn't bring himself to say it.

"Much older brother," he said, finally finishing that sentence.

Gerri giggled at him. A genuine small laugh, without any tears, and Gavin smiled.

"That's not true."

"It is true. Do you even know how old I am?"

"Yes. You're 44 years old. You just had a birthday four months ago, which you celebrated all alone, without so much as a cupcake because Trey was away at school, and you don't tell your detectives when your birthday is."

He narrowed his eyes.

"How do you know all that?"

A sexy smile slid across her lips.

"I'm a detective. I find shit out."

"Hmm. And that number doesn't give you pause? The fact that I'm 16 years older than you?"

"Only for half a year until my birthday. Then we're 15 years apart."

Gavin rolled his eyes. "And it doesn't bother you?"

"Should it?"

"Gerri, you are closer in age to my 19-year-old son than you are to me."

"So?"

"So? You probably have more in common with him than you do with me! That doesn't bother you?"

"No. Why should it? Age is just a number, Gavin. A record of how long you've been on this earth. As long as both people are legally adults, age has absolutely no bearing on love or sex!"

They stared at each other for a moment, and Gavin wasn't sure how to take her views.

"And you don't honestly believe that I have more in common with a college boy, do you? I mean, you're not seriously entertaining the idea that I might suddenly find myself attracted to your son, right?"

Gavin didn't answer those questions. But hearing her say them, he couldn't deny that the possibility had crossed his mind, back when he was telling himself all the reasons why they shouldn't get involved.

"Because... don't get me wrong, Trey's a nice boy. But he's just that. A boy. I need a man who can handle me. The way you just did."

She trailed a single finger from his chest down to his pubic hair, and his dick stood up and said hello.

"If it makes you feel any better, my 29th birthday is in two months."

She grinned at him, and Gavin laughed out loud. He pulled her to him and kissed her, long and deep. His hands roamed her body as his tongue explored every inch of her mouth. Then he pulled back and looked at her face.

She'd said she loved him, and that she had for a long time. Gavin wasn't sure what to do with that information, but he knew he didn't want to take it for granted or take advantage of it. She was trusting him with her heart, and he took that responsibility seriously.

"You need to go?"

Her question pulled him out of his thoughts and brought him back to the now.

"What?"

"Well, it's dinner time, and I know Trey is staying with you."

"Oh." He shook his head. "Trey has gone out with some of his old high school buddies tonight. About ten of them were doing pizza and movies at Mark's parent's place."

"Ah. So that's how you're here past dinner time."

"Speaking of dinner though... did you eat?"

"No."

Gavin sighed. "You've got to take better care of yourself."

"I just haven't had much of an appetite."

"Well, if you don't eat, you'll let the grief run you down. We can't have that."

Gerri smiled at him. "Are you going to feed me again?"

"That depends. You got anything besides soup in that kitchen of yours?"

She appeared to think about it, and then made a face.

"I haven't shopped in a while."

"Where do you keep your take-out menus?"

9

Isaac:
My girl better not have a
scratch on her this morning

Pete:
Who dis?

Isaac:
The man who's gonna kick your
ass if you hurt my car

Pete:
No hablo ingles

Isaac:
Don't forget to pick me up
or you won't hablo at all

Pete:
Yeah yeah

Isaac ended the text conversation with his partner and then stuck his head out the doorway, checking to make sure Sidney was still in the kitchen. She was cooking their breakfast, and Isaac knew he only had a few minutes. He needed to do this fast. He found the contact in his phone and dialed.

The phone rang only a couple of times before she answered, and Isaac could barely make out her words through the decidedly un-lady-like yawn.

"It's a little early, Ike. I'm only halfway into my first cup of coffee."

Isaac rolled his eyes. His little sister was famous in their family for not being a morning person.

"How do you run a business if you hate mornings, Em?"

"The beauty of running your own business is being able to set your own hours. My hours don't begin until my second cup of coffee."

"Well, sip fast because I need your help."

There was a slight pause, and Isaac could hear that Emily perked up when she responded.

"My help? With what?"

"Picnics."

"Huh?"

"I want to take Sidney on a little backyard picnic, and I was..."

"Aww!" She interrupted him with a loud girly squeal. "That's so sweet. Where'd you get such a romantic idea?"

"I looked up romantic date ideas on the Internet."

All the girly excitement quickly left her voice.

"Oh, my God, Ike. The Internet?"

"Hey. I found some really good ideas that way. And you just gushed all over the first one."

"All right, all right. So, what do you need help with?"

Duh. Hadn't she been listening?

"Picnics."

He could hear the exasperation in his own voice.

"What about them?"

Emily sounded just as irritated with this conversation as he felt.

"Well, what kind of food goes into one?"

"What? The Internet didn't tell you that part?"

Isaac let out an overly exaggerated sigh.

"You know what? I started to call Bree instead, but I figured she's busy with the baby and all. But what the heck, I'll take my chances. Thanks anyway."

"No! Don't bother Bree. I got this."

Isaac smiled. He knew pitting her against their sister-in-law's prowess in the kitchen would trigger her competitive streak.

"Now let's see... picnic food. Hmm," Emily hummed. "Well, there's always the basic sandwich and chips route. Or even the old standard fried chicken and potato salad route. That's always a good one. But if you're going for romantic, you need sexy foods."

"Sexy food?"

"Yes. You know... foods that you can eat with your hands and feed each other. Little nibbles, like an assortment of cheeses and crackers, grapes. Oh! And strawberries with cream or even chocolate sauce."

"Cheese and crackers? Really?"

"Well, not just plain cheese and crackers, Ike. It'd be a variety of cheeses, and fancy crackers. Maybe a couple of meats, like salami and prosciutto, or even smoked salmon."

"You're talking about like one of those antipasto things."

"Well, I was actually thinking more of a charcuterie, but yeah. Same principle."

Isaac's head was starting to spin.

Was he getting way out of his depth here? He just wanted a simple little picnic in his backyard with the woman he loved.

"A char what?"

"Breakfast is ready, baby!" Sidney yelled from the kitchen.

"I'll be right there!" he yelled back. Then to Emily he said, "I gotta go. Listen, thanks for the um... ideas. I really appreciate it."

"No problem. Hey! Have you heard from your friend lately?"

"My friend?"

"Yeah. Special Agent Dork. What's his name?"

Isaac's lips twisted. He knew that she was well aware of his name.

"I thought you were into that dork. What happened?"

"Nothing happened. We flirted at your place on game night; made a date to go out. And then he canceled on me, citing work reasons. Never called me back. Totally ghosted. I guess he wasn't into me."

She tried to hide it, but Isaac could hear the genuine disappointment in her voice.

"That is not the vibe I got from him, Em. He's interested in you. If he said he's working, then he probably is."

"I don't know."

"Isaac?" Sidney called again.

"Yeah, I'm coming, Sid." To Emily he said, "I gotta go, Em. Thanks for your help."

"Yeah. You too. Say hi to Sid for me."

"Will do."

He ended the call and hurried out to the dining table where Sidney sat eating her breakfast.

"Your pancakes are getting cold.

He took his seat and poured syrup on his pancakes and fruit.

"Sorry. I was talking to Emily on the phone."

"Oh. What about?"

Isaac took a bite of his food and glanced at her.

"She thinks a certain FBI agent is trying to give her the brushoff. She wanted my take on it. I told her that wasn't the vibe I got from him. In fact... I saw them kissing in one of my futuristic visions."

"Really? Intrigue and romance. Tell me more."

Isaac grinned at her and took another bite.

"No, seriously. Tell me more. I mean, I was witness to some pretty shameless flirting during our game night a few weeks ago, but you didn't tell me you actually saw them together in a vision."

Isaac nodded. "Yeah. The kiss I saw was pretty hot and steamy too. I don't actually care to see it again, thank you very much."

Sidney laughed, and Isaac smiled at her. He was happy to see her feeling better.

They ate in silence for a few minutes, and he thought about his picnic plans and whether or not he should proceed.

"So tonight is your late day at the shelter, right?"

"That's right. Dinner will be late. I'll pick up some take-out on my way home."

Isaac took her hand and looked into her eyes.

"You know what? Don't worry about dinner tonight. I'll take care of it."

"You will?"

"Yep. Leave it to me."

From outside they heard a car horn, and Isaac immediately recognized it as his car.

"There's Pete. I've gotta go."

He leaned in and kissed her lips. Then he stood and clipped his gun to his hip and gathered his things.

"Be safe today."

Isaac looked down at her and lightly ran his thumb over the small bruise on her right cheek. The swelling was down, but it was an angry shade of purple this morning, setting off ripples of rage in Isaac's stomach.

"You do the same, darlin'. No more kung fu or gun slinging for you today, okay?"

Sidney giggled. "I make no promises."

He kissed her again and then left the house.

Outside, he walked to the driver's side of his car, where Pete sat behind the wheel.

"Get out of my car."

"Come on, just get in. We're going to be late."

"Get out of my car, Pete."

"Ah, jeez. You are such a control freak."

Pete unhooked the seatbelt and got out of the car, grumbling all the way, and Isaac tried to hide his amusement.

"Your car likes me better than she likes you," Pete said as he walked around to the passenger side.

"In your dreams."

Isaac slid behind the wheel, adjusting the seat for his long legs. Then they took off.

Once they got to the station, he stole a few minutes before roll call to place another personal phone call.

"Isaac?"

"Hey, Bree. How you doing this morning? I apologize if I'm interrupting something important with the baby."

"No, you're fine. Isla is down for her morning nap. What's going on?"

"Well, I got this silly idea to take Sid on a little backyard picnic tonight, and..."

"Oh, that's not silly at all. It sounds sweet. And romantic! She's going to love that."

Isaac grinned at her enthusiasm.

"Well, I was talking to Emily about what food to eat, and she suggested some kind of char... charcu... something or other?"

"You mean a charcuterie tray?"

"That's it! And I wondered if that's something I could buy somewhere instead of having to make one myself? I was hoping you might know the answer to that."

Bree wasn't simply an amazing cook. When Adam met her, she was the head chef at a successful catering company. When it came to food, the woman had all kinds of skills.

"As a matter of fact, I do know where you can get a beautiful and delicious one. Me!"

"You?"

"Yes. Let me make you one!"

"Oh, no, no, no. Bree, I don't want to bother you with this. You've got so much going on with the baby and everything."

"Nonsense! Ike, I would love to do this for you. Let me do it as a thank you for getting Isla and me through the delivery safely. Please?"

"Are you sure?"

"I'm positive. And I've even got most of what I'll need right here. What time do you need it by?"

"Um, well. I can come pick it up after work tonight. Say about six?"

"Perfect. It'll be ready and waiting. But hey... what's the occasion?"

"No occasion. I just wanted to do something nice for her. Something romantic, like you said."

"A romantic backyard picnic? You will score very high points for this one. Make sure you have a nice comfy blanket to spread in the grass."

"Good tip. Hey, thanks again for doing this. You're sure it's not a problem?"

"It's going to be so much fun! Go to work. I'll see you this evening."

He thanked her again and ended the call. Then he got up, not wanting to be late for the morning briefing.

"Taylor. Vega."

Isaac turned to see Gavin Hayes coming their way.

"We were just headed to the morning briefing." Isaac chucked a thumb in the direction of the briefing room.

"Skip it." Gavin handed him a piece of paper.

"What's this?"

"College student at Cleveland State came home to find his roommate slaughtered. Castrated, just like the other two."

"Wait." Pete held up a hand. "Cleveland State? Not Case Western?"

"Yep."

He looked at Isaac with an oh-this-is-bad expression.

"You thinking it's our missing bachelor number three?" Isaac watched him carefully.

"Aren't you?"

Isaac shrugged a shoulder. "Only one way to find out."

"Let's go."

"When you get back, I want a full update."

Isaac glanced at the information on the slip of paper — dorm name and room number. Then he nodded at his boss.

He and Pete hustled from the pit and down to the waiting unmarked cruiser.

When they finally arrived at the dorm, the place was swarming with a crowd of onlookers, and a handful of uniformed campus cops trying to keep them contained to the lobby of the building.

"Shit," Isaac mumbled, staring at the small mob. Then he took a breath and braced himself. Pete shot him a look.

"Allow me."

His partner turned toward the crowd and raised his badge.

"All right, people." Pete's voice was forceful as he called out. "Part like the Red Sea. *Now!* Don't make me ask again."

The small mob did as they were told, making a path in the lobby, and Isaac followed Pete through them and up the stairs to the third-floor dorm room.

"I'd say thanks, but I think you enjoyed that."

"It was fun." Pete grinned at him.

Isaac chuckled and stepped into the room.

"Wow."

Blood was everywhere.

Blatant signs of a struggle.

Dead, half naked body across the bed.

He scanned the area with a hawk-eyed gaze.

"This guy fought back. Our killer wasn't able to knock him out and transport him to a second location."

"Nope." Pete looked at the body. "But he did eventually get what he wanted. Dude's junk is cut clean off. Just like the other two."

"Yeah." Isaac looked around at the blood and scanned the floor and the area around the body. "Exactly where is the... um, junk?"

He and Pete looked around.

"Uh, we haven't located it yet, Sergeant."

Isaac looked at the CSU tech and felt his eyebrows lift to the sky. Was she for real?

"What? Did the killer take it like a souvenir?"

The tech shrugged her shoulders and turned back to her task.

Donning blue latex gloves, Isaac and Pete joined the careful search of the dorm room.

"Found it!"

The other CSU tech sounded victorious, like he'd just won a new car in a game show.

Isaac watched him carefully lift the severed genitals from a small trash can behind the desk. The man stared at it with a scrunched-up expression.

"It's flattened. Like it's been stomped on or beaten."

"Like tenderizing a piece of meat?" the female CSU tech asked.

Isaac looked at Pete. "We're looking at some serious revenge here."

"No shit."

Isaac snapped a picture of the victim's face for their case board.

"Who found the body?"

"Guy's in the dorm room next door with Officer Jackson," the tech said, carefully putting the mangled genitals into an evidence bag.

Isaac and Pete ventured to the dorm room next door, where he nodded at Officer Jackson. Then he flashed his badge at the young man sitting on the small couch, head in hands.

"Detectives Taylor and Vega. You are...?"

"Doug. Doug Henley."

The kid looked up at him with wide eyes that didn't seem to be focusing on anything, and Isaac thought maybe he was in shock.

"And you live in the other dorm room with the victim?"

"Yes. Mike is my roommate. We met freshman year when we were paired together in Biology Lab."

"And his full name?"

"Michael Rivers."

Isaac and Pete shared a glance.

"That's the missing third man from the high school case," Pete said.

Isaac nodded, then turned back to Doug.

"I'm assuming he wasn't like this when you left this morning?"

Doug looked up at him again. “I just got back to campus this morning. I’d been in Cancún with my parents for two weeks.”

“So you have no idea how long he’s been here like this?”

“No, sir.”

“Was he scheduled to be here all this week, or had he gone on vacation like you?”

“No, he was staying here. Said he’d use the quiet to study for his biochem exam or something. He was still taking classes this summer.”

“He have any enemies you know of? Anyone he’d been having trouble with?”

Doug appeared to think about it.

“There was this jock who threatened to kill him once over a girl. But that was over a year ago now. I don’t think there’s anyone currently looking to kill him.”

“Did Mike ever tell you about being accused of rape when he was a senior in high school?”

“What? No, I... he never mentioned that.”

“Did he ever mention a Bobby Cook or Craig Wentworth?”

“Yeah. They’re his friends. They both go to Case Western. He wanted to transfer there too at one time. Not sure why he stopped pursuing that.”

“Did you know Cook and Wentworth?”

“I met them through Mike. They all went to high school together. Why are you asking about them? Did they do this to him?”

Doug sounded horrified at the prospect, and Isaac shook his head in response.

“No. They didn’t hurt Mike. They’re dead.”

“What?”

“Killed in the exact same manner.”

Doug turned an alarming shade of green, then he lowered his head, bending over at the waist. No doubt attempting to stave off the nausea.

Isaac motioned for Pete to hand over one of their cards.

"Please don't leave town, as we may have more questions in the near future. And if you think of anything else that might be helpful, no matter how small, give us a call."

They stepped out into the hallway and Isaac looked at his partner.

"We need to dive deep into that old rape case. Seems someone's getting revenge."

"Yeah, I'll bet the killings stop now that all three of the accused and acquitted are dead."

"Unless our killer decides to go after the victims lawyers, or even the judge." Isaac didn't like the idea of that, but it needed to be pointed out all the same. "Do we have a current location of their alleged rape victim?"

"No. But I'm on it."

They headed for the stairs.

"Good. That's where we need to start."

At the foot of the stairs in the lobby, Pete took the lead again, and Isaac grinned to himself.

"Coming through, people," Pete called out. "You know the drill!"

The small crowd parted again to let them through, allowing Isaac the freedom to walk through them without the fear of being touched.

Outside the building, he gave his partner a sideways glance. Pete smiled, but refused to look directly at him.

He was turning out to be the best partner Isaac had ever been paired with. Certainly the most accepting of his touch issues and the crazy psychic shit. They might make a good team after all.

They marched back to the car in silence, and Pete stared at his cellphone the whole time. Once in the car, Pete finally looked up.

"Lakewood Mental Institution."

Isaac looked him in the eyes. "Mental Institution?"

"Yep. Apparently, she's been there for the last five years almost."

"So, she's been there since the rape?"

"It would seem so."

Isaac sighed and started the car. He hated this case. As he punched the destination into the cruiser's GPS system, he shook his head. He hated everything about this case, and he didn't even have all the facts yet.

The institution was local, on the outskirts of the city, and they fought lunchtime traffic to get there. When they walked through the glass doors, Isaac was reminded of the last mental institution he'd visited just a few weeks ago during the lullaby case, and how his traveling companion, Special Agent Emmett Fox, hadn't given the receptionist a chance to try and stonewall them.

He pulled his credentials from his pocket and flashed them at the receptionist behind this desk.

"Detective Sgt. Ike Taylor. This is my partner, Detective Pete Vega. We'd like to speak with Amber Camden."

He eyed the woman with a steady I'm-not-playing-games-here gaze, refusing to take no for an answer. The girl seemed trapped in his stare for a few seconds. Then she quickly picked up the phone.

Isaac had no idea who she spoke with, but two seconds later, a woman with short blond hair came from around the corner. She was tall and stocky. The kind of woman one might refer to as corn-fed.

"Detectives? I'm Josephine Turner. Head nurse of the hospital. How can I help you?"

"We'd like to speak with a patient. Amber Camden."

"Well, is there some problem with her family? Some news you wish to give her?"

"I'm afraid the details are a police matter." Isaac stared at her, trying to gage the reason for her odd question.

"Well, I'm sorry, detective. But speaking with Amber Camden is out of the question."

"I will come back here with a court order, if I have to."

"I'm afraid that wouldn't do you any good. You see, Detective... Amber Camden doesn't speak. She won't be able to answer any of your questions."

Isaac and Pete looked at each other.

"You mean she's mute?"

"It goes deeper than that." Josephine motioned for them to follow her, and they walked slowly down the hall.

"It's not simply that Amber is mute. At one time, she was a perfectly normal teenager. But when she came to us, she had recently suffered a very traumatic event. Her selective mutism was the result of that trauma."

"That trauma being her rape when she was a senior in high school?" Isaac asked.

"No. The inciting incident for her mutism was the humiliation she suffered in court during the trial of her *alleged* rapists. After they were acquitted, she never spoke another word. Still hasn't. She simply sits and stares. She's in an almost catatonic state. It's been over four years now."

Josephine stopped walking and gestured to the room on their left.

Isaac turned and noted that they were at the open doorway of a patient's room. A frail young woman with mousy brown hair sat in a chair facing a window.

Isaac glanced back at Josephine, who nodded.

He took a breath and then stepped inside the room, walking slowly toward the woman.

"Amber? Amber Camden?"

There was no response.

"Amber, I'm Detective Ike Taylor. I'm here with my partner, Detective Pete Vega."

He pointed to the doorway where Pete still stood.

"We'd like to talk to you about... well, about the men who hurt you."

Amber never moved.

Never acknowledged him.

Never even blinked.

Isaac looked at Pete, who gave him an I-got-no-clue-what-to-do-now look. He turned back to Amber and tried again.

"Amber... the three boys who hurt you? They're all dead now. Do you know what could've happened to them?"

Amber didn't flinch at the news. He wasn't even certain she could hear or comprehend a word he was saying.

Isaac sighed, and walked back to the door.

"Thank you for allowing us to try, Nurse Turner."

"You're welcome. I'm sorry she can't help you. Although I can't say that I'm sorry to hear her rapists are gone, though. Whatever they did to her was cruel enough to land her in here, so they couldn't have been very nice young men."

"No. I don't suppose they were. Thank you for your time."

He and Pete left the building and headed for the car.

"Since Amber can't talk to us about her old rape case, we're going to have to find someone who can."

"Well, all three accused rapists are dead, so what've you got in mind?"

"I think we need to talk to her male relatives — father, brothers, step-father, uncles, cousins..."

"Uh, you realize that could potentially be a whole lot of people, right? Especially on top of the pertinent people connected to each of our victims."

"You got a better idea? Because yes, we do need to speak with those closest to each of our victims, but we also need answers about this rape case, and her family can give them to us. In fact, the very nature of the crimes makes it more than likely that someone in her family is our revenge killer."

10

Sidney pulled to the curb in front of the Hope House and got out of the car. Every step up the walk reminded her of the previous night and the way that sneaky bastard had cupped her chin, leaned in, and kissed her.

"The nerve," she mumbled to herself.

And then telling her that she *wanted* him to kiss her!

Oh, if he showed up at the shelter today, she just might be tempted to sock him in that smug, smarmy grin of his.

At least Isaac had come to her rescue. Not that she'd needed him to. But he was there, like always, being wonderful.

That brought a smile to her lips, and she thought about how sweet he'd been to her the past few days. He'd been her rock since their loss, and she wasn't sure she could've gotten through it without him. She truly loved that man.

She stepped through the front door of Hope House in an instantly better mood. On her way to the back office, she spotted Zoe and two of the residents in the living room.

"And there's our conquering heroine now!"

Zoe sounded chipper as she motioned to her, and Sidney got

the distinct impression that she'd been the topic of their discussion.

"Good morning."

"Good morning to you."

She smiled at them and then continued on to the office to put her things away. She wasn't at all surprised when Zoe followed after her.

"I hear you were really quite something last night. Taking on Ann's drunken husband in an actual fist fight!"

"It really wasn't that dramatic." Sidney sat down at her desk.

"That's not what those present have been telling me. Julie called me first thing this morning. And then when I got here, Ann and Tyneesha can't shut up about it. They say you were like some badass out of an action movie. And now I see for myself that you've got the bruises to prove it."

Sidney looked up at her, dumbfounded. Was that really what Ann and Tyneesha thought? Because she certainly hadn't felt like an action hero last night. She lifted a hand and lightly touched her bruised cheek.

"Well, it... it was just... instinct, I guess. A reflex."

Zoe shook her head.

"Um mmm. Women who've been abused don't reflexively spring into action when faced with an irate male. That's something that only comes with careful training and determination. And I know you've been taking self-defense classes and the like. I think last night, we're finally seeing the results of all your hard work in that area. Well done, Sidney."

Sidney took a proud, but uneasy breath and let it out slowly. She hadn't thought much about her defensive actions last night. After it all happened, she'd been much too preoccupied with how her feelings about loosing the baby had played into the rage she'd directed at Ann's husband. But hearing Zoe talk about her training now gave her an unfamiliar sense of pride in her ability to take care of herself.

And others.

She'd defended them all last night, and she'd prevailed.

A small smile erupted on her lips.

She'd done it.

She could honestly say she'd kicked a man's ass.

Granted, that man had been weakened by his drunken state, but that didn't matter. She'd faced him and won.

Her smile grew bigger.

"Thanks, Zoe."

"You're welcome. Now... what's this I hear about the strange tension between you and Lance Tobey in the midst of everything that happened last night?"

Sidney's smile vanished, and she rolled her eyes at the mention of him.

"Julie told me she thought she'd walked in on something pretty heated when the police arrived. She said you looked extremely pissed."

"Julie's a little chatterbox, isn't she?"

"Don't blame the messenger, Sidney. Julie was doing her job of keeping me informed of what went on overnight. Now, tell me what happened."

Sidney sighed and crossed her legs, leaning back in her desk chair. Then she looked her boss in the eyes.

"First, he did something inappropriate. And when I called him out on it, he *said* something very inappropriate. So, yes, I put him in his place with a few choice words. That's when Julie and the police showed up."

"And your fiancé."

"Yes. I'd sent Isaac a text right after the incident with Ann's husband, and he showed up right after the officers did, to check on me."

"Well, back up a bit. What inappropriate thing did Lance do that upset you?"

Sidney hesitated and sighed.

"When he was tending to my wounds, he kissed me."

Zoe's eyebrows shot for the roof.

She rushed forward and sat on the corner of Sidney's desk.

"He kissed you?"

"Yes."

"Oh, my God! Was it good?"

Sidney stared at her.

"It was unwelcome, Zoe! And when I pointed out why it was unwelcome, he said that he believed things weren't going well in my relationship. Like that somehow gave him permission. And, that's a notion he could've only gotten from lurking in the doorway the other day when we were talking."

Zoe's expression fell, but Sidney kept ranting.

"Then he had the nerve to say that maybe I was so upset because I secretly *wanted* him to kiss me!"

"Oh, boy."

"Yeah! That's when I really let him have it, and I pointed out that he was treating me like the inferior-weaker-sex-playthings that Neanderthal-bullies always accuse women of being."

"Ouch."

"Yeah, well, he had it coming. Trying to tell me I don't know my own mind? Of all the degrading, condescending, self-esteem-killing things to say to a formerly abused woman!"

"Okay. I can see we're still a little hot about this issue."

Zoe stood and moved over to her own desk.

"Can you blame me?" Sidney stared at her. "Zoe, come on. I know you've got this little crush on him, but..."

"I don't have a crush!"

"...please tell me that you understand why I'm so pissed off. The guy acted every bit as bad as Ann's husband, only without using his fists!"

Zoe sighed, and Sidney could hear the disgust in that sound.

"Shit. That is not what I wanted to hear."

"I know. And I'm sorry, but... if you could've heard his words and seen the smug smirk on his face." Sidney's tone was softer when she said, "Felt the humiliation he tried to lay on me."

"I'm so disappointed. I thought he was better than that. Tell me, was his behavior bad enough to terminate his volunteer work here?"

"Terminate?"

That word made her look up and give Zoe her full attention.

Zoe nodded.

"Well, I can't have him volunteering here and speaking to the residents the way he spoke to you, can I? Makes me wonder if he's made anyone else feel uncomfortable in the past."

Sidney sighed. She didn't want to get anyone fired. Even if it was just a volunteer position for him.

"I honestly don't know if he was deliberately trying to demean me, or if he just wanted to save face after being turned down."

"Well, either way, he said all the wrong things, didn't he?"

"Well, that's certainly true."

Zoe seemed to study her for a moment before she spoke again.

"The decision is yours, Sidney. If you feel uncomfortable around him after last night just let me know, and I'll take care of it."

Sidney stared at her. How was she supposed to respond to that? If she were being truthful, almost from the moment she'd met him, the good doctor had made her skin crawl with imaginary chiggers. But she'd learned to push that unease aside and ignore him, for the most part.

"Let's just see how it goes for now, okay?"

"All right. If you're sure."

Zoe left the office then, and Sidney got to work on some of the administrative tasks she handled every day. She pushed all thoughts of the previous night behind her. Well... as much as the dull throb in her right cheek would allow.

She worked steadily through to lunchtime, when she stopped

and went into the shelter's kitchen and heated up a cup of noodles.

Once lunch was over, she gathered the math worksheets she'd printed off and met with Beth's daughter, Kylee, at the kitchen table. Beth sat nearby, quietly watching while Sidney talked Kylee through the sample math questions and then encouraged the girl to work on the others on her own.

The look of sheer joy on Kylee's face when Sidney gave her a good score on the completed worksheets was priceless. She actually wasn't certain who was prouder — Kylee or her mother.

When they were finishing up, Ann came into the kitchen.

"Thanks for all your help, Miss Sidney."

"You are so welcome, Kylee. We'll work on word problems tomorrow, okay?"

"Okay."

"Thank you, Sidney." Beth took Kylee's hand and ushered her out of the kitchen.

"It was my pleasure."

"Sidney?"

She looked up at Ann, who stared at her intently, wringing her hands and working her bottom lip.

"What is it, Ann?"

Ann pulled out a chair and sat beside her at the table.

"I'm so sorry, Sidney. For the mean bruise and the cut on your face."

Sidney waved a dismissive hand.

"It's all right, Ann. None of what happened last night was your fault. Not a single part of it. Okay?"

Ann nodded and looked down at the table. Then she glanced around, as if making sure no one was around to hear them before she looked Sidney in the eyes.

"I heard... um."

"It's okay. What'd you hear?"

The woman ran a hand through her lifeless blonde hair and licked her lips before trying again.

"I heard that you got away from your abuser. That you disappeared or something... went underground and fled across the country? Is that true?"

Sidney wasn't sure how Ann came across that information, but it wasn't a big deal. She'd shared her story with Zoe and with other residents freely.

"Yes, that's true."

The air in the small kitchen grew thick, and Ann glanced around again.

"Could you..." She paused and quietly cleared her throat. "Could you help me and my kids disappear? Like you did? Could you help us get away from Donald?"

The hairs on Sidney's arms stood at attention like soldiers.

She shivered from the goosebumps.

Sidney stared at her, not knowing how to respond.

Helping other battered women get away from their abusers was the growing passion in her heart, wasn't it?

"Let me give it some thought. I'll get back to you in a day or two."

"Oh. Okay."

"If I agree to this, Ann, there are some things you would have to agree to. Some rules. Otherwise, helping you will be pointless."

"I'll do anything. Whatever you say. Just please help me! Help me get my babies away from him, Sidney. He is dangerous. He will kill me someday if we don't get away from him."

"Okay, okay."

She grabbed the woman's hand to calm her down, and stared into her eyes. What she saw there was terror.

A terror Sidney knew only too well.

"The first step is money. Do you have any stashed away? Any you can get your hands on? A joint bank account, or some you can borrow from a relative or a friend?"

"I have a few hundred dollars hidden in my room upstairs."

"You're going to need more than that. A lot more."

"I-I can get more. I'll pay you whatever you want!"

Sidney shook her head.

"The money's not to pay me, Ann. You're going to need money to get away. Gather as much as you can."

Ann nodded. "Okay. I can get more. I can borrow some from my friend, Sheila."

"All right. We'll talk again soon."

Ann squeezed her hand tight.

"Thank you, Sidney. Thank you so much!"

She got up and rushed from the kitchen, and Sidney took a deep breath.

What had she just agreed to?

She walked back to her desk in a preoccupied fog, thoughts and ideas forming and twisting in her mind. Sitting down at her desk, she pulled out a legal pad and began making notes — a list of rules that Ann, or any other resident who might ask in the future, would have to agree to if Sidney were to do this. They were tactics she had used herself. Ideas she had given a lot of thought to while she was lying in that lonely hospital bed Damien had put her in.

She also made a list of things Ann would need to succeed if she tried this. Things like fake IDs and papers — birth certificates, and such — for her and her kids. She tapped her pen against the pad and wondered where in the world she would get those things.

Before she'd run, it was fairly easy. She'd known exactly where to go. But here in Cleveland she had no clue. And she couldn't ask Isaac.

Could she?

The possibilities swirled around in Sidney's mind all day long. She thought of almost nothing else, functioning on auto-pilot throughout paperwork and the normal day-to-day tasks of helping to run the shelter.

She carried on conversations with Zoe, all while having a silent-running dialogue with herself, ticking away in her head. Going over the ins and outs of putting together a foolproof secret plan of action to help other battered women slip away like ghosts and free them from their abusers.

Was she crazy?

Was this an absolutely insane thing to get herself into?

Could she really pull it off?

She worried that she was casting herself as some sort of modern day Harriet Tubman — someone who'd been abused and oppressed and who'd broken free, now on a mission to help others do the same. But really... wasn't that her duty?

If she knew the way to freedom, shouldn't she feel obligated to lead others?

It was a question that plagued her all the way home that evening. On the one hand, the prospect of helping others in this manner excited and invigorated her. On the other, it was a scary thing to consider. So many things could go wrong. There were so many moving parts to think about.

She sighed when she pulled her car into the short driveway.

Yep. This was crazy.

Her stomach growled, reminding her that it was past dinnertime. And that thought reminded her that Ike was taking care of dinner tonight since he'd gotten home before her.

She was fumbling with her keys at the front door when it suddenly swung open and Isaac stood there smiling at her, those sexy dimples welcoming her home.

"I thought I heard your car."

He reached for her hand and pulled her in for a slow, knee-buckling kiss.

"How was your day, darlin'?"

Sidney smiled at him and took note of the casual way he was dressed — comfy pair of jeans that were ripped at one knee, plain white t-shirt that emphasized his biceps and his impressive torso, and bare feet. He looked relaxed and sexy and completely comfortable in his own skin. A state she knew he only reached when he was alone with her.

"It was... interesting."

"Oh, yeah?"

"Mmm hmm."

"Well, I want to hear all about it. But first, why don't you go get out of your work clothes while I finish up dinner prep?"

Sidney inhaled, taking a generous sniff.

"I don't smell dinner being cooked. What are we having?"

Ike chuckled. "That is a surprise. Just go get into something comfortable and meet me in the sunroom."

"The sunroom? Are we eating in there?"

"No more questions. Off you go."

He gently prodded her along, playfully swatting her tush when she moved.

She loved when he was in this mood. Frisky, fun-loving, and just a little mischievous. Perfectly relaxed with himself. That's when his real personality was able to shine.

She entered their bedroom and made quick work of getting out of her work clothes. Alfred Hitchcock leapt onto the bed with a loud *meow,* demanding attention.

"Hey, there, Mr. Hitchcock. How's the best kitty in the world today, huh?"

Sidney gave the kitten a liberal scratch and was rewarded with a deep contented purr.

She pulled on a comfy pair of yoga pants and one of Ike's many long-sleeved t-shirts. Then she slipped on a pair of flip-flop sandals and left the bedroom.

In the sunroom she smiled at Isaac.

"Reporting as ordered."

"Requested," Ike corrected her. "I requested, not ordered."

"Tomato, tomahto."

"Well, one's a lot nicer than the other, and I would never try to *order* you to do anything."

"Duly noted. Now feed me. I'm starving."

Her stomach growled right on cue, like it was backing her up, and they both laughed. Isaac took her hand and led her outside to the patio.

When he side-stepped the small café-style table sitting there and walked down into the yard, Sidney wondered what was going on. It didn't take her long to figure it out.

On the back lawn, he'd spread out a red and white plaid blanket, beside which she spotted a small bucket of ice that cradled a bottle of something sparkling. Two champagne flutes sat at the ready.

In the center of the blanket, spread out like a feast, was a large charcuterie board piled with several different cured meats, an assortment of cheeses, fancy crackers and baguette slices, fresh strawberries, grapes, thin slices of pear, and fresh figs, dried apricots, cream cheese stuffed olives, marinated artichoke hearts, and walnuts sprinkled into every tiny nook. It was both breathtaking and mouth-watering. And so artistic it made her want to weep.

"Isaac!"

Her voice was all breathy and girly, even to her own ears, but it couldn't be helped.

"How did you do this?"

"I'd like to say I slaved in the kitchen for hours, but we both know that'd be a lie."

Sidney burst into excited giggles.

"I did, however, spend an hour or so looking up romantic date ideas on the Internet. And then I annoyed my sister and my sister-in-law until they agreed to help me. Does that count?"

Sidney stared up at him. He was so damn cute when he was unsure of himself, all bashful and sexy.

"Yes. That definitely counts."

"Whew!"

Still holding her hand, he stepped onto the blanket and folded his long legs, gently pulling her down with him. They settled on the blanket and Sidney got a better look at their picnic.

"This looks absolutely delicious! Did you buy it somewhere?"

"Come on, now."

His southern accent dropped heavy, and Sidney grinned.

"Why would I do that when we have a chef in the family?"

"Ah. It's all making sense now. Bree is the artist of this masterpiece." She popped a walnut into her mouth and watched Ike pour them each a glass of the non-alcoholic champagne.

"Well, honestly... I did call her to ask if she knew where I could buy something like this. And she offered to make one for us. I tried my best to decline. I told her I didn't want to bug her or interfere with baby Isla's schedule or anything. But she insisted. Said for me to think of it as a thank you for getting her and the baby through that crazy delivery."

"Aww, that was sweet of her. And so are these figs. Oh, my God, this is all so good!"

Isaac laughed. "I was going to offer up a toast before we dug in, but I guess that's out."

Sidney laughed out loud.

"I'm sorry, baby. I'm just hungry." She held up her glass. "What shall we drink to?"

Ike held up his glass and stared at her with those mesmerizing light grey eyes of his.

"To the most beautiful woman in the world."

Sidney's heart melted to the point she thought it might ooze from her pores and seep into the blanket.

"Isaac."

She lifted a hand and brushed her fingertips over the lingering bruise at her right cheek.

Sidney was no stranger to bruises on her face. She'd suffered that and more at the hands of her former husband. But she'd never had a man stare at her in that state and tell her she was beautiful.

Isaac took her hand, gently pulling it away from her bruise. He brought her fingers to his lips and kissed them. Then he leaned in, brushing his lips over her cheek.

"You are the springtime, Sidney. The sunshine and the soft breeze. You are my everything, darlin'. The most beautiful woman in the world."

He lightly clinked his champagne flute to hers and took a sip, staring into her eyes, and Sidney's belly quivered. Who was this man? This amazingly sweet, smart, sexy man who loved her. Where had he come from? And most importantly, what had she ever done to deserve him?

She took a tentative sip of champagne, her eyes still locked on his.

"I love you, Isaac. I love you so much."

"I love you," he smiled. "Now. Eat up. I hear someone out here is very hungry."

She giggled at him and then turned to their dinner.

They ate in silence for a few moments as they explored the delicacies Bree had made for them, nibbling and noshing and feeding each other.

"So. Tell me about your day. Why was it so interesting?"

His question brought her up short, and Sidney stopped mid-chew.

Her mind raced wondering how best to tell him what was going on. She swallowed and quietly cleared her throat.

"Well, a surprising thing happened today."

"What's that?" Ike took a bite of peppered hard salami.

"Ann... she's the resident whose husband did this."

She motioned to her cheek, and Ike's grey eyes darkened like the coming dusk.

"Well, she came to me today and asked if I could help get her and her kids away from him. Help her run, you know? Like I did."

Isaac swallowed down another bite and nodded.

"What'd you tell her?"

"I told her I'd think about it. I mean, it's not something you can do on a whim. If you really want to get away from that kind of situation, you have to plan. And when I ran, it was just me. But she's got two small kids to think about. She would lose any kind of support system she might have in place here. There's a lot to think about."

She shook her head, going back over it all again in her mind.

Could she really do this?

"There is a lot to think about," Ike echoed her words. "But why do I get the feeling you've already made up your mind?"

Sidney lifted her gaze to his. He was staring at her hard. Studying her.

"Well, it..." She hesitated. "I mean, I..."

Her voice trailed off again, and she searched for the words.

A slow grin tipped the corners of his lips, but it was tempered with the concern she saw forming in his eyes.

"You've already agreed to help her, haven't you?"

Sidney licked her lips. Was he going to be upset with her?

"I just feel like it's my duty to help."

"Your duty?"

"See, the question I've been asking myself all day is... if I know the way to freedom, why shouldn't I feel obligated to lead others to it?" She reached out and took hold of his arm. "Ike... if I can help someone in a highly abusive situation to break free from their abuser and build a new life for themselves, shouldn't I do that? Shouldn't I help them the way you helped me?"

"But Sid, I didn't help you run. You were already on the run when I met you. I simply helped keep you safe from that bastard."

"Yes, but if it hadn't been for you, Ike, Damien would have killed me. I have no doubts about that. And when Ann tells me that man will kill her if she doesn't get away, I believe her."

"Okay. Well, have you thought about everything that an undertaking like this would entail?"

"Yes! I've thought of nothing else all day. I have a notepad in my purse with a list of rules and tactics and ideas. Things to look into and research, like bus depots and routes, and what's needed for border crossings into Canada and Mexico..."

"Border crossings?"

"Yes."

"Wow. You're not playing around. You have given this a lot of thought today, haven't you?"

"Yes, I have. And that stuff is easy. The hard part is going to be figuring out the best place to get fake IDs and papers. When I fled from Damien, it was fairly easy. I knew the people to ask. I knew the area. But now?"

She sighed and shook her head.

Isaac leaned back, his gaze falling to their half-eaten picnic, and Sidney could see his mind working.

"Sid... are you asking me a question?"

Sidney toyed with a fig half before she looked up at his eyes.

"No. I mean, I... I know that you could probably point me in the right direction, given your job and all. But I would never want to put you in a difficult position."

"I'm glad you realize that it would be a difficult position for me. That means I don't have to tell you that what you're proposing right now is illegal."

Sidney sunk her teeth into the fig, the sweet juices of it tempering the bitter bite of his words.

"I know buying fake IDs and papers is illegal, baby. But it's a necessary part of fleeing an abuser."

Ike reached out and took her hand again. He leaned forward, staring into her eyes.

"I am so damn proud of you, Sidney. And I applaud what it is you're wanting to do. But it's so dangerous. A million different things could go wrong, and I'm not sure how I could help you."

"I understand that. I would never expect you to help me. This is my thing."

"I'm talking about legal help, darlin'. If, by some chance, you were arrested for obtaining fake papers, even if they were for someone else, you could go to jail for that. Or what if Ann's irate husband shows up demanding to know where she is? Or what if you unknowingly help a mother who doesn't have legal custody take a child across state lines? That's accessory to kidnapping. Or if you..."

"I get it, Ike! It's dangerous. Don't you think I've taken that into consideration?"

She didn't mean to yell. She hadn't meant to raise her voice at all. But she also hadn't expected his objections to be so frightening.

"I'm sure you have. In fact, I'm sure you've probably thought about this thing from every angle imaginable. But you've had hours to mull this all over, whereas I'm just now hearing about it. You gotta give me a few minutes to catch up here, okay?"

He let go of her hand and turned away, looking out at the sunset. Sidney wondered what was going through his mind, and she watched him pile a small wedge of baguette with a piece of white cheddar and a slice of pear, and take a bite. It was crazy, but even the movement of his jaw while he chewed was unbelievably sexy. And right now, after he'd just pointed out the pitfalls of her idea, his sexiness annoyed her.

She huffed out an exasperated breath and looked toward the sky.

The sunset was beautiful, all pink and purple and golden. The rays kissed his honey blond hair, giving him an adonis-like glow that put the twilight to shame. He was so freaking handsome.

"Isaac, I don't want this to be a problem between us."

He slowly turned toward her, reaching out to caress her sore cheek.

"This is not a problem, darlin'. You're just quietly blowing my mind, becoming the badass I've always suspected you to be, that's all."

Her smile was slow, and she could feel it splitting her face in two.

"You say the sweetest, most romantic things, Ike Taylor."

"Me?"

"You."

"Nonsense. What the hell do I know about romance?"

Sidney looked around at their sunset backyard picnic.

"I'd say you know a lot more than you think."

"I just like to do stuff to put a smile on that beautiful face. Is that romance?"

"I think that qualifies." Sidney smiled and leaned in for a kiss.

What was meant to be a sweet meeting of the lips turned fevered and urgent in an instant. His mouth tasted like pears, and their tongues danced and twirled.

She felt Ike's fingers slip into her mass of curls, his hand cradling the back of her head. His other hand snaked around her waist, gently pulling her closer as the kiss deepened.

Before she knew what was happening, Sidney was on her back on the soft blanket, and they were making out like a couple of teenagers. He nibbled on her bottom lip while their hands explored each other's bodies like it was all new.

She shivered when his lips moved around the rim of her ear and then down to her neck, and her fingers trembled as she fumbled with the hem of his t-shirt, searching for warm flesh.

Isaac groaned when she made contact with his skin, and Sidney smiled. The bulge in his jeans became insistent, and Sidney rocked her hips forward, craving the friction.

One large hand reached beneath her t-shirt and cupped a needy breast. Sidney whimpered as his lips found hers again. He rolled a nipple between his fingers and Sidney's back nearly bowed off the blanket.

The movement must have stirred something within him,

because his lips left hers and he pushed her t-shirt up, exposing her breast. His lips replaced his fingers, sucking her nipple in forcefully. Sidney cried out, rocking her hips against him. Her fingers tightened around strands of his hair, and she pushed her breast closer into his face.

She had no clue how long the sweet torture went on. All she knew for certain was that dusk was giving way to darkness when the mouth at her breast slipped away, leaving her bereft. Isaac looked down into her eyes.

"We should probably stop before we go further than the doctor recommended, huh?"

It took a few seconds for his words to make sense in her dazed mind.

"Hmm?" Still panting, she searched his eyes. "Oh. Yeah. Probably so."

With a parting kiss, he sat up and ran a hand through his hair.

"Well, I guess we should get the remnants of dinner inside and put away."

Sidney sat up and straightened her shirt.

"Yeah, let's do that."

They stood and Ike gathered up the charcuterie board and the champagne bucket, and Sidney folded the blanket and snatched up the glasses and followed him inside.

In the kitchen they put away the leftovers, and Isaac grabbed her hand and pulled her in for a quick turn around the kitchen.

Sidney giggled at him.

"What are you doing?"

"Dancing."

"But there's no music, Ike."

He pulled out and twirled her under his arm, bringing her back in close.

"Maybe not. But I figure I need to get in all the practice I can before our wedding."

Sidney grinned up at him.

"You want to dance at our wedding?"

"Of course. Don't you?"

"Well, yes, I do. But I didn't think you would. I mean, I know how problematic that could be for you."

"I know. But I was hoping maybe we could work around that. Like maybe... I don't know. Maybe we could dance to a few songs before we open up the dance floor to everybody else? That way, it wouldn't be so hazardous for me."

Sidney smiled. "I love that idea."

"Yeah?"

"Yes. It's perfect. And I love that you want to dance at our wedding. I know that's something you're doing for me, and I love you for it."

"It's not just for you, Sid."

"No?"

"No."

He gave her that bashful I'm-about-to-bare-my-soul-to-you look that she loved, and Sidney gave him her undivided attention.

"See, the truth is... until that night when you made me dance with you here in the kitchen..."

"Yeah?"

He hesitated, like he was trying to find the right words.

"Well... until that night, I had never danced before."

"Never?"

"Nope. I mean, you were right, I'd always wanted to. I love music, I always have. But I also knew that, for me, dancing was just too risky. I couldn't risk someone accidentally touching me or brushing up against me."

He sounded so forlorn, and Sidney touched his face.

"Anyway... after that night when you made me dance with you, I realized how much I enjoyed it. Moving my body so freely. It was incredible, Sidney. And you gave that to me."

He stared down into her eyes with such reverence, and Sidney's heart felt like it might explode with love.

"So, yeah. I want us to carve out a small block of time where we can dance to a few songs at our wedding without the worry of anyone else being on the dance floor with us."

"Consider it done."

She stood on her tiptoes and gave him a quick kiss on the lips.

"Come on." Still holding her hand, he led her from the kitchen, turning off the light as they went.

"Where are we going now?" Sidney asked, hearing the smile in her own voice.

"I'm putting you to bed."

He flashed that sexy double-dimple smile over his shoulder at her.

"If I'm lucky, I might be able to get to second base again."

11

"I'm going to give Bree a call today and thank her for the amazing picnic dinner she made for us last night."

Isaac smiled and stared at Sidney from over his coffee cup. Nearly twelve hours later and she was still gushing about how wonderful their backyard picnic had been. A sense of triumph swelled in his chest at the thought that he'd done something to please her. His idea had put a smile on her face, and that was all that mattered.

"I'm glad you enjoyed it, darlin'."

"I did enjoy it! It was such a sweet surprise. Romantic and delicious. And I'm not just talking about the food."

Her tone turned flirtatious, and Isaac set his cup down and gave her one of those arched eyebrow looks that women seemed to love.

"Are you flirting with me, Ms. Fairchild?"

"Me? No. I'm just commenting that the kisses last night were particularly scrumptious, that's all."

"Oh, I see. Well, delicious kisses could be on the menu every night if you'd just marry me already."

"I have every intention of marrying you, Detective Taylor. I'm just trying to find the right place and time."

"Um hmm."

"Wait. Are you implying that you'll withhold all future kisses until we're married?"

Isaac grinned. "Well, I would. I do like that suggestion and I think it could be an effective means of coercion to set a wedding date. However, I don't think I personally could survive without your kisses for a single day. So..."

Sidney giggled, and he smiled at the sound as he leaned in and kissed her lips.

"On that note, I need to get out of here and get to the station."

"I need to get moving too."

They stood and cleared the table of their breakfast dishes.

"Hey, when you do speak to Bree, be sure and thank her again for me, would you?"

"I will."

Isaac holstered his gun at his hip and gathered his things. Then he pulled her into his arms for another kiss, this one slow and lingering.

"You have a good day."

"You too. Be safe out there."

"I always am. Love you."

"I love you back, baby."

He gave her ass a quick squeeze and then he headed for the door.

He purposely got to the station a little early and walked the back hallways in search of someone. When he spotted him, a jolt of anxiety shot through him. He walked over to where he saw the man putting the large industrial mop away in the service closet.

"Hey, Milton. How's it going?"

Milton George was an old confidential informant of Isaac's. At least, he had been when he lived on the streets. But after he was witness to the same gangland shooting that Sidney had witnessed, Isaac had done what he could to help the man start over. Including arranging Milton's job with the janitorial service that cleaned the city's police stations and court buildings.

"Ike! Hey, man, how you doing?"

"I'm good. How are things going for you around here? Job still working out?"

Milton smiled, and Isaac thought about how great it was to see the man doing so well. It was like he was a new person.

"Oh, the job is great, Ike. It's hard work, but I enjoy it. The way I see it, keeping this place clean and tidy is important. I do my part so that you officers can do your part to keep the peace."

"Teamwork makes the dream work, right?"

"That's right. You know, it feels good to have a purpose again, Ike. I'll always be grateful you helped me find that again."

"It was my pleasure, Milt. Hey, listen, I've got a question for you." He glanced around to make sure no one else was within hearing distance.

"What's up? Did I do something wrong?"

Milton suddenly looked worried.

"No, no. Nothing like that. I was just wondering if you might be able to give me a little information. You know... kind of like old times."

"Oh. Sure." Milton glanced around too, and moved in closer. "I'll help if I can."

"What do you know about a janitor named Savage?"

Isaac kept his voice low, and he nodded a greeting at a passing patrol officer.

Milton blanched, and his expression told Isaac that he wasn't surprised to be asked.

"Burle Savage. That's his name."

"You know him?"

"Yeah. He makes me uneasy."

Isaac knew Milton George to be a decent judge of character, so his ears perked up.

"How so?"

"Let's just say that his name suits him well."

"Has this guy given you any trouble?"

Milton shook his head. "No, not me. I stay out of his way. But..."

He paused and glanced around again, and Isaac could see the dread on his face.

"What is it, Milt?"

"Well... I heard him threaten our boss once."

"What kind of threat?"

"A violent one. He threatened to beat him until he stopped breathing. He said he'd done it before, and he wasn't afraid to do it again. I think the only reason the boss doesn't fire him is because he's terrified of him."

Isaac took a deep breath and nodded. Milton's words reinforced what his flash had already told him about Savage.

"All right. Thanks a lot, Milton. I appreciate it."

"You won't tell him I told you all of this?"

Isaac grinned at him. "You know me better than that, my friend."

Milton smiled. "Yeah, I do."

"Have a good day."

"You too, Ike!"

Isaac hurried up to the fourth floor, taking the stairs two at a time, and scooted into the morning briefing just as Lieutenant Hayes called it to order. His attention during the briefing wasn't worth shit. His mind was preoccupied with everything Milton George had shared with him about Savage.

He wasn't sure why it bothered him so much. Hell, it wasn't like he wasn't used to having the particulars of more than one case crowding his mind at the same time. Lord knew every detective in the entire CPD homicide division had half a dozen open cases sitting on their desks at any given moment. And that was even when they were fully staffed.

But something about the flash he'd seen when Savage's arm had touched the back of his hand disturbed him on so many levels.

The brutality of it.

The inhumanity.

The look on Savage's face as he beat the homeowner. Like he was enjoying himself.

Bodies stood all around him, and Isaac was jolted back to the here and now. He stood and followed everyone out into the pit and headed to his desk.

"What's going on, partner?"

Isaac looked up at the sound of Pete's voice.

"What?"

"I said what's going on? You got that look."

"What look?"

"That look." Pete pointed to Isaac's face, and then sat down. "The one that says something's on your mind."

Isaac sighed. He wasn't ready to bring Pete in on this yet. He wasn't even sure what *this* was, and he wanted to be sure. He may have gotten to a place where he wasn't trying to run from his abilities anymore, but that didn't mean he was eager to trot them out like dancing bears at a circus for everyone to gawk at either.

"Nothing. Just wondering where to begin this morning with Amber Camden's family members."

He sat down and began leafing through the papers on his desk, searching for the list he'd made the day before of the girl's male family members, and where to locate each of them.

"Well, she's got a dad and two brothers, right?"

"Right." Isaac looked over the list and confirmed the number of brothers. "Not to mention a step-father and several uncles and male cousins."

"I say we start at the top and work our way down."

Isaac nodded. "Father it is then. Let's go."

"Where we headed?" Pete asked once they were in the unmarked cruiser.

"Paul Camden works at an ad agency downtown. We'll go there first. One brother manages the appliance store on Buckeye Road, and the other one works from home doing medical billing or something. He's out in Fairfax."

"You're still set on one of them being our killer?"

"It's the only thing that makes any sense. Unless you're suggesting that Amber Camden snuck out of her room at the institution and did it herself."

Pete chuckled. "Now that sounds like the plot of a very twisted movie, doesn't it?"

"It does indeed. Not to mention the fact that she'd have to have superhuman strength on top of the ability to fool all the medical staff at that place, and her family that comes to visit."

Those words rattled around in Isaac's brain for a couple of seconds.

"You know, Pete... we should head back to the institution at some point and get a look at their visitor log. Find out who Amber Camden's regular visitors are. It's a long shot, but it might tell us something useful."

"I'll make a note of it." Pete thumbed in a few keys on his cellphone.

They navigated the morning traffic and pulled to the curb in the heart of downtown, and got out of the car. They entered the ad agency building with badges at the ready.

"Detective Sergeant Ike Taylor. My partner, Detective Pete Vega. We need to speak with Paul Camden."

The receptionist blinked at him, and Isaac wasn't sure if her non-response was fear or shock. It didn't matter. Either way, he needed her to move.

"Ma'am?"

"Yes? Oh. Yes, of course! Right away."

She picked up a phone then and spoke softly into it. Isaac shot a what-the-heck-is-wrong-with-her look Pete's way, to which Pete rolled his eyes.

"If you'll follow me, please."

She stood and came around the desk, giving Isaac a shy smile. They followed her across the vestibule and down a short hall. Then she stopped and ushered them into a small conference room to their right.

"Mr. Camden will be right down to meet with you. Can I get you anything, Detective Sergeant?"

"No, thank you."

"Willa. I'm Willa Cooper."

She tossed her dark blonde hair over her shoulder and smiled. Isaac shoved his hands into his pockets and glanced at the floor before he looked at her again.

"Thank you, Ms. Cooper."

Was this for real? Was she flirting? With *him?*

"Nothing for me, thanks."

Pete's flippant response brought a soft pink blush to Willa Cooper's cheeks.

"Right."

She backed out of the room giving Isaac one last glance over her shoulder.

He couldn't have stopped the surprised grin if he'd tried. Women didn't typically flirt with him. Not until Sidney, anyway. She'd been the first woman to flirt with him in a very long time. He wasn't any good at flirting back. That's why he still couldn't believe that he'd actually gotten that woman to fall in love with him.

Wait.

Was this the proper response?

A young, attractive woman openly flirted with him, and all he could think about was flirting with the woman he loved. Was that right?

"Okay, you can wipe that cheesy grin off your face now, Mac Daddy. She's gone."

"Mac Daddy? Wow. Okay."

"Whatever. She obviously needs glasses."

"Obviously."

The door opened, and a man walked in dragging the weight of the world behind him. Something about the concern in his eyes touched Isaac.

"Detectives? I'm Paul Camden. What's wrong? Has something happened to Scott or Jonathan?"

"Your sons are fine as far as we know, sir. But we're investigating a triple murder that's led us to the rape your daughter suffered several years ago. We have some questions for you."

Isaac motioned to the conference table, and they all moved over and took seats.

"I don't understand," Paul said as he settled in the chair and ran a hand through his graying brown hair. "How could a murder case lead you to my daughter's rape? Does this have something to do with DNA?"

"No, it doesn't. Mr. Camden, the three men who were prosecuted for raping your daughter were each found dead within the last 72 hours. The bodies of all three men were grossly mutilated."

"Oh, my God. Mutilated how?"

"That's not important. What is important is that we have reason to believe your daughter's rape is central to our investigation. We've been to visit Amber at the institution, and we know..."

"You went to the institution and bothered Amber with this?" The man's tone was suddenly harsh, all civility gone.

"It was the logical place to begin our investigation, sir."

"And did you get what you wanted? Was she able to answer your questions?"

He glared at Isaac.

Isaac calmly studied his face.

"You know that she wasn't."

"No, she wasn't. So your next step was to come harass me, is that it?"

"You're first on our list to speak with. I'm sure you can figure out why."

Paul suddenly stood and swiveled around, clutching the back of the camel-colored leather chair like he was trying to rein in his anger.

"I'm sorry, Detectives, but you won't see me mustering up any sympathy for the animals who raped my daughter and killed her spirit. They may as well have cut her heart out that night. The end result was the same. You say they're dead now? Well, I say hallelujah! They got what they deserved."

Isaac stared at him, sizing him up. Paul Camden was of medium height and build, and even though his anger and righteous indignation would've carried him far, Isaac couldn't see him performing the acts necessary to kill their three victims. Not alone anyway.

"Sit down, Mr. Camden."

"Why are you here, Detectives? Do you think I killed those boys?"

"Sit. Down. Mr. Camden."

The man stared at him for a long moment. Then he sighed, and his shoulders fell at least a foot. He maneuvered around to the seat of the chair and slumped down onto it.

"I'm sorry. I didn't mean to yell. I just get so angry when I think about what they did. How they hurt my baby girl."

Paul broke down into tears, and Isaac took a deep breath, mentally pushing the profound sorrow away. He began building a wall with concrete blocks in his mind. It was a technique his grandad had taught him. A trick to keep other people's emotions from overpowering his own.

It was the part of his psychic abilities that disturbed him the most — well, besides the telekinesis, of course — the excessive sense of empathy he felt when other people's emotions were running high.

He quietly cleared his throat and addressed Paul Camden again.

"Mr. Camden, I'm going to be straight with you right now. Because of the particularly brutal nature of these murders, we believe that someone close to Amber is the killer."

Paul Camden's head jerked up and he stared at him.

"So, you're here to what? To arrest me? But I haven't done anything!"

"We're here to ask where you were on these dates, at these times."

He tore a page from the small notebook he carried, and slid it across the table. The estimated times of death for each of the three victims. Paul picked up the paper and studied the dates and times. His gaze bounced between Isaac and Pete.

"Well, these times are all middle of the night. I was home each night."

"Anyone that can corroborate that for us?"

"My wife."

Isaac nodded. Not a great alibi.

"Did you and your wife watch any TV on those nights? Make any phone calls, or have any contact with others during those times?"

"No, we usually turn in around 11 most nights. They were normal nights... nothing unusual or different."

"And you don't know of anyone who might've been angry enough to go after the men who raped your daughter and got away with it?"

Paul hesitated.

"I can't say that. I mean, honestly? We were all angry when those jackasses got off scot free. Carl and I don't usually agree on much, but I'll tell ya... that day we were both so angry. If Judith hadn't talked us down, I think we might've collaborated on a little payback."

"And Carl is Amber's step-father?"

"Yeah. Carl Maddison. Judith married him about two years after our divorce. Much as I hate it, he's been a really good step-father to my kids."

"Who else was angry enough to join that collaboration?"

"Everyone. My sons. My brothers. Judith. My wife, Lisa. We were all ready to lash out."

"But no one acted on it back then?"

"No."

"So, why do you think someone waited over four years for their revenge, Mr. Camden?"

Paul looked Isaac in the eyes.

"No. What you're saying can't be right. My family was devastated when those boys got off four years ago. And Amber never spoke another word, Detective. Not one word. But we all rallied around her, we didn't go off planning the ultimate revenge. No one in my family did this. They couldn't have."

"Not even Amber's older brothers, or the step-father who was angry enough to join forces with you when the verdict came down?"

"No! My sons wouldn't do this. Please... don't speak with them. It was hard enough on them when this happened. Please don't open up those old wounds."

"I'm sorry, Mr. Camden, but we have to speak with everybody close to Amber. And we would appreciate it if you did not call and warn them that we're coming."

Isaac stood, prompting the others to follow suit.

"We'll be in touch, sir. Don't leave town. We'd hate to have to track you down if we have more questions."

Pete handed the man a card. "If you think of anything that might be useful, give us a call."

They left the building and climbed back into their car.

"What's your gut saying?" Isaac asked.

Pete sighed. "I don't think he did it."

"I don't either."

"But he did get nervous when you suggested his sons may have something to do with this."

"I caught that too. Either he knows something outright, or he's just genuinely scared that his sons may have done this."

"On to the sons then. Who do we take first?"

"They're fairly close together in location. Might as well hit Fairfax first."

Isaac pulled into traffic and navigated away from downtown, heading for the Fairfax suburb. As he drove, something occurred to him. He shot a glance Pete's way.

"You know, Fairfax is awfully close to University Circle, where body number one was found."

Pete glanced at him and nodded. "It is. And Wade Park, where body number two was discovered, is a mere mile away."

Isaac stopped at a red light and glanced around the intersection.

"Body number three was downtown at Cleveland State. That's roughly ten minutes from anywhere in Fairfax."

"Proximity to the crime scenes doesn't make them guilty, Ike."

"No. It doesn't."

They drove on in silence, although Isaac's mind worked over the disturbing details of the crime scenes. If this case was connected to Amber Camden's rape, they were clearly looking for someone close to her. Only a loved one would go after her attackers so brutally.

They pulled up at the curb of a mid-century two-story in the residential neighborhood and got out.

"I'm going to let you take the lead on this one."

Pete's head jerked in Isaac's direction.

"Really?"

"Yeah."

"Why?"

Isaac fought the grin tugging at his lip.

"Because you're my partner and you need the experience."

Pete didn't respond as they moved up the walkway.

"Is there a problem?"

"Not at all. Which brother is this?" Pete reached out and rang the bell.

Isaac looked at his notes.

"Jonathan Camden. He's the younger of the two."

It took a few moments for the door to open. When it did, a young man in his late twenties or early thirties with medium brown hair and blue eyes looked at them.

"Can I help you?"

Pete held up the badge that hung around his neck like bling whenever he was on duty.

"Jonathan Camden?"

"Yes, that's me."

"Detective Pete Vega. This is my partner, Detective Sergeant Ike Taylor. We'd like to speak with you about your sister, Amber."

"Amber?" The man's demeanor went from passive to engaged in the span of two seconds. "Is she okay? Has something happened?"

"She's fine, Mr. Camden. But the three men who were tried and acquitted for raping her are all dead."

Isaac stood by and observed. It wasn't that long ago that he was in Pete's shoes — a fairly new detective with something to prove to himself. But Pete was doing a great job.

"Wait." Jonathan held up a hand. "Are you telling me the assholes responsible for putting my sister in that institution are dead?"

"That's exactly what I'm saying. May we come in? Or would you prefer to do this on the porch in front of your neighbors?"

The man blinked and opened the door wider, gesturing for them to step inside.

"After you."

Pete pointed inside, and then followed after Jonathan. Behind him, Isaac smiled to himself. Remembering not to turn his back on the subject being questioned was rule number one.

He followed them inside, where Jonathan showed them to the living room. He gestured toward the couch.

"Please, sit down. How can I help you?"

Jonathan sat down in a chair opposite the couch, leaving it for Isaac and Pete. Once seated, Pete leaned in.

"Mr. Camden, what can you tell us about your sister's ordeal?"

Jonathan blew a huff of air through his lips.

"I don't even know where to start. It was a nightmare for my family. My sister came home from a high school party and stepped into the room like Carrie after the bloody prom. We knew something had happened, but she wasn't exactly up for talking about it."

He ran a hand through his hair, and Isaac noted how much this man looked like his father.

"My mom insisted on taking her to the hospital. That's where she finally told my mom what had happened. Those boys were arrested a few days later, for all the good it did. It's like none of the authorities took Amber's story seriously. And each of those boys, their parents had a lot of money and influence. They hired this shark of a lawyer who was hellbent on making my sister out to be some slut! They made a fool of her in court. Made her sound..."

He paused and fought hard not to get emotional.

"They made her sound cheap and dirty. And Amber was just so traumatized by it all that she broke down. She turned inward, where she felt safe, you know? She went inside herself where no one could hurt her again."

Jonathan wiped his face with a gruff hand. Isaac took a deep breath and closed his eyes for a quick moment, silently pushing Jonathan's grief and sorrow away. He mentally stacked a few more concrete bricks to the wall in his mind.

"Mr. Camden," Pete continued. "Where were you during these times?"

Isaac handed over the piece of paper torn from his small notebook, and Pete passed it on.

Jonathan took the paper, but his gaze never left Pete's.

"You want to know where I was? What? You think I had something to do with killing those animals?"

Isaac watched Pete level his gaze at Jonathan.

"I didn't say that, Mr. Camden. But it's our job to pinpoint the whereabouts of everyone close to Amber at the times of the three murders, yes."

"So that you can get justice for those boys, right?"

Isaac felt more than saw the unease settle in on Pete's shoulders, and he couldn't blame him. They both knew where Jonathan was going.

"Well, where the hell is Amber's justice, huh?"

Jonathan glared at them. He kept his voice at a respectable level, but Isaac could see the battle within him. This man wanted to yell and rage against them.

"Those assholes raped her! Then they publicly humiliated her and walked away like she was some piece of shit stuck to the bottom of their shoes. If someone killed them, good. They deserved it. What they don't deserve is your justice!"

To his credit, Pete never batted an eye at Jonathan's harsh words. He kept his cool and calmly repeated his question.

"Where were you during the times on that paper, Mr. Camden?"

Jonathan gritted his teeth and turned away, searching for peace perhaps. Then he looked down at the paper in his hand.

"These times are in the middle of the night. I was here, sleeping."

"Can anyone corroborate that?"

"Well, I live alone."

"So that's a no."

"No. No one but my dog. But I didn't do this!"

"Do you have any idea who might have?"

Jonathan hesitated for only a split second.

"No."

But it was enough for Isaac to pick up on. One glance at Pete and he knew his partner had picked up on it too. Pete leaned in closer.

"What was that, Mr. Camden?"

"I don't know who did this."

"Are you sure?"

"Yes, I'm sure."

Pete nodded and leaned back. Isaac nodded when his partner's eyes met his again.

"Thank you for your time, Mr. Camden." Pete stood and handed the man a card. "If you think of anything that might help, no matter how insignificant, please give us a call."

Isaac stood next to him. "And don't leave town. We may have more questions in the future."

Jonathan showed them out. When the door closed behind them, Isaac looked at Pete.

"What's your gut say?"

"Gut says he's lying."

"Good. Your gut is right." Isaac walked down the porch steps toward the car. "What else did you pick up on?"

"If he didn't do this, he knows who did."

"Yep."

They got into the car and headed for the appliance store to

find brother number two. Inside the store they went straight to the first salesman they spotted.

"Detectives Taylor and Vega. We need to see Scott Camden."

The scrawny man looked shocked, but before he could say a word, another man came toward them.

"It's all right, Tommy. I've got this."

The scrawny man walked away, and Isaac looked the newcomer over. He was taller and slightly more robust, with the same light brown hair and blue eyes as the other Camden men.

"I'm Scott Camden, and I already know why you're here."

"How's that?" Pete asked.

"I saw on the news where those three douchbags had been killed. I knew it was just a matter of time before you guys came sniffing around. And before you ask, no. I didn't do it. But I'd sure like to buy the guy or girl who did a drink."

Isaac handed over a piece of paper.

"Mr. Camden, where were you during these three times?"

Scott studied the paper and then huffed out a breath, almost grinning.

"You gotta be kidding me?"

"Nope. Not kidding."

"Well, these times are all in the middle of the night. I have to get up at 5:30 every morning to come open up the store by 7. I was at home sleeping."

"Can anyone corroborate that?"

"Yeah, my girlfriend, Sharon. We live together."

Isaac carefully handed over his small notepad. "Name and number where we can speak with Sharon."

"Jeez," Scott mumbled, taking a pen from his shirt pocket, and scribbling down the information.

"Since you didn't kill your sister's rapists, I don't suppose you know who did?"

"I've got no clue." Scott handed back the notepad. "But I'd really love to thank them when you find them."

"Right. Thank you for your time. Stay local. We may have more questions for you later."

Outside the store, Isaac shook his head and started for the car.

"Same song, different verse. I didn't do it, I don't know who did it, but they're great, and the dead guys don't deserve justice anyway."

Pete opened the passenger side door and looked at him from over the top of the car.

"You kinda can't blame them though. If what happened to Amber happened to my sister, I'd want the guys who did it dead too."

"Enough to lie to protect the killer?"

"You think Scott Camden knows who did this?"

"I think the father believes his sons did this. And I think both sons know who actually did it, but they aren't talking."

"Is that your psychic powers at work, or just a hunch?"

Isaac slid into the drivers seat. When he'd strapped on his seatbelt, he looked at Pete, who was just closing the door.

"It's just a hunch. But it's an educated one. The way Jonathan Camden hesitated when you asked if he knew who did this. There was something in his eyes and his tone of voice. And just now, with Scott Camden. The way he came at us loaded and ready."

"You think his only-a-matter-of-time speech was rehearsed."

"I do. But we can't prove it."

"So we keep moving down the list? Move on to the step-dad?"

"Moving on."

They carried on throughout the morning, running down all of Amber Camden's closest male relatives and getting much the same responses. Not surprisingly, none of them had much sympathy for the dead boys, and Isaac couldn't fault them. They were still grieving the loss of Amber — a girl who wasn't dead, but who may never come back to them.

It was a bitch of a case. And now all the players had been silenced in one way or another.

Isaac sat at his desk mulling over all the interviews they'd conducted, and his stomach growled, reminding him that they'd skipped lunch to get through them all.

Pete suddenly pointed the eraser end of a pencil his way.

"So, I'm thinking... since our questioning of Amber's male relatives didn't yield us much of anything, I think it's time we go back and question those close to the victims. Other than that and digging into the court transcripts of the rape case, I don't know what else to do."

Isaac didn't respond for a moment, and he rocked back in his chair, thinking.

There was something he could do that might help. But even the thought of it made everything inside him scream.

He couldn't explain it. But he knew instinctively that touching the victims was the wrong way to go. Somehow, he knew that he wouldn't be able to take it. The lingering trauma of touching the four little girls during the Lullaby case still tore him to shreds with every nightmare. He didn't want to make an already horrible situation worse.

But they didn't have much of a choice right now, did they?

He blew out a heavy sigh.

His voice was flat and resigned when he finally looked at Pete and said, "I know what else we can try."

12

"Why don't we break for lunch before I do this?"

Isaac was stalling and he knew it.

Pete knew it too.

"Look, Ike... you don't have to put yourself through that. Not for this case. We'll find a foothold some other way, man."

Isaac sighed. He appreciated that his partner understood the risk he was taking. But he wasn't sure there was another way. Three men were dead, and they had exactly zero leads so far. And yeah, those men may have been scum, but it was his job to find who killed them.

"Either way, I could use a sandwich or something."

"Okay. Let's hit the taco stand down the street."

Isaac was about to respond when he glanced up and spotted Burle Savage rounding the corner pushing a mop bucket.

Talk about scum.

Savage wrung out the mop and stepped into the break room.

"Actually, Pete... I have something I need to do, so I'll see you back here after lunch."

"Whatever."

Pete got to his feet and headed for the stairs.

Isaac stood and slowly made his way to the break room. He waited at the door and watched while the man mopped up a spill.

With every second that ticked by, his grandad's words of instruction echoed in his head with the things he needed to concentrate on so that he could tell if what he'd seen before was in the past or in the future.

Sterling had made it sound so easy. Like breathing. Isaac wasn't so sure.

When Savage turned to leave, Isaac took a breath and stepped inside.

"Whoa!"

The collision was quick, but effective, and Isaac fought not to double over when blades of fire ripped open his gut.

In the flash that followed, Savage swung.

The billy club splattered Savage's cruel face with blood.

Isaac reared back, bouncing into the counter in the break room.

"I didn't see you there, buddy! I'm sorry."

Savage rushed forward, arms reached out to help steady him.

Isaac drew back and quickly raised his hands in a don't-come-any-closer stance.

"I'm all right. *Don't.* Touch me!"

Savage stopped and stared at him, his face going hard as stone.

"Well, you don't gotta be shitty about it. I did apologize."

Isaac clutched the counter behind him and tried to steady himself with thoughts of Sidney.

"Apology accepted."

"You're one of them jumpy types, ain't ya?"

Isaac took a deep breath, finally filling his lungs with air and gratitude.

"Not really. I just don't like to be touched." He straightened up to his full height and stared Savage in the eyes. "You gotta problem with that?"

"I got no problem."

Savage's gaze locked on his, and Isaac got the feeling they were now playing some twisted game of who'll-blink-first. Isaac had no intention of being the one to look away. He stared the slightly shorter man down.

An evil grin slithered across Savage's face, then he slowly turned for the door.

"Cops," he mumbled under his breath.

"What was that?"

"What?" Savage returned the mop to its bucket and looked back at Isaac.

"I thought you said something."

"Nope. Nothing."

He watched Savage slink out of the break room and down the hall, and then he sagged against the counter behind him once more, taking another deep breath.

He wasn't certain if he'd done it right or not, but the flash felt like the future to him. Like something Savage was looking forward to with great anticipation.

Unfortunately, that knowledge brought with it many more questions than it answered.

He needed to talk to Sterling again.

He took off through the detectives pit and hurried down the four flights of stairs and out to his car. On the way, he stopped at the vending machine down by the exit doors and grabbed an energy bar.

He had no intention of actually going anywhere. He simply needed a quiet, private place to talk. He dialed his grandad and put the cellphone in the holder, then he opened up his energy bar and took a bite.

"Why, hello there!"

Isaac looked up at the phone screen and smiled. "Hey, Grandad. How you doing?"

"Oh, I'm doing just fine. How 'bout yourself?"

"I'm okay. Hey, is this a bad time? I don't want to interrupt your daily chess game with Maynard."

His grandfather had a long-standing date to meet his friend, Maynard Jennings, by the pond at their retirement village, where they would play a game of chess before lunch.

"Oh, I've got a little time. What's on your mind?"

"Well, I've got a question for you."

"Shoot."

"I did what you said and touched that guy today, concentrating on the information that I wanted to know."

"Right. Did it work?"

"It did. I was able to tell that the flash I had was a vision of the future."

"Excellent! See, I knew you could do it."

Isaac shook his head and took another bite.

"It was weird, Grandad. I could actually feel this guy's anticipation. He's looking forward to..." He stopped himself and just shook his head once more. "Sorry. You don't need the gory details."

"I'll take your word for it. So what's your question?"

"Well, now that I know for sure that it is the future, I was wondering if there was a way that I could find out a location for this future event? I thought about going to Geneviève and asking her, but..."

"Oh, sure there is."

"There is?"

"Yeah. All you gotta do is freeze what you're seeing and step outside your target's head to examine the scene."

Sterling said the words like he was telling him to put one foot in front of the other. As though it was no big deal, and Isaac stared at him on the screen.

"Do what now?"

Sterling chuckled. "Okay. Let's start at the beginning."

"Yes, please. And go slow. Act like I'm a five-year-old."

Sterling laughed again.

"Okay. First, just relax. You don't have to touch anyone for this, so there's no anxiety needed. It's just you and the memory of the vision you already had."

Isaac nodded and set aside the empty energy bar wrapper. He took a deep breath and tried to let the tension seep from his shoulders.

"Now, close your eyes and think back on that vision you had when you touched this man."

Isaac nodded again and closed his eyes. He was reluctant to see the flash again, but he was eager to learn any tricks his grandfather had to teach him. Especially if they could help him to live a better life with his monsters.

"Okay now, do you see it? The vision?"

In his mind, Isaac saw through Savage's eyes as he walked up to the stranger's door and knocked.

"Yes, sir."

"Is it playing out in your mind's eye, just like before?"

That door opened, and the homeowner greeted Savage with a curious smile.

"Yes, sir, it is."

"Freeze it. Just like you're pushing a pause button."

"But I don't know how."

"Yes, you do. Just push pause, Isaac."

"But Grandad..."

"Just pause the picture."

"But..."

Before he even finished the word, the image stopped. Savage and the home owner frozen in time.

"I-I don't... know..."

Words failed.

Silenced by awe.

"It's paused, yes?"

"Yes, sir."

Wonder. That's what he heard in his own voice now. Wonder.

"Good. Now... this is the tricky part."

Isaac licked his lips and waited.

"Step outside of your target's point of view."

What?

"My target?" He could hear the frustration, and the Tennessee accent, creep in beside that wonder.

"The eyes you're seeing through, that's your target. Step out of his point of view and look at the scene objectively. Like you're watching a movie."

"I can do that?"

"You can. Try it now."

"But how?"

"The same way you move an object with the power of your mind. You simply do it. Don't think about how. Just walk toward wherever it is you want to go in that scene. Picture yourself standing there."

Isaac opened his mouth to protest. But instead he felt himself step to the side, out of Savage's body. Out of Savage's head space.

Astonishment rippled his insides like the the brisk wind across Lake Erie in the winter.

"Holy shit!"

The whispered words held so much disbelief.

"You're out. Good. Now look around and find what you need."

"What I need?"

"A location is what you're after, right? An address? A landmark? Something of the sort?"

"Right."

Isaac glanced around, still not believing this was actually happening. Not knowing where to begin, he took a step further away from the frozen Savage and felt something snap inside him.

His vision blurred.

His mind rocked.

Voices swirled around him as the frozen scene suddenly jerked forward.

He blinked and opened his eyes, slightly panting.

"What the hell?" He looked around his car, and at his cellphone. Sterling smiled at him. "What just happened?"

"You snapped back."

"What?"

"That wasn't bad for a first try. How'd it feel?"

"Weird as fuck. Forgive my French, sir."

Sterling laughed. "No forgiveness needed. It is a bit disconcerting at times. You'll have to try again to locate the information you need."

"I have to ask... how in the world did you ever discover that you could do that?"

"The same way I learned everything I know. From my mama. Your great-grandmother, Abilene Taylor. She was a fiery thing, and so proud of all she could do with her mind. She made learning about our abilities fun and special. But she was careful to school me on the ways of the world too. She knew that not everyone would understand, and that we couldn't go flaunting the things we could do in front of just anybody."

"I wish I could've known her."

Isaac sat back in the driver's seat and wondered, as he often did these days, what his ancestor hypersensitive psychics had been like.

"Oh, I wish that too. She would've loved you, for sure."

Isaac smiled, and then glanced at the clock on his dash.

"I should try this again before I have to head inside."

"A word of caution."

"Yes?"

"Once you master freezing the scene playing out in your mind, you may find that you're only able to hold it for small periods of time."

"How small?"

"Well, you just saw it for yourself. 15 to 20 seconds. With practice, you may be able to get it up to 30 seconds, but not much more than that. The trick is to learn to freeze the scene at exactly the right moment, so that when you do step outside your target point of view, the information you're after is close by. That way you don't waste time searching."

"That makes sense. Thank you, Grandad. For everything."

"You are more than welcome, Isaac. Call me anytime."

After they ended their call, Isaac took a few deep breaths and prepared to try again.

"The same way you move an object with the power of your mind. You simply do it."

His grandad's words came back to him.

"Easy for him to say."

The words brought back his clumsy attempts to move the salt shaker the other day. Sterling made it sound like it was so easy. Second nature. Isaac wondered if he'd ever get to that point.

But one psychic step at a time.

He blew out a sharp breath and closed his eyes. The flash came back to him easily, the scene playing out like before. Seeing through Savage's eyes, he approached the door and knocked.

The door was answered by the meek homeowner and his curious smile.

Savage forced his way inside, knocking the man to the floor.

Savage whipped out an old-fashioned billy club, and bent over, club raised high.

Isaac hit pause.

The scene froze.

Astonished, he stepped to the side, leaving Savage's point of view.

Quickly, he scanned the area. They were in the foyer of the house, a staircase straight ahead, a formal living room off to the left. To the right, beside the staircase there was a table with a lamp and some envelopes.

Mail!

Isaac moved closer to have a look, wishing he could sift through it, but he knew instinctively that he wasn't able to actually move things in this state.

As luck would have it, the envelope on top was a utility bill. A bill with an address in clear view.

Yes!

Committing the address to memory, he glanced up at the mirrored clock hanging over the table and noted the time.

The snap happened more smoothly, zapping him back into Savage's point of view in an instant. Before the man could strike his first blow, Isaac opened his eyes, yanking himself out of the violent vision.

He silently panted and tried to calm the rush of his heart. Then he grabbed a pen and scribbled the address down on the small notepad he kept with him.

The things his grandfather could do with the power of his mind were incredible, and Isaac wondered if he'd ever be able to learn it all.

"The same way you move an object with the power of your mind. You simply do it."

Sterling's words came back to him a second time, and Isaac could no longer ignore them. The telekinesis was the biggest, scariest monster he could imagine, and it sounded like his grandad had turned his into a pussycat.

The salt shaker jerking across the counter came to mind once more.

Isaac's gaze darted around his car. He spotted the pen he'd just used sitting in the cup holder of the center console where he'd dropped it. Repositioning in his seat, he stared at the pen, and thought about his grandad's words once more.

"You simply do it. Don't think about how."

Don't think about how.

He concentrated on the pen and pictured it moving.

Nothing happened.

He reached out his right hand toward the pen, glancing around outside the car to make sure no one was around. Then he licked his lips and concentrated on the pen once more.

His right hand began to tingle.

He pictured the pen moving.

The pen spun around the rim of the cup holder as if he'd given it a push with his finger.

"Hah!"

Astonishment kicked him in the stomach.

Isaac practically leapt backward into the driver's side door, as if trying to get away from it.

He'd made the pen move.

Had he made that pen move?

Did that just happen?

"Holy shit."

This was ridiculous. Telekinesis wasn't real. People couldn't make things move with the power of their minds.

Except he could. And he did.

He'd done it four times so far, and his grandfather claimed all the hypersensitive psychics in their family had the ability too.

He turned his right hand palm up and studied it. Why had it tingled like that?

He didn't remember it tingling when he'd made those cement blocks fly through the air. He didn't remember it tingling when he made that gun turn on Jeffery Schiffer either.

This was insane. He couldn't think about it right now.

He left his car and headed back inside the building.

Back on the fourth floor, he got to his desk surprised to see Pete already there. He was even more surprised to see the white paper bag waiting for him.

"What's this?"

Pete looked up at him.

"Well, usually when you say you have something to do at

lunchtime, it involves some psychic shit, and it means that you don't have time to grab an actual lunch. So, I brought you a taco."

Isaac stared at him, fighting hard not to smile. He sat down and unwrapped the unexpected treat, examining it closely.

"I didn't spit in it, if that's what you're looking for."

Isaac grinned. He couldn't stop it.

"Thanks, partner."

"No problem. Hey, you and Sidney are still coming over for dinner tonight, right?"

"Oh, is that what this little show of kindness is? A bribe?"

"Just an insurance policy." Pete smiled and Isaac laughed.

"Yes, we're coming."

"Cool."

"As long as you agree to do something for me."

Pete rolled his eyes. "Now who's bribing who?"

"It's not a bribe. Call it a favor. I scratch your back..."

"...you stab mine," Pete finished, cutting him off.

Isaac grinned and took a bite of his taco.

"What do you want?"

"I want you to join me on a stake out tonight after dinner."

"A stake out?"

"Yep."

"Who we after?"

"You remember the janitor that accidentally touched me the other day?"

"Aww, shit!" Pete flopped back in his chair and then stared at him. "Psychic Batman?"

Isaac responded with a look, and then took another bite of his taco.

Pete sighed and leaned forward again.

"What've you got?"

Isaac popped the last of his surprise lunch into his mouth and then proceeded to talk Pete through everything he'd seen in his flash, and learned from Milton George about Burle Savage.

"Jesus," Pete whispered. "What is wrong with people anymore?"

"I don't know. I feel like I'm asking myself that question every single day lately. So, are you in?"

"I'm in."

"Good. I was thinking..."

Isaac's cellphone rang and he was surprised when he looked at the caller ID.

"Hang on, Pete." He leaned back in his chair and hit the button. "Fox?"

"Taylor. Hello."

"Hey. What can I do for you?"

He heard Special Agent Emmett Fox take a deep breath on the other end of the line, and he immediately regretted taking the call.

"Well, I was just calling to, um..."

"Yes?"

"Well, I was wondering if maybe, there might be... uh..."

"Might be what?"

There was a pause, and Isaac rolled his eyes, finally understanding where this awkward conversation was going.

"Look, Emmett..."

"I was wondering if there might be another family game night coming up that I could invite myself to?"

The agent finally spit the words out in a rush, like they wouldn't come out at all if he didn't give them a shove.

Isaac sighed and then chuckled to himself.

"Next one's not for another couple of weeks, and it's at my brother's house. But you know, in the meantime, you could just man up and call my sister to reschedule your date."

There was a deflated sigh from Emmett.

"You heard about that, huh?"

"I heard more than I ever wanted to. She thinks you ghosted her."

"Damn. I was afraid of that."

Isaac wanted to be a good friend and ask what happened, but he really didn't want the details. He'd already been through this twice this week — once with Pete, then with Hiroshi. He did not want to become known as the go-to guy for his friend's relationship problems.

"We've been busy as hell around here putting together a RICO case against a suspected trafficking ring."

Emmett provided the details without Isaac asking. But now, he was intrigued and couldn't help himself.

"Drug trafficking?"

"Drug and human. Our guy on the inside has gathered evidence that Martelli is heavily entrenched in both."

"You have a man on the inside of Boston Martelli's organization?"

Boston Martelli was a wealthy businessman who had his hands in several different pots around the Cleveland area. Everything from real estate to import/export to finance. And it had long been rumored that he was tangled in deep with organized crime.

"We have two, actually."

"Wow. I wasn't aware the FBI was currently investigating Martelli. Not seriously anyway."

"Good. We've tried to keep it completely under wraps. I'm only telling you because I want you to know that I did not intentionally set out to hurt your sister. When I met her, I had no idea that this case would heat up so fast. I've been swamped."

"I understand, Emmett. And I'm sure Emily would understand too. Just call her and explain. She's a reasonable sort."

"Was she very angry?"

"She called you Special Agent Dork."

"Ouch."

Isaac could hear the grimace over the phone.

"Yeah. Do better. I'd hate to have to kick your ass or something."

Emmett laughed out loud and Isaac smiled.

"Get back to work, Fox. And call my sister."

"Will do. Thanks, Ike."

"Yep."

He ended the call and turned back to Pete.

"Enough horsing around. We've got victim's families to interview."

"So did you change your mind about touching the vics to glean any useful information?"

Isaac looked at Pete and sighed. "Yeah, I think I have. At least, for now. I just don't want to put myself through it."

"You'll get no push back from me. I have no idea what you go through when you do that, but I know it can't be easy. We'll get through this case without any of your psychic trickery."

Isaac grinned and they stood up to head out for more questioning. Before they could take the first step, Isaac's extension rang. He held up a finger to Pete and sat back down to pick up the receiver.

"Detective Sgt. Taylor."

"Sgt. Taylor, this is Officer Rodney Hamilton, from the Domestic Violence unit. We spoke the other night at the women's shelter. I took your fiancée's statement."

"Yes, I remember. What can I do for you Hamilton?"

"Just a courtesy call, Sgt. I wanted to let you know that we've picked up Donald Mowbray. He's currently in a cell down in central booking."

Isaac's ire spiked in an instant.

"What are you charging him with?"

"Assault and battery. Trespassing. Violating a protection order."

Isaac's jaw clenched. First degree misdemeanors.

Not that they weren't serious crimes. They all were. But it meant that the asshole who'd hit Sidney would only do about six months behind bars if convicted. And he'd most likely make bail and be back on the street within 24 hours to wait for his court date.

"Have you notified my fiancée, or the dirtbag's wife yet?"

"Not yet. I thought you'd want to tell your fiancée personally. I can call her if you wish."

"No, I'll take care of it. Thanks."

"No problem."

Isaac hung up the phone and stared at his desk for a moment.

Seething.

He wanted to go downstairs to the jail and visit Donald Mowbray. He wanted to teach the man a lesson he'd never forget. He wanted to leave the man huddled in a corner whimpering and begging for the pain to stop.

He wanted Donald Mowbray to think twice about putting his hands on a woman ever again.

"Everything all right, Ike?"

Pete's voice cut through his anger. He looked up at his partner.

"Patrol picked up the asshole who manhandled Sidney at Hope House the other night. He's down in a cell."

"Ooh. We going downstairs for a minute?"

Isaac thought about that question for a long moment.

The longer he thought, the more his right hand began to tingle with the oddest sensation. He had no clue where it came from or how, but he instinctively knew that he could do some real damage with that tingling hand and his growing skills in telekinesis.

Oh, how he wanted to go downstairs to Donald Mowbray's cell and try it out.

But Sidney had begged him not to.

"No. Let's get to work."

He stood and headed for the stairs. He had a killer to catch.

13

Gerri Miller smoothed a hand over her jeans and straightened her blue buttoned-down shirt. She didn't want to do this. She didn't want to walk through that door and face that man with the piercing, probing eyes and the blunt questions. But she knew she had to. She had no choice.

She took a deep breath and knocked.

The door opened and Dr. Clark Newman smiled at her.

"Detective Miller. Right on time. Come in."

Gerri stepped into his office squeezing her hands together.

"You sound surprised."

"What's that?"

"That I'm on time. You sound surprised about that."

Dr. Newman smiled and gestured to the chair in front of his desk.

"Not at all. But I am pleased you decided to keep this appointment today. I was beginning to think you wouldn't come back."

He sat in his desk chair and leveled that intrusive gaze at her, and Gerri shifted in her seat. She toyed with a loose thread at the end of her sleeve.

"Actually, I... I did think about quitting."

"I see. Why were you thinking about quitting?"

Gerri stared past him and concentrated on the yellow in the abstract painting on the wall behind him.

"Because I... I just didn't know if I could come back here and do this job without Curt. I mean, without seeing him everyday."

She grinned at a stray memory of her partner.

"He was the biggest pain in my ass sometimes, but he was a good partner. A good teacher. He taught me a lot about being a good detective."

She paused and tried to swallow around the large, jagged stone in her throat.

"You're talking about him in the past tense."

"What?"

She looked at Dr. Newman, hearing the puzzlement in her own voice.

"The last time we talked, you could only speak about Curt Dorn in the present tense. As if he were still here. You're using the past tense now — 'he *was* a good partner.' It means you're finally accepting Curt's death."

"Oh."

Gerri looked down at her hands.

"It's a good thing, Gerri. It means you're not stuck anymore. You're moving forward."

A tired sigh escaped her, and she slumped back in the chair and folded her arms.

"It doesn't feel like a good thing."

"I know. But it is. And you'll see that eventually. So tell me, what brought you back? You thought about quitting, yet here you are. What changed your mind?"

"I love my job."

Gerri shrugged her shoulders and finally looked Dr. Newman in the eyes.

"I love being a detective, and I'm good at it. I worked hard to get here, and to prove that I could do the job just as well as any man. And I know Curt wouldn't want me to quit."

Dr. Newman nodded. "I'm glad you came to those realizations, because they're all very true. Yes, you are a good detective. Yes, you worked hard to get here. And no, Curt would not have wanted you to quit."

Gerri mirrored his nod and then unfolded her arms and looked down at her hands again, twisting her fingers together. She knew this process was necessary if she wanted to be cleared to go back to work, but she wondered how much she could, or should, say to this department shrink.

"I..."

She stopped and thought better of it.

"Gerri? What were you going to say?"

"I just... well, I... I've been thinking about transferring to another precinct."

Dr. Newman sat back and stared at her.

"I see. Is this about being reminded of Curt here at this precinct?"

Gerri hesitated. Would he report anything she said to the chief? Would their conversation be stored in her file for anyone to read?

"Partly. Fresh start and all that."

"What's the other part?"

She suddenly met his gaze. She knew it was risky, but she had to ask.

"That doctor patient confidentiality thing... that's in play here, right? You're not going to take what I say to the brass and report me or anything?"

Dr. Newman frowned and then a slow smile turned up the corners of his lips.

"No, Gerri. I am employed by the city of Cleveland, not the

police chief. And even if I were employed by Chief Branson, everything we say in these sessions stays between you and me. I'm *your* doctor. So yes, that doctor patient confidentiality thing is most definitely in play here."

Gerri took a relieved breath and sat forward.

"Good. Because I need someone to talk to."

"That's why I'm here. It's my job to be someone you can talk to, without fear of judgement or fear of being reported to the higher ups. Why are you thinking of transferring?"

Gerri hesitated still, searching for the right words.

"I've been thinking about transferring because... well, because it would make things easier. For my love life."

"Your love life?"

Gerri nodded. "I'm..."

She stopped herself. Should she really do this?

"I'm involved with my boss."

"Oh."

Newman's eyebrows lifted, then his gaze drifted off to the side and he breathed in that air of discreetness allies always did when they realize the unflattering truth about you.

"Who knows about this relationship?"

"No one but you. And it wasn't an actual relationship until recently. Until after Curt died."

"I see. Well, my question to you is, do you think it's wise to make such a big decision based on a relationship that's still so new?"

"The thing is it's not new."

"But you just said..."

"I know, I said it wasn't an actual relationship until recently. And that's true, in the... *physical* sense."

"I see."

The awkwardness in Dr. Newman's tone told her that he did, in fact, know what she was implying.

"But the feelings, the connection, the magic. That's all been there for a very long time. So long that I have no doubt in my mind that I love him. I love him enough to switch precincts so that we can be together without worrying about how it might look to the brass. Gavin's been very worried about his position as Lieutenant if this should come to light."

"And if he's no longer your immediate supervisor there's nothing to worry about."

"Exactly."

"Well, relationship help is not exactly my area of expertise, Detective, and I'm not about to pass judgment on what you or anyone else does with their love lives. But if it's my advice you're asking for, I can give you that."

Gerri smiled at him. "Yes. Please."

"All right. Here it is. Having zero information on what's happened between the two of you... I would first caution you that, despite your feelings, this relationship is still very new. And it would be unwise to make such an important decision as switching precincts based on who you love."

Gerri sighed and closed her eyes.

"That said," Dr. Newman continued, "have you thought about looking at the in-house job postings?"

Gerri looked up at him, and her insides jiggled like jelly.

"The in-house job postings." She repeated his words like a parrot. A pleasantly shocked parrot. "No. I hadn't thought of that."

Dr. Newman shrugged. "You might be surprised at what's listed there. After all, the objective here is for Lieutenant Hayes to not be *your* lieutenant anymore. Correct?"

Gerri smiled a smile that she felt on the inside. A smile that was genuine and rejuvenating. A smile that she hadn't experienced in weeks.

"Yes! That is the objective. Thank you for pointing that out, Dr. Newman. I don't know why I hadn't thought of it."

"You're too close to the situation. Not to mention you've been through a lot. You're grieving. You're not thinking objectively. And it's all perfectly normal behavior."

Gerri laughed, and it was a light-hearted sound she hadn't heard from herself in a long time.

"I'm going to check those postings while I'm here."

"I think that's a great idea. And since our time is almost up, I think you should go do that now."

She stood and gathered her things.

"Thank you, Doc. I was so nervous about coming here today, but right now I feel more hopeful than I have in weeks. Thank you!"

"You're welcome. I'm glad I could help."

She rushed for the door.

"But Gerri!"

"Yes?" she turned back toward him.

"I'll still need to see you again next week."

"I know. Once a week until you feel I'm ready to go back to work. I understand. And I won't cancel on you again."

"All right. Have a good day."

Gerri left Newman's office on the second floor and walked around the corner. Beside the door to the dispatch office, was the huge bulletin board where employees posted everything from roommate searches to wedding invitations. But it also had a section that was reserved for department news, and a regularly updated listing of positions that would soon be opening up within the department.

Gerri's breathing shallowed as she stepped closer and studied that list. It was a long shot, and she knew it. There was a good chance that there'd be nothing she was qualified for. Or worse, only positions she'd be overqualified for. But she was grateful to Dr. Newman for the suggestion all the same.

A listing caught her eye, and a slow smile sent a warm fuzzy zip of excitement up her spine.

She jotted down the particulars of the job listing in the notes app of her cellphone. Then she headed for the stairs and went up to the fourth floor.

She'd feared that stepping into the detectives pit would be as difficult as it had the last time she was here, right after Curt's death. But somehow all she felt was welcome. A familiar sense of comfort and belonging wrapped around her like a warm shawl.

She stepped further in, staring at her desk and trying not to envision Curt sitting at the adjoining one. Before her emotions could get the best of her, she heard her name.

"Hey, Miller! You back?"

Gerri looked up to see Keisha Harris, one of her fellow female homicide detectives, coming toward her with a big smile.

"Harris! Hey, how are you?"

She gave her friend a hug and spotted a few other familiar faces now turned their way. One she didn't see though was Keisha's partner, Gary Barker.

"I'm good."

"Where's Barker?"

"In the hospital with a bleeding ulcer."

"What? No!"

"Yeah. He'd lost so much blood they had to give him a transfusion that first night. A lot of us went down and donated blood in support."

"Why didn't you call me? I would've donated."

"Oh, don't worry about it. We all know you've been dealing with a lot. Besides, it's been crazy around here the last few weeks. Barker's ulcer, Wheeler had hernia surgery, so he's out too."

"He is?"

"Yeah."

Across the pit, Gavin Hayes stepped out of his office and spoke to another detective, handing him a file. He looked surprised to see her, and he smiled and started walking toward them, but Gerri wasn't able to return his smile.

"Wait. So you guys are down four detectives right now?"

"Well, yeah."

Gerri bit her bottom lip and glanced around the pit. Why hadn't Gavin told her they were so short handed? Why had he listened to her go on and on about quitting or transferring when they obviously needed her to get back to work as soon as possible?

Breaths suddenly didn't come so easy when guilt sat on her chest like a ten-ton elephant.

"Now you look familiar. Hey, didn't you used to work here?"

The voice came from behind her, and Gerri turned to see Pete Vega smiling at her. Ike Taylor came up the stairs right behind him.

"Hey, Vega!"

She gave him a hug.

"You look good."

"Thanks."

She turned and hugged Taylor too.

"Whoa!"

He jumped and froze.

The surprise of it caused Gerri to jump in turn, and her cheek brushed against his.

"Swoo!"

He inhaled a sharp breath and hunched up, as if in pain.

"Oh, my God, Ike! I'm so sorry. I completely forgot. I don't know what I was thinking."

"It's okay. It's okay."

"I'm so sorry."

"I'm fine. Don't worry about it. It's good to see you."

Even as he smiled at her he shot a heated look over at Gavin, who'd joined them just in time to see her blunder in touching Ike. Gavin's grin slid off his face, and Gerri wondered what that weirdness was all about.

"Pete's right. You're looking good, Miller," Ike said to her. "How you feeling?"

"Oh, I'm okay. Getting there, anyway, according to Dr. Newman. I just came from an appointment with him. He's not ready to clear me just yet, but he says I'm making good progress."

"That's all we can ask for then," Ike said.

"I guess. I'm really sorry you guys are so short handed right now though. I had no idea." She looked right at Gavin when she said it. He met her gaze, but looked away quickly, glancing once again at Ike.

"Aw, we'll get through it," Pete said.

"Yeah. Well, I should get going and let you all get back to work. Maybe I'll swing by the hospital and say hey to Barker. Is he okay to have visits?"

"Oh, yeah. Cleveland Clinic, room 213. Tell him I'll be by after my shift." Keisha gave her arm a pat. "I've been relieving Becky each evening so that she can go home and have dinner with their girls and put them to bed."

"That's sweet of you."

"That's what partners are for, right? It was good to see you."

"You, too. It was good to see all of you."

"See you later, Gerri," Pete said.

"Take care of yourself," Ike said.

She waved at them all and then headed for the stairs. She glanced back in Gavin's direction, and her stomach fluttered when she saw him watching her. Then she went down the stairs and headed out.

When Gerri was gone, Isaac looked at Gavin.

Gavin stared back at him for a moment, the air around them crackling with tension. Then without a word, he turned and walked back to his office.

Pete walked away, oblivious to anything wrong.

Isaac huffed out a soft breath and shook his head, then he

followed Pete to their desks, wondering what the hell he'd just seen.

He sat down and began to look over the notes he'd taken during their latest round of interviews.

They'd spent the afternoon speaking to the family members of each of their three castrated victims, as well as a few students from both campuses who'd been close to the vics. None of what they'd learned sparked any hints, clues, or breakthroughs in their case. It was clear they needed to regroup and come at this case in a different way, but for the moment, Isaac was at a loss.

A loss made more confusing by the flash he'd just seen when Gerri Miller's cheek had briefly brushed against his own when she'd hugged him. The good part was that Gerri was a decent person, so the pain had been minimal. But the flash. Well, that was another story.

What the hell had he seen exactly?

How long had it been going on?

And most importantly, what were they thinking?

Unable to concentrate on the work before him, he got up and headed for Lieutenant Hayes' office.

The door was open. He stepped inside and closed it behind him, then he stood in front of the desk and stared at his boss.

Gavin never looked up, his attention focused on the paperwork he was filling out.

"We should talk, sir."

Gavin sighed, dropping the pen, and finally looked up at him.

"What did you see, Ike?"

"Is Gerri wanting to transfer out because of you?"

He knew it was an extremely personal question, and he knew that Hayes could easily pull rank and tell him to mind his own eff'n business, or worse. But he had to ask.

Gavin sat back in his chair and folded his hands together.

"Have a seat."

Isaac took a seat in the chair across from Hayes' desk. It was strange, but he was getting used to being Hayes' sounding board and his confidant. Since his recent promotion to sergeant, Hayes seemed to be pulling him in a lot more.

"Tell me what you saw when Gerri touched you."

Isaac ran his hands over his thighs and hesitated for a beat.

"I saw the two of you... you know. In bed."

Gavin closed his eyes and lowered his head for a second before he met Isaac's gaze again.

"How long?"

Isaac couldn't stop himself from asking.

"The sex, not long. Just a few days. The feelings? Several months."

Gavin shook his head, as though he couldn't believe it himself.

"I have fought so hard to avoid the situation I'm in right now. But it's like... once Curt Dorn died, I worried about her so damn much. And I purposely stayed away from her for as long as I could. That's why I hadn't gone to see about her after his funeral."

Gavin stopped and shook his head again, and Isaac could feel the turmoil bubbling up inside him. He took a deep breath and pushed his boss' emotions away, and began reenforcing that imaginary concrete wall in his mind.

His boss' weird headspace lately made so much sense now.

"You realize the dangers here, sir?"

Gavin's gaze snapped back to Isaac.

"Of course I do. Why do you think I've been fighting it for months? I could be demoted over this relationship. I could lose my job. Not to mention I have Trey to think about."

"Well, Trey's almost a grown man."

"Yeah, well he's still mostly kid on the inside. And he's been through a lot in the last year and a half with the divorce, and his mother remarrying and having a new baby. And now I'm going to spring a girlfriend on him? One who's *half* my age."

Gavin paused and ran both hands over his close-cropped hair.

"Gerri is closer to Trey's age than she is to mine."

He looked Isaac in the eyes, and Isaac got the feeling he was waiting on a reaction of some sort.

"Look, Lieu... I'm one of those people who thinks that age is just a number. The fact is, Gerri may be closer to Trey's age in numbers, but the fact that she went to the police academy right out of college and has been on this job for the last seven years puts her closer in age to you in all the ways that matter."

"I'm not sure I follow your logic, Ike."

"Well, think about it. The things she's seen and done on this job has given her an education that someone like Trey will never have, unless he decides to become a cop himself someday. At this point in their lives, she has much more in common with you than she does with him."

Gavin stared at him for a moment, and Isaac could see his mind working. He slowly began to nod.

"I guess I never thought of it that way."

"Is she bothered by the age difference at all?"

"No. She thinks I'm making more of it than it is."

"I tend to agree."

"You don't seem shocked about this at all, Ike."

Isaac shrugged a shoulder, realizing that he was now squarely involved in yet another conversation about a friend's love life.

"Frankly, I don't give a shit who you sleep with, sir. But I would hate to see you face any backlash over it. And I'd really hate for you to lose your job over it."

Gavin nodded.

"I take it this is why Gerri was wanting to transfer out and go to another precinct?"

"Originally she wanted to transfer just to get away from me. She said it was too painful being around me everyday and not be able to be with me."

"Wow. Sounds like whatever's between you two is serious."

Gavin nodded again and stared past Isaac's head, like he was looking into the future.

"Feels like it could be, if it's given a chance."

"Then maybe you should. Give it a chance, I mean."

"After we... crossed that line? Gerri actually offered to go through with the transfer to another precinct solely so that we can be together."

Isaac nodded. "Sounds reasonable."

"Does it, though?" Gavin met his gaze again. "I mean... can I really ask her to do that? Uproot her life to another precinct, just to protect my career? Somehow that feels like a jerk move, you know? Like I'm telling her my career is more important than hers."

Isaac was shaking his head before Gavin even finished his sentence.

"But you're not asking her, Lieu. She's volunteering. And if I've learned anything about women, I've learned this. When it comes to matters of the heart, they don't make big life-changing moves unless it's important to them. So if she's volunteering to switch precincts so that your career won't be jeopardized, she's doing it because being with you is important to her."

Gavin stared at him and grinned.

"Since when did you become the love guru?"

"Hell if I know. But damned if I haven't been drawn into the love lives of three other men this week besides you. Each of you asking for my advice, or my help in some way. Like I'm not still the socially awkward misfit with touch issues who just happened to get lucky when a beautiful woman decided she loved me."

Gavin laughed out loud, and Isaac smiled.

"I guess desperation leads us dumb men to strange places sometimes."

"Yeah, it does," Isaac agreed.

Then he took a breath and leveled a serious gaze at his boss.

"Listen, Lieu... as someone who spent a whole lot of years alone and lonely, my best advice to you would be to choose happiness. If Gerri makes you happy, if you feel like what you have together can become something real and lasting... take the chance. Let her transfer. Make it work. Choose happy."

14

Sidney scribbled furiously, dumping all the information flooding her brain onto the legal pad. There were so many ideas flowing, so many things to add to the checklist, to the rules, to the plan.

She'd been at her desk for several hours, lost in the idea of helping battered women escape from their abusers. She'd made pages and pages of notes, and gone over the ones she'd made the other day too, adding things and making revisions.

She paused and put down the pen. She shook her hand and wiggled her fingers, looking over the list she'd made. It was a series of questions for anyone expressing interest in her services. The first question was the hardest.

Are you sure?

So simple. But a person's response to this one question would determine their success in getting away and staying under the radar. Because in order to succeed, they would have to completely sever ties with everyone in their present lives. Everyone — including parents and siblings and friends — in order to stay safe, and to keep loved ones safe from their abuser.

Sidney had been lucky in that respect. By the time she ran

from Damien, he'd completely isolated her from her Aunt Bobbie and her cousins. They were the only family she had besides her brother, Simon. Since Simon had been overseas in Japan at the time, when she ran, she just ran. She didn't have a problem severing ties with anyone.

"Hmm. But you're not in hiding anymore, Sidney. And Damien is dead. Which means Aunt Bobbie and your cousins aren't in any danger from Damien anymore."

Zoe walked into the office and glanced at her.

"Were you saying something, Sidney?"

"Huh? Oh, sorry. I still have a bad habit of talking to myself sometimes. It started after my mom died when I was in high school. I used to talk to her, and it made me feel better. And that eventually turned into talking to myself. I did it a lot after I ran from Damien and was in hiding."

Zoe sat down at her desk across the room and smiled at her.

"I can understand that. I used to talk to Hope that way after she died."

"Your sister." Sidney nodded, remembering the story of the sister Zoe named the women's shelter after.

"Sometimes I still do."

Sidney was about to respond when a timid knock came at the open door. They both turned to see who it was.

"Ann. What can we do for you?"

"Actually, I was hoping to speak to Sidney if that's all right."

"Of course, come on in." Zoe waved her inside.

"Um...well..."

"Oh, I forgot." Zoe popped up from her chair like bread from a toaster. "I have something I need to take care of. Excuse me."

She winked at Sidney on her way out the door, leaving her alone with Ann.

Sidney stood and crossed the room to close the door so they could have some privacy.

"Why don't you have a seat, Ann."

"Okay. You said you wanted to see me. Is something wrong?"

"No, nothing. I just wanted to talk to you again about your request. You see, I need to know how serious you are before I agree to help you."

"I'm very serious. I told you that! If the kids and I don't get away from Donald, he is going to kill me. And I can't leave my babies alone with him. Please!"

Sidney felt for the woman. She motioned again for her to sit down, and then she took her seat and picked up the legal pad from her desk.

"Ann, I'm going to ask you again. Are you sure you're ready to do this? Because you're going to have to cut off all contact with everyone you know. All of your family, your friends."

"Well, I can contact them once the kids and I are settled somewhere."

"No! You can't. That's what I'm trying to tell you. When you run, you have to leave your current life behind you, for good. Otherwise there's no point."

All the color drained from Ann's cheeks, and Sidney was certain she was about to faint.

"I don't understand. Why can't I just let them know that we're settled somewhere?"

"Let me explain. Let's say you run across the country and settle in someplace, like Portland for instance. Then you contact someone here and let them know that you and the kids are safe in Portland. A month later, Donald gets drunk and decides he wants his family back. So he pays a visit to whomever it is that you called, and he threatens them. Or he flat out beats the shit out of them until they give him the information he's after. What do you think happens next?"

Sidney didn't think Ann could get any paler, but she did.

Then her chin trembled.

"Then I won't tell them where we are. They can't give him any information if I don't tell them where we are."

"No, they can't. But do you think that will stop Donald from trying to beat it out of them anyway? The point is, when Donald realizes you and the kids are gone, he may be the type to say, 'oh well, good riddance,' and let it go. But he might be the type to stop at nothing to track you down and drag you back home. Or do something worse than drag you back. Which type do you think Donald is?"

Ann licked her lips and wiped a stray tear from her cheek.

"My mom is elderly. She was so happy when I told her that the kids and I had come here. She made me promise never to go back to Donald again. I couldn't talk to her again? Ever?"

"There are ways you can get a message to a loved one. But it can't be through conventional means. Nothing that Donald could monitor and trace back to you. Think of it as being in the witness protection program. The idea is to keep you and your kids alive and safe from the criminal who wants to kill you."

That explanation seemed to settle Ann, and she nodded and took a deep breath. Sidney could see the woman running everything through her mind.

"Ann?"

When Ann finally met her gaze, Sidney leaned in and placed a comforting hand on her arm.

"Are you sure you still want to do this?"

The woman bit her lip, and more tears began to swim in her eyes. But Sidney saw something else bloom there too. Determination and resolve.

"I have no choice. After our last fight, he told me that I had no power. I had begged him not to hit me in front of the children anymore. To at least send them to their rooms first. He said that he would kill the children to punish me if I tried to tell him what to do again. They were sitting right there; they heard every word. And we all knew that he meant it."

Sidney's stomach lurched, and she closed her eyes.

"When he went to work the next morning, I got myself

together and I called Dr. Lyman. She'd treated me once in the ER and told me about this place. She said she could get me and my kids in here, and to call her if I ever changed my mind. So that's what I did. I got my babies out of that house and away from him. And now I have to keep them safe. I'll do anything."

Sidney nodded and gave her arm a squeeze.

"Okay. Then I will do all I can to help you. Are you still gathering money?"

"Yes. My friend, Sheila, gave me a few thousand dollars. And I have some jewelry I can take to the pawn shop to sell."

"Good. Set aside all the money you can, you're going to need it. Now, your next assignment is to pick two places. One to run to, and one to say you're from when others ask. And they will ask, so learn all you can about your fake hometown."

Ann nodded, staring at her with intensity.

"Okay."

"The next move is mine. I have some things to put in place before we do this. But that'll also give you time to study your fake hometown, gather money, maybe visit your mom."

Ann nodded again, and Sidney wasn't certain she was processing everything.

"I've thrown a lot at you. Do you have any questions?"

"No, I've got it. Pick two places and learn all I can about one of them. I understand. It makes so much sense, I never would've thought of these things on my own. Thank you."

"Don't thank me yet. We've got a long way to go."

A knock sounded at the door, and Zoe stuck her head in.

"Everything all right in here?"

Sidney smiled at her and then glanced back at Ann.

"Yes. Everything's good."

Ann stood. "I'm sorry. I didn't mean to kick you out of your office. I just wanted to ask Sidney's advice."

"No, it's perfectly all right. I hope I gave you enough time to talk."

"Yes, just enough. Thanks. And thank you, Sidney. For everything."

"You're more than welcome, Ann. I'm sure everything will work out the way it's supposed to."

They watched her leave the office and then Zoe turned to her with a curious expression.

"What was that all about?"

Sidney hesitated. "She just wanted to talk about her issues with Donald. She feels really bad about what happened. I think the bruise on my face makes her feel guilty every time she sees it."

"Well, that's understandable."

"I keep telling her that what happened wasn't her fault, but she feels responsible."

"The poor thing. It's good of you to spend some time easing her mind." Zoe went back to her desk and got to work.

Sidney turned back to the checklists on her desk and thought again about everything they were planning. She needed to know where to get her hands on believable fake IDs and other papers, because Ann was going to need them.

It was the most important piece of this puzzle, and Sidney was determined to figure it out.

Her mind stayed focused on it the rest of the day as she went about her normal routine and made time to sit down with Beth's daughter, Kylee, to work on the child's math skills.

By the time her day came to an end, she was tired and not much in the mood for dinner with friends. But she'd promised Jada, so there was no way she was going to back out.

She straightened her desk and gathered her things.

"Well, I'm out of here."

Zoe looked at her from across the room.

"Oh, that's right. You have dinner plans to get ready for tonight."

"Yes. So I'll see you tomorrow."

"Have a good evening!"

"You, too."

Sidney left the office and headed out, saying goodbye to a couple of the residents she passed on her way to the front door.

Outside she pulled her keys from her purse and headed for her car, parked on the street. As she neared it, something about its appearance was off somehow. It wasn't until she got right next to it that she understood why.

Both tires on the passenger side were flat.

"You've got to be kidding me," she said out loud to no one.

Had she run over some nails on the way to work?

She had no idea how to change one tire, let alone two of them. She walked around to the driver's side to put her things in the car and stopped short.

All four of her tires were flat.

"Son of a bitch!"

It was an aggravated groan, but the second the words floated out of her mouth, fear barreled down on her like a charging bull, the sharp horns of it stabbing at her stomach.

The tire she was looking at had a long gash.

Her tires weren't just flat, they had been slashed.

Someone had done this deliberately.

She glanced up and down the street and her heart began to race.

Retracing her steps, she walked back to the sidewalk and pulled out her cellphone to call the one person she always reached for when she needed to feel safe and loved.

"Hey, Sid, I didn't forget. Pete wouldn't let me. So I'll be leaving the station in ten minutes."

She could hear the playfulness in his tone. It was comforting.

"Isaac..."

It was the only word she could push past the tight grip fear had on her throat. But somehow, he heard the distress in her voice.

"Sidney what's wrong?"

"My car. My tires have been slashed."

"What?"

"All four of them."

"They're flat?"

"Yes, but someone did this! I can see the cut marks."

"You're at the shelter?"

"Yes."

"All right, stay put. I'm sending a tow truck to take the car to a repair shop, and I will swing by and pick you up. I'll be right there."

"Okay."

She ended the call and stood there staring at her tires. She glanced up and down the street once more, and then she checked out the tires on Zoe's car, as well as a few others that were parked on the street. None of the other cars had been targeted, just hers.

She walked back up to the house and took a seat in the chair on the porch. Who could've done this? And why?

That question brought two people immediately to her mind. Ann's husband, Donald. And Dr. Lance Tobey.

Donald could be pissed that she'd pulled a gun on him. Not to mention the fact that she'd knocked him on his ass in front of his wife. Yeah, he could be angry enough to slash her tires.

Lance Tobey, on the other hand, was probably not that vindictive. Slashing someone's tires wasn't usually the kind of thing someone did after they'd been jilted, was it?

She lost track of time as she sat there mulling it all over, and was slightly startled when Zoe stepped out onto the porch.

"I thought I saw you through the window. What are you still doing here?"

"Waiting for Ike and a tow truck. My tires were slashed."

"What? Are you sure?"

"Oh, I'm sure."

"But who would've done such a thing?"

"I don't know."

"Oh, Sidney. You don't think it could've been Ann's husband, do you?"

Zoe glanced back at the door to make sure no one was around.

"He did cross my mind, but I just don't know."

She stood up when she spotted Isaac's metallic dark blue Mustang GT coming down the street.

"Ike is sending a tow truck to get the car, so if you see one out here, you know why."

"All right. Please be careful. I don't like the turn things have taken around here."

Sidney nodded. "I don't really care for them myself. Have a good evening, Zoe."

She left the porch and joined Isaac in the street, where he had knelt down to examine her tires.

"Hi, baby."

"Hey, darlin'." He stood and wrapped an arm around her waist and pulled her close, kissing her forehead. "You okay?"

"I'd be lying if I said I wasn't a little rattled. But I'm fine. What do you think?" She gestured to the car.

"Well, you're right. They've definitely been slashed. All four of them. I'm going to walk around a bit and look at the other cars on this street. See if any others were hit."

"I checked Zoe's and a couple of others, but I didn't see any damage."

"Well, let me have a look. Why don't you go on and get settled in my car? I'll be right back."

He took off, walking down the street, and Sidney watched him scrutinizing each of the cars that were parked on the road. By the time she'd gotten into his car, he'd gone down quite a ways. She watched him cross to the other side and start back up the street, checking out the cars on that side as he made his way back to his car.

He opened the door and slid in beside her.

"Well?"

"Nope. No other cars have slashed tires, or fresh damage of any kind."

"So my car was targeted on purpose?"

Isaac's head bobbed from side to side.

"We still don't know that for sure. I mean it could be that some kids came down the street and picked a car at random to vandalize. Long shot, but it happens. I mean, do you know of any enemies who might want to give you a hard time?"

There was a certain amount of levity to his voice and she knew that he was only trying to make her feel better. But she couldn't shake the feeling of impending doom.

"Only Ann's husband, Donald."

"The asshole who put his hands on you a few nights ago and marred that pretty face of yours."

She silently nodded.

"Yeah, I thought of him too."

There was something in his voice when he said the words that gave Sidney an uneasy feeling.

"But I got a call from Officer Hamilton informing me that they'd picked up Donald Mowbray this afternoon and charged him with assault and battery, among other things. He's in a jail cell downtown, so unless he did this right after you got to work this morning, — which I suppose is entirely possible — it wasn't him."

Fear and dread ran over Sidney like tires leaving skid marks.

Isaac started the car and pulled onto the street, heading for home.

"Don't we have to wait for the tow truck?"

"No. I've already given them all the information. They'll pick it up and get it to the repair shop, then they'll deliver it to the house once the tires have been replaced."

"Wow. That's some service."

Isaac smiled and flashed those dimples at her.

"It's a garage owned by the same company that maintains the police cruisers. They like to keep the cops' business, so they add a few perks and a discount if you have a badge. It's still not going to be cheap to have all four of those tires replaced though."

"I was afraid of that."

He reached over and took her hand, then brought it to his lips and kissed it.

"Don't worry about it. You'll have your car back by tomorrow, and it'll be fine."

She slumped back against the seat and held tight to his hand all the way home.

15

"Ah!" Pete flinched from the hot steam and dropped the dutch oven lid to the counter with a loud *clang*. He gave the *Picadillo* a good stir and replaced the lid.

He was a nervous wreck.

He glanced across the kitchen where Julieta was setting the table for seven. She wore an amused expression that he knew she was trying to hide.

"Te estas riendo de me, mamá?"

"No, *mijo*, I'm not laughing at you. But it is fun to see you this way."

"What way?"

"Nervous. Anxious. Excited. Maybe a little scared."

"Oh, you like that I'm scared! My fear amuses you?"

Now she did laugh out loud, and Pete smiled at the sound. He wanted this night to go well, but he also wanted his mother to be at ease and happy. He wanted her to love Jada and Charlie as much as he did. And he really wanted Mateo to love them too.

Mateo.

Where was that kid?

"Mamá, have you seen Mateo? He still hasn't come down yet."

"He was getting dressed. I think he's just as anxious about tonight as you are."

"Really? Why?"

Pete lifted the lids on two other pots, checking that everything was ready.

"Why do you think? He wants to please you, Pedro."

Pete shook his head and looked at her.

"You know, sometimes I feel like you and I are talking about two very different people when it comes to that kid. You make it sound like he wants nothing more than to be with me, but..."

"And you make him sound like he's the enemy that you must conquer and tame."

Her words rendered him speechless, like he'd been punched in the gut.

That wasn't how he felt about Mateo.

"Is that how I make him feel, *mamá?* Because that's not how I feel about him. I love that kid. I don't want him to feel like he doesn't matter to me."

"So tell him that sometime. *Mijo*, you have to remember that Mateo has had nothing but disappointment in his young life. He's never known his father. His mother loved her drugs more than she loved him, and now she's in prison. Mateo will be a grown man by the time Paulina is up for parole. He knows that I won't be around forever. You are all he has in this world."

"I hate it when you talk like that. You are going to be here for a long, long time, *mamá*."

"From your lips, to God's ears. But don't change the subject. Mateo just needs to know that you will always be there for him. That there is one person in his life who won't leave him."

The sliver of an idea ran through his system like a river. A notion he'd thought about more than once lately. But now was not the time to discuss it. Not when they were expecting company at any minute.

"I'm starving." Mateo said as he entered the kitchen and headed for the stove. He lifted the tin foil on a batch of *tostones*. The crispy fried plantain slices were the kid's favorite.

"You touch one of those *tostones* and you're in big trouble." Pete pointed at him.

"But Uncle Pete..."

"Not one! We will wait for our guests. You are not going to starve to death in the next ten minutes. Out of the kitchen."

He pointed again, this time to the door.

"But..."

"Out!"

Mateo stomped out of the room, and Pete did one last check on his waiting meal. He'd made a big batch of easy and delicious *Picadillo* — a ground beef dish made with bell peppers, tomato sauce, and the finest Puerto Rican spices — to be served with rice, black beans and the tostones. There was even a pineapple rum cake for dessert, but Julieta had made that.

Pete was looking over his handiwork one last time when the doorbell sounded. He nearly jumped out of his skin.

He rushed to the door and swung it open. For one single perfect moment, all of his anxiety melted away when Jada smiled at him.

He took her hand and kissed her cheek as he ushered her inside.

"I'm sorry, we're late."

"No, you're not. You're right on time."

He smiled and looked her over. She was wearing a burgundy-colored dress that matched the shade of her lipstick and gave her a modest, chaste look. The kind of dress one might wear to impress the mother of the man you were dating.

"You look beautiful."

"Thanks."

"Hey, Pete."

"Hey, Charlie, how's it going? Up top."

He raised his hand, and Charlie reached up and high-fived him.

"It's going okay."

The kid glanced around the entryway where Julieta stood nearby. Pete noticed Mateo hung further back, quietly watching everything.

"Jada, Charlie... this is my mother, Julieta Vega. *Mamá*, this is Jada Lopez and her son Charlie."

"Hello, *Señora* Vega. It's so nice to finally meet you. Pete says the sweetest things about you all the time."

Jada shook Julieta's hand.

"Well. My Pedro is a sweet boy."

Julieta glanced at him, and Pete's cheeks turned warm. He was only grateful that Ike wasn't there yet to witness his embarrassment.

"Y esto debe ser...?"

And this must be?

Julieta let her question dangle and stared at Charlie, and Pete knew his mother was testing to see if the child knew any Spanish. Not embracing one's culture was a deep-seated pet peeve of Julieta's. She had always insisted on speaking their mother tongue in the house when he and Paulina were growing up.

"Yo soy Carlos. Pero prefiero Charlie."

I am Carlos. But I prefer Charlie.

Julieta smiled broadly, and Pete knew Charlie's perfect Spanish had just helped Jada clear a major hurdle where his mother was concerned.

"Welcome Charlie. It's good to meet you." Julieta gestured to where Mateo was hovering near the living room. "This is my grandson, Mateo. He's just a couple of years older than you, but I think you'll be great friends."

She motioned for Mateo to come closer.

Mateo stepped over to them and gave Charlie a half-hearted wave.

"Hey."

"Hey."

"Uh, you two have something in common." Pete pointed to each of the boys, and in the back of his mind he couldn't help but notice that his stomach felt so loaded down with bricks. He understood it. In his heart, he knew that this first meeting between the boys was every bit as important as the meeting of his mother and Jada. He wanted it to go well.

He needed it to go well.

"Charlie loves anime. And Mateo, you love comics."

"That's not exactly the same thing, Uncle Pete."

Mateo gave him a deadpan stare.

"Well, no. But Charlie's favorite show is *My Hero Academia*. And I know for a fact that you like that show too, and you've used it as inspiration for your own comics."

He turned to Charlie. "Mateo likes to draw his own comic books. They're really good! Mateo, why don't you show him?"

He knew he was working too hard, and he could tell by the expression of horror on Mateo's face that the kid didn't appreciate being put on the spot. Pete opened his mouth to say something else and the doorbell sounded.

"Oh, thank God," he huffed under his breath. "Excuse me."

He hurried to the door and whipped it open.

Ike and Sidney smiled at him.

Okay, Sidney smiled. Ike just looked annoyed, which was normal.

"I'm so glad you're here," he whispered and waved them inside.

He ushered them into the living room, where the awkward silence greeted him like a dear invited guest.

"Ike and Sidney, you know Jada and Charlie, of course. But this is my mother, Julieta Vega, and my nephew, Mateo."

Ike waved. "Good to meet you, ma'am."

Sidney gave Jada a friendly hug and then shook Julieta's hand,

and Pete was instantly glad of the warmth she brought with her. Small talk seemed to be a specialty of hers, and it didn't take long before she had his mother laughing at some comment she'd made.

Pete marveled as he watched her. To him, Sid and Ike were total opposites. A true odd couple. In fact, he often wondered what the heck she was doing with his weird partner in the first place.

But what did he know? They said opposites attract, didn't they?

"Well, something smells delicious, Pete," Jada said.

"Yes! Dinner is ready, so if you guys want to move to the kitchen."

"Finally. I'm starving." Mateo grumbled.

Pete shot him a look.

Julieta led them all to the kitchen, and Jada took Pete's arm, pulling him to the side.

"Take a breath, Pete."

"Huh?"

"It's going to be fine. The boys. Your mom. It's all going to be okay. So take a breath and calm down."

"Are my nerves that obvious?"

"I feel like you're going to explode at any minute."

Pete laughed out loud.

"Okay, I get it. I know something that might help though."

"What's that?"

He leaned in and kissed her lips, his tongue gently teasing hers.

"I wanted to do that when I first opened the door, but we had an audience then."

Jada smiled and touched his face.

Then he took her hand and led her to the kitchen with the others.

Earlier, when he was cooking, he'd watched as Mateo helped his mother put the removable leaf into the center of the round kitchen table, instantly enlarging it. Then he'd helped Mateo bring the extra chairs up from the basement. The furniture wasn't fancy, but it was homey and comfortable and real.

Just like the meal he'd prepared.

Everyone took their seats and Pete noticed that Isaac looked extremely uncomfortable — shoulders hunched, elbows in close to his sides like he didn't want to risk touching anyone.

"Mateo."

When his nephew looked up at him, Pete used his hand to motion for him to scoot his chair a little to the left.

"What?"

Pete shot him a don't-argue-just-do-what-I'm-telling-you glare, and gestured again.

Mateo glanced to his right and looked Isaac over.

"Ohh. You're the weird partner Uncle Pete is always fussing about, aren't you?"

Everything inside of Pete stopped — heart, blood, breath — done.

Heat radiated from his shoulders to his ears, and he knew that he had to be red as a tomato.

I'm gonna freaking kill that kid!

The thought floated through his mind just as Ike looked from Mateo to Pete, and back to Mateo again.

Mortified.

Pete was completely mortified.

"Yeah, that would be me," Ike said, nodding at Mateo.

Mateo scooted his chair to the left.

Ike scooted his chair to the right, closer to Sidney. Then he looked back at Mateo and grinned.

"Thanks for the extra room."

"Sure."

Pete exhaled and turned to the food on the stove.

"So why don't you like to be touched?" Mateo asked.

Pete swiveled back around.

"Mateo!"

"What?"

The kid looked genuinely innocent and curious, and Pete wanted to throttle him.

"It's all right, Pete." Isaac quietly cleared his throat and looked at Mateo. "Um, the simplest explanation is that... well, I um..."

"He has a condition that makes him super sensitive to physical touch. It's really rare."

Sidney jumped to Isaac's rescue with an explanation that sounded more like a medical condition than psychic one, and Pete watched his partner heave a silent sigh of relief.

Mateo studied Ike for a moment longer, looking him over once more as if trying to spot the condition for himself.

"Cool."

Pete shook his head and went back to his task.

"Is it true you live next door to Jada and Charlie?"

"That is true. We live right next door to each other." Isaac nodded, and Pete glanced over, wondering why Mateo was questioning Ike so much.

"That's actually how I met your uncle, Mateo," Jada chimed in. "At Ike and Sidney's house warming party a few months ago."

Mateo nodded, staring at her stone faced. "So it's their fault."

Quiet descended over the table, and Pete turned to see everyone looking uncomfortable.

"That was a joke," Mateo mumbled. He looked down at the table with a jeez-lighten-up glint to his eyes.

Isaac laughed and shot Mateo a look of appreciation that told Pete he liked the kid's dark humor. Relief ran through Pete, and he carried food to the table.

He placed large platters and serving dishes of the meat, rice, beans, and tostones in the center of the table.

"We don't stand on ceremony around here. Please help yourselves. All I ask is that you try some of everything." He looked up at Ike. "I'm talking to you, Ike."

"Have you met me? You should know by now that I like to eat. I'll try anything."

Pete filled everyone's glasses with fresh lemonade before he finally sat down. Conversation stopped once all plates were full and everybody dug in. Pete glanced around the table, waiting for reactions.

"Wow. This is really good."

"Thank you, Sidney."

"Why am I eating raisins and green olives together in ground meat and thinking it's delicious?" Ike asked the question with the most serious of expressions as he examined his food, and Pete couldn't help but laugh.

"Because it is!"

"It's the sweet and salty together. It works somehow." Sidney nodded, agreeing with him. "What is this called?"

"It's called *picadillo*. Very flavorful, but very simple. You'll find variations of it all through Latin American cuisine. I love it over rice, like this. But it can also be used as a filling in *pastelillos*, or empanadas."

"*Pastelillos* are the best!" Mateo exclaimed.

"My gramma makes those," Charlie chimed in. "They're so good."

Pete was ecstatic to see the boys agree on something.

Jada looked at Pete, a sly smile on her face. "You cooked this?"

"I did."

"No way."

Her smile did things to him.

"I may not be as good a cook as you, or as *mamá*, but I know my way around a kitchen. *Mamá* made sure of that, right?"

He smiled at his mother.

"It was the only way I could be sure you wouldn't starve once you moved out of the house."

"And I learned from the best cook in the world."

He winked at her. He was buttering his mother up, and she knew it. But he loved the proud smile on her face.

"Well, I would love any tips or recipes you'd care to share, *Señora* Vega." Jada said. "Pete raves about your cooking all the time. I do okay in the kitchen, but I'm always looking to improve."

"Oh, I'm sure you do just fine."

Was Pete mistaken, or did he feel a frost moving in?

"Ah, well, Jada has a lot on her plate besides cooking, *mamá*. She works full time for a doctor's office downtown. She's the head nurse there; she oversees the other nurses and acts as the office manager. And on top of all that, she's a great mom to Charlie."

Charlie nodded in agreement as he chewed.

"Pete, stop. You're making me sound like a saint."

"Well, no, I just mean..."

"We know what you mean. And trust me, no one is as great as you just made me sound. But I do appreciate it."

She smiled at him, and Pete's insides turned into a gooey sticky mess.

"So, Isaac, Pedro tells me that the two of you will be getting a commendation for stopping a crime while you were off duty. What is this about?"

"Oh, well, a few weeks ago Pete and I just happened to be in the right place at the right time. It was a sexual assault in progress. I guess the victim said some nice things about us when she gave her statement, and that prompted our Lieutenant to recommend us for the award."

Pete listened to Ike roll out the explanation like nothing extraordinary had happened that night. Like it hadn't been his psychic abilities that had led them to the crime in question.

"Where did that happen?" Mateo asked.

"It was outside a bar on the east side," Ike continued.

"I thought Uncle Pete said you don't drink alcohol."

"I don't drink alcohol anymore."

"Then what were you doing at a bar?"

"We'd gotten a tip," Pete jumped in. "About this guy, the one that was about to commit the crime. We got a tip about him."

It wasn't a lie. They had gotten a tip. A tip from Ike's psychic abilities.

"But how, if you were off duty at the time?"

"You are full of questions tonight. Eat your dinner."

Mateo made a face and turned back to his dinner plate.

"So this award?" Julieta resumed her earlier line of questioning. "There is a ceremony we can attend, yes?"

"Usually, yes, ma'am. There's a ceremony twice a year where they hand out those things and invite the officer's family and loved ones. The officer gets a certificate he can frame and a medal in a fancy little box to display. And the tiny bar pin that comes with the medal looks impressive on the dress uniform."

"Ah. I bet Pedro will look very handsome with the bar on his dress uniform."

"You know, I just bet he will."

Isaac grinned at him, and Pete rolled his eyes. Whose idea was it to invite his annoying partner to dinner anyway?

"Yeah, like when you got that commendation for saving the drowning kid at Lake Erie," Pete pointed out. Turnabout was fair play after all.

"You did?" Mateo asked.

"Oh. Well, it was just a freak thing, really. Sidney and I were boating with my brother and sister-in-law when I saw these two kids on another boat fall over into the water. I just dove in and helped, that's all."

"Don't be so modest, Ike." Sidney touched his arm and looked at Mateo. "He swam nearly 175 yards out to where the boy had drifted, and pulled him back to the boat. Then he administered CPR to get the boy breathing again."

"Whoa!" Mateo looked at Ike with big, round eyes.

"That's almost two football fields!" Charlie sounded just as shocked.

Sidney nodded.

"Sidney exaggerates." Ike looked at her and shook his head. "It was really only a few kilometers or so."

"Don't listen to him." Pete grinned. "He's just trying to protect his secret identity. See, he doesn't know that he can fully trust you two yet."

"Pete..."

Isaac's tone held a warning of some kind, Pete was sure of it. But he couldn't let the moment slip away from him. One good tease deserved another, didn't it?

"It's okay, Ike. They're cool. You can tell them who you really are."

Isaac sat back in his chair and eyed Pete.

"Who is he, Pete?" Charlie asked, sounding properly intrigued.

Pete sent Isaac a grin that said, 'I win', and Isaac glowered at him.

"Boys, you are looking at... Super Cop!"

"Super Cop?" Mateo's tone indicated he was clearly unimpressed.

"That's right. Ike here holds the highest closed case record in the entire Cleveland Police Department."

"What's that mean?" Charlie asked.

"That means that Ike has successfully closed more cases than any other detective in the city."

"Really?" Mateo was now slightly impressed.

"Yep." Pete answered.

Mateo looked at Ike. "So you solved more cases than anybody?"

Isaac sighed. "So they tell me. I don't keep track."

"How'd you do it?"

"How?"

"Were your psychic powers involved?"

A cannonball struck Pete in the gut.

Damn that kid and his questions, questions, *questions!*

"Psychic powers?"

Jada, Charlie, and his mom all spoke at once, and Pete just wanted to shrink down into the chair, slip away under the table and go hide. This is what he got for sharing things with his nephew.

Ike and Sidney looked at each other.

"You're psychic?" Jada stared at Isaac. Then she looked at Sidney. "He's psychic?"

"I'm really sorry, partner." Pete glared at Mateo. "I guess I never told Mateo that you didn't want the entire world to know."

"Oops." Mateo turned contrite eyes at Ike. "Sorry."

Isaac set his fork down and reached over to take Sidney's hand. They shared a look, and Pete finally began to realize that Sid was like an anchor for his strange partner. Opposites or not, she gave him something he needed. Something he lacked. And Pete suddenly understood the mystery of their connection.

Isaac made Sidney brave.

Sidney made Isaac whole.

"It's all right." Isaac glanced around the table. "Psychic is not a word I fancy. But unfortunately, it is the word that best describes it. And yes," he looked at Mateo. "A lot of times my... abilities play a big role in my job."

There was dead silence around the table and Pete really wanted to kill Mateo for making Ike uncomfortable.

"As long as you continue to watch out for my Pedro, I don't care that you have the sight." Julieta smiled at him.

"The sight. I haven't heard anyone but my grandfather use that term."

"That's what we called it in the olden times," Julieta laughed and then she looked Ike in the eyes. *"La vista. La vista de la oscuridad? O la vista de la luz?* Which one do you possess, Detective?"

Pete could only describe Isaac's expression perplexed.

Ike opened his mouth to speak, but hesitated a beat and then quietly cleared his throat.

"My Spanish isn't all that great, ma'am. But I think you said sight of darkness or sight of light?"

"I did."

"The only answer I can give you is both. The things I see are often dark. But I use my abilities for good. To shed light on the awful deeds done in the dark."

Julieta nodded. "*Sí*. I can see this inside you. I think you are a good man, Isaac Taylor. Pedro is lucky to have you as a partner."

Isaac grinned at her. "Well, you know, I tell him that all the time, but he doesn't want to hear it."

Laughter went around the table, and Pete rolled his eyes.

"Oh, come on! Don't tell him things like that, *mamá*. It's hard enough to work with him already."

"You love working with me, and you know it."

"I hate working with you, and don't you forget it!"

Dinner passed by with a constant flow of chatter after that, and Pete relaxed when he realized that everyone seemed to be having a good time. Aside from Mateo's endless questions about Ike and police work, both boys appeared to be on their best behavior. Too bad they didn't spend much time talking to each other though. Pete was really hoping they would hit it off, but so far that prospect wasn't looking so hot.

They devoured Julieta's pineapple rum cake after dinner, and when they were cleaning up afterwards, Pete was ecstatic to see Jada and Julieta laughing and talking as they loaded the dishwasher and put away the leftovers.

"Thank you so much for a lovely evening, Pete. Dinner was absolutely delicious!"

"Thanks, Sid. And thank you for coming."

He kissed her cheek and then looked at Ike.

"I'll see you in a few hours, I guess."

"Yep. See you then."

Ike turned around and waved at Mateo and Charlie who were both sprawled out on the sofas in the living room with eyes glued to the flat screen.

"Bye boys."

They said goodbye to Jada and Julieta and left.

"Well, Charlie and I should be leaving too." Jada motioned for Charlie to get up. Then she turned to Julieta with a smile. "Thank you so much for having us, *Señora* Vega."

"Please call me Julieta."

"Julieta." Jada nodded. "This was fun. Maybe sometime you and Mateo could come to my house for dinner?"

"That would be lovely. Right, Mateo?" Julieta looked at the kid, and Pete watched as Mateo shrugged a shoulder.

"I guess."

"Okay," Pete sighed. "I'm going to walk Jada and Charlie to their car. I'll be right back."

He followed them outside and Jada gave Charlie the keys so that he could unlock the door. He ran ahead, leaving Pete and Jada alone for a few minutes.

"Well, I think that went well."

She smiled at him, and Pete pulled her into his arms.

"Despite me acting like an idiot half the night, I agree."

"Why were you so nervous? Did you think your mom wouldn't like us?"

"I don't know what I was thinking. I just... I don't know, I wanted the two of you to love each other. And I expected Mateo and Charlie to have some missteps, but it turns out they barely said more than two words to each other."

"Pete, they're kids. They'll find their own rhythm. We can't expect them to be best friends right off the bat, and that's okay. They don't have to love each other just because we do. It would be unrealistic and unfair of us to expect that of them."

"What did you just say?"

"I said it would be unrealistic..."

"No, no, no. Not that part. The part right before that?"

Jada tried to hide a smile.

"I said we can't expect them to be best friends right away."

"Mmm... I'm pretty sure you said something else in between those two things."

"No, I didn't."

"Yeah, you did."

"Nope."

"I heard something else in there, I'm sure of it."

"Well, then you should get your hearing checked because I don't know what you're talking about."

"Riiiight." He nodded. "Okay. Guess I was hearing things then."

"I guess you were."

He smiled and stared into her big brown eyes. Then he leaned in and kissed her, tightening his arms around her.

The car horn sounded, making them both jump about a foot.

They turned to see Charlie laughing from the passenger seat.

"I have to go."

"All right. You drive safe."

"I will."

He watched her walk to the car and open the driver's door.

"Hey, Jada?"

"Yes."

"I love you too."

The wickedly wild smile that lit up her face was quickly tempered and wrestled into submission, and Pete loved the way she tried to pretend she wasn't just as crazy about him as he was about her.

She blew him a kiss and slid behind the wheel. He watched them drive off and then went back inside the house.

"Well, what did you think?" he asked when he joined his mom and Mateo in the living room.

"Jada is a very nice girl, *mijo*. And Charlie's Spanish is excellent. We had an entire conversation over dinner while you all were talking about something else."

Pete chuckled at her.

"Oh, and I love your partner. I meant what I said. He's a good man."

"Great, I'll tell him you said so. Again."

"He and Sidney make a lovely couple. She's funny, that one. I like her. She invited me to their wedding."

"That's great. We'll all go together. What'd you think of Jada, *mamá?*"

"I said she's a very nice girl."

"That's it? Just very nice?"

"What do you want me to say, Pedro?"

"I want to know what you think of her."

Julieta sighed.

"She's beautiful. She's smart. She's a good mother. She is obviously completely in love with my son. I approve."

Hearing the words lifted a ten ton weight off his chest, and Pete took a deep breath. He turned to Mateo with a smile.

"What about you? What did you think?"

"I think your partner is kinda cool. He's definitely weird, but in a cool way. Those light grey eyes of his are creepy as heck though, especially when he stares right at you! They make the whole psychic thing much more believable, and kinda scary at the same time."

The kid sounded fascinated, and Pete couldn't believe it when he kept going on and on about it.

"And you know, it's strange, but did you notice that his fiancée has weird eyes too? Maybe they're, like telepathic or something. I think I might write something like that into my comic book. Two new heroes that have psychic powers that only work when they're together, and their eyes glow!"

"Okay, that's great. I'm glad they've inspired you. But what'd you think of Jada?"

"Oh." Mateo shrugged a shoulder. "She's pretty, I guess."

Before Pete could respond to that, Mateo turned and left the room.

He headed upstairs without another word, and Pete let out a defeated sigh.

16

"This isn't half bad, Dad."

"What do you mean, not half bad? Man, this is gourmet food I cooked for you! Grilled salmon and garlic smashed potatoes, salad."

Trey laughed out loud, and Gavin couldn't help but smile. The one thing he was proudest of in life was the relationship he shared with his son. His only child.

But Trey wasn't a child anymore, he was a grown man now, just like Ike Taylor had pointed out. A grown man who'd be starting his second year of college soon.

Gavin looked Trey over while they ate in silence.

"So, there's um..."

Trey stopped talking and stuffed a forkful of potatoes into his mouth, and Gavin didn't like the look of worry on the boy's face.

"There's what, Trey?"

"Well, there's something I've been wanting to talk to you about, Dad."

"Oh? Well, there's something I'd like to talk to you about too. But you go first."

"No! You go ahead."

"Trey... what is it?"

Trey sighed and his shoulders fell a few inches. He moved the food around on his plate and Gavin got the feeling he was searching for the right words.

"Okay, you're making me nervous now, Trey. What's up?"

"Well... what would you say if I told you I wasn't sure I wanted to stay on the pre-law track at school?"

Gavin let out the breath he'd been holding and chuckled.

"Why is that funny?" Trey frowned at him.

"It's not funny, and I'm not laughing at you. But it's nowhere near as upsetting as what I thought you were about to say."

"Why? What did you think I was going to say?"

"Something worse."

"Worse like what, Dad?"

"I don't know. Worse like you'd gotten some girl pregnant."

Trey made a raspberry sound with his lips.

"No chance of that. The girls at Ohio State don't seem to be feeling my charms," Trey joked.

Gavin grinned. "Oh, no?"

"Naw."

Something about the way he said that gave Gavin pause, and he studied his son.

"Any, um... any *guys* feeling you? Maybe?"

Trey looked at him with wide eyes.

"What?"

"I'm just asking."

"No. You know I'm not gay, Dad. I told you the first time I had sex! You gave me the whole condom lecture beforehand."

"I know, but kids are experimenting a lot these days. I just thought I'd ask."

"Any experimenting I do will be with girls, okay? I'm way too big a fan of boobs to go play for the other team."

"All right. Good to know."

Trey shook his head like he couldn't believe they were having this conversation. Then he took another bite of his food.

"Man, I thought you were going to be really upset."

"Trey, if you want to change your major at school, that decision is up to you. I want you to study to be whatever you want to be. The only thing that would truly upset me is if you said you were dropping out of school altogether."

"No, I'm not dropping out."

"Okay, good." Gavin grinned and took a bite of salmon. "So, tell me what you're thinking of switching to. Is it political science itself that you're not liking? Because, you know, you can major in something else like criminal justice or even history and still have a good foundation to go to law school."

"I know that."

"Or maybe it's law school that's lost its appeal for you?"

"Sort of. I was actually thinking about switching to psychology."

"Psychology?"

"Yeah. I really enjoyed the two psych classes I had this year. And I've been looking into job prospects for psych majors. Did you know that just as many psych majors get admitted into medical school as biology and chemistry majors?"

"No, I did not know that."

"And psychology is a perfect field of study for not only psychiatry, but also for neurology and even pediatrics!"

Gavin stared at Trey and slowly smiled.

"My son, *the doctor?* You're switching from pre-law to pre-med. Is that what you're telling me?"

Trey stabbed at his salad with his fork and smiled.

"I'm thinking about it. But I wanted your opinion."

Words failed him for a full minute. Finally, he looked at his son and smiled.

"Trey, I think it's wonderful! And I believe that you can do absolutely anything you set your mind to. So, if this is what you want, I'm behind you every step of the way."

Trey beamed from ear to ear.

"Thanks, Dad!"

He shoveled the forkful of salad into his mouth, and Gavin laughed and turned back to his own plate.

"Your turn."

"What?"

"You said that you had something to talk to me about too. What was it?"

"Oh."

Gavin's stomach seized, and he forced down his mouthful. He set his fork down. To stall for time, he took a long slow sip of his wine. Then he quietly cleared his throat.

He could do this.

He had to.

He looked Trey in the eyes and took a deep breath.

"So, I was wondering, um..."

How should he word this?

"Well, how embarrassing would it be for you if your old man started dating again?"

Trey made a face that Gavin couldn't place.

"Seriously?"

"Yeah, seriously. I want you to be honest with me."

"It wouldn't be embarrassing at all, Dad."

Gavin stared at him.

"Not at all?"

"No. Not at all. Honestly? I feel like you deserve to be happy after everything that Mom put you through."

Trey's words touched a place in Gavin's heart that he knew only his son could reach. He looked down at the table for a few seconds before he met Trey's gaze again.

"I appreciate that. But what if I was dating a much younger woman. A woman actually closer to your age than to mine?"

Trey's eye brows lifted up like they were attached to helium balloons. Then they quickly crashed down like they'd fallen from the sky.

"How close to my age?"

"She's 28. So she's nine years older than you. But that makes her 16 years younger than me."

His stomach did a funny flip floppy thing, and he watched Trey work that math out in his mind.

"Do you really like her? Do you have much in common? Is this just some fling for her? Or for you?" Trey stopped and gave him a sheepish grin. "I guess I have a lot of questions."

Gavin nodded. "That's all right. I understand. And yes, I do really like her. I like her very much. We have a lot in common actually. We see the world in a similar way, we both work at the precinct. And no... as far as I'm concerned this is not a fling."

"What about her? Is it a fling for her?"

"I love you, Gavin. We have dangerous jobs, no matter what precautions we take; and I don't want to miss my opportunity to tell you how I feel about you."

Gerri's words floated back to him on a sweet memory, and Gavin shook his head.

"No. It's not a fling for either one of us."

"Well, then... what I said earlier stands. You deserve to be happy, Dad. If she does that for you, I say go for it. You're both adults so who cares about the age difference?"

Gavin's heart took off like it was being carried away by an eagle.

"I'm really glad to hear you say that, Trey. Thank you."

"You didn't exactly need my permission."

"No. And I wasn't asking for it. But I'm glad to have your blessing."

"So who is she? Do I get to meet her while I'm home?"

"Actually, you've already met her. Like I said, we both work at the PD."

"Oh. Who is it then?"

"Gerri Miller."

Trey's eyes bugged out like a giant beetle.

"Hold up!"

He held up a hand, palm out, as if to say stop.

"You're talking about all the right curves, dark brown skin, *beautiful,* super hot female detective. *That* Gerri Miller?"

Gavin laughed, but he couldn't miss the swell of his own chest at his son's description of her.

"Yeah, that's her."

"Wow!" Trey sounded more than impressed. "Way to go, Dad!"

Gavin laughed again.

"I had no idea that she'd caught your eye."

"If she doesn't catch a man's eye, that man is either gay or dead. And now she's with my dad. *Ugh!*" He balled his fists over his eyes. "I did not need that visual!

Gavin nearly doubled over in laughter.

He'd missed this while Trey was away at school — their easy playful rapport. When Trey was growing up, he'd kept Gavin laughing every day. It had been the one thing he looked forward to most when he'd come home after a long day of police work.

When dinner was finished, he helped Trey load the dishwasher and clean up. Then once Trey went upstairs to his room, Gavin pulled out his cellphone and placed a video call.

His stomach did that flip floppy thing again the instant her face filled his screen. Damn, she was beautiful.

"Hi."

"Hey."

"What's going on?"

"I just had a very enlightening conversation with my son."

"Oh? What about?"

"You."

"Me?"

"You."

"Should I be worried?"

"Nope. Not unless you take offense to being found beautiful by a young college man."

"I take offense if all a man sees is my looks."

"If all a man sees is your looks then he's missing out on something truly special."

Gerri's lips turned up into a Mona Lisa smile.

"Did you just call to sweet talk me, Lieutenant?"

"No. I called to invite you to dinner with me and Trey sometime soon. I'd like for us to all get together before he goes back to collage."

Gerri's smile grew bigger. "I'd love to."

Pete checked the time on his cellphone.

"Last time we did this it was just after midnight too."

Isaac nodded at Pete's comment, but he didn't say anything. He kept his eyes on the house in question.

"Well, don't you think it's weird that a lot of crimes seem to happen right around that time?"

Isaac looked over at his partner in the passenger seat and shrugged a shoulder.

"I guess they don't call it the witching hour for nothing."

"Hmm. I wonder if anybody's ever done a study on that."

"The best time of night to commit a crime? Oh, I'm sure somebody somewhere has done it."

"Probably."

"So what was the verdict on dinner? How'd your mom and Jada get along?"

"They got along great. I think my mom genuinely likes her. She called her smart and beautiful, so I guess those are good marks."

"Congratulations. What about the other matter?"

"Mateo and Charlie?"

"Yeah."

"I don't know. I mean, they barely said two words to each other the whole time. You were there. Did you see them even acknowledge each other?"

Isaac thought about it for a second.

"Now that you mention it, no. I didn't."

"Yeah. Jada says that's just a kid thing, and that we can't rush them. That we can't force them to be friends just because we love each other. I don't know."

"I think she's right. They probably just need to spend a lot more time together, you know? To warm up to one another."

Pete seemed to think about that.

"Yeah, maybe. Hey, listen. I'm really glad you and Sidney were there. It did help take some of the pressure off all of us."

"We enjoyed it."

"My mom has decided she loves you, for some odd reason. She thinks you're a good man."

Isaac chuckled.

"And Mateo thinks you're some kind of weird psychic superhero. I'm pretty sure he's writing you into one of his homemade comic books."

"Sweet. I always wanted to be a comic book character."

Pete snickered. "Well, thanks again for coming."

"No problem. The food was really good."

"As promised."

"I'm sorry we were a little late getting there. Sidney had some trouble at work."

"Again?"

"No, no. It's not what you're thinking. There was no irate husband this time. At least not in that fashion."

"I don't follow."

Isaac sighed. He shifted in his seat and kept his eyes on the house under surveillance.

"She came out of Hope House this afternoon to find all four of her tires slashed."

"Slashed? Like with a knife?"

"Slashed."

"What the hell, man?"

Isaac shook his head. "I don't know, but it didn't sit well with me."

"I'm sure it didn't. You thinking it was that guy from the other night. The one she put the beat down on?"

"He's the only one who came to mind. Guy like that was probably good and pissed to be put in his place by a woman."

"Yeah, not to mention humiliated. She kicks his ass and pulls a gun on him. All in front of his wife, who he beats on a regular basis."

"But honestly, we have no way of knowing for sure if it was him. I mean, don't forget that he was picked up by patrol earlier today, and charged with assault and battery, trespassing, and violating his wife's restraining order."

"Which means he maybe didn't have the time to slash Sid's tires. Without knowing where patrol picked him up or tracking his movements today, we can't say with certainty that it was him."

"Exactly."

"But who else could it have been, Ike?"

"I don't know. But now I'm sorry I didn't go down and pay him a visit in lockup. I should've gone down there and kicked his ass myself for putting his hands on Sidney. But she begged me not to."

Pete glanced over at him.

"Could you really do that, Ike?"

Isaac's gaze snapped to Pete with a jerk.

"Are you fucking kidding me? He manhandled the woman I love and left bruises on her face. What do you think?"

"No, I absolutely get the motivation. I don't blame you there. But I meant, with your touch issues and all?"

Ike's voice was ice when he said, "That's what leather gloves are for."

The anger that had been brewing since the incident suddenly threatened to boil, boil, boil to the surface. His stomach bubbled with it.

He turned his gaze back to the house just in time to see Burle Savage cross the street, moving toward it.

"Right on time. Let's go blow off some steam."

They waited until they saw the light come on in the entryway of the house, then crept from the car. The front door opened, and the homeowner greeted Burle Savage with that curious smile Isaac had seen in his vision.

He and Pete inched closer to the front door, hidden by the hedges that lined the walkway.

"Can I help you somehow?"

"You gotta nice house." Burle Savage's voice was calm.

"Thanks. We like it. But it's awfully late, sir."

"Can I come in?"

"What? No. I don't know you. What do you want?"

"Your house."

Savage made his move.

He shoved the homeowner hard in the chest.

The man fell backwards and hit the floor.

Savage stepped inside and whipped an old-style police billy club from the back of his pants. Then he leaned over, billy club held high.

Isaac and Pete rushed in, guns drawn.

"Cleveland police! That's enough, Savage! Put the club down."

Savage froze, mid swing, eyes wild.

He turned to see Isaac's gun pointed at his head.

Pete snatched the billy club from Savage's hand.

Savage looked Isaac in the eyes.

"I know you."

"Yeah, you do."

"You're that cop. The jumpy one who doesn't like to be touched."

"That's right. And you're the janitor who keeps bumping into me. You should've been more careful."

Burle Savage was going to bolt. Isaac could see it in his eyes.

His right hand began to tingle.

The man lunged for the door.

Isaac raised his hand and slapped the air.

The door slammed closed.

Savage fell into it.

Pete used Savage's awkward fall to their advantage and pounced.

A moment later, he was cuffed and being hauled to his feet.

Isaac's veins pumped with power, the surge of it hammering his lungs and winding him. But through his astonishment, he couldn't miss the what-the-fuck-just-happened look that Pete shot his way.

Isaac ignored it and turned his attention to the homeowner, who was still on the ground balled into a corner. He knelt down beside him.

"Are you all right, sir?"

"Y-yes, I'm fine. What's happening?"

"Lawson?"

A woman crept down the stairs, wide-eyed and clearly shaken.

"I'm okay, honey. The police are here."

"What on Earth is going on?"

She sounded frantic, and Isaac helped the man to stand.

"This man was attempting a home invasion, ma'am. He assaulted your husband and forced his way inside. My partner and I have him in custody now, everything's okay."

"Oh, my God! Thank goodness you were here."

They took a statement from the homeowners and left them with their card.

As they herded Burle Savage to the car, Isaac looked at him.

"Why'd you do this? What was your end game? Were you going to rob them? Kill them?"

Savage turned cold eyes on him.

"Just something to do. It's fun. I like messing with them, making them beg, hearing them scream and cry. It's especially fun if there's a female at home."

He grinned an evil grin that Isaac felt in his soul.

"I wanted to try it again with a rich person. Nicer house."

"You're a sick fuck, you know that?" Pete glared at him and practically shoved the man into the backseat. Savage only laughed, and Pete shut the door and turned to Isaac.

Isaac braced himself for what was coming.

"I know that I give you a hard time about this off-duty Psychic Batman thing we've been doing. But I gotta tell you, it feels good to be part of getting trash like this off the streets."

"I agree."

"That said... what the hell did I just see back there?"

"What do you mean?"

"I mean I... I thought..."

He paused and stared at him, like he couldn't put it into words. Or didn't want to.

"Thought what, Pete?"

Pete opened his mouth to say more, but only stared at him instead.

"Pete?"

"Nothing. Forget it."

Isaac nodded, relieved.

"Let's get him to the station. Robin."

"Very funny."

17

The next morning, Isaac woke early and showered. He dressed in a pair of black swim trunks and a long-sleeved Cleveland Cavaliers t-shirt. It was his day off and he had big plans.

When he came out of the bathroom, Sidney was still asleep. He smiled and carefully climbed back onto the bed.

Head propped up on his elbow he laid beside her and watched her sleeping.

She was so beautiful that sometimes he had to pinch himself.

What had he done in his crazy life to deserve someone like her? He would never understand it. What in the world was she even doing with him? How had he gotten so lucky?

He reached out and gently took one of her dark brown curls and twirled it around his finger.

Sidney stirred and her eyes fluttered open. When the sunlight streaming in through the window hit them, they sparkled like champaign-colored diamonds, enchanting him.

She smiled.

"That's not allowed. Watching me sleep is against the rules, mister."

"Oh, it is?"

"Yes."

"Sorry. I've never heard about these rules you speak of. I didn't get a copy of that document. And I'm certain I would never have agreed to something like that."

"What are you doing?"

"Watching you sleep. I thought we'd just established that."

Sidney giggled. "I mean, why are you watching me sleep?"

"Duh. Because it's impossible not to. You're too gorgeous. The question should be how can I look at anything else but you?"

Sidney rolled her pretty eyes.

"You have to get up and get showered," Isaac said, still playing with her hair. "We've got a big day."

"We do?"

"Yep."

"Doing what?"

"Well, since it's my day off, and since it was near impossible for us to get a day off together, I figured the occasion called for a special outing."

"I agree, in theory. But what did you have in mind?"

"Well, I know how much you used to love going to the beach and being near the ocean back in California. You said the beach was your refuge back there. Your happy place. I also know that you've really missed not being able to do that since you've been in Ohio. And I want to show you that Lake Erie has it's charms too. So, we're spending the day at the beach."

She smiled at him. "Really?"

"Really."

"Which beach?"

"I was thinking we'd go to the beach at Lakeview Park."

"I don't think I've ever been to that one."

"Perfect. That means we have to go. Get dressed. I'm making breakfast."

"You're cooking?"

She sounded shocked, and a little afraid. Isaac grinned.

"I can cook a few things without burning 'em."

"Like what?"

"Like scrambled eggs and toast."

He kissed her lips and hopped off the bed.

"Get up. Get dressed."

"I'm getting, I'm getting."

He left the room and ventured out to the kitchen.

Meow.

"Well, good morning to you too, Mr. Hitchcock. I can pour cat food. I know I can't burn that. Come on."

The kitten trotted along behind him and waited patiently while he filled up the dish with the dry cat food he preferred in the morning.

"There you go."

The kitten dug in, and Isaac turned his attention to breakfast.

By the time Sidney came out wearing a pair of denim shorts and a lightweight sweatshirt, he'd already tossed out a bad batch of eggs and was cutting up some melon and strawberries.

"Okay, now before you say anything, we have toast with butter and jam, or that chocolate spread you like. And fruit. We've got strawberries and grapes and melon."

"What happened to the eggs?"

"Well, they didn't scramble up too well, but we don't need 'em, really."

"Did you burn them?"

"No! I didn't burn them. I just couldn't get all the shells out."

Sidney giggled and helped him get their breakfast ready for the table.

He watched her top the toast with the chocolate spread and slices of strawberries and banana. Then she put the cantaloupe and grapes into two bowls and added some fresh pineapple chunks.

"Breakfast is served."

"How'd you do that?"

"You did all the prep work. I just helped."

"You salvaged the mess I was making."

"That's my job, baby."

He laughed at that. They sat and ate their breakfast in silence for a few moments. Then he looked her over.

"You're wearing that to the beach?"

"Yeah." She looked down at her attire. "Is something wrong with it?"

"Well, no. I just thought you'd wear a bathing suit, that's all."

Sidney lifted her sweatshirt all the way up over her boobs and revealed a blue and white stripped bikini top.

"Did you just flash me, darlin'?"

"Yes, I did."

"Um hmm." Isaac stared into her eyes. "You'd better look out when our two weeks of abstinence are over."

A sexy grin slid over her lips, and Isaac just wanted to reach out and grab her.

"Is that a threat, Detective?"

"Just a fact, ma'am."

She took a bite of melon and Isaac shook his head and turned back to his breakfast.

They turned up the radio and sang along to the oldies for the entire half-hour drive to the beach at Lakeview Park.

Isaac looked over at Sidney while she was bopping to The Marvelettes and smiled. He loved seeing her happy and smiling, and he was so hopeful that she might finally be bouncing back from her incredible sadness over losing their baby.

He reached over and took her hand, and she smiled at him and kept on singing.

When they reached the beach and found a parking space, Sidney hoisted the tote filled with towels and other supplies onto her shoulder while Isaac grabbed two beach chairs and the small cooler with drinks from the trunk of the car. Then he took Sidney's hand.

"Is that a rose garden?"

She was transfixed by the huge blooming circle that heralded the entrance to the beach.

"Yeah, it is. You want to go have a look?"

She looked up at him. "Are we allowed?"

"Of course. It's there to be enjoyed. Come on."

He led her over to the garden, where he spent the next several minutes just smiling and watching her marvel at and sniff all the different colored roses.

"This place is beautiful! How many varieties do you think are planted here?"

Isaac shrugged a shoulder.

"A couple hundred, at least."

"I have never been to a beach that had a rose garden to greet you."

Isaac laughed and took her hand again, leading her out of the garden. They got to the top of the steps that led down to the beach and stopped.

"Look at that."

He nodded toward the lake. The morning was glorious — blue skies, bright sun, gentle breeze. There were already a few boats on the water, and mild waves crashing into the break walls.

"Now that's a view," Sidney whispered.

"Yeah, it is." Isaac glanced around at the small patches of people dotting the sand. "Let's go find a semi-secluded spot so I can have a chance at relaxing for a while."

"Okay."

They descended the steps down to the sand and made their way across the beach.

"Oh, there's a lighthouse!"

She pointed to the Lorain Lighthouse in the distance, and Isaac grinned.

"Yeah. Pretty cool, huh?"

When they found a suitable spot that was far enough away from other people for him to feel comfortable, Isaac set up the beach chairs — the kind that sat low to the sand and sort of reclined — and put the cooler in between them, like a table.

Then he had to stop his tongue from hitting the sand when he looked up to see Sidney remove her sweatshirt and shimmy out of her shorts. The woman knew how to fill out a bikini.

She sat down on one of the chairs and pulled a tube of sunscreen from her straw bag, and proceeded to rub a dollop into first one shapely leg, and then the other.

Isaac shook his head and looked out at the water. Then he pulled his t-shirt over his head and set it aside.

"Would you mind?"

She was holding out the sunscreen to him and smiling in that I'm-sexy-and-I-know-it sort of way that always drove him the right kind of crazy.

Who was the idiot who decided to come to the beach and torture himself by looking at her gorgeous body in a tiny bikini all day?

Oh, that's right. It was him.

He was the idiot.

"Of course not."

He took the tube of sunscreen and she turned around. He put a small blob of the stuff in the palm of his hand and rubbed them together before beginning.

The moment he touched her skin he saw a vision of the future. One he didn't understand, and didn't particularly like.

A crying baby boy covered in blood and clinging to him.

Cops and police tape.

Sidney with tears in her eyes.

"You'd better put some of this on too, you know? You don't want to burn."

"Huh?" Isaac snapped out of his vision and finished rubbing sunscreen onto her back and shoulders.

"I said you should put some on too, so you don't burn."

"Oh. Right."

She glanced over her shoulder at him.

"You okay?"

He forced a smile. "Yeah."

Sidney turned her body around and stared into his eyes, and Isaac knew what was coming. She could read him like a book, and he often wondered if that was because of their extraordinary psychic bond, her being his shield and all.

"You saw something just now when you touched me, didn't you?"

He sighed and glanced out at the water.

"Yeah, I did. Only I have no clue what I saw or what it means."

"Well, what was it?"

Isaac shook his head and finally looked back into her eyes.

"I don't know, darlin'. Just a bunch of jumbled images is all. You know I don't like to speculate about them until I can make heads or tails out of what I've seen."

She stared at him.

"Was it something bad?"

"Sidney..."

"All right, I know. Well, if you change your mind, I'll be sitting right here soaking up the sun."

He grinned. "I'll remember that."

He watched her lean back in the chair and stretch out her sexy legs. She looked out at the water and breathed in deep.

Isaac did as she suggested and put on the sunscreen, still mulling over the things he'd just seen in that flash. None of it made any sense to him.

Why would that little boy have blood all over him?

And who was he?

And why was he clinging to Isaac so tightly?

What were all the cops doing there? Wherever 'there' was.

And most importantly, why was his Sidney crying?

He had no way of knowing if all of those images were connected in some way or not. Maybe one had nothing to do with the others. Although, his flashes had never worked that way before. Not even the futuristic ones.

For now, he shut it down. Pushed it away to the back of his mind and leaned back in his chair. He shoved his toes into the sand and looked out at the lake.

The sound of the waves, and the gulls calling overhead, and the chattering of the people... the beach had a definite hum all its own, and there was something about it that Isaac found so soothing. It was as if stress wasn't allowed to enter here. The tightness in his shoulders slowly melted in the morning lake sun.

"Hey, Sidney?"

"Hmm?"

"How are you doing, darlin'? I mean, really. We haven't talked about the miscarriage since that night in the grocery store parking lot, after you'd just kicked that guy's ass."

Sidney opened her eyes and looked over at him.

"I'm okay. I'm still sad. But something tells me that I'm always going to be sad about what happened. It's just something that I'm going to have to learn to live with. And I know it'll take time. But for now, I'm okay."

"Good."

"How are you?"

"Me?"

Sidney nodded. "You lost a baby too. How are you doing?"

Isaac took a deep breath and blew it out slowly.

"I'm okay. Honestly, I've just been so worried about you."

"Please don't worry. I'm sad, but I'm okay, Ike. I promise."

He reached out and caressed her face, staring into her eyes.

"Besides, all the weird stuff going on at work is giving me something else to focus on instead of feeling sorry for myself."

"Oh, speaking of that. I got a text from Eddie at the garage. Your tires have been replaced and they'll be dropping the car off later today. I told him to just leave the keys in the mailbox if we're not home."

"What about the bill? Don't we need to pay them?"

"Already done. I had them charge it to my credit card."

"But Ike, I should pay you back for that. Tires aren't cheap."

"It's no big deal, Sid. I already have a card on file with this garage, so it was just easier. And I got the tires at a discount because I work at the PD. Plus, we decided we were going to merge our bank accounts into one joint account after we're married anyway, so what's mine is already yours."

She smiled at him, but he could still see the uncertainty in her eyes.

"Are you sure you won't let me pay you back?"

"Oh, I'm positive."

She laughed and rolled her eyes.

"So, tell me. Have there been any other strange things going on at Hope House lately?"

"Well, I guess that depends on what you consider strange."

"I consider four slashed tires strange. I consider an angry husband now being charged with assault for hitting you strange. I consider you pulling your gun on this same man strange.

"Gotcha."

"So?"

"So?"

"Have there been any other *strange* things going on there? Anything that might make you believe there's a pattern of odd behavior?"

She seemed to study him for a second.

"You don't think any of this is random, do you?"

"I'm just looking at it all from a cop's perspective. It's two fairly major incidents too close together. If it were me... I'd be writing everything down in a notebook of some kind. Keeping some sort of record of odd behavior so you have it to refer back to if you need it."

Sidney looked out at the water, and Isaac could tell she was thinking about his suggestion.

"Now, it could be that the irate husband has nothing at all to do with the slashed tires."

"And we have no way of knowing? There's no way to find out if he's the one who cut my tires?"

"Not really. Not unless Zoe, or one of Hope House's neighbors on that street happened to pick something up on a security camera."

"And I know for a fact that Zoe doesn't have any kind of security system there. After what happened with Diane and Tom Billings, I asked Zoe to give some thought to possibly hiring a security detail."

"Not a bad idea. That would certainly cut down on incidents like the one you just went through. Most shelters would never have the budget for something like that, but Hope House is privately funded by Zoe and her family."

"Yeah, but she's concerned that the residents would be spooked by big male security guards lurking around. I suggested she look into female security guards. You wouldn't happen to know of any outfits that hire females, would you?"

"Not off the top of my head, but I can look into it for you."

"That would be great."

He smiled at her and leaned back in his chair, crunching the sand up beneath his toes. Beside him, Sidney was silent for a moment. Then he heard her take a deep breath, and something inside him went on alert, bracing for whatever curve ball she was about to throw him.

"So, I'm moving ahead with my decision to help Ann and her children get away from her abusive husband."

Isaac's stomach tightened.

He looked over at her, but didn't reply.

"I know you don't like the idea, but I just really feel like it's something I have to do."

The tightness became almost painful.

"I don't want you to be angry with me over this, Isaac."

"I'm not angry, Sidney. I'm in awe of you. And I'm proud of you, and I'm terrified about what you could be getting yourself into. I don't want you getting cozy with people who traffic in false papers. I don't want you getting mixed up in anything illegal at all."

"I understand that, but..."

"I worry about you so much just working at Hope House. I mean, you had to pull your gun on some asshole there just a few days ago."

"I understand your reservations, Ike. I do. And I completely get it. All of your fears are totally valid. But this is happening. Helping women escape their abusers is my calling. It's my destiny. And I intend to go through with it."

The painful tightening in his stomach grew to a dull, throbbing toothache kind of pain. The kind of pain he knew he'd have to learn to live with.

"Then you have to see it through. I'll help you however I can, short of breaking the law."

Sidney reached for his hand.

"Thank you."

Isaac brought her hand up to his lips and kissed the back of it. Then he turned toward the water.

"You want to take a walk along the water's edge?"

Sidney smiled at him.

"Sure. If you do."

He stood and reached out to help her up.

They were quiet on their walk, and Isaac looked down, focusing on the water hitting their ankles, and the imprints his feet were making in the wet sand. But the whole time, his mind raced.

He couldn't stop himself from obsessing over the things Sidney had said. Part of him was proud as hell and endlessly impressed with her determination to see this thing through. But the bigger part of him worried. How the hell was he supposed to keep her safe if she was going to run around willfully courting danger?

"I can't get over that rose garden at the beach entrance."

"Hmm?"

Isaac glanced down only to see her gaze fixed in the direction of the rose garden. He smiled.

"I didn't know you liked roses so much. I guess I've never really sent you flowers before, have I?"

"No, I don't think you have."

"Are roses your favorite flower?"

"Actually, my favorite flowers are orchids. But I do like roses very much."

"What color rose is your favorite?"

"Mmm. I think the pale pink ones. Or the ones that are super pale pink, like almost white, but the center petals are much darker pink. I don't know what they're called, but they're so pretty. So innocent looking."

"So, why are orchids your favorite?"

"I don't know. I guess because they look so delicate and fragile. But they're not delicate at all, they're very strong, resilient flowers."

"Sounds like you just described yourself, darlin'."

Sidney smiled up at him, and he pulled her close, wrapping his arm around her as they made their way down the beach back to where they left their gear.

They hung out on the beach for hours, chilling and relaxing into the late afternoon. Slowly, Isaac's semi-secluded corner of the beach began to fill with other people, some of whom set up their beach towels a little too close for his comfort.

"You ready for lunch?"

He glanced over at Sidney, hoping she wouldn't mind calling it a day, or at the very least, moving to a different spot.

"I could eat. Should we pack it in and head home for lunch?"

"Actually, I thought we could have lunch here."

"Here?"

"There's a café inside the bathhouse there." He chucked a thumb over his shoulder toward the building where the concession stand stood. "They have a pretty good menu of sandwiches and salads. Fresh lake perch."

"Really?"

"Yep. You game?"

"Sure."

Sidney put her shorts and sweatshirt back on, and Isaac pulled on his long-sleeved t-shirt. They gathered up their beach gear and carried it back to the car and put it away. Then they walked hand-in-hand back toward the building across the parking lot from the rose garden.

Inside they were seated by the windows with a spectacular view of the lake and the beach down below.

"What looks good to you?"

Isaac studied his menu already knowing that he was going to order the fried perch wrap.

"Sid?"

He looked up when she still didn't respond. Her gaze darted around the room, taking in all the details, and Isaac could see her mind working as she studied the place. He had no clue what she was seeing that he didn't.

"Sidney?"

"Hmm?" She finally turned back to him. "I'm sorry, what did you say, baby?"

"What's going on?"

"Nothing. I was just looking at the place. This is beautiful."

"Yeah, the view is great."

"Not just the view, the whole place is nice."

Isaac looked around and nodded.

"Do you need a few more minutes to look at the menu?"

A smiling waiter appeared at their table.

Isaac motioned for Sidney to go first.

"Oh. Um..." She looked at Isaac. "You said something about fresh perch?"

Isaac grinned and looked at the waiter. "We'll both have the fried perch wrap."

"Awesome. What can I get you to drink with those wraps?"

"Ginger ale for me. Water for the lady."

"Sure thing."

"Excuse me." Sidney stopped him before he could get away. "Can you tell me if you ever rent this place out for events?"

"All the time. I'll get you the information and number to call."

"Great. Thank you!"

The waiter walked away.

Sidney looked at Isaac with a triumphant smile, and he playfully narrowed his eyes.

"What just happened here? What's that smile for?"

"This is the place, Ike."

"The place?"

"Yes."

He stared at her sexy smile until her meaning dawned on him.

"Oh! *This* is the place? Really?"

She nodded, her smile getting bigger.

"This is the place. The beautiful beach, the views from this terrace restaurant with the lighthouse in the distance. That rose garden! This is definitely the place."

"Okay. So are we talking inside this building? Or maybe in the rose garden?"

"I haven't worked out all the details yet."

"Here you go." The waiter brought over their drinks and handed Sidney a brochure. "All the information is in there, along with a number to call to reserve a date for your event."

"Thank you so much."

He walked away, and Isaac lost Sidney again for a few moments as she devoured the information inside the brochure.

"According to this, they have lots of weddings here."

"Great."

"Ooooh! They allow park permits to rent a section of the beach."

She looked up at him with pure unadulterated excitement in her beautiful eyes, and Isaac couldn't help but smile. He had no clue what had sparked that fire, but he loved it.

"Rent a section of the beach, huh?"

"Yes. That's it!"

"That's what? I need you to spell it out for me, darlin'."

"We'll rent a section of the beach for the ceremony, Ike. We can get married right out there on the beach, take photos in the rose garden, and have the reception here in the Sunset Terrace venue. It's perfect!"

She sounded so happy that all Isaac could do was smile at her.

"If it's perfect for you, then it's perfect for me."

"Let's find out if someone's available to talk to us about dates while we're here."

Isaac laughed. "Whatever you want, Sidney."

Whatever she wanted.

He would move heaven and earth to give it to her.

18

Sidney was still riding high the next morning.

They'd set a wedding date.

And it was barely two months away.

The event planner at the beach venue thought they were crazy, but Sidney didn't care. She floated through her morning routine as though she were in a dream. She remembered making breakfast for her and Ike. She remembered Ike kissing her before he left for work. But she couldn't recall their breakfast conversation for anything. Her mind was much too cluttered with beach wedding ideas and wondering if she could talk Bree into helping her pull this thing together so quickly.

She dressed in a pair of black leggings and a light purple tunic-style blouse, zipped up her black wedge booties and headed off to work.

Her car was sitting in their small driveway when they'd gotten home from the beach yesterday, keys waiting in the mailbox just like Ike said, and Sidney couldn't help but give her tires a double look before she climbed behind the wheel.

She thought of nothing but wedding plans on her way to work, and wondered where the heck a girl went for a decent white dress in this town.

The flashing red and blue lights punctuating the siren coming up fast behind her snapped her out of her giddiness.

She pulled to the curb on the right and stopped, expecting the marked police cruiser to zoom past her in pursuit of someone else. Instead, it pulled in behind her, and Sidney's belly tumbled over itself.

Her first thought was Isaac.

Was he all right? Had he sent someone to find her?

Then another, more sensible, thought settled in.

Had she done something wrong?

"Stay calm, Sidney," she mumbled to herself. "Remember everything Ike told you to do in this situation, and just stay calm. Everything's going to be okay."

She glanced in her rearview mirror.

She couldn't be certain, but the cop appeared to be female. When the door opened and the officer started for her car, Sidney's heart rate sped up. She hit the button to let down her window, and then put both of her hands on the steering wheel, giving it a good squeeze.

When the officer stepped up to her window, Sidney smiled.

"Good morning, officer. I have a Concealed Weapons Permit, and my gun is in my purse."

Without a word the officer stepped back, unsnapped her holster, and drew her gun.

"I need you to slowly step out of the car and put your hands on your head."

The gun wasn't pointing directly at her, but still Sidney's heart took a flying leap down into her stomach.

"Of course."

She'd known this could happen.

Isaac had explained the procedure to her in great detail. What an officer would do — and what Sidney *should* do — if she were ever pulled over while she had her gun with her. But even knowing the procedure and the wherefores and whys, her hands were trembling when she slowly opened the car door.

She stepped out of the car and put her hands on her head.

"Turn around."

Sidney did as she was told. She knew what was coming next.

Handcuffs.

Isaac had told her that would most likely happen. Especially if she were stopped by a one-man car. It was for the officer's safety and for hers. But it still opened up a hallow pit of humiliation within her.

She closed her eyes as the officer pulled her hands behind her back and secured the cuffs.

"Where's the gun?"

"In my purse. The purse is on the passenger side floor."

The officer walked around the car to the passenger side.

Out of the corner of her eye, Sidney spotted a second police car pull in behind the first one. She closed her eyes again. It was for the officer's protection, she knew. Back up, in case Sidney was some big time cop killer or something.

Isaac had this same kind of back up everyday.

It was what she had to tell herself to stay calm.

The man she loved was a police officer, just like these officers. They wouldn't hurt her as long as she stayed calm and did what they asked her to do.

She opened her eyes and watched the female officer secure the gun from her purse.

"Where's the gun permit?"

There was no politeness in her tone of voice. Just business.

"It's in that same purse. In the pocket behind my driver's license."

The officer searched her purse, pulling out her license and the gun registration. She returned the purse to the car and closed the door. Then she headed for her cruiser with a glance at Sidney.

"Hang tight."

Sidney nodded and watched the woman's every movement. She got back into her cruiser, no doubt running the registration for the gun, and most likely her license. As she waited, Sidney wondered what the hell had prompted this stop in the first place. What had she done that put her on this cop's radar?

She had been awfully distracted with her wedding plans. Maybe she had run a red light and not known it? Had she been driving erratically?

After what seemed like forever, the officer got out of her cruiser and came toward her again.

"Turn around."

Sidney turned around and breathed in deep when the handcuffs came off.

"Thank you for your cooperation, Ms. Fairchild."

"Of course."

"Who does the FOP emblem on the rear license plate belong to?"

She was referring to the small round disk that most officers attached to their rear license plates. It alerted other officers that the owner of the car in question was also either an active duty police officer or a retired one, or that the driver was the spouse or child of an officer.

"My fiancé. He's Detective Sergeant Isaac Taylor at the 3rd precinct."

The officer's face blanched noticeably, and Sidney wondered what that was about.

"Your information."

She handed Sidney back her license and CCW permit.

"Thank you."

"Ms. Fairchild, I stopped you this morning because you made an improper lane change back there."

"I did?"

"Yes, you did. Failure to signal."

"Oh. I'm so sorry."

"I'm writing you a citation."

She scribbled something down on her citation booklet and tore out Sidney's copy, handing it to her.

"Please pay better attention in the future."

"Yes. I will."

The officer handed over Sidney's gun and dipped her head in greeting. Then she hustled back to her cruiser and drove off.

Sidney looked around wondering what the hell that was all about. Then she got back into her car just as the second police cruiser pulled away. She returned her gun, license and permit to her purse, and stuffed the citation down in there with them. Then she secured her seatbelt and headed to work.

She arrived late, but only by a few minutes. Still completely puzzled by the whole ordeal, she went straight to the office and flopped down in her desk chair.

It wasn't even nine o'clock in the morning, but it had already been a long hard day.

"This does not bode well, Sid," she mumbled to herself.

"Talking to yourself again?"

Zoe smiled at her when she breezed into the office.

"Give me a break, I've had a rough morning."

"Cry me a river. Remember that summer flu bug we were talking about a few days ago?"

"Yeah?"

"Well, Tyneesha has it. I've been sanitizing the place from top to bottom all morning, praying that it doesn't spread throughout the house. Tyneesha promises to stay in her room so that she doesn't spread it around. I had to call Lance Tobey to come check on her and give her something. I just wanted to give you a heads up, in case you run into him. He's not here yet, but he is expected sometime before noon."

"Great. That's in keeping with the theme of my morning."

"Sorry."

"It's okay. Don't sweat it."

She turned to the papers on her desk.

"The good news is that Ike and I set a wedding date yesterday."

The sing song quality to her own voice made her smile.

"Did you!"

"We did. August 29th. Save the date."

"Of this year?"

"Yep."

"Oh, that's soon!"

"Yes, it is."

"Why the rush?"

"We're two adults in our mid-thirties. Why wait?"

"Well, I don't know. I mean, is there some reason *not* to wait?"

She gave Sidney a funny probing look, and Sidney laughed.

"I know what you're insinuating, Zoe, and the answer is no. I'm not pregnant." She sighed and beat a pencil eraser against her desk. "I wish I was."

"Oh?"

Sidney looked her in the eyes, and something inside her said it was time. She took a deep breath and gathered her courage.

"I had a miscarriage, Zoe." Her voice was soft and halting to her own ears, but she'd said it. Out loud. "A week ago. That's why I missed those two days."

"Oh, God. Oh, Sidney, I'm so sorry. And here I am being flippant."

"No, it's okay. You didn't know."

"Are you okay? Should you even be back at work?"

"I'm fine. I am. The doctor just wanted me to take it easy for 24 hours, so I did him one better and made it 48. I'm good."

Zoe stared at her for a moment.

"I'm really sorry. I know what you're going through. I had a miscarriage. Well, actually I had two miscarriages before our blessings were born."

"You did?"

Zoe nodded. "It's not an easy thing to get over. Especially when you've been trying to get pregnant for so long. We finally did in-vitro."

"Oh? You were having difficulties getting pregnant?"

"My husband and I tried for three years. When the only two pregnancies we managed on our own resulted in miscarriages, we sought professional help. IVF brought us our twins. Megan and Maurice."

She pointed to the picture behind her desk. Sidney had seen the picture of two smiling teenagers a million times, and she knew Zoe's kids were older now.

"I don't think I knew Megan and Maurice were twins."

"Yep. We got one of each with one IVF treatment, so we stopped."

Sidney smiled at her.

"Were you and Ike trying to get pregnant?"

Sidney shook her head.

"No, it was a total surprise. We were both slightly terrified at first, but we were warming to the idea when..." Her voice trailed off and she paused. "Anyway, we both realize now how much we'd like to have a child together."

Zoe smiled at her. "I suppose if there is one good thing about miscarriage, it's that. It helps you realize how badly you want to be a parent."

Sidney nodded as Zoe's words sunk in.

"Well, I'm going to go check on Tyneesha again. Try to get her to eat something." Zoe stood and headed for the door again.

"Hey, Zoe?"

"Yes."

"Thank you."

She smiled at her. "If you ever need to talk about it, you know where to find me."

"I do. Thanks."

Zoe left the office, and Sidney let out a long, sad sigh. That was the first time she'd talked about the miscarriage with anyone other than Isaac, and it felt cathartic somehow. Like she was finally ready to let go and move on.

She wiped a few wayward tears from her cheeks, and then she got to work.

The morning passed into afternoon without incident. At about half-past twelve, Sidney was in the kitchen when she heard Dr. Lance Tobey's voice in the hallway talking to one of the residents.

She headed for the office and made eye contact with Zoe as she passed her in the hall.

"Lance! Thank you for coming on such short notice," Zoe called out and rushed toward him.

"Sorry, I'm late. I got caught up in traffic."

"That's no problem, but I'm glad you're here. Tyneesha is upstairs and feeling very poorly. Let me show you to her room."

Sidney glanced back and spotted him watching her as Zoe took his arm and herded him toward the staircase. She appreciated her boss' efforts in keeping him out of her orbit.

She closed the office door and made a point of staying put at her desk in order to minimize her chances of running into him. She busied herself with staff scheduling, and printing out new worksheets to help Beth's daughter.

About an hour later, Zoe came into the office with a tired expression.

"He's gone."

"Was he able to help Tyneesha?"

"He says it's definitely the flu. He left her some menthol to rub on her chest, and some cough drops. And he said to keep her drinking clear fluids." Zoe flipped through the stack of mail in her hands as she spoke. "He thinks with lots of rest, she'll be back on her feet in no time."

"Good."

"Oh, here's a package for you."

Sidney looked up from her computer screen.

"A package?"

"Yes. It was in the mailbox."

Zoe handed her the small, nondescript, brown box addressed to 'The Future Mrs. Ike Taylor.'

"That's odd."

"What's that?"

"Look at the way it's worded. The future Mrs. Ike Taylor? Who would send me something addressed that way?"

Zoe shrugged a shoulder. "I don't know. Maybe your beloved?"

Sidney examined the box. There was no return address.

"I don't think Ike would go to the trouble of mailing me something here."

"Your future sister-in-law maybe? The one who brought the food by and ended up giving birth here. What's her name again?"

"Bree Taylor."

"Yes, her. Maybe she sent you something."

Sidney shook her head. That didn't make any sense to her either.

"Maybe."

"Well, there could be a card inside. Or at least a clue of some sort. Open it."

Sidney searched for the letter opener on her desk and used the very tip to puncture the tape on the box, slicing down the middle. Then she opened it up.

It took her mind a few endless seconds to comprehend what she was seeing.

A small stuffed puppy — mutilated with dirty, matted fur.

The eyes were ripped off.

The stuffing was coming out.

And crawling on top — the biggest, hairiest, brown spider.

Panic in her mind and fear in her gut battled like wild dogs.

Sidney screamed, leaping from her seat like a shot.

The box fell to the floor.

The spider crawled out.

Zoe screamed in solidarity. Then she went running to her desk for the heaviest book she could find.

Sidney couldn't wait that long.

With a loud karate yell, she stomped on the big creepy crawly with her wedged-heeled bootie.

Zoe stared at her, hard-covered dictionary raised above her head.

Ann and Beth came running, stopping in the doorway to gape at them.

Panting, Sidney looked at Zoe.

"I'm afraid to look."

"Raise your foot. If it's not dead, the dictionary's ready."

Sidney nodded frantically. Then she took a breath and raised her foot.

"Oh, thank God!" Zoe breathed a loud sigh of relief. "You got him."

"Ahh!"

Sidney took a step back and flopped down into her chair.

"What just happened?" Beth asked.

"Where did that huge thing come from?" Ann chimed in.

"Good question!" Zoe looked from Ann to Sidney. "What the fuck was that?"

"How the hell am I supposed to know? You brought the box in here! Was it in the mailbox?"

"Yes. I told you, I found it in the mail. Addressed to you."

"No. It was addressed to the 'Future Mrs. Ike Taylor.'"

"Well, that is you!"

"Yes, it's me. But who the hell would send something like that in the mail?"

Zoe threw up a hand. "I don't know."

"Oh, my God." A thought hit Sidney's brain.

"What?"

She got up and maneuvered carefully around the squished spider. Then she picked up the box and studied the outside of it more carefully. Not only was there no return address. There was also no postage, no post office stamp. Nothing.

"I don't think someone sent this through the mail at all. I think someone simply put it inside the mailbox."

"Who would do that?"

Sidney grabbed a pencil from her desk. Then she bent down and used the end of the pencil to shove the stuffed animal back into the box. She took a deep breath and did the same with the fat, dead spider.

"Yeewl!"

The creeped out sound came with a shiver of her entire body. Then she closed up the box and looked up at Ann and Beth.

"Can one of you find me a plastic bag to put this in, please? Ziplock if we have it."

"Sure."

They both hurried from the doorway, and Sidney stood up.

"What are you doing, Sidney? Why not just throw it away?"

"Because it's evidence. I'm bagging it up to give to Ike."

"Evidence? Of what?"

"Harassment. This, on top of my tires being slashed. It might not be related, but... it could be."

Zoe placed her hands on her hips.

"Oh, heavens. I never thought of that."

"I'm not sure I would have either, but Ike and I just had a conversation about this yesterday. He said that I should keep a record of any strange things going on here."

Zoe glanced at the door and then lowered her voice when she said, "Do you think it could be Ann's husband?"

"The thought occurred to me. I think he's still in jail though. And how would he know who I'm marrying?"

There was another thought that occurred to her as well.

Dr. Lance Tobey.

He was just there, after all. Who's to say he couldn't have dropped the package in the mailbox before he walked in the door?

"Here you go, Sidney."

"Thanks."

She took the plastic bag from Beth and placed the box inside, zipping it up tight. Then she put it on the corner of her desk and looked at Zoe.

"It's officially been the worst day ever."

Zoe fought to hold in her laughter, finally letting it burst forth.

Sidney shook her head and joined in because... well, it was better than crying.

19

Isaac floated out of the briefing room that morning and over to his desk as if his chest were filled with helium. And why not? The most beautiful woman in the world was going to marry him in just two short months. Less than that even.

Oh, yeah. Happy wasn't a big enough word for what he was feeling.

"What are you doing right now?"

Isaac looked up to find Pete staring at him in the most peculiar way.

"What?"

"That strange sound. The one coming from your mouth. Is that whistling? Are you whistling right now?

"Yeah, so I was whistling. What of it? Am I not allowed to whistle?"

"Oh, no, you're allowed. But you usually don't."

"I whistle."

"No, you don't. Because whistling implies that you're in a good mood. Which you usually aren't. And it implies that you like people and that you're approachable. You hate people, *and* you're most definitely not approachable. So why are you whistling?"

"I'm approachable."

"No, you're not."

"And I don't hate people."

"You don't like them."

"I like them fine! Although I don't particularly like you at the moment."

Pete laughed out loud, and Isaac rolled his eyes.

He knew only too well that Pete often enjoyed giving him a hard time simply for the fun of it. What Pete didn't know, and what Isaac could never let him know, was that he secretly enjoyed the ribbing. It was nice having a good rapport with his partner. It made it easier to work together.

"What's got you in such a good mood, Ike?"

"Well, it's certainly not you, that's for sure."

"Touché."

He sat down at his desk and ignored Pete's question.

"Well?"

"Well, what?"

"What has you whistling this morning, man?"

Isaac sighed. "Sidney and I..."

"Wait! If this is a sex thing, I don't want to hear it. I don't need that visual in my head."

"I don't want that visual in your head either! Now, you asked me a question. Do you want to hear my response or not?"

Pete grinned at his aggravation. "Please, continue."

"I was going to say... Sidney and I finally set a wedding date yesterday."

"Oh, for real?"

"Yes."

"Congratulations, man!"

"Thank you."

"So when's the special day?"

"August 29th."

"Of this year?"

"Yep."

"That's fast."

"Not fast enough for me. I tried to talk her into going to Vegas for the weekend, but she wasn't having that."

"That's no surprise. Chicks don't like the Vegas wedding route for some reason."

"I've noticed that. Can't imagine what turns them off about it."

"I'll tell you what turns them off about a Vegas wedding."

Isaac and Pete both turned to see Gavin Hayes standing at their desks.

"What's that, Lieu?"

"It's not special enough. Women want their weddings to be special, and Vegas doesn't feel special enough for them. Especially if she's never been married before."

Isaac pointed a finger at him.

"Now that makes sense. How do you know this stuff?"

"Well, I was married before, remember? I think every engaged man tries the Vegas weekend suggestion at least once during the wedding planning stage. I take it Sidney hated the idea?"

"Pretty much, yeah."

"Well, not that your wedding woes aren't important, but what's going on in your mutilated college boys case? Got an update for me?"

Isaac and Pete glanced at each other.

"I'd like to say yes, but that'd be a flat out lie, sir. We've interviewed the family members and close associates of all three victims, not to mention the family of the young lady the three were accused of raping back in high school. None of it brought us any closer to a suspect."

"You don't have anyone of interest? After all that?"

"No, sir. Not yet."

"How sure are you that these deaths are related to that old rape case?"

"Seeing as the killings were centered on those three men, and no one else is dead..."

"And the rape is the one thing all three boys had in common..." Pete interjected.

"We're reasonably sure," Isaac finished.

"Well, something's not adding up, Sgt. I'd hate to tell you to start over and interview all those people again, but..."

"Don't worry, Lieu. You know me. I'll always find a new angle to explore. Even if I have to use my unconventional means to find it."

"That's good, because it seems we may need your unconventional means on this one."

He gave Isaac a pointed look and then headed back to his office.

Isaac sighed and glanced at Pete.

"Is it time to touch the vics?"

Isaac rocked back in his chair and didn't answer. He didn't want to resort to touching the victims, not yet. He knew that eventually the time would come when he would have to use his abilities in that way again. But not now. This case didn't warrant it. At least, that's what he kept telling himself.

There had to be something they were overlooking. *Someone* they were overlooking. They just hadn't looked in the right place yet.

The right place.

He pointed a finger at Pete.

"What was it I asked you to make note of about the institution?"

Pete picked up his cellphone and checked his notes.

"That we need to go back there and ask about Amber's regular visitors."

"Right. Let's do that. In fact, while we're there let's talk to every member of that staff that has regular contact with Amber."

"You think one of them could be our killer?"

"I'm just trying to find a new angle to explore."

"Let's go."

They got up and headed out.

Luckily, the traffic was just hitting that sweet spot between the morning rush and the lunch rush where things calmed down and moved at a nice normal pace for a couple of hours. He loved it when things weren't bumper-to-bumper.

They made it to the Lakewood Mental Institution in record time. Inside at the front desk, Isaac flashed his badge at the same receptionist from the other day.

"Detective Sgt. Ike Taylor, this is my partner, Detective Pete Vega."

"Yes, I remember. What can I do for you today, Detectives?"

"Well, we'll be needing a number of things actually. First, we'd like a list of everyone who has visited with Amber Camden in the last six months."

"Oh. I'm not sure if that information is restricted."

"It's a matter of public record, ma'am, not part of Amber's medical file. It's not restricted information, and I will come back here with a court order if I have to."

"Yes, sir." The receptionist's cheeks pinked up like she'd been slapped. "What else do you need?"

"We're going to need to speak with anyone on staff who had regular contact with Amber Camden. Everyone who's involved in taking care of her on a daily basis."

"I'm going to need to consult with Josephine Turner for that. She handles the schedule and staff rotations, so she'd have that information."

"Do what you gotta do."

He fixed her with a steady stare, making it clear that they were not leaving until they got what they had come for. The girl picked up the phone and spoke softly into it. He couldn't hear what was said, but watched her float a few nervous glances up his way.

Two minutes later, the same stocky corn-fed woman from their last visit came around the corner wearing a frustrated scowl.

"Detectives? You've come back?"

"Nurse Turner, sorry to bother you again."

"Not at all. Lindsey is going to make a copy of Amber's visitors log for you." She motioned to the receptionist. "I understand you wish to speak with any staff who helped take care of Amber?"

"That's right."

"May I ask why?"

"We're investigating a triple homicide. The CPD believes in leaving no stone unturned when it comes to murder."

"Of course. Well, that's quite a few people over the course of her time here. We are talking years, after all. How far back would you like me to go?"

"Let's say the last six months."

"Very well. I can set you up in the boardroom if you like. You can conduct your interviews in there."

"That would be great. Thank you."

She led them down the hall to a small room where the long, polished table and chairs dominated the space.

"We have our staff meetings in here, so you should be comfortable. And it should give you ample privacy for your interviews. I'll send in the first in a few moments. Would you like the others in fifteen minute intervals?"

"Just send in the first. We'll let you know when we're done and ready for the next."

"Very good."

"Thank you for your cooperation."

Josephine only gave a curt nod. Then she turned and left the room.

"There is something about that woman that I can't put my finger on." Pete stared at the door she'd just disappeared through. "But I feel like she's hiding something."

Isaac looked at Pete and grinned.

"Your instincts are getting better all the time, young padawan."

Pete rolled his eyes at the term.

"Oh, so now you're the Jedi master?"

"That's right."

"Bullshit."

"Well, one of us has been a detective for over nine years, while the other is still a little wet behind the ears. I think that makes me the Jedi master and you the padawan."

"Whatever. You're such a nerd."

"Sticks and stones, Pete."

"Grow up."

Isaac huffed out a breath. "This coming from the same guy who teased me about whistling an hour ago?"

"The difference is that my teasing was funny. Yours is just awkward."

"I am a very funny guy."

"No, you're not."

"You're just jealous because you don't have my Jedi skills."

"Honestly, I'm not sure I'd want your Jedi skills, Ike."

Pete looked at him, and Isaac knew they weren't talking about Jedi mind tricks. He sighed and glanced over at the door before looking Pete in the eyes again.

"No. You would not."

Pete nodded and a moment passed between them.

"So... you think there's something fishy about Nurse Ratched too?"

"I do. She's been very accommodating since we met her, but there is something. It's in her tone of voice, the weight of her stare. Something about her just feels... off somehow. Almost like she's trying too hard to be helpful. Maybe so that we won't suspect her of anything."

"She is a big, healthy girl."

"Yes, she is. Although I'm not sure she'd possess the upper

body strength to string up victim number one to that tree. Not by herself anyway."

"Now there's an angle we haven't really discussed."

"More than one person?"

"Yeah. I mean you mentioned Amber's brothers possibly knowing who our killer is, but what about the possibility that they were actually in on it?"

"I think the possibility that the killer had help is more than good. I mean, think about it... victim number one was tied, spread eagled to a wide tree trunk. Hiroshi says the autopsy suggests that the victim was incapacitated by a blow to the head before he was strung up and killed. Now how much effort would it take for one person to handle all that dead weight? They'd have to subdue him, transport him, and then string him to that tree."

"That's a whole lot of work for just one person."

"Yes, it is. Not saying it couldn't be done, but... it'd sure be a hell of a lot easier with a second set of hands and muscle power, now wouldn't it?"

Pete nodded just as someone knocked on the open door. They turned to see a male orderly standing in the doorway.

The man was of average height and build, and looked as though he were perturbed to have been summoned.

"I was told to come speak to the detectives in the boardroom."

"Yes, sir. That's us." Isaac motioned for him to come in further. "I'm Detective Sgt. Ike Taylor. This is Detective Pete Vega. We'd like to ask you a few questions."

The man stepped into the room, clearly guarded. Pete motioned for the man to sit at the head of the table.

"Your name, sir?"

"My name is Randy Luden. What's this about?"

Isaac and Pete each took seats on either side of him.

"Mr. Luden, we're investigating the murders of three men.

Bobby Cook, Craig Wentworth, and Michael Rivers. Do you know any of them?"

Randy Luden shook his head.

"No. I don't think so. Did they work here or something? Is that why you're questioning us?"

"We'll ask the questions, if you don't mind. We understand you've had a hand in taking care of Amber Camden during her stay here. Is that right?"

"Amber Camden? Yeah, that's right. I help get her out of bed and into her wheelchair. Stuff like that."

"How long have you worked here, Mr. Luden?"

"Going on five years now, I guess."

"So, you were here already when Amber Camden first came to stay here?"

"I suppose so."

Isaac nodded. "And during that time, have you ever known Amber to speak?"

"No, sir. Amber never says nothing."

"Does Amber ever get up and move around on her own?"

"No, sir. One of us always has to get her up and into her wheelchair or her bed. I mean, she can move and walk on her own. She just don't want to no more."

"She doesn't want to?"

"No, sir. I heard her doctor say once that she's just lost the will to do for herself. It's like that old saying, you know? All the lights is on, but ain't nobody home. It's like Amber just ain't home no more, and don't nobody know if she'll ever come back."

Isaac nodded. It was way more information on Amber's medical condition than they would likely get from anyone besides her doctor."

"Mr. Luden, do you know how Amber came to be here?"

"Well, sure. Everybody here knows the story. Sad, sorry business, that was. Those boys got off scot free after what they done. It weren't right."

"No." Isaac studied Randy Luden for a moment, assessing whether or not he might possess the upper body strength to pull off this heinous triple murder. "No, it wasn't right. Mr. Luden, are you aware that those very same boys, young men now, were all recently murdered?"

He hesitated for a fraction of a beat.

"Well, yes, sir. I may have heard tale about that around here lately."

"And what is that tale exactly? What are people saying about it around here?"

"Just that it was karma coming back to bite those boys where it hurts, is all. You won't find no sympathy for 'em around here. No, sir."

Isaac looked him in the eyes.

"So, you think they got what they deserved?"

"Alls I know is that if something like that happened to someone I loved, I'd want 'em dead. Wouldn't you, Detective?"

Isaac stared Randy Luden in the eyes.

"I suppose I would."

Randy Luden nodded in agreement.

"You wouldn't happen to know who set that karma in motion, would you Mr. Luden?"

"No, sir."

"Would you tell me if you did?"

Randy appeared to think about that for a moment.

"No, sir, I don't think I would."

Isaac glanced at Pete, who raised his eyebrows in response.

"Thank you for your time, Mr. Luden. Please tell Nurse Turner we're ready for the next one."

They watched the man leave, and Pete rapped his knuckles on the tabletop.

"You believe he doesn't know anything?"

"I do." Isaac looked at him. "You don't?"

"I don't know. I mean, he didn't seem like he had any special attachment to Amber or anything."

"No, he didn't. I get the feeling Randy Luden's a man who comes to work, does his job, and goes home. He pays attention to the work gossip, but he's not really a part of any of the hospital cliques. He knows what's going on, but for the most part he stays out of the office politics."

"Let me ask you something, Ike — padawan to Jedi master."

Pete grinned, but Isaac could see the seriousness in his eyes.

"What?"

"All that you just said about Randy Luden..."

"Yeah?"

"Was all of that police work, or was there a certain amount of psychic Jedi mind tricks involved?"

Isaac put a quick stop to the curl of his lips and looked down at the table.

Part of his job as the senior detective was to teach his new partner everything he knew. And as the new sergeant of the homicide division, he felt like that obligation was now doubled. So he owed it to Pete to be honest. He looked his partner in the eyes.

"Pete, I'd be lying if I said the psychic thing didn't play any part in me doing my job. It does. Every single day. Sometimes in small ways, sometimes in much bigger ways. It's inevitable because I can't turn it off. But honestly, that was mostly just watching and listening. The body language, the small tells that alert you when someone's not being truthful, the voice inflection. All things you can and will pick up over time."

"You make it look so easy."

"I'll take that as a compliment."

"That's how it was meant."

"You gotta remember, I've been a detective for almost ten years now. I didn't start out knowing everything. Hell, I still don't know everything."

"Yeah, well you..."

"Excuse me?"

They looked up to see a young woman, roughly in her late twenties or early thirties, standing in the doorway. She was short and pleasant looking with her starched white scrubs and blue cardigan. Her hair was pulled back into a ponytail tied with a red ribbon. She even wore one of those old-fashioned nurses' caps on her head. She looked as though tiny woodland creatures helped her get dressed in the mornings, like Snow White. If Snow White were a nurse in a mental ward.

"Hello. I was told to come speak with the detectives in the boardroom. I'm Freya Altman."

"Come in, please."

Isaac stood and motioned her to the seat Randy Luden had vacated. She took her seat and folded her hands in her lap.

"Is this about what happened to those three young men? The ones from the colleges?"

"As a matter of fact, it is." Isaac took his seat and looked at her. "I'm Detective Sgt. Taylor; this is Detective Vega. What do you know about those three young men, Ms. Altman?"

"Only what they're saying around here. That those are the three young men who hurt Amber Camden, and what they did to her sent her here."

"So you didn't know about that until the three men were murdered?"

"Well, I knew that something traumatic had happened to her, and I'd heard whispers and rumors ever since she came here, but I'd never gotten the full story until this week."

"I see. And you take care of Amber often?"

"Oh, everyday just about. Well, during the daytime hours anyway. My shift is over at four."

"So you're usually working when Amber gets visitors, correct?"

"Yes. Oh, and she's got a great support system. Her mother comes about twice each month. Her father too. And on her birthday, her whole family comes together with a cake and balloons. It's so sweet. If only the poor girl would respond to them."

"She never responds? Not to any of them?"

"No. So sad."

"Ms. Altman, have you ever seen or heard Amber respond to anyone?"

She shook her head, but then stopped, and Isaac could see her thinking.

"Ms. Altman?"

"There was this one time..." Her voice trailed off, like she was trying to remember the details, or maybe just questioning what she'd witnessed.

"What happened?"

"I was walking by her room... you know, on my regular rounds to give out afternoon meds?"

"Yes."

"It was the strangest thing. I heard someone talking, so I stuck my head in her room."

She paused again, sparking Isaac's impatience.

"And?"

"Well, her friend Danny was visiting. And he gave me the strangest look when I walked in. Almost worried like. I asked him if they were having a nice visit... you know, just being polite. And he joked that the conversation was a bit one-sided."

She smiled.

"Why was that strange, Ms. Altman?"

"Well, because when I was in the hallway walking by, I... I remember hearing him say something like 'of course I'm sure.' As if he were responding to a question she had asked him. Only... she couldn't have."

The woman seemed truly puzzled.

Isaac and Pete exchanged a look.

"And who exactly is this Danny person?"

"Oh, Danny Broderick. Amber's BFF." She giggled. "That's

what he says. He comes all the time. Usually two or three times a week, every week since Amber was admitted."

Freya Altman nodded, her smile confirming what she thought of Amber Camden's BFF.

"He's never missed a visit. Well, except of course those two weeks right after his transition surgery. It was amazing! He was still recovering and in a certain amount of physical pain, yet he still came faithfully. He's so dedicated to her. I wish all of our patients had the support system she does. It really makes..."

"I'm sorry." Isaac held up a hand to halt her running commentary. "His transition surgery?"

"Oh. Yes, well, I probably shouldn't have said that. Patient confidentiality and all. But, of course, he's not a patient here, so I don't suppose it matters."

"No, I don't believe it does. So please explain."

"Well, Danny Broderick is transgender. When Amber was first admitted and Danny would come visit, he was Dannielle then. His transformation is remarkable."

"And Danny and Amber were best friends in high school?"

"Oh, yes! To hear Danny tell it, they were fast friends from the moment they met in the fifth grade. He's such a sweetheart. There are pictures in Amber's room... you know, family pictures and the like? Well, there are a few pictures of her and Danny, back when he was Dannielle."

Isaac nodded. "Thank you for your time, Ms. Altman. You've been extremely helpful."

"Oh, I have? Wonderful."

When she was gone, Isaac looked at Pete.

"Did you pick up on anything during that interview?"

"Oh, yeah. Seems we need to find this Danny Broderick who went to high school with Amber and our three victims."

"Yes, we do. Anything else?"

Pete nodded. "Yeah. It almost sounds like Amber does, in fact, respond to someone."

"It sure as hell does."

Interviews at the mental hospital took up the rest of their morning, but nothing they learned was as intriguing as the discovery of Amber Camden's BFF. Well, nothing except a little nugget dropped by one of the nurses that head nurse, Josephine Turner, was apparently very fond of BFF Danny Broderick. Fond enough to have invited him over for a home cooked meal on more than one occasion.

Isaac and Pete took that knowledge back to the PD with them. They walked into the detectives pit after lunch determined to explore this new angle from every single side.

"Okay. Here's the plan."

Isaac pulled out his desk chair, sat down, and pointed at Pete.

"You take Josephine Turner, find out everything you can. I'll take Dannielle/Danny Broderick. Let's pull them both apart and see if we can find a murderer between them."

"I'm on it."

They worked steady for the next couple of hours. Finally, Isaac glanced around to make sure the area around him was people free before he raised his arms and stretched out his back.

"Tell me something good, Pete."

Isaac settled back in his chair and looked at his partner expectantly.

"Give me something we can use."

Pete sighed and looked up.

"Well, it seems that Josephine Turner is a pedophile."

"What?"

"Well, not registered, or anything. But there is evidence that she likes 'em young and pretty."

"We talking girls or boys here?"

"Boys. Fifteen years ago, before getting a nursing position at

Lakewood Mental Institution, she was a school nurse at one of the area high schools. She was fired for getting a little too friendly with the male students who would venture into her nurse's station."

"Criminally friendly, or just 'we've gotten complaints' friendly?"

"Several complaints from several different boys about improper touching. And one rumor about her performing fellatio on a minor that was swiftly heading the criminal route. So, the school board acted preemptively and let her go."

"No criminal charges ever brought?"

"Nope."

"Huh. Okay."

Isaac tried to work out how that information fit into this current case. He was certain it did somehow, he just had to figure it out.

"What about you? You finding anything of note?" Pete asked.

"Oh, yeah. Seems Dannielle Broderick and Amber Camden were as tight as two little girls could get from the time they were preteens. Dannielle was tall and awkward, and of course, picked on mercilessly all through school. Which, in turn, made Amber her protector. Then at the start of their senior year, Dannielle cut off all her hair and started dressing like a boy, which only made things worse."

"Of course."

"Through all those changes though, Amber stuck by her side. Seems she encouraged Dannielle to be her true self."

"That's real friendship."

"The girls were at a high school party when the rape happened. According to Dannielle's statement at the time, the three boys cornered them outside as they were leaving, and herded them out to the shed. She claimed that *she* was their target, that the boys threatened to show her that she was a girl once and for all. Amber tried to help her fight them off, but they were overpowered."

"Wait a minute," Pete frowned at him. "You're telling me Dannielle was raped by these guys too?"

"According to her statement."

"But I don't remember seeing anything about that when we researched the trial itself."

Isaac shook his head.

"No. She later dropped the charges because she didn't want to go through a trial and be humiliated when they inevitably made her sexuality an issue. So, Amber went through the trial ordeal alone."

"Wow! No wonder Danny now visits her multiple times a week. He probably feels majorly guilty for hanging his best friend out to dry like that."

"I'd imagine so. Especially since Amber was always the one protecting him when he was Dannielle. And to me, that all sounds like a motive for slicing their shit off."

"Agreed."

"Now, add to that the fact that, after his transition surgery, Danny Broderick has become a body builder and a personal trainer."

"Which means he, more than likely, possesses the upper body strength needed to pull off the murders."

Isaac pointed a finger at him as a thought occurred to him.

"And he's young enough that he might just catch the eye of a certain boy-loving nurse."

"So you're thinking maybe Josephine Turner was Danny Broderick's accomplice?"

"Stranger things have happened."

Pete nodded. "I like it."

"Me too. Now all we have to do is prove it."

20

Sidney stared at the package of cheese tortellini on the kitchen counter. Isaac would be home any minute now, and she needed to get dinner started.

Only she couldn't.

She couldn't move. She was much too preoccupied with everything she had to tell him to focus on dinner.

What would he say?

How would he react?

Would he be angry?

How angry?

Angry enough to hit her?

"Of course not!"

She sucked in a deep breath. She hated herself for even thinking it.

"Isaac would never do that, Sid. Isaac is *not* Damien. He is nothing like him."

He could never be like him.

Isaac was kind and loving and gentle. Protective. Strong.

Authoritative when he had to be.

Powerful when his abilities took center stage.

But cruel, mean-spirited, or sadistic? Isaac was none of those things. It wasn't in his nature.

She jumped about a foot when she heard his keys jingling in the front door.

Meow.

She stepped out of the kitchen into the living room in time to see Alfred Hitchcock run to the door like a happy dog greeting its human.

"Hey, there, Mr. Hitchcock. How was your day?"

She smiled at his friendly tone, and the loving way he carried the cat into the living room scratching its head.

"Hey, darlin'."

"Hi."

He leaned in and kissed her lips, and Sidney forced a smile for him. But he wasn't buying it. She never knew if it was his psychic skills, or if he simply knew her so well, but she could never hide anything from him. He read her way too easily.

"What's the matter?"

"I... had an eventful day, that's all."

"Why? What happened? Are you okay?"

"I'm fine."

He caressed her face. "No, you're not."

"Okay, I'm not. But I don't want to bombard you with everything as soon as you walk in the door. Why don't you get comfortable and I'll get dinner started. We'll talk over food."

She turned to head back to the kitchen, but Isaac gently grabbed her arm, stopping her from retreating. He set the cat on the floor and then led Sidney over to the sectional sofa. When they sat down, he took both of her hands in his.

"Talk to me. What happened today?"

Sidney took a breath and tried to relax her shoulders. Why was she still so unsettled?

"Well, first I got a ticket this morning on the way to work."

"A ticket for what?"

Irritation crept into his voice, and Sidney withered a little.

She hated upsetting him.

And she hated herself for reacting this way. She knew her response had zero to do with him, and everything to do with her past abusive relationship. She was conditioned to cower to her significant other, and she hated that.

"The officer said that I made an improper lane change."

"And he wrote you a citation for that?"

"She. And yes, she did. But the upsetting part was that she pulled her gun and made me get out of the car. And she handcuffed me."

Isaac took a deep breath, and Sidney could see the vein in his temple bulge. He was pissed.

"You told her about your gun?"

"As soon as she came to the window, just like you said."

He nodded. "Was she gruff with you? Or unnecessarily an ass?"

"Well, she wasn't polite. But no, she wasn't an ass either."

"That's something at least. But I can't believe she actually wrote you a citation for an improper lane change. We never did that unless the person was driving erratically. We'd always just let them off with a warning. Did she see the FOP emblem on the car?"

"She did, and she asked who it belonged to. When I told her who my fiancé was, she kind of blanched and then just gave me my gun back and walked away."

"Yeah, that was her 'oops' moment. Improper lane change."

He mumbled and fussed under his breath for a few more minutes, and Sidney steeled herself for the conversation to come. Once he stopped venting and looked at her, she licked her lips.

"There's more?"

"Yes."

"You seem rattled, Sidney. What the hell happened?"

"Well, something else did happen today, but..."

"But what?"

"But I think I need to back up a few days and tell you something else first."

"Start wherever you need to, just tell me what's wrong."

"Okay so... you remember the night that Ann's husband showed up drunk and I pulled my gun on him?"

"Yes." He ran his thumb over the fading bruise on her cheek.

"Well, something else happened that night that I didn't tell you about."

Isaac's eyebrows scrunched into a frown, giving him an almost fierce appearance.

"What happened?"

"Lance Tobey, remember him?"

"The doctor that volunteers at Hope House? He bandaged the cut above your eye that night."

"Right, him. Well, even before that night I... I could tell that he was interested in me. He stares at me and always tries to engage me in conversation. Something about him gives me the creeps."

"What did he do?"

Sidney bit her bottom lip to stop it from trembling.

"He kissed me that night, after he bandaged my cut. It was totally unsolicited, and I put him in his place as firmly as I could."

"Did he try to force himself on you?"

Isaac's lips were a hard, thin line, the vein in his temple even more prominent.

"Just the kiss. I stood up and moved out of his reach. And then I blasted him, first because he knows I'm engaged, and then because he acted like an ass when I protested. I have not seen him since. Until today. Zoe called him about a sick resident, so he came this morning."

"And?"

"And, I purposely stayed in the office the whole time, so that I didn't have to speak to him or deal with him at all. But... well, once he was gone, Zoe brought in the mail."

"Go on."

"In the mailbox was a small package addressed to 'the future Mrs. Ike Taylor."

"Odd way to word that."

"I thought so too. Inside the package there was a mutilated stuffed animal with torn, dirty fur, and the eyes ripped off. And there was a huge hairy spider crawling around inside. Like a tarantula or something."

"What?"

Isaac sounded horrified.

Sidney stood on shaky legs and walked into the hallway where she'd left the box. She brought it back to the living room and handed it to him. It was still sealed inside the bag she'd placed it in earlier.

Isaac pulled a blue latex glove from his pocket and slipped it on. Then he unzipped the bag and pulled out the small box, opening it up with one hand. He carefully examined the contents — the mangled stuffed puppy, and the smashed spider.

"What the fuck kind of sick message is this supposed to be?"

"That's what I want to know."

"You say this spider was alive?"

"It was when I opened the box. Scared the shit out of me! When I dropped the box, he crawled out and I stomped on it."

"And you think this jilted doctor left this in the mailbox for you?"

"Well, he came to mind because he'd just been there. And there's no return address or even a post office stamp on the package."

"No, there isn't. So whoever it's from just placed it in the mailbox."

"That's what I was thinking."

"Who else has touched this box and the contents?"

"Well, Zoe brought it in from the mailbox. So just her and me. And whoever sent it."

"Good."

He put everything back into the box and returned the box to the bag.

"Get your things."

He stood and grabbed his keys.

"Where are we going?"

"Where do you think? I'm taking you and your little box of goodies here to the PD. With this, and the pictures I took of your slashed tires, we're going to file a harassment report."

Sidney sighed. "Not again."

"You know the drill, Sidney. We need a record of the escalating harassment in order to make a case."

"I know, I know. I just... I hate this step."

"Most people do, but it's necessary."

"Are you angry? About the kiss?"

Isaac stared at her, and for once Sidney felt like she couldn't read him. The expression on his handsome face was inscrutable.

"Did you kiss him back?"

"Hell no, I didn't kiss him back. I wanted to slap him!"

"Then yes, I am angry. But I'm not angry at you."

"I'm sorry that I didn't tell you that night."

"I am too. Because I want you to trust that you can tell me anything, always. You do know that, don't you?"

"Of course, I do."

"Good. But for the record, I'm also glad you didn't tell me that night, because the way I felt then, I might have turned the car around and gone back there to kick his ass."

Since she'd known him, he'd always been protective where she was concerned, but this was only the second time she'd ever heard him threaten to kick someone's ass. Both times over her.

In a way, it was comforting to know that this mild-mannered man who had drastic issues with physical touch, would be willing to get into an actual brawl with someone just to keep her safe. Weird, but it only made her love him more.

Once she got herself together, he took her by the hand and led her out to his car.

Sidney watched him while he drove. His jaw was tight, and he clutched the steering wheel like he was trying to strangle it. They drove straight to the police station where he worked, and Sidney held tight to his hand as they waited for the elevator. Inside it, he kept his eyes on the numbers overhead.

They got off on the fourth floor, and Sidney recognized it from when she was here once before. This was the detective section where Isaac worked.

Still holding her hand, he marched her through the area they called the pit.

"Hey, Ike. Didn't I just say goodbye to you at shift change?"

"Yeah, you did. But it turns out I got some business to take care of. Oh, hey. Palmer, this is my fiancée, Sidney Fairchild. Sidney, this is Sasha Palmer. She also works homicide."

"Hello." Sidney smiled at the woman.

"And that's her partner, Lynn Driscoll." Isaac motioned with a lift of his chin.

"Nice to finally meet you, Sidney," Lynn said, with a smile.

"Finally?" Sidney looked from one to the other.

"Well, we'd heard the rumors that 'Mr. Don't Touch Me,' here had a woman, but we didn't really believe it," Sasha said with a wink. "Now here you are."

"Yeah, yeah. You ladies are real funny. Get back to work."

"Will do, Sarge. Good to meet you, Sidney."

"You, too."

When they walked away, Sidney looked up at him.

"An all female detective team?"

"Yeah."

It was a statement of fact, but Sidney heard the question in that one little word.

"It just surprises me. Are they... effective? I mean, are they good at the job?"

"Palmer and Driscoll are an excellent detective team. Why do you ask?"

Sidney shrugged a shoulder, and a small wave of jealousy crashed through her belly.

"I just wonder sometimes if I could do your job. I know the answer to that is no."

"But why would you want to do my job, darlin'?"

"I wouldn't. It's not about that. I just... I wonder if I'd ever be brave enough."

"Brave enough?"

She nodded.

"You mean brave enough to take on a drunk irate husband at the women's shelter and knock him on his ass? Or you mean brave enough to take on the daunting task of helping that asshole's wife get away from him so that she and her kids can live a normal happy life without him beating the shit out of 'em every other day?"

Sidney looked up into his intense grey eyes and felt her chest swell just a little. How did he always know the right thing to say to make her feel good about herself?

"Trust me, Sidney. You are braver than you give yourself credit for."

She couldn't look away from his eyes. They held her in place.

"Sgt. Taylor?"

He looked away and the spell was broken. Sidney let out a long slow breath and followed him over to a desk manned by a red-haired man in his mid-thirties.

"Detective Casey, you got a minute?"

"Sure thing. What can I do for ya?"

"Well, it seems I've got myself something of a harassment case. And I thought about taking it to patrol, but what's the point of that when I know it's eventually going to end up here on the fourth floor anyway?"

"I see your point. Have a seat, Sarge. Whatcha got?"

Isaac motioned for Sidney to sit in the chair beside Casey's desk. Then she watched him pull over an empty chair and sit down beside her.

"Detective George Casey, this is my fiancée, Sidney Fairchild."

"Nice to meet you, ma'am."

"You, too." Sidney smiled at him and glanced at Isaac.

"Casey here works in the Violent Crimes division," Isaac told her before he turned back to Casey. "Now, Casey I know that this isn't violent yet, but it's escalating quickly, and I don't like the direction it's going, so..."

"I understand. Lay it out for me."

"Sid's been having some strange occurrences at work."

"I'm sorry to hear that, Sidney. What's been happening?"

She told him everything then. All about the deal with the slashed tires and the sick box of goodies. Isaac handed over the box and its contents as evidence, and even forwarded the pictures he'd taken of her slashed tires.

"And do we think this could be a coworker harassing you? Maybe someone that you had words with recently?" Casey asked.

Isaac looked at her, waiting for her to answer, and Sidney's stomach rolled.

"Actually there are two people that came to mind as possible culprits."

She explained then about Ann's angry husband, pointing to her fading bruise for reference. And she told him about Lance Tobey and how she'd jilted his affections. Detective Casey took their report and told them that he would look into it personally.

When they finally left the PD over an hour later, Sidney climbed into the car and crumpled with exhaustion. She sighed, and Ike started up the car.

"Here."

She looked up and he was holding out a slip of paper to her.

"What's this?"

She took the paper and unfolded it. A name and number.

That's all the information the paper contained. She looked Ike in the eyes.

"He's not cheap. But he does convincing work. And he's discreet."

Still puzzled, Sidney stared at him until his meaning became clear. This was the name and number of someone who could provide her with false papers to help Ann get away.

"Isaac..."

"This cannot come back to me in any way."

He cut her off before she could say anything more.

"So the less we discuss it, the better. Just be careful, Sid."

"I will."

She knew the position she was putting him in. She knew how difficult it was for him to watch her willfully do something against the law. And she knew that she loved him even more for his willingness to help her however he could.

She strapped on her seatbelt, and he pulled out into traffic without another word. In fact, the further he drove, the longer his silence stretched, and Sidney wondered what was going on inside his mind.

She couldn't blame him. She had done a lot lately to upset him. She knew that he wasn't happy about her decision to help Ann get away from her abuser. And he really hated that she was going to be doing business with criminals in order to help Ann. Now he had an image of her kissing another man in his head.

"Let's face it, Sid. He isn't talking because he's angry. He can't even look at you."

Those thoughts tore her up as they drove on in silence.

Was he really so angry that he couldn't talk or look at her right now?

She sighed and turned her gaze out the window.

Isaac took her hand.

Birds took flight and angels sang songs.

She looked at him, and he kept his eyes on the road. But he

held her hand as he drove on, lightly rubbing his thumb over her skin.

She smiled and glanced out the window again. This time with a lighter heart.

Suddenly it dawned on her that they were heading out of Cleveland.

"Isaac? Where are we going?"

She asked the question more than once. His only response was a quick glance at her from behind the wheel.

She had no clue what to make of it. And she had no clue where they were. Glancing around, she didn't recognize anything. Not a single landmark. Finally, she couldn't take it anymore.

"Isaac. Please tell me where we're going.

"We're here."

She glanced around again.

"Where?"

"Woodmere."

"Woodmere?"

She'd heard of it. She knew it was a village in Cuyahoga County, about half an hour from downtown Cleveland. But she'd never had occasion to go there before.

"What are we doing in Woodmere?"

"Coming here."

She glanced out the window as he pulled to a stop in front of Tiffany & Co. Then her gaze shot back to him.

"Well, obviously I need to put a ring on it so that other men will back the hell off. I need to tag you as taken."

The southern drawl that became more prominent when he was excited or agitated made his words sweeter than honey, and Sidney smiled at him.

"We're ring shopping?"

"I'm sorry that I didn't do this sooner, Sid. With everything going on, it just kept slippin' my mind. It's certainly not because I don't want to marry you. I'd rush you off to Vegas tonight if you'd let me."

"I know that. And I wasn't worried about not having a ring yet. I knew we'd eventually get to it."

"Well, we're getting to it right now. I want all the men in the world to know that you are no longer available."

He got out of the car and came around to open her door. Sidney couldn't wipe the silly grin off her face as he took her hand and led her into the store.

"Good evening. May I help you?"

The woman was impeccably dressed and very polite as she smiled at them.

"Yes, we're in the market for an engagement ring," Isaac told her.

"Wonderful, congratulations!"

"Thank you."

Giddy ripples of happiness and joy fluttered in her belly. She was the best kind of lightheaded and she loved it.

"Let me show you to our wedding collection."

They followed the woman to the back of the store where she waved a sweeping hand over a long glass case.

"Please feel free to browse. I'm here if you have any questions, or if you find one — or a few — that you'd like to try on."

"Thank you," they said in unison.

The woman walked away, and Isaac turned to her.

"Pick out whatever you want."

"Whatever I want?"

Surely he didn't mean that.

"Whatever you want."

Sidney narrowed her eyes at him and then turned to the glass case. There were so many beautiful rings in all shapes, sizes, and colors of dazzling. It was as if someone had captured the stars and put them under glass.

She started at the far end and moved slowly down the long

case, meandering away from the larger, more ostentatious stones. What did she need with a seven-carat sparkler worthy of Elizabeth Taylor? She didn't need anything nearly that fancy. When it came to jewelry, she was much more of a dainty kind of girl. In fact, she could make do with something small and inexpensive. Something simple and modest. Something...

Oh!

Her gaze and her forward movement stopped. Both snagged on the sweetest, most lovely ring she'd ever seen.

"Something catch your eye, darlin'?"

"Hmm? Oh, well... I just..."

"Find something you'd like to try on?"

Their helpful saleswoman was back, and before Sidney could stop her, she had the back of the case opened with her key.

"Which one can I show you?"

"Oh. Well, I just thought it was pretty, but I don't need to try it on."

"Nonsense." Isaac looked at her with a frown. "Sidney, we're here to get you an engagement ring, and I want you to have something you love. Which one caught your eye?"

"That one there," she pointed. "In the middle."

The saleswoman pulled out the ring with a knowing smile.

"You have excellent tastes. A two carat, cushion cut diamond set in a delicate half carat pavé diamond band, for a total of 2.5 carats. This one is white gold, but we also have it in rose gold, yellow gold, and platinum. Do you know your ring size?"

It took Sidney a moment to register the question.

"Um, yes. I wear a size five."

The woman checked the ring and smiled.

"What a coincidence. This is a five. It must be fate."

She handed the ring to Sidney, but Isaac quickly took it from her.

"I botched it the first time, so I want to do this properly."

He took her hand and knelt down before her on one knee.

Sidney bit her bottom lip, but it was no use. The tears came anyway.

"Sidney Fairchild, will you marry me?"

A hush fell over the store. Even the walls waited with bated breath.

"Yes, I will marry the crap out of you!"

The three salespeople on duty and the sprinkling of customers all erupted into polite applause and smiles, and Isaac slipped the gorgeous ring onto her finger.

It fit like it was meant to be there.

Isaac stood and looked down at her. Placing his fingers at her chin he lifted her gaze up to him and kissed her lips.

"You happy with it?"

"Yes, I am. But Isaac, we can't get this ring."

"Why not? You love it."

"I do love it, it's so beautiful. But it's too much."

"What do you mean?"

"Isaac!" She glanced at the saleswoman, who lowered her head and took a step back to give them some privacy. "Did you happen to get a glimpse of the price tag?"

"Yeah, I saw it."

He sounded so cavalier about it.

"That's it? You saw it?"

"Yes."

"Ike, this ring is over $9,000 dollars."

"I know how much it costs, Sidney. And it's okay."

"It's okay?"

"Yes."

She opened her mouth to say more, but she had no words. She also had no delusions about what Isaac made on a police salary. She knew his new promotion to sergeant had come with a pay raise, but that raise couldn't have been much.

"Sidney, listen to me."

Isaac pulled out one of the stools situated next to the glass case and sat her down. Then he sat down next to her and took both her hands in his and looked into her eyes.

"Before you came into my life, I spent a lot of lonely years living like a hermit. I did my job, and I put my money in the bank. I had a nice TV. A car. But I didn't spend my money going out, or going on trips and all that kind of thing. And you of all people can attest to the fact that I didn't splurge on my living space back then."

Sidney giggled as thoughts of his old dingy one-bedroom apartment sprang to mind.

"Now, I may not ever come close to being in my brother, Adam's, tax bracket. But I actually do have a nice cushiony nest egg saved up. And it has more than enough to cover our wedding rings. Okay?"

Those light grey eyes flashed at her in that way that always made her insides feel like jelly. The dimple heavy smile made her swoon. Damn he was fine.

And he was all hers.

"Okay."

He turned to the saleswoman and gave her a taste of that million-dollar smile.

"May we see some wedding bands that would go great with this ring?"

"Certainly. Will you be needing a band as well, sir?"

"Yes. And if it could match her band, that would be perfect."

21

"Pete says they have to qualify on the shooting range twice a year. It's like a big test to make sure they can still shoot good and hit their target."

Charlie sounded like he knew all about it.

"And if they don't pass the test, they can't carry a gun anymore. It means they lose their jobs."

"So? Why do you care?"

Mateo just sounded annoyed.

"I just think it's kinda cool is all."

"Like you know what cool is."

"Pete's a great shot, so he doesn't worry about it. He shoots almost as good with his weak hand as he does with his dominant hand. The S.W.A.T. Team captain even asked him to think about joining the team, but Pete wasn't interested."

"I know he's a good shot, okay. He is *my* uncle!"

Mateo's tone was defensive, and Pete glanced up into the rearview mirror, scoping out the scene in the backseat.

"I know he's your uncle. You don't have to keep telling me. That's like the third time you've said that."

"Well how 'bout you just shut up about him. You act like he's your dad. Like you're in love with him or something."

"Hey. We don't tell each other to shut up." Pete raised his voice and realized he'd been doing that a lot tonight.

"I do not!"

"You do too."

The argument continued, like Pete hadn't said a word.

"Do not!"

"Quit acting like such a baby!"

"I don't act like a baby!"

"Yeah, ya do."

"Do not!"

"Do not, do not, " Mateo mocked. "That's exactly what babies say."

"No, it isn't. And I'm not a baby!"

"Well, you sure cry like one."

Pete gripped the steering wheel. He was ready to scream.

They had done nothing but argue the entire night, and he wasn't sure what he was more tired of — hearing their constant bickering about the stupidest things, or having to get after them for it.

Since his conversation with Ike about the boys needing to spend more time getting used to each other, Pete had decided to try and ease them into that. So he'd suggested taking both the boys out for a movie and pizza.

Jada had loved the idea. She'd even praised Pete for being thoughtful and caring. He'd felt like a hero.

But the bickering had begun almost from the moment he and Mateo had picked Jada and Charlie up for their date. They argued over who was in who's space in the back seat on the way to the theater. They argued over which snacks to buy and which seats to choose at the theater. After the movie, they argued over which of the ninjas was the greatest. They argued over pizza toppings, and soft drinks, and radio stations, and, and, and...

His head was pounding. He'd spent the night playing referee, verbally pushing each of them back to their respective corners. And Jada didn't even seem to notice. Occasionally, she would interject with a calm word that seemed to stop both boys in their tracks. Sanity and quiet would prevail for several minutes, and then the bickering would begin again.

It was a vicious cycle that Pete was ill equipped to handle.

What had he been thinking?

Was he nuts for even attempting to make them a foursome?

The boys obviously hated each other, so maybe it was just as well that they didn't try this again.

He pulled to the curb out front of Jada's house and parked the car with a heavy sigh. Then he turned around and stared at them.

"Boys!"

The bickering stopped and both boys looked at him.

"Time for the arguing to stop. Jada and Charlie are home."

Jada turned in the passenger seat and smiled at Mateo.

"Goodnight Mateo. I'm so happy you came out with us tonight. This was a lot of fun! Maybe you'd like to do it again sometime?"

Mateo shrugged his shoulders and stared at her, his expression saying things Pete couldn't make out.

"Sure."

"Great! You have a good night, okay?"

"Okay."

She shot a hopeful look Pete's way, and Pete wondered how she managed to do that. He got out of the car and opened the door for her. That was important to him — to show both of the boys by example the way to treat a lady.

He helped her out of the car, and Charlie shot out of the back seat.

"Here, Charlie." Jada handed the boy the house key. "What do you say to Pete?"

"Thanks for the movie and pizza, Pete. It was fun!"

The kid ran ahead to the house, giving Pete a moment alone with Jada.

"It was fun?"

Jada laughed. "Yes, it was. Charlie enjoyed it. I think they both did."

"How can you say that? The boys did nothing but argue."

"Oh, they acted like kids. They're fine."

He blew a huff of air through his lips.

"Well, I'm exhausted from playing referee all night."

Jada placed her hands on his chest and looked into his eyes.

"Pete, you've got to relax and stop trying to force this. Dinner the other night went really well. Your mom and I found common ground, and I think we even bonded a little bit. And the boys are just boys. They'll figure it out."

Pete wrapped his arms around her and pulled her close.

"I just want the boys to be as crazy about each other as I am about you. That's all. Something tells me that being around you and Charlie might be a good thing for Mateo. I just want it to work out."

"And it will. But you've got to let it happen naturally."

Pete sighed and leaned in to kiss her lips.

She placed her hands on either side of his face.

His hand slid down her backside as their kiss deepened, and her back hit the closed front door. Pete pinned her there, his lips moving across her skin to her ear.

Her soft sigh at his ear shot straight down to his dick.

And then the car horn sounded, making them both jump.

"I'm going to kill that kid."

Jada giggled. "I have to go inside anyway."

Pete groaned. They still hadn't resumed the sexual side of their relationship yet — mostly because Charlie was always around — but Pete knew the day was zooming closer.

He kissed her once more and then stepped back. Jada opened

the door and stepped inside. She waved to him and blew him a kiss before she closed the door.

He walked back to the car in a haze of love, confusion, and frustration.

He slid behind the wheel and started up the car, glancing to the passenger seat where Mateo now sat.

Before he even pulled onto the street, he was already giving his nephew an earful.

"Could you have been any ruder tonight?"

"Would it have killed you to smile at least once? Or maybe *pretend* to have a good time?"

"Jada was being so nice to you. Couldn't you have responded in more than one syllable grunts?"

"Everything that came out of Charlie's mouth, you pounced on. You never gave the kid a break!"

Mateo never responded.

Not one word.

He just slumped down in the seat and looked out the window.

By the time he pulled into the driveway of their house, Pete felt like a heel for laying into him. Jada was right. He had to stop trying so hard. And he had to stop making Mateo the bad guy. They would never become the foursome he wanted if Mateo felt bad about it, right?

"Ah, you're home. *Como estuvo la pelicula?*" Julieta asked as soon as they walked into the house. How was the movie?

"It was good," Mateo responded in his typical teenaged monotone. He walked over and kissed his grandmother on the cheek. "I'm going to bed."

He turned for the stairs without another word.

Pete watched him go and flopped down on the couch.

"Algo salió mal?"

He stared at her.

"Did something go bad? Uh, yeah... I think so. The boys bickered and argued all night long. The only time they didn't was during the movie. They fought over everything, even what pizza toppings we should order, and which ninja in the movie was the greatest."

Julieta smiled. "Sounds like they had a great time."

Was she for real?

"That is exactly what Jada said. But the bickering drove me nuts! I couldn't relax and have a good time because I was so worried about their constant arguing."

"*Mijo*, kids are just like adults. They need to feel each other out a bit. And they do that by bickering and pushing each other's buttons. It's how they relate to the world and each other while they're learning how to become adults. Remember the way you and Paulina used to argue?"

Those words brought a torrent of memories, good and bad, rushing to his mind, and he couldn't help but smile.

Back in the day, his big sister had been his best friend in the world. But there were times when they would fight like dogs and cats from hell — screaming at each other, bickering, trading punches and barbs.

He stood and bent over to kiss Julieta on the cheek.

"Gracias, mamá."

"For what?"

"For reminding me what it's like to be a kid. Good night."

"Buenos noches, mijo." Goodnight my son.

Pete left her and went upstairs. He stopped at Mateo's door and knocked.

"Yeah?"

He opened the door and stuck his head in.

"Hey. Can I come in for a minute?"

Mateo sat up from his reclining position on top of the covers and lowered his headphones. He gave Pete a withering look, and Pete closed the door behind him and pulled over the straight-backed chair from Mateo's desk. He turned it around backwards and straddled it to sit down.

"Listen... I want to apologize for my rant on the way home. I want you to know that it had nothing to do with you. That was all about me being a nervous wreck over this whole thing."

Mateo gave him that same expressionless stare he'd given Jada, and Pete watched it slowly morph into curiosity.

"What whole thing? Why are you nervous?"

Pete sighed. "I just need to remember that, just because I love Jada, I can't expect you and Charlie to get along right off the bat. Or at all, really. No matter how much I may want you to."

Mateo twisted his lips and looked down at the bedspread, and Pete could see his mind working. He really wished the kid would be more forthcoming with his thoughts because trying to guess was getting Pete nowhere.

"I like Charlie okay."

It was a mumble delivered with the signature shoulder shrug, and Pete was left open-mouth-shocked.

"You do?"

He could hear the blatant disbelief in his own voice.

"Yeah. I suppose he's like an annoying little brother, maybe. I always thought it might be kinda cool to have one. Tonight I got to know what it'd be like. It was kinda fun."

Pete stared at him, still trying to understand exactly what had happened tonight.

"Wait, so... are you telling me that you actually enjoyed tonight? You had fun?"

"Charlie and me had a lot of fun. That's why I didn't understand when you started yelling at me on the way home. I didn't know what I did wrong."

Mateo sounded forlorn, and that was a punch to Pete's heart.

"Charlie and *I*."

"Charlie and I," Mateo repeated.

"And you didn't do anything wrong, Mateo. I wasn't yelling at you. I mean, I was, but... But I'm sorry about it. I didn't mean to make you feel bad."

Mateo looked at him with what Pete could only describe as puppy dog eyes, and it did something to him.

"Sooo... how come Charlie knows so much about police stuff, and how you're a good shot and all that? You never tell me that kind of stuff."

Mateo's question was laced with a hefty dose of jealousy, and Pete looked him in the eyes.

"Well, that's because Charlie's always asking me questions about being a police officer. He wants to hear my stories about different things like the shooting range, and what it's like to arrest people, and if I've ever had someone shoot at me. Things like that. Lately, you don't seem to care much for my job, so I don't talk about it with you."

"Oh."

Mateo looked down at the bedspread again, and Pete watched him.

"I think your job is cool."

"You do?"

He found that hard to believe. But then he remembered the way Mateo had questioned Ike during dinner, asking him all sorts of police related questions.

Mateo nodded.

"Some of my friends... well, my old friends. They didn't like cops. But I think that's because they were always doing bad stuff."

"I think you're right about that. And I gotta say, I'm glad you're not hanging out with those guys anymore. I know the things they do look cool and they seem like badasses, but... they're not going to be so cool in prison. And that's where most of them are heading."

"I know."

"You're smarter than that, Mateo. The way you love to read and draw. You can be anything you want to be, if you work hard enough."

"Do you really believe that?"

"Hell, yeah, I believe it. I believe in you. You got the smarts and the talent to be anything you want to be."

Mateo's gaze drifted around his room, and Pete smiled when he saw a spark of curiosity and wonder in the boy's eyes. The sight ignited the strangest flame of hope and pride in his chest. Where the hell had that come from?

"Well, I've got to work in the morning. You get some sleep."

He was about to stand when Mateo surprised him with another question.

"Uncle Pete?"

"Yeah?"

"Are you going to marry Jada?"

Pete's butt hit the seat of the chair with a soft thud, and all the air left his lungs.

The kid could sure surprise him with the things that came out of his mouth sometimes.

But this wasn't about Jada. Not really. He understood that now.

This was about him and his nephew. What was it his mom had said about him thinking in terms of being Mateo's guardian some day?

He licked his lips and looked Mateo in the eyes.

"Whether I do or not makes no difference, Mateo. Because you and I are a package deal. Where I go, you go."

Mateo's lips twisted into a pout again.

"That's not true. Grandma is my guardian. Not you."

There was nothing Pete could say to refute that. Julieta was his legal guardian. And maybe it was time they looked into that.

"I'm not going anywhere, Mateo. No matter what happens, you are stuck with me, kid. Okay?"

"Okay."

Pete left Mateo's room and went back downstairs to the living room where Julieta sat knitting and watching TV. She looked up and smiled at him.

"I thought you were going to bed, *mijo*."

"I am, but I wanted to talk to you about something first."

"Qué es?" What is it?

"How would you feel if..." He hesitated and wondered if she would be offended by the suggestion. Maybe he should leave it alone.

"Pedro? If what?"

"What would you think if I suggested we look into transferring legal guardianship of Mateo over to me?"

Julieta stared up at him for a long moment, and Pete wondered what his mother was thinking. Finally she set her knitting aside and looked into his eyes.

"Are you sure about this?"

Pete sat down beside her.

"I've just been thinking that it might help Mateo to know that he's stuck with me forever. No matter what, you know? I mean, you were saying that he needs to know that his place in my life is permanent. And I want to show him that he's not a burden to me. That this is something I want."

A slow smile spread across Julieta's face, and Pete thought he saw a mixture of pride and relief in his mother's eyes.

"I think that's a wonderful idea, *mijo*."

"Yeah?"

"Yes."

"Are you sure, *mamá?* Because I don't want to step on your toes or take Mateo away from you or make Paulina angry or anything. I only want what's best for Mateo."

"I know that, Pedro. And Paulina will see that too, eventually. But honestly... she has no room to object. Even if she did, there's nothing she can do about it from behind bars, is there?"

"I don't think so. But I'll have a lawyer look into it."

"Dad? Seriously, take a deep breath and chill. *Please!*"

They sat in a booth near the back window in the greasy diner Trey loved. Gavin's heart pounded in his chest like he was beating a big bass drum.

Trey was right. He needed to chill out. Badly. But he couldn't seem to take in a breath deep enough to make his heart slow down.

God, what had this woman done to him?

He looked down at the table and clasped his hands together on top of it.

He felt ridiculous. Like a twenty-something bringing a girl home to meet his folks for the first time.

"I'm not so sure this was a good idea."

"It's gonna be fine, Dad. Why are you being so weird about it?"

"Because it's a weird situation, Trey. Do you know how long it's been since I even went out on an actual date? And now I'm sitting here in a diner with my nearly grown son, waiting for my... my... aw, hell, I don't even know what to call her!"

"Girlfriend." Trey's tone was teasing. "We call them *girlfriends*."

"Very funny, wise guy."

"Well..."

"Yeah. Just wait until you bring someone home to meet your old man in a year or two. Then we'll talk about this day."

Trey laughed at him, and Gavin shook his head. Then his gaze fell on the front entrance just as the door opened and Gerri Miller stepped in. The bells over the door chimed, and it was like music from heaven heralding her arrival.

Still unable to take a proper deep breath, Gavin huffed air from his chest and stood. She was dressed in a white skirt that sported a jagged hemline that danced around her calves, and a matching top. Her hair hung loose around her shoulders, and Gavin realized that he'd never seen her this way before — all feminine and sweet and girly.

She walked toward him with a smile.

"Hi."

"Hi, yourself. You look amazing."

He leaned in and kissed her lips, not giving a damn that his son was watching their every move.

"Thank you."

He gestured to the booth and stepped aside so that she could slide in across from Trey. Then he slid in beside her.

"Um, you remember my son, Trey."

"Of course." She smiled at him and stretched out her hand. "Good to see you again, Trey."

"Yeah. You, too."

"And thank you for the dinner invitation. Your dad said this was your idea."

"No problem. Thanks for coming. And thanks for making my dad goofy."

Gavin shot him a look.

"Who you calling goofy?"

"You!" Trey shot back. Then he turned to Gerri and flipped a thumb in Gavin's direction. "I've never actually seen my dad this happy and goofy before you."

Gavin chuckled. But then a strange look came over Trey's face and Gavin suddenly wondered what the boy was thinking about. Trey fixed him with a curious stare, the kind of stare that makes you want to rethink your whole life.

"I guess I never really knew the truth, did I?"

"What do you mean, Trey?"

"I never realized before that you and mom... your marriage wasn't a very happy one, was it?"

Gavin was shocked his son was finally asking that question. He was even more shocked to be having this conversation in front of Gerri. But he would never lie to his son. He slowly shook his head.

"No. No it wasn't. In fact... the only good thing that came out of it was you."

Trey was silent for a moment. Then he slapped on a smile and looked Gavin in the eyes.

"Well, it's good finally seeing you this happy, Dad. It looks good on you."

Underneath the table, Gerri grabbed Gavin's hand and gave it a light squeeze. Gavin looked into her eyes for a moment and then he gave her hand an answering squeeze.

"Hello, everyone. Here are menus." The waiter handed them each a menu to look over.

Trey looked at Gerri.

"You're not a vegetarian are you, Gerri?"

"Nope. Bring on the meat."

"Well then you're in for a treat. This place makes the best cheeseburgers in the world!"

"Is that so?"

"It is."

"Your dad tells me you love this place."

"Oh, my God, they're so good!"

"Good, because I'm starving."

Gavin looked at her. "*You're* starving?"

"I am."

"After all the times I've had to practically tie you down to get you to eat. Now, you're starving?"

"In my defense, I wasn't at my best when you were trying to get me to eat. Besides, I'm told this place has the best burgers in the world."

Gavin laughed, and when the other two joined in, he felt his body letting go of the anxiety. This was going to be the best dinner date ever.

———

Emmett Fox pulled up outside a brown brick house in Kamm's Corners. Something about the cookie-cutter nature of all the cute little brick homes reminded him of gingerbread houses. A whole neighborhood of gingerbread. Not that he typically paid attention to such things, but he'd be willing to bet that at Christmastime the whole neighborhood would look like a candy land with colored lights everywhere.

He checked his appearance in the rearview mirror and fought against the flutter of butterflies in his stomach. His level of nervousness tonight had him truly undone. He couldn't explain it. He didn't get nervous about this type of thing. Women didn't make him nervous. In fact, nothing much did.

Maybe chasing down killers.

Certainly, gunfights.

Never women.

Not until tonight anyway. Not until Emily Taylor.

Just the thought of her had him keyed up and he had no clue why.

Maybe because he'd flubbed their last attempt at a first date so badly, and then had to call her brother to gage Emily's level of pissed.

He shoved that thought aside and got out of the car and made his way to the front door wondering if he should've taken the time to press his jeans. Not that they were wrinkled or anything. The thought made him roll his eyes, and he reached out and rang the bell before he could obsess over his attire anymore.

The door swung open, and he stared into her bright blue eyes and sweet smile. He'd almost forgotten how gorgeous she was.

Golden waves framed her lovely face and she looked like an angel staring back at him. His gaze traveled down, taking in the short, pale yellow dress with tiny pink and red flowers on it. The thin straps exposed her bare shoulders, and his gaze drifted lower to her bare legs and high-heeled sandals. Wow was the only word registering in his mind, but he swallowed it down in an effort not to embarrass himself.

"Hi."

She smiled at him, and his self-control evaporated.

"Wow."

It was all he could say.

Emily frowned and looked down at her dress.

"Is this okay? You didn't indicate a dress code or anything."

Emmett hesitated, forcing his mind and his mouth to work together.

"You look amazing."

"Thanks."

She smiled at him again, and Emmett fought to pull himself together. This woman made him stupid, and that had never happened to him before.

"Let me just grab my purse."

She disappeared for a few seconds, and he silently chastised himself for acting like a moron. When she returned and stepped out the door, she was carrying a small purse and wearing a short denim jacket.

"So, where are we going, G-man?"

Emmett grinned at the term. "How do you feel about pizza?"

"Pizza?"

He could tell from the sound of her voice that it wasn't what she'd been expecting.

"I love a good pizza. When I first got this posting, I was overjoyed to find a place that makes the most delicious pizza. It's called Niccolo."

"Hmm. I've never been."

She sounded skeptical and Emmett thought about choosing someplace else. He really wanted this date to go well.

"Well, they have a great dinner menu too if pizza's not your thing."

"No. Pizza sounds great."

She smiled, but she sounded less than convinced. Emmett led her to the car and opened the door for her. Before she got in, she picked up a single long-stemmed pink rose he'd left on the passenger seat and looked up at him.

His whole face heated up like an oven.

"Oh. I got that for you. I thought maybe a full bouquet would be too much for a first date, but a single rose was classier. And then I forgot to bring it to the door with me."

The smile that slid over her slightly pouty lips lit up her pretty face, and his fluttering heart.

"I'm a little nervous," he admitted.

"I didn't think G-men got nervous."

"Well, this one does. Especially tonight."

"I'm going to take that as a compliment, Agent Fox."

"As you most certainly should, Ms. Taylor."

He watched her sexy legs fold into the car, and once he was behind the wheel they pulled out into traffic. Their drive to the restaurant was peppered with polite chit chat about nothing — the weather, their workday. Then he quietly cleared his throat and glanced at her.

"I want to apologize again for canceling the last time we were scheduled to do this. It's just this big case we've been working on. It's gotten crazy real fast, and I'm..."

"It's okay, Emmett. Really. I know how important your work is."

"Thanks for being understanding."

When they were finally at the restaurant and seated at a secluded table in the corner Emily looked around with an assessing gaze.

"Well I don't know what the food is like, but it smells wonderful in here."

Emmett smiled at her. "I know, right?"

"Welcome. Can I get you something to drink?"

They looked up at their waiter and Emmett motioned to Emily.

"A glass of red wine, please."

"You know what... why don't you just bring us a bottle of merlot?" Emmett glanced at her for approval, and she smiled, which gave him a huge measure of relief.

"Very good." The waiter nodded. "And are we ready to order, or would you like some time?"

"We don't need time." Emily spoke up, surprising him. And then she shocked him even more when her blue eyes met his. "What's your favorite pie here?"

Emmett smiled. "Well, you can't go wrong with the supreme. Sausage, pepperoni, and veggies. Simple, but out of this world."

"Perfect."

They ordered a large supreme, and once the waiter was gone Emily turned to him.

"So... you're not from Cleveland, are you?"

Emmett shook his head.

"I'm not even from Ohio. I was born in upstate New York, raised in Boulder, Colorado. Studied biology at Yale. Turned down a spot at Harvard Medical School and joined the FBI instead."

"Wow." Emily sounded impressed.

"My father was not pleased."

She seemed intrigued. "So, why'd you do it? Why the FBI?"

Emmett sighed and thought back on that time in his life. "I don't know. It was just that... no matter how hard I tried, I just couldn't see myself in a hospital setting. Practicing medicine. Holding people's lives in my hands. My ego is not big enough for that job."

Emily laughed out loud and he smiled at the sound of it.

"What? Why's that funny to you?"

"It's nothing. Just... don't ever say that to my dad or my oldest brother, okay?"

An embarrassed groan escaped him.

"Let me guess. Doctors. Both of them."

"Yep."

He chuckled. "Thanks for the warning."

The waiter set their glasses on the table and poured their wine. Then he left the bottle on the table. They thanked him in unison as he walked away.

"Yeah, my dad's a doctor too. That's why he was pissed when I walked off that path."

Emily took a sip of her wine.

"Mmm. My dad got one of us to follow, so I guess he's happy."

"What kind of medicine are they in?"

Emmett studied her face, fascinated by the way her nose crinkled when she talked.

"Daddy's in sports medicine. He works for the Cleveland Indians organization, although he keeps threatening to retire."

"Really? That's cool."

She shrugged a shoulder. "If you're into that sort of thing."

He smiled at her disinterest.

"Not a baseball fan?"

"Sports aren't really my thing. My brothers are mad for all things sports related though. Indians, Cavs. Even the Browns. They love them all."

"And how many brothers do you have exactly?"

"Three. Adam... he's the doctor. An orthopedic surgeon. Married to the sweetest Suzy Homemaker you ever want to meet, and just had his first child. Then there's Isaac, whom you know all about. And finally Oliver, the photographer." She smiled at her rhyme. "And also my twin."

"Twins! Really?"

"Yep. I'm older by eight whole minutes."

Emmett laughed. "So are you two close? That's probably a silly question, huh?"

Emily nodded her head from side to side as if weighing his question.

"Mmm. Somewhat. We were very close when we were little. And we do often do that twin thing where I'll get a mysterious bout of achiness and chills, for example, and come to find out, he's the one who has the flu. But our lives have taken different twists and turns though."

"How so?"

"Well, Oli likes to live life on the fringe. His friends aren't what I would call criminals exactly, but they're not really people I'd care to hang out with either."

"That's too bad. But he was at Ike's house though, wasn't he? The night we met?"

"Yeah, he was there."

"So he does come around sometimes?"

"He does. He and Ike recently had a breakthrough. A thawing of tensions, if you will."

"Hmm. Bad blood between them?"

"Not exactly bad blood. It's just that Isaac's always been a little... well... self-contained. It's because of the whole psychic thing, you know? The pain that comes when he touches others sometimes. It's kept him sort of on guard for most of his life. Kept him from really getting close with anyone, family included. In fact, until meeting Sidney, Ike's been like this tragic figure for as long as I can remember."

Emily sounded as though she felt sad for what her brother had been through, and it was Emmett's turn to be intrigued. Although he couldn't help but feel like he was prying into Ike's personal life.

"I can't even imagine," he said quietly.

"It's only been recently that he's become more comfortable in his own skin, you know what I mean?"

She looked up at him, and Emmett nodded.

"I think finding Sidney had a lot to do with it. Well, that and reconnecting with our grandpa, who has the same weird psychic abilities, if you can believe that."

Their pizza arrived at their table, piping hot and smelling delicious, and their conversation was halted for a few moments as she served them each a large slice. Emmett took the time to reflect on the interesting things she'd shared about her family — and about Ike in particular. But he wanted to know more about her.

"Oh, my God. Mmm." The exclamation was uttered around a mouthful of pizza. "You're right. This pizza is incredible!"

He smiled at her.

"Didn't I tell ya?"

After a bite of his own, Emmett looked at her.

"So, tell me about Emily Taylor. What's she like?"

Emily smiled and set her slice of pizza down and wiped her hands with a napkin before picking up her wine glass.

"Oh, she's a world of contradictions, that one."

"Oh, yeah?"

"Yeah."

Both her expression and her voice were full of mock gravity, and Emmett grinned.

"She's silly, but also serious and business minded. Intelligent, but also spontaneous and fun-loving. Girly, but also raised with three brothers, and therefore more than capable of burping the alphabet, and making crude noises with her armpit."

Her words brought Emmett up short and he stared at her.

Then he laughed harder than he'd laughed in a long time, nearly doubling over with the best kind of stomach spasms.

He wiped tears from his eyes and said, "I think I'm going to enjoy getting to know her."

22

"Oh, come on. You've got to be fucking kidding me!"

Sidney sighed and pulled her car to the curb, putting an end to the blaring siren. The flashing lights continued though, as the black and white police cruiser pulled in behind her.

She lowered her window and placed her hands firmly on the steering wheel, thoughts of yesterday morning's humiliating handcuff and car search events swirling in her mind.

The male officer approached her window and Sidney smiled at him.

"Good morning, officer. I have a Concealed Weapons Permit, and my gun is in my purse."

"Thank you for the information, ma'am. Can I get you to step out of the car and put your hands on your head, please?"

"Yep."

Sidney did as she was told, holding her tongue the whole time the officer instructed her to turn around and place her hands on the trunk of her car. He performed a quick and unceremonious pat down of her body.

"Where is your purse, ma'am."

"On the passenger side floor."

"Thank you. Stay here."

He retrieved her purse, extracting the gun, her permit, and her license. Then he approached her again.

"All right, ma'am. Your CWP appears to be in order. And I do see that you have an FOP emblem on your back plate, here. Who does that belong to?"

"My fiancé. Detective Sgt. Isaac Taylor of the third precinct."

"Very good, ma'am."

"That would be your precinct too, is that right? Officer Garfield?"

Sidney glanced at the name tag on his uniform.

When his cheeks pinked up like she'd slapped him, she felt a small measure of satisfaction. Too bad she hadn't thought to ask the same question of the female officer from yesterday.

"Yes, ma'am, this area of the city is in the third precinct, and I'm aware who Detective Sgt. Taylor is."

His chest seemed to deflate a little, and his gaze dropped down to the citation booklet in his hands before he looked her in the eyes again.

"I pulled you over because you failed to come to a complete stop back there at the stop sign. I normally write citations for that, but out of respect for Sgt. Taylor I'm going to let you go with a warning today. Just make sure you pay better attention while you're driving."

He tore a page out of his citation book and handed it to her.

Sidney took the slip of paper from him.

"Of course. Thank you, officer Garfield."

He gave her a quick nod and handed over her purse. Then he got back in his cruiser and drove off.

Sidney stood there for a few moments, staring at the ground.

Twice in so many days.

Coincidence?

She'd stopped at that stop sign.

She was sure of it. So, what the hell was going on?

She got back in her car and continued on to work, fuming the whole way. She walked into Hope House completely distracted by the puzzling encounter, and wondering if the one from yesterday had anything to do with this one today. Mostly she wondered what the hell it all meant.

"Everything okay?"

She looked up at the sound of Zoe's voice.

"I'm sorry, what?"

"Well, you slammed that drawer closed with a lot of force. Who are we mad at?"

Sidney stared at her and then looked down at her desk where she'd just put her purse away in the bottom drawer.

"Sorry."

"What's wrong?"

Sidney sighed. "Nothing. Just a frustrating morning. Traffic and crap."

"You sure?"

"Yes. I'm sure." Then she smiled and crossed the room to Zoe's desk. "Can I help you with anything this morning?"

She held out her left hand in a dramatic fashion, rocking it back and forth so that the stone could catch the light.

Zoe's lips formed a perfect O, but no sound came out. Then she reached for Sidney's hand, bringing it closer for a better look.

"Sidney! It's stunning. Oh, do you love it?"

"I do! It's so gorgeous I can't stand it."

"How did he give it to you? Was it romantic?"

"He gave it to me like a rock star. Or an actor, or some other wealthy millionaire type."

"What do you mean?"

"Well, it started off as a really crappy night because I told him all about the strange package that came for me..."

"Eww! I'd almost forgotten about that."

"Yeah, well, when I showed it to Ike, he took me immediately to the police station to file a harassment report."

"That was probably a good idea, don't you think?"

"I suppose. But anyway... on to the good part."

"Okay!"

"So, we left the PD and he just started driving. And he wasn't saying much, so I assumed that he was really upset. And I kept asking him where we were going. Finally he stops the car in Woodmere, of all places, right in front of Tiffany & Co."

"No!"

"Yes! He said that he obviously needed to put a ring on it so that other men would back the hell off. His words."

"You told him about the kiss."

"I did."

"Wow."

"Well, I felt like I had to. Especially after the super-scary creepy crawly package. I mean, the fact is, that box was hand-placed in our mailbox. It didn't go through the post office. And Dr. Lurker had just been here."

Zoe shook her head.

"I just can't believe that Lance would do such a thing. I'm going to be so angry and disappointed if he did this. I'm sorry, but I've known him a long time."

"I know he's your friend. And I don't want it to be true either."

"But you don't like him."

"I don't like the way he always looks at me like I'm a steak and he's starving."

Zoe laughed, and Sidney smiled.

"Anyway... Isaac took me into Tiffany's and told me to pick out anything I wanted."

"Ah, hence the millionaire rock star reference."

"Exactly. Then, after I chose this beauty, he got down on one knee — right there in the jewelry store — proposed all over again and slipped it on my finger."

"Aww! I had no idea that man of yours was such a romantic."

"Neither did I, but it was perfect."

"I'm so happy for you!"

"Thanks!"

"But I'm also worried."

Sidney stared at her. "What? Why?"

"All of the strange things happening. Your tires, that package. I mean, what's next?"

"Don't ask that question! Don't *ever* ask that question; it's like tempting fate."

Zoe laughed at her, and Sidney grinned and left the office.

She went in search of Ann and found her in one of the bathrooms upstairs, cleaning her little girl's face and hands.

"There you are."

Ann looked up and smiled at her.

"I think more oatmeal and jam ended up on her face than in her belly."

Sidney giggled. Then a pang of longing fluttered somewhere inside her when Ann kissed the top of her daughter's head.

"Okay, go play. But stay here in the room."

"Okay, Mommy."

They watched the little girl walk over to her coloring book and crayons in the corner of the bedroom, and Sidney turned to Ann.

"I'm sorry, is this a bad time?"

"Of course not. Is this about... you know?"

"Yes. I've located someone that does convincing work on false documents, so I'm going to need your picture."

"My picture?"

"For a fake ID and passport. Actually, I'll need photos of the children as well."

"Oh. Right." She ran a self-conscious hand through her hair. "I look a fright. But I guess, most people do on their driver's licenses, don't they?"

Sidney smiled. "I know I do. Look, the picture doesn't really matter much in the long run. It's not like you're going to keep it and frame it. We just need something to attach your new name to. It's only temporary."

"I know. I get it. Let me just um... run a brush through my hair or something."

"Okay."

Sidney waited while Ann made herself slightly more camera ready. Then she took a couple of headshots with her cellphone, and snapped a couple of Laney and Ben as well.

"These should be perfect," she said, looking at the pics on her phone. "I'll let you know when I have an update."

"Okay. Sidney?"

"Yes?"

"Thanks again. For all you're doing."

Sidney smiled at her. "You're welcome."

She left Ann's room and went back downstairs to the office, where Zoe was gathering her planner and a couple of files into her bag.

"Oh, Sidney. I'm off to my meeting with the chairwoman of the Women's Business League. We're going to discuss a program that will allow for business mentors to come in and do some coaching for residents entering the work force. You know... resume writing, interview tips, asking for a raise, that sort of thing."

"Oh, yes. We've talked about that before. That would be a wonderful program if you can arrange it."

"Wish me luck. And hold down the fort."

"Will do."

When Zoe left, Sidney closed the office door and hurried to her desk. She dug out the slip of paper Ike had given her with the name and number of the document forger. She took a deep breath and then dialed. The phone rang only once.

"Yeah?"

Not the friendliest of greetings.

"Is this Ronan O'Dwyer?"

There was hesitation on the other end of the line, a caution that Sidney could feel in her bones. She suddenly wondered if he would turn her away because she was female.

"Who's asking?"

The voice was distinctly Irish. The tone was distinctly suspicious.

"My name is Sidney Fai..."

"I don't want yer last name."

"Oh. All right. Well, then you can just call me Sid."

"Are ya a copper, Sid?"

"A copper? Oh. You mean a cop. A police officer?"

"Aye."

"No. I'm not a cop. I'm in social work."

"How'd ya get this number, Sid the social worker?"

How was she supposed to answer that? I'm not a cop, but my future husband is. That would go over well.

"From a friend."

"And why would this friend send ya ta me?"

"Because I asked him where I could get my hands on some false documents."

"And he just tossed me name out, all casual like?"

"Well... no. Not at first. Not until I'd brought the subject up a few times. I think he didn't take me seriously at first. And then he just wanted me to be careful, so he gave me your number because he said you do good work. Convincing and discreet."

Hesitation again. She could almost hear him thinking.

"What is it yer wantin' from me, Sid the social worker?"

"A driver's license. Birth certificates and passports for a woman and two small children."

"Well, did yer friend tell ya that I don't work fer pennies, Sid?"

"He said you weren't cheap."

"He told ya true. The three passports will run ya two hundred a piece."

His three sounded more like 'tree', but Sidney got the gist.

"One hundred for the driver's license. One fifty for each of the documents. Another hundred fer me time and labor. That's twelve hundred and fifty total. Ya still interested?"

Sidney blew out a silent breath. $1250. She closed her eyes and silently prayed Ann had that much to spare.

"Yes. I'm still interested."

"Payment is due when I deliver yer papers, then. Delivery happens on neutral ground. Public place."

"That sounds acceptable."

"If I deliver yer papers and I don't get paid, delivery has a bad ending fer you."

"There's no need for threats, Mr. O'Dwyer. You'll get your money. If this goes well, I may even become a repeat customer."

"I'll hold up me end of the bargain. All will go well as long as you hold up the end of yers."

"All right then."

"I assume ya have pictures for me?"

"Yes, I do."

"Are they digital?"

"They are."

"Text them to this number once we hang up, along with any special details you want on the documents, like cities, names, and dates."

"Oh. Right. It may take me a half hour or so to collect that information."

"Tsk, tsk, tsk. Always come to me prepared, Sid the social worker. Otherwise yer just wasting me time."

"I'm sorry."

"I'll let it slide this once. But if ya come back fer more, make sure ya remember."

"I'll remember."

"Get the info to me quick. Within the hour. The sooner ya do, the sooner I can get started."

"Okay."

"I'll text ya with a meetin' place fer delivery in two days. Maybe three."

Maybe *tree*. His Irish brogue made her smile, despite the nervousness nibbling at her stomach.

"Thank you, Mr. O'Dwyer."

Another pause. Like he was thinking it over.

"The name's Ronan."

Before she could respond, the line went dead. Sidney stared at the cellphone for a moment and then got up to go find Ann. She had cities and names and dates to choose for her and her children, and Sidney had every intention of getting that information to Ronan O'Dwyer as quickly as she could.

Once she'd passed on Ann's chosen information to O'Dwyer, Sidney got to work. Her day was fairly routine, and she was more than happy about that. She'd had enough bad surprises to last a good long while.

She'd just delivered a bowl of chicken noodle soup upstairs to Tyneesha, who was finally on the mend, and was heading down the stairs when she saw Zoe open the front door.

"Oh, my goodness!" Zoe exclaimed.

"You know, it didn't dawn on me until right now that this might not be a great idea."

There was no mistaking that slight southern drawl, and the sound of it made Sidney's heart skip, trip, and flip.

"Isaac?"

She hurried down the last few stairs and rushed to the door.

One look and she immediately understood Zoe's exclamation.

He stood there holding the biggest, most beautiful bouquet of pale pink roses she'd ever seen. The kind with the pale pink outer petals and the darker pink centers. The kind she'd told him she favored when they were walking along the beach.

"What have you done?"

She reached through the open doorway and practically pulled him inside.

"Well, I took an hour for lunch and thought I'd spend it with you. So I got us a couple of those Cobb salads you like so well from the deli." He held up a bag in one hand. "And as I was leaving there, I saw this little florist shop, and I remembered what you said about your favorite roses."

"Isaac..."

"I described them to the florist, and she gave me these. I hope they're the right kind."

"They are exactly the right kind. They're beautiful."

She took the flowers from him and then kissed his lips.

Zoe quietly cleared her throat.

"Oh." Nervous laughter bubbled out of her and she gestured to her boss. "Zoe, this is my fiancé, Isaac Taylor. Ike, this is Zoe Ridley, my boss."

"Hello, ma'am."

Isaac kept both hands on the bag containing their salads and made no move to shake Zoe's hand.

"I believe we've actually met once or twice before."

"We have?" Zoe sounded shocked. "I mean, I know you were here for the whole Tom Billings debacle, but I was unconscious then."

Isaac chuckled. "I'm glad you're feeling better."

"You and me both."

"I was actually referring to several years back when I was still in uniform. I worked in the domestic violence unit for a short time. I was here at Hope House on a few calls back then."

"Oh, gosh. Is that right?"

"Yes, ma'am."

"Small world and all that."

"Yes."

"You know, you do actually look familiar."

"You've probably seen him sitting on my desk." Sidney smiled at her.

Zoe laughed.

"That's right! You have a picture of him sitting there. I see it everyday!"

They all laughed.

"Well, it's nice to finally meet you, Detective. Sidney talks about you all the time. And congratulations on your engagement."

"Thank you. I hope I'm not interrupting your work. Like I said, I didn't even think that this might not be a good idea until I was here."

"Nonsense. Actually, I think the residents feel safer with a cop in the building. Plus, it might help them to see a healthy relationship. Enjoy your lunch."

She left them and headed for the kitchen.

Sidney looked up at him.

"I'm sorry. I should've called and asked if this was okay."

"Are you kidding? Isaac, this is the sweetest surprise."

"You sure?"

"Yes! Thank you for the roses. They're so lovely."

He ran his thumb over her cheek.

"They pale next to you, darlin'."

Did women actually swoon in real life? She needed to know because if not, then she was probably about to faint or something.

"Come with me."

She took his hand and led him into the office and over to her desk.

"Have a seat. I'll be right back."

"Okay."

She took the roses into the kitchen where Zoe was helping Ann and Beth to prepare lunch for their little ones.

"Do we have any vases around here by any chance?"

"Oh, Sidney. Those are gorgeous!" Ann stared at the bouquet in delight.

"Did your fella give 'em to you?" Beth asked, smiling.

Zoe handed her a vase from under the sink.

"He did. Thanks."

She filled the vase with water and placed the roses in. She leaned in and inhaled the fresh fragrant scent.

"Is he always so sweet to you?"

Beth's tone was one of wonder, like someone had just told her that unicorns exist. The sound of it tugged at Sidney's heart. Had the woman really never experienced a man being kind to her?

Sidney looked her in the eyes.

"Yes, he is. And it's... taken some time to get used to. In all honesty, I'm still not. Used to it, I mean. I'm afraid to upset him sometimes, because... well, we all know why. But then I remind myself that he's not Damien. He's not going to react with his fists, no matter what I say or do."

"How do you know that for certain?"

The fear in Beth's voice was heartbreaking.

Sidney glanced down at her roses and thought about Ike. About the goodness inside his heart, the love and gentleness.

"I just know."

She left the kitchen and headed back to the office, where Isaac had their lunch all laid out on her desk. Two Cobb salads with balsamic vinaigrette, and two bottles of sparkling water.

She set the roses on the corner of her desk, and then sat down to eat.

"I can't believe you did this."

She glanced at him and took note of the satisfied smile on his handsome face.

"What's gotten into you lately?"

"What do you mean?" He took a bite of his salad and frowned at her.

"I mean, you've become Mr. Romance all of a sudden. That wonderful backyard picnic, the most amazing day at the beach where we made wedding plans, and then picking out my gorgeous engagement ring and our wedding bands. Now, two dozen roses hand delivered to my place of business, along with lunch."

Isaac's eyebrows shot up, and Sidney grinned and took a bite of her salad.

"Are you complaining about the romance, Ms. Fairchild?"

"Absolutely not. I'm enjoying the romance very much, Mr. Taylor. I'd just like to know what brought it on."

"Well, maybe I've always been romantic and you just never knew it. Maybe I never knew it until you came along. Maybe..." He pointed his fork at her as he thought about it. "Maybe I've simply never had anyone in my life to shower my romantic tendencies on."

They stared at one another for a long moment, and Sidney decided that last theory was most likely right. And that in itself carried a certain sort of sadness.

"So, how's your day going, baby? Any progress on your castration murders?"

"We have a new person of interest we're looking into right now. And we're starting to suspect our killer had help."

"So you're looking for more than one person?" Sidney took a sip of her water.

"We think so. We keep trying to pick him up for questioning, but he keeps eluding us."

"And this person of interest. Does he have a connection to the girl in the mental hospital? The old rape case you mentioned?"

"He does indeed."

"So, you were right about it all stemming from that rape case?"

"Seems that way. And if we're right about our person of interest, then this case has a doozy of a twist."

"Really? I can't wait to hear about it."

Isaac finished off his salad in record time and put his container into the empty bag.

"What about you? Any new developments in the harassment case?"

"Ooh, it's a case now."

"It is in my book. Slashed tires and that tarantula package. Hell yeah, it's a case."

Sidney swallowed a bite and debated on whether or not to say anything. Finally she put down her empty container and licked her lips.

"Well, I'm not sure this is part of the harassment or not, but..."

She sighed, letting her shoulders fall heavy.

"But what, Sid?"

"I was stopped again this morning on my way to work."

"What? You were pulled over? Again?"

Sidney nodded. "Yes."

"And?"

"And, I did what you said and told the officer up front that I had a CWP and my gun was in my purse. Just like last time."

"And he made you get out of the car."

"Yes."

"Did he cuff you?"

"No. And he didn't pull his gun on me either. He was much nicer than the female cop who pulled me over yesterday."

"Then what happened?"

"Same drill. He located my purse, secured the gun, found my license and my permit. Then he said he'd pulled me over for failure to come to a complete stop at a stop sign."

"Bullshit!"

"Which I know that I stopped at!"

"Did he give you a citation for that?"

"He said out of respect for you he was letting me off with a warning." She reached for her purse in the bottom drawer of her desk and pulled out the citation. "He gave me this."

Isaac took the yellow slip of paper from her and looked it over.

"Andy Garfield."

He read the signature out loud, and Sidney stared at him.

"Do you know him?"

"No. But it's a big precinct and we work in different departments. Different floors."

"He claimed to know you."

Isaac looked at her. "That doesn't mean much. Patrol is a lot more aware of who the detectives are than the other way around. Mostly because there's just so many patrol officers. No way to get to know them all personally unless you happen to work on one of the cases they've caught."

Sidney nodded. "That makes sense."

She cleared away the last remnants of their lunch. While she worked, she could see Isaac's mind spinning. He was looking at the body of evidence, coming at it from all available sides, attempting to put the puzzle pieces into place.

"Two shit citations, two days in a row. Both on your way to work in the morning."

He was mumbling to himself, and Sidney wondered if he'd picked up the bad habit from her, or if this was his way of working through a case. She suspected the latter, and she found it fascinating to watch him work.

"Slashed tires. Big hairy spider in the mail. What do they all have in common?"

"Ike?"

"Two citations. Slashed tires. Creepy package for future Mrs. Ike Taylor."

"Isaac?"

"Hmm?"

"You're going to be late getting back to work."

He glanced down at his watch and then looked at her.

"I don't think your troubles are the angry husband you beat up, or the jilted doctor who forced a kiss on you."

"You don't?"

"No."

"Then who?"

"Something about it screams Natalie Bains to me."

Sidney stared at him, completely lost.

"Who is Natalie Bains and why the hell is she pissed at me?"

Isaac leaned back in her desk chair and folded his arms over his chest.

"Natalie Bains is a toxic harpy that's obsessed with me for some odd reason."

"Obsessed with you?"

"She's the one who reported us to Internal Affairs about our relationship, and caused me to have to go through that IAB inquest."

"Ohh! *That* Natalie Bains."

"Right."

"Well, still... what is she pissed at me for?"

"Because you have me, and she doesn't?"

Sidney cocked her head at him and grinned. Then she reached out and lightly ran her hand over his.

"Not that you're not all kinds of sexy, baby. And any woman would be lucky to have you. But do you really believe she'd come after me like this just because you turned her down?"

Isaac's response was immediate and held zero humor.

"Yes, I do. I know that you're joking right now, and believe me, I know how laughable it is that a sane woman would go to these lengths over someone like me. But we're not exactly talking about a sane woman. Natalie is evil and vindictive. Lieutenant Hayes and I even have reason to believe she's a dirty cop. And that she's deliberately put you in harm's way before."

"What?"

Icy fingers of dread zipped up Sidney's spine.

This wasn't funny anymore.

"What do you mean she's put me in harm's way before?"

"You remember after our first date when we took you into

police protective custody after your car blew up, and the safe house we had you in was compromised?"

"That's kind of hard to forget."

"Yeah, well... we believe Natalie is the one who gave up the safe house location to Nacio Rivas-Solis. He sent his men there to try and kill you. But he never would've found you if he hadn't gotten help from someone on the inside. We can't prove it, but we believe that someone was Natalie Bains."

"Holy shit."

"Yeah. And just a few weeks ago, during the Lullaby Killer case, she stopped me in the hallway and made a thinly veiled threat against you."

"What?"

Sidney heard the alarm in her own voice, and she stood and paced around her desk.

"What kind of threat, Isaac?"

"It was vague. She asked how you were liking your new job here at Hope House."

Sidney stopped and looked at him.

"I don't follow. Where's the threat in that?"

"The threat is that her question came at a time when you had just gotten the job here. Like maybe two days after you started. Early enough that someone like her shouldn't have known anything about where you worked."

"So... you think she was watching me? Following me?"

Isaac nodded. "And I asked her what she was doing keeping tabs on you."

"What did she say?"

"She tried to say I was paranoid, but we both knew I wasn't buying her bullshit. I went straight to Hayes with my suspicions."

"And?"

"And he suggested that I keep a record of it. Take it a step further and file a harassment report if I wanted to, but honestly there was nothing we could do. Officially, she hadn't done anything we could prove."

"So where does that leave us now? I mean, I'm assuming there's nothing to really tie her to my slashed tires or that creepy package."

"Well, I don't have an official word on that yet. I know Detective Casey was having that box of nasties tested for fingerprints and fibers and anything else that might help. But I haven't heard anything from him yet. I'll check on that when I get back to the precinct."

Sidney wrapped her arms around herself. Why was she shaking?

Isaac stood and stepped around her desk and took her into his arms.

"Hey. I don't want you to worry too much about this, okay? I'm going to take care of it."

Sidney looked up into his eyes. "How can you ask me not to worry? I just found out some bitch who's obsessed with my fiancé is most likely the person who's been harassing me. And she's a cop! She could have me arrested on some bogus charges if she wanted to."

"No, it's not going to get that far. Give me your citations. Both of them. I'm going to take care of this as soon as I get back to the PD."

"What are you going to do?" She pulled the other citation out of her purse and gave it to him.

"I'm going to handle it."

He pulled her close again, and Sidney settled into him.

"I don't like this, Ike."

"I know. I don't like it either. But at least we know now what's really going on, and who's really behind all of this."

"But do we? I mean, you seem so sure."

"I am. I can't tell you how, but I know it's her. I can feel it.

Something about those citations just put it all into perspective for me."

He kissed her lips and looked into her eyes.

"I've got to get going or I really am going to be late. But don't worry. I've got this."

"Okay."

She walked him out to the front door.

"Thanks again for lunch. And for the flowers. They made my day."

He kissed her again, this time lingering, and Sidney moaned as their tongues caressed.

"I'm glad you like them. I'll see you at home, okay?"

"Okay. Stay safe."

"Love you."

"I love you back."

She watched him leave the porch and get into his car, and after he'd driven away Sidney sighed. Somehow her predicament seemed worse. More sinister. And all she could do was trust that Isaac had it under control.

Isaac put Sidney's citation copies into his pocket and slid behind the wheel of his car. Then he glanced at her in the doorway before he drove off and headed back to the PD.

He stewed about it the entire way back — all the stress, worry, and fear Sidney was going through. It pissed him off. And now to know that Natalie was behind it all.

Well, to suspect she was.

There was the off chance that Sidney was right, and he was simply jumping to conclusions. Yes, Natalie had made threats against Sidney in the past, but it could just as easily be that arrogant doctor Sid had jilted doing all these things, couldn't it?

In fact, the more he thought about it, he realized that there could be an even worse scenario playing out here.

What if Sidney was being attacked on two different fronts?

Just like last time.

When he'd met her, Sidney was being stalked and terrorized by her abusive estranged husband. But she was also being hunted down by a ruthless drug lord who'd wanted her dead because she'd seen something she wasn't supposed to.

What if Natalie was behind the two bogus citations, but someone else was behind the other, more nefarious acts of harassment?

He didn't like that idea. Hell, he didn't much like either prospect, but he couldn't discount either one of them.

He pulled into the back lot of the police station and marched inside. He headed straight to the detectives section on the fourth floor, and from there he turned left and ventured into the narcotics section.

He stood and glanced around, his gaze darting around the space, searching for the vile she-snake. He spotted her rounding a corner, heading for her office.

He followed after her.

She glanced his way just as she stepped inside, and the bitch grinned as she tried to close the office door in his face.

Isaac pushed the door open with his fist. It made a soft *thud* against the doorstop. He stepped in and closed the door behind him.

Natalie smiled, her bright red lips parting to reveal perfect white teeth.

"I knew you'd come forcing your way into my office eventually. Finally realize you want me? You want to screw me on my desk?"

"In your dreams."

"Then what are you barging in here for, Ike? I have work to do."

He pulled Sidney's two citations from his pocket and tossed

them onto her desk.

"What are those?"

Her tone was super sweet and innocent, and laced with arsenic.

"You know exactly what they are. What'd it take? What did you bribe your buddies with to get them to harass Sidney this week, huh?"

"My buddies?"

"Your friends in the patrol section. Officers Tammy Hunt and Andy Garfield. They each pulled Sidney over on her way to work the past two days, writing her shit citations for an improper lane change and failure to come to a complete stop. You know what I'm talking about."

He couldn't help the rise of his voice, and he really wanted to snatch the smug smile off her face.

"I'm sorry, Tammy who?"

"And since you've been keeping close tabs on her, you know full well that Sidney just got her Concealed Weapon Permit. So you figured it'd be fun to have your buddies pull her over and search her car. Were you parked somewhere watching when Officer Hunt pulled her gun on Sidney and cuffed her when she got out of the car? You probably got a big ol kick out of watching Sid be humiliated like that, didn't you? Did you and Officer Hunt have a good laugh about that one afterwards?"

"I have no idea what you're talking about, Ike. Maybe this is one of your psychic delusions or something. You should get that checked."

"You know what my psychic delusions get right every single time? Recognizing your noxious handiwork when I see it."

"It sounds to me like your girlfriend needs to learn how to drive."

"Sounds to me like you need to grow up and learn how to stop being a world class bitch."

"Ooh, such language! What's the matter? Is your girlfriend not liking her new job? Too many creeps hanging around there?"

"Yeah, and apparently one of them is you."

"Me?"

"I know you slashed her tires, Natalie. And you sent her the creepy box of goodies addressed to the future Mrs. Ike Taylor. Damn! I knew you were jealous, but wow. What's your long term plan? You planning to harass her up until the wedding, or are you still going to be pulling this shit on our tenth anniversary?"

Natalie's cheeks turned as red as her lipstick, and Isaac knew he'd struck a nerve.

Bingo!

There was only one person harassing Sidney, and he was looking at her.

"Get the fuck out of my office, Ike! I don't have time for this shit."

"Neither do I. This stops and it stops now, you understand me?"

"Or what? You can't prove a thing. I haven't gone anywhere near your precious girlfriend. Yet."

"Is that another threat?"

"Another? Whatever do you mean?"

Isaac stared at her and snatched the citations from her desk.

"I'm done playing. This game is over."

He turned for the door.

"Is it?"

Her tone was a challenge.

A dare.

Isaac turned and looked at her.

"Oh, yeah. It's done."

He left her office and went back to the pit. But instead of heading for his own desk, he went in search of his boss. He knocked on the open door of Gavin Hayes' office.

"Ike. What can I do for you?"

He walked in and closed the door behind him.

"I just wanted to give you a heads up, sir."

"About what?"

"I'm going to be filing a formal complaint with IAB over Natalie Bains' continued harassment of Sidney and myself."

Gavin put his pen down and looked up at him.

"Thank you for informing me."

Isaac nodded.

"May I make a suggestion," Gavin asked.

"Sure."

"Start at the beginning."

Isaac nodded again. "I plan to gather the old report I filed when she made that veiled threat against Sid a few weeks back."

"Good. But that's not what I'm talking about."

Isaac walked closer to Gavin's desk and sat down in one of the vacant chairs across from him.

"What were you referring to?"

"I think you need to include mention of the IAB inquest you went through as her first act of harassment. After all, she is the one who reported you and sparked the whole inquest in the first place."

"Can I do that?"

"I don't see why not. Her reporting you was an act of harassment, was it not?"

"It was to me."

"I wish there was some way we could include what happened at the safe house, but there isn't."

Isaac shrugged a shoulder.

"Doesn't matter. The things she's done lately are bad enough. The good part is that Sid and I already filed a harassment report about it all with Detective Casey, so there's a record of it. I'm going to gather all of that, plus anything that Casey may have found, and take it all upstairs to IAB."

"Do I even want to know what else she's done?"

Isaac rolled his eyes. Then he sat back and filled his boss in on all the things Sid had been through in the last several days.

Gavin shook his head when Isaac finished his tale.

"Well, they'll have to drag Officers Hunt and Garfield in for questioning. And those two probably won't be too happy about that. Which means..."

"Which means they'll go bitching to Natalie about it," Isaac interrupted.

"And then she'll come bitching to you."

"Let her." Isaac shrugged a shoulder.

He and Gavin stared at each other for a moment.

"Well, thanks again for the heads up. I appreciate you letting me know. That way if IAB calls on me, I won't be blindsided."

"Yeah. I guess I should update Pete as well, in case they might go to him."

"Probably not a bad idea."

"Thanks, Lieu."

"Yep."

When he finally got to his desk, Isaac filled Pete in on the new developments in Sidney's weird occurrences at work, and what he planned to do about it.

"Natalie Bains? For real?"

"You sound skeptical."

"No, not skeptical. I totally believe she's capable of it. I just can't believe she'd go so far. I mean, what's her endgame? What's the point of harassing Sidney? Especially if her real beef is with you?"

Isaac lifted a hand, palm up, before it flopped down onto his desk.

"Probably because she knows it's the quickest way to get to me. Mess with the woman I love? The woman she feels like I chose instead of her. I don't know."

"Well, if IAB comes to me, what should I say?"

"Depends on what they ask. Just tell them what you know."

"I don't know much. Just what you've said here."

"Tell them that. I just wanted you to be in the loop."

"Well, thanks for that, I guess."

Isaac nodded. "Enough of Natalie Bains for now. We've got a killer to find."

"Yeah, about that."

"You find something?"

"Maybe. I was going back through Josephine Turner's financials..."

"And?"

"And I saw that she recently spent nearly two hundred dollars at a local hardware store."

"What'd she buy?"

"Rope. And lots of it. Duct tape. Zip ties."

"A kidnapping kit."

"You got it. Also hedge shears. The big ones."

"Maybe that was before she and Danny settled on a weapon. When did she make this purchase?"

"Three days before our first victim was strung to that tree trunk."

"Any chance the store still has video footage from that date?"

"Only one way to find out."

"Okay, why don't you go to the store and check on that footage."

"What about you?"

"I'd feel a lot better if we had a murder weapon in hand. So, I'm going to do a little digging into it. If what Hiroshi says of the murder weapon most likely used on our three vics is true, then we're looking for some kind of machete or kukri or something similar. I'm going to look at places that sell those kinds of things. I doubt there's a whole lot of demand for something like that, so maybe a store will remember a recent purchase of one. Might get lucky."

"Okay. Good hunting."

"You, too."

23

Two days later, Sidney sat on a park bench in Old Brooklyn across from the swing set. The text had said to come alone and bring the cash in an envelope. The text hadn't given her much time either, insisting she be on that bench in just twenty minutes. So she'd collected the money from Ann and high tailed it out of Hope House.

She sat trying to catch her breath, eyes darting all around her. Twenty minutes was no time at all when you were still learning your way around a new city.

Kids screamed and laughed. The sound of it working wonders toward calming her nerves. Whoever this Ronan O'Dwyer was, he certainly wouldn't pull anything frightening with children around.

Would he?

She drew in a deep breath and glanced down at the time on her cellphone.

She'd parked her car right at the twenty minute deadline and then had to power walk through the unfamiliar park to find the playground.

She was late.

Nearly two minutes to be exact. But surely, he wouldn't count that against her. He wouldn't leave and forfeit this transaction just because she'd been a little late in getting to the park bench.

"Oh, please still be here," she whispered to herself, still looking around the park.

She glanced down at the time on her phone once more.

Five minutes.

It was now five minutes past the time she was supposed to have been there. How long should she wait for him?

She sat back and crossed her legs. If he didn't show at least she'd have a few moments of quiet time in a lovely park.

That's what she told herself. But the spike of anxiety threatened to keep her in fight or flight mode, ready to box or bolt with her next breath.

As she glanced off to the left, a man sat down to her right.

Startled, Sidney turned and looked at him.

Ronan O'Dwyer was short and stocky, and dressed very casually in a rumpled pair of dark khakis and a denim shirt. He had the hands of a factory worker. A well worn leather flat cap sat atop his close-cropped red hair at an angle, and two sharp brown eyes peered out from beneath it. He was younger than Sidney had imagined, and nothing like she'd pictured.

He set a lightweight jacket on the bench between them, and Sidney noticed a large manila envelope underneath it.

"Sorry for the delay, but ya don't look like the pictures on the documents. I had to watch ya fer a bit to make sure ya were here fer me."

"The documents aren't for me."

"So I gathered. Tell me, Sid. What does a social worker need with forged documents?"

Sidney watched a pair of little girls on the swings and thought about his question.

"Well social work involves helping people. Sometimes it involves helping people to protect themselves."

"Ah. So ya help them run to safety, do ya?"

This question brought a new wrinkle of thought to Sidney's mind, and she frowned.

"Is knowing what your documents are being used for a requirement for you?"

"Not at all. Ya simply intrigue me. It's not often someone so good seeks my services."

"Maybe I'm not as good as you think."

Ronan chuckled, and the sound of it irked her.

"Don't play games, lass. We both know this is your first foray into the dark side."

Sidney grinned. She was beginning to enjoy being underestimated by men. Men who didn't think she could stand up for herself or others.

"Sorry to disappoint you, Mr. O'Dwyer, but you don't grow up where I did and come out pure as the driven snow. You are not the first forger I've dealt with. Only the first in this state."

"Well, now I'm doubly intrigued."

He turned and looked directly at her, and Sidney met his gaze.

Ronan picked up the jacket between them and put it on, leaving the manila envelope behind.

Sidney placed the manila envelope inside her purse and replaced it with the envelope of money.

"You will get rid of any remaining pictures you may have from me, right?"

"Already shredded and deleted. Along with the texts and phone logs."

Without another word, he picked up the envelope of money and walked away.

Sidney let out a slow sigh and settled back on the bench. She sat there for a long time just watching the children play. Then she gathered her purse and phone and headed back to her car.

On the drive back to work, she thought about those kids on the playground. Something about them sparked a memory of being at the park at that age, her mother seated on a bench nearby.

"Watch me, mommy!"

Cartwheels were never so much fun as when she had her mother's full attention.

She didn't get many trips to the park when she was a kid growing up in Compton. She knew things were different now in her old hood. Better. Safer. But back then, the parks were no place for children.

It was weird how one stray thought could lead you down a rabbit hole of memories and emotions. The park led her to thoughts of her mother. Which, in turn, led her to thoughts of what her life was like after her mother's death.

And that, of course, led her back to her Aunt Bobbie. Her mom's sister. The woman who had taken her in after her mom was killed by a drunk driver.

She hadn't spoken to Aunt Bobbie in about three years. Not since Damien had threatened to break her jaw if she told the woman anything else about their relationship.

He'd been so stealthy in his campaign to isolate her from her loved ones. So stealthy that Sidney hadn't even realized what was happening until it was too late.

She'd thought many times about contacting Aunt Bobbie back when she was in hiding from Damien, but she couldn't risk it. Now that he was gone and her life was settled and she wasn't living in fear anymore, she knew it was past time to reach out.

She pulled to the curb outside Hope House and parked the car. Then she grabbed her cellphone and dialed, hoping that the number hadn't changed.

It rang three times before the familiar voice answered.

"Hello?"

Sidney opened her mouth to speak, but her emotions robbed her voice. Tears sprang to her eyes.

"Hello?"

If she didn't respond soon her aunt would hang up. She took a breath and forced sound from her mouth.

"Aunt Bobbie?"

A long heavy silence followed.

"Oh, my God. Sidney?"

A smile erupted on Sidney's face.

"Yes. It's me."

"Oh, my God. *Sidney!* I thought... oh, never mind what I thought. Child, how are you? *Where* are you?"

Sidney laughed through her tears.

"I'm good, Aunt Bobbie. Things are great actually."

"Oh, honey. Where are you? The last I heard from Simon, you were on the run from that son of a bitch who was beating you."

"Yes."

"But that was so long ago..."

"Yes, I know, and I'm sorry it's been so long. But, I'm free now, Aunt Bobbie! Damien is gone, and I am wonderful."

"What do you mean he's gone? Where is he?"

"He's dead. He can't hurt me anymore."

"Dead?"

"Yes."

A tense pause.

"Honey, what did you do?"

Bobbie's tone was tight and low.

Sidney laughed again. "I didn't kill him, Auntie. I promise. It's a very long story, and I can't wait to tell you all about it. But I just wanted you to know that I'm all right."

"Well, are you here in California?"

"No. I live in Ohio now."

"Ohio?"

"Yes, Simon is actually here in Ohio too."

"What?"

"We're just four hours from each other, which has been great."

"When did he leave Japan?"

"Only a few months ago. Listen, there's so much to tell you, but right now I have to get back to work. Is it okay if I call you later tonight after I get home? I'll tell you everything then."

"Are you kidding me? Of course, call me back later! Can I save this number?"

"Yes. This is my cellphone number. Save it. Use it often. Share it with Erika and Tika."

She'd missed her two cousins as much as she'd missed her aunt, and she couldn't wait to reconnect with them.

"Oh, they will love that!"

"Okay. I have to go. I'll call you later. I love you!"

"Oh, Sidney, I thought we'd lost you. I love you back honey."

She ended the call and got out of the car. She entered the shelter with fresh hope blossoming in her chest.

24

The next morning, Gavin stood in the briefing room looking out over his dwindling troops. He'd just handed out a couple of assignments to the already taxed detectives of his unit, and now it was time for the big news. News he knew would be met with a mixed bag of emotions.

"Finally, I have an announcement to make, so quiet down."

He waited for them to give him their undivided attention. When all eyes were on him, he took a deep breath.

"I am sorry to inform you that we will be losing Detective Gerri Miller, effective immediately."

A low rumble of chatter went around the room.

"Yes, it is disappointing. However, it's not entirely bad. Gerri has chosen to transfer out of the Homicide Unit and take a position in the Special Victims division of Violent Crimes. So, while we will lose her expertise in Homicide, she will still be here at the 3rd precinct, and I believe she'll be on day shift, so you will still see her face around here on the fourth floor."

Another rumble of chatter interrupted him again, and he raised his voice slightly in order to be heard above the din.

"Two new detectives will therefore be joining our team to fill the voids left by Miller and Dorn. Detective Jack Runyan will be transferring in from the 5th precinct Violent Crimes division, and the other, Officer Lonnie Spencer, will be rising from patrol, in-house. Now... due to the loss of Miller and Dorn, as well as Barker and Wheeler both being out for health reasons, there will have to be some significant shuffling of teams in order to pair our two new hires with seasoned detectives."

More chatter began, and a couple of hands shot in the air before Gavin could go any further. He had a good idea what was coming next.

"Yes, Harris?"

"Forgive the interruption, Lieu, but what does that mean exactly?"

"I haven't worked out all of the details just yet, but it means exactly what you think it does. Exactly what I just said — there will be some significant shuffling of teams in the near future."

"So we're all getting new partner assignments, sir? Whether we want them or not?"

"Harris, if you can figure out a way to keep everyone with their current partners and still pair the new hires with seasoned detectives, let me know."

She didn't like his response, but Gavin didn't know any other way to do this. The fact was, they were simply too damned short-handed right now to do it any other way.

"Sir?"

"Yes, Walker?"

"Is this significant shuffling only going to affect the day shift, or will the night shift homicide detectives get shuffled too?"

"Are you volunteering for night shift, Detective?"

"No, sir. Just asking."

A soft laughter went around the room.

"I did begin my search for new detectives by offering the day shift to all those currently working nights. None of them were interested in the switch. However, a couple of them were open to filling in for a short time until the day shift is back fully staffed. So they may come into play over the next few weeks. I'll just have to see how my reshuffling efforts go."

He glanced around at them all and noted a few worried expressions. He understood it, but it couldn't be helped.

"All right, dismissed. Let's be safe out there."

He marched for the door and exited the room before most of them had even had a chance to stand. He went straight to his office almost dreading the headache that shuffling his detectives around was going to cause.

But the reason for it made him smile.

Not all of it, of course. Not the part about Curt Dorn dying. But the part where he got to be with Gerri freely and not worry about jeopardizing his career?

That part he loved.

He plopped his paperwork down on his desk just as Ike Taylor stepped inside his office.

"Got a second, Lieu?"

Isaac closed the door behind him and walked toward Gavin's desk.

"So, this transfer? I take it that has something to do with your new relationship status?"

Gavin pulled out his chair and sat down, but the grin on his face told Isaac everything he needed to know.

"We had dinner together with Trey the other night."

"Oh yeah? How'd that turn out?"

Isaac took a seat in the chair across from Gavin's desk.

"It went great actually. Trey said he thought it was high time I moved on and found some happiness."

"Cause he's a good son."

"He and Gerri really hit it off too. And you were so right."

"Of course, I was. About what exactly?" Isaac grinned.

Gavin chuckled at him.

"About Gerri having more in common with me due to this job. It's funny, but she and Trey could not be further apart. It's..." He paused, like he was searching for the right words. "It's like she's my age."

Isaac shook his head. "Let it go, Lieu. That age thing. Just let it go. Don't even think about it. It means nothing in your relationship."

"I'll try to embrace that."

"Good. I'm happy for you both."

"Thanks."

"I'm sorry we'll be losing her though."

"Yeah. I'm sorry that couldn't be helped."

"You went with my suggestion and hired Lonnie Spencer."

"I agreed with your assessment of his file. Good detective material. I also took it a step further and spoke with his current sergeant, his current lieutenant, and his current partner. I'm confident we can build him into a good homicide detective."

"Good." Isaac nodded. "About this reshuffling thing you were talking about in the briefing..."

Gavin held up a hand, and Isaac stopped mid-sentence.

"I know what you're going to say, Ike, and you don't have to. Pete Vega seems very open-minded about your psychic stuff, and I think you've actually warmed to him quite a bit. So, don't worry. I won't be busting up the two of you."

"Thanks for that. We're finally working really well together, so I appreciate it."

Gavin nodded and folded his hands on top of the desk with a sigh.

"I was toying with the idea of bringing Palmer and Driscoll up from nights permanently and moving the two new hires into their spots, busting up the other night shift team to make two new teams. That way the new blood is on nights, and the day shift gets two seasoned teams who work well together."

"Meaning me and Pete, and Sasha and Lynn?"

"Right."

Talking about the two female detectives brought to mind the memory of Sidney asking how effective the all-woman detective team was.

"That way we'd have two seasoned teams and two restructured teams on days," Gavin continued. "But, neither Sasha Palmer nor Lynn Driscoll wanted the permanent move to the day shift. They like working nights."

"Go figure. Well, what about Cruz and Polanski?"

"Palmer and Driscoll were my first choice. Apart from being the senior detectives on night shift, they have the better record. Besides, Cruz and Polanski weren't interested in the switch either."

Isaac shrugged. "Some people love working nights."

"I guess. And I'm all for trying to make everyone happy with their shifts if I can, but it doesn't solve my problem."

Isaac sighed and gave it some thought.

"Well, there is another option, sir?"

"I'm open for suggestions."

"Since one of the new hires is actually a seasoned violent crimes detective, why not simply partner the new hires together?"

Gavin stared at him, not blinking.

"I mean, it's not like this Runyan fella is going to need the training, guidance, or hand-holding that a brand new detective would. And it's not like he's coming from another city, or another state where they do things a little differently than we do. He's just coming from across town. He already knows how the CPD operates, and violent crimes isn't all that different from homicide."

The ghost of a grin hit Gavin's lips before he lowered his head, and Isaac wondered what was going on. When Gavin finally looked up, he was quietly laughing.

"Wow."

"Sir?"

"I have been so turned around by this whole thing with Gerri that I'm obviously not thinking straight."

Isaac grinned. "It's all right, sir. It happens to the best of us."

"Damn. What has this woman done to me, Ike?"

"Don't worry. The stupid will wear off eventually. Just give it time."

Gavin laughed out loud, and Isaac couldn't help but join in. He'd never seen his boss in such a state before. It was kind of nice. He stood and headed for the door.

"Pete and I have a pair of killers to catch."

"A pair?"

"We're pretty sure our killer had an accomplice. And we've been hitting a wall in trying to bring our suspect in for questioning, so we've got a small sting operation in motion for today. I'll update you when we have 'em in custody."

"I'll look forward to it."

Isaac got to his desk just in time to hear Pete end a phone call. He looked up at Isaac with an almost gleeful expression.

"That was our lookout at the institution."

"Nurse Freya Altman?" Or Gossipy Snow White, as he thought of her in his mind. "Does that mean what I think it means?"

"She says Amber's BFF just showed up for his regular visit."

"That's our cue."

They high tailed it out of the pit and snagged a two-man patrol car to join them. Then they raced across town to the Lakewood Mental Institution.

After instructing the two uniformed officers on what was

about to go down and who their target was, they rushed inside, badges at the ready.

They moved with precision, knowing exactly which room they were headed for.

In the hallway across from Amber's door, they saw nurse Josephine Turner speaking to a tall, dark haired young man that Isaac recognized from pictures he'd found during their investigation as Danny Broderick.

The instant the pair looked up and spotted them, the man bolted.

He took off down the hallway, and the chase was on.

The unfamiliar corridors were like running through a maze. Danny led them this way and that, finally ending up in Amber's room.

When they caught up to him, Danny was kneeling at Amber's feet, holding her hands, and speaking softly to her.

Panting, Isaac and Pete looked at each other, and Pete pulled out his handcuffs.

"Wouldn't it have been a whole lot easier without the sprint through the hallways, Danny?" Isaac asked.

Danny grinned. "I needed a few moments to accept my fate."

Isaac motioned to Pete with a nod of his head.

"I'm going to need you to stand up, Mr. Broderick. You're under arrest for the murders of Bobby Cook, Craig Wentworth, and Michael Rivers. You have the right to remain silent."

While Pete continued to recite Danny Broderick his rights, Isaac looked and saw nurse Josephine Turner watching intently from the hallway. When she caught him staring, she put on her most distraught face.

"I can't believe it. He's such a nice young man. So caring and loving toward Amber. I can't believe he'd do something like this, Detective."

"Really? Even though you helped him?"

"What? Helped him! Why, I never..."

"We have video surveillance of you and Danny buying tools for your revenge murder spree, so save your lies for the coming trial jury, okay." He looked at the two uniformed officers standing behind her in the hall. "She's coming with us, gentlemen."

They took her into custody, and Isaac turned his attention back to Danny.

"Where's the murder weapon, Danny? What'd you use? Machete? Kukri?"

"The machete is back in my father's knife collection, where it belongs. He's a real enthusiast. You can't imagine how many times I fantasized about taking one of them to school and exacting justice. So, I finally did."

Isaac made a mental note to seek a warrant to search Danny Broderick's father's home.

"I have to ask. Why'd you do it, Danny? More importantly, was it worth it?"

The young man laughed, but it was a sad sound, devoid of joy.

"Seriously? I'd do it all again, because I love her."

He stared at Amber, and Isaac slowly began to nod.

"That's what all this has been about, isn't it? They hurt the woman you loved. You've been in love with Amber since high school."

"Since before that, actually."

Danny's voice was sad and smug, and he kept his eyes on Amber as she sat, unmoving, in her chair.

"I fell in love with her when we were children. I didn't give a shit about what those small-minded, homophobic, neanderthal assholes did to me back then. But I could not let them get away with what they did to her. I went to her brothers, mistakenly believing that they had backbones. But they were no help at all. *Pussies!* But Amber stood up for me for years when I was too weak to do it myself. So, for once, I was going to be her champion. I did what no one else was willing to do. Not even the cops. I did it because I love her, and I would do it again."

"But you're going away now. You won't be around to visit Amber anymore."

Danny smiled, and a lone tear rolled down his cheek.

"That's okay. We've said our goodbyes. We knew this could happen. But we knew it had to be done. Didn't we, my love?"

Amber's vacant eyes lifted to Danny's, and Isaac could swear he saw the ghost of a smile hint at her lips. As her gaze drifted back to her lap, he saw tears fall. It was the only sign of life Isaac had seen from her.

He glanced at Pete, who's expression of astonishment must've matched his own.

They ushered Danny from Amber's room and handed him off to the waiting officers. As they followed them out of the building, Isaac huffed out a breath and shook his head.

"It's too bad we can't arrest Amber herself, since she was obviously in on the plan."

"Do you really think she was aware of what was going on?"

"Don't you? You saw that look she gave him in there. She knew full well what he was up to."

"That look was creepy, if you ask me."

"Agreed."

"And what about Amber's brothers? Seems you were right about them knowing exactly who the killer was."

"And they'll have to be charged with something. Obstruction of justice at the very least."

"They could've saved us a lot of time if they'd just given us his name from the beginning. I don't get people sometimes."

"Me either. But at least we got him. We got them all."

They transported Danny and nurse Turner downtown to the station and sent them off to central booking with the two uniformed officers. Then Isaac went in search of Lieutenant Hayes. He was almost to Gavin's office when someone grabbed his arm with force and attempted to pull him in the opposite direction.

"You son of a bitch!" someone snarled.

Thanking God for his long sleeved dress shirt and jacket, Isaac yanked his arm free.

He spun around and glared at Natalie Bains.

"What the hell is your problem?"

"My problem is you!"

She waved a severely wrinkled sheet of paper in his face.

"You reported me to Internal Affairs for harassment?"

"You bet your ass I did. I told you this little game of yours was done."

"They're bringing me up for an inquest, you asshole! You're playing with my career now."

"Oh, like you played with mine when you reported me for improper conduct with a witness? It's okay for you to mess with my career, but now you're pissed because I've served your shit right back to you?"

"Your career was never going to be in jeopardy over sleeping with a witness! But you've leveled a serious charge at me here, and they're going to be looking at me hard over it."

"Well, you should've thought about that before you started your little games."

"Are you trying to get me fired?"

"You're trying to terrorize the woman I love, and I am not letting that happen. Whatever your beef was with me, you should've left her out of it!"

"I am so sick of you and your precious little girlfriend!"

"Good. If you're so sick of us, then leave us the fuck alone!"

"All right, that's enough!"

Gavin's deep baritone got their attention, and Isaac glanced around the pit to see that they'd been putting on one helluva floor show with their screaming match.

"Sergeant Bains, I suggest you get back to your section."

"I'm going, Lieutenant." Her heated gaze found Isaac again. "This isn't over, Ike."

"The hell it's not. You come near me or my fiancée again and I'll file a restraining order against your ass. Won't that look nice to IAB during your inquest?"

"You cock sucker."

"I'm not the one always chasing dick, Natalie, that's you."

"Enough!" Gavin snapped.

"Crazy bitch," Isaac mumbled before he walked away, effectively ending the show down. He walked into Gavin's office and plopped down in the chair and waited for his boss to join him.

He knew the instant Natalie was gone and Hayes was headed his way because he could hear the not so low rumble of chatter and whispers out in the pit. They'd be the talk of the entire precinct by day's end.

Gavin closed the door and walked over to his desk chair.

"What the hell was that?" he asked, sitting down.

"Apparently she just got her inquest notice from IAB. I'm sure she had a fun time explaining it to Lt. Dunbar when it landed on his desk."

Dunbar was the Lieutenant over the narcotics division, and also Natalie's boss. Isaac also knew that Lieutenant Hayes didn't care much for the man.

"Better him than me. I'm starting to think that woman has a screw loose."

"I just want her to leave Sidney alone. That's all I care about."

"Yeah, well, take a little advice from me on this. You might want to keep Sidney close for the next few days, because that woman is dangerous."

25

"Three tickets to Helena, Montana, please."

Sidney glanced around the Sandusky bus depot, attempting to keep a careful watch on her surroundings. It was one of the personal safety tips that Pete Vega had drilled into her mind during the self-defense course he taught at the YMCA. A course Sidney had taken to heart and excelled at.

That course had been the first step in her evolution from victim to warrior, and had done wonders for her self-esteem and her sense of bravery. Both attributes that she never would have attained without first meeting Isaac.

"Your tickets, ma'am."

"Thank you."

She gathered the tickets and walked briskly back to her car, eyes scanning her surroundings the entire way. The sky was just beginning to darken, and she slid behind the wheel with a pounding heart.

"Here. Consider the bus fare my gift."

She handed the tickets to Ann, who sat in the passenger seat. Her children were bundled in the backseat, watching their mother with great curiosity, and Sidney guessed, a fair amount of fear.

"Oh, Sidney, I should pay you. That couldn't have been cheap."

"Nonsense. You need to save your money. You're going to need it, and I know the documents ate a big chunk of what you had."

"My mom gave me more. When I told her what was happening, she gave me several thousand and told me to find a place where we could live safe and happy."

Sidney smiled at her. "That's amazing. I'm happy you got to spend some time with her."

"Me too."

"Now, tell me the plan one more time."

Ann glanced in the backseat at her babies and inhaled a deep breath.

"We take the bus to Helena, Montana, where I buy a used clunker car with cash so that there's no paper trail."

"Then?"

"We drive across the boarder into Calgary, Canada."

"Right. Then?"

"And we live below the radar."

"Next step?"

Ann gave her a blank look, as if she couldn't remember. And Sidney reached up and tugged on one of her own curls.

"Oh, yes! Most important. Change my appearance."

"Yes!"

Ann took another breath, to steady herself, Sidney supposed.

"There are so many details, Sidney. I don't know if I can do this."

"You're a mother, Ann. A good one. I believe you can do anything if it means saving their lives." Sidney gestured to the backseat.

Ann nodded.

"Here."

Sidney handed over the large manila envelope that held their new forged papers, and Ann tucked it safely into her bag.

"One more thing."

"Yes?"

"When you get yourself settled somewhere, find a local self-defense class and throw yourself into it. You'll be surprised what it can do for you."

Ann smiled. "Will it make me an action heroine like you?"

Sidney chuckled. "It might not make you an action hero, but it can bring you all sorts of wonderful things, like confidence, bravery and self-esteem."

Ann nodded. "I'll remember that."

They got out of the car then and made their way inside the terminal to the boarding area. Once they found the right bus, Ann turned around and engulfed Sidney in a bear hug.

"Thank you for everything, Sidney."

"You're welcome, Ann. I mean Angela."

Ann looked at her and smiled.

"Yes. Angela. I always loved that name. Ann is so boring."

"I'll expect a postcard at the shelter in a few months from Angela Mason. Which I will read, savor, and then burn so that there's no trail back to you."

"And then you'll get a message to my mom?"

"As promised."

"Okay." She glanced around. "Looks like we're boarding. Come on, kids. Tell Miss Sidney goodbye."

"Bye, Miss Sidney," the kids said in unison. Then, to Sidney's shock, Laney rushed toward her and wrapped two chubby arms around her knees in the sweetest hug.

"Thank you, Laney. You take care of your mommy, okay? She's going to need your help."

"Okay."

Sidney watched as they boarded the bus and got settled in their seats. She waited and waved them off as the bus pulled away, praying for their safety and success. Then she left the depot and headed back to her car.

Her footsteps echoed on the pavement.

As she crossed the parking lot, the sky grew darker.

Her pace quickened.

She clutched her purse, reassured by the outline of her gun.

She shot a safety glance at the backseat when she slid into her car. Then she locked the doors as soon as she was inside. Starting it up, she hit the 'home' button on the fancy GPS system Isaac had insisted on getting her, and then she pulled out of the lot and headed straight for home.

When she walked into the house just over an hour later, Isaac was pacing the living room.

"Sidney!"

His tone was laced with what Sidney could only call relief. He rushed forward and wrapped his arms around her.

"Isaac? What's wrong?"

"I was getting worried. You're over an hour late. I didn't think you were working so late tonight."

"Well, I wasn't working exactly. I mean, I was, but I wasn't."

"What?"

"It's a long story."

"You're okay?"

"Yes, I'm fine, baby. What's wrong? You seem rattled, Ike."

He sighed and turned around, pacing again.

"I didn't know what to think. And I texted you, but you didn't respond. So I called, and nothing."

"I'm sorry. I didn't get a text or a call." Sidney pulled out her cellphone. "Shit. It's dead. I'm so sorry."

"No, it's okay."

"Ike, did something happen? What is it? Here. Come sit with me."

She took his hand and led him over to the couch.

"What's wrong?"

He let out a heavy sigh, and she ran her fingers through his hair. A move that always seemed to have a calming effect on him. Tonight was no exception. His soft moan was right on cue.

"I had a run in with Natalie Bains today at work. She's on the warpath because I filed a harassment complaint against her with Internal Affairs. So when you were late getting home, and then I couldn't get you on the phone..."

"Oh, baby."

"My mind just went to the darkest places is all. I'm sorry."

"No, don't apologize for worrying about my wellbeing. If you didn't worry, it would mean you didn't care."

He turned his head and kissed her lips.

"I love you, Sidney. You know how much I do care."

"I do know, and I love you back."

"And when that bitch went off on me today..."

He let his sentence dangle, and Sidney knew he was reliving whatever horrible things must've been said.

"Afterwards, Lt. Hayes warned me to keep you close, seeing as we both know how vindictive and obviously off kilter Natalie Bains is."

"And then I go and make myself unreachable for an hour. I'm sorry, Ike."

He placed his hand on hers, lacing their fingers together.

"It's all right. I'm just glad you're home safe and sound." He brought her hand to his lips and kissed it. "So were you working or not? You seemed confused on that point."

Sidney grinned. "Well, I forged ahead with my plans for Ann. The resident who wanted help getting away."

"I see."

"I contacted Mr. O'Dwyer and got what she needed. And tonight, I drove her to a bus depot in Sandusky."

"Sandusky? Why there?"

"One of their lines goes from here to Montana."

"And that's her destination?"

"No. Her destination is a little further north."

"As in across the boarder."

It wasn't exactly a question, but Sidney silently nodded.

"Well, did she get off okay?"

"She did."

"I hope things work out for her."

"Yeah, me too. I'm going to be on pins and needles waiting for word."

"Is she supposed to get word to you?"

"We have a system set up."

Isaac nodded, and Sidney wondered what he was thinking. For a long moment only silence passed between them. Silence and a tension so stiff she could feel the abrasiveness of it on her skin, like sandpaper.

Then Ike looked into her eyes.

"I'm proud of you, darlin'."

Relief washed over her, soothing the sandpaper roughness like water over a sandcastle.

"Really? You're not mad?"

"I'm not mad. I'm in awe of you."

Sidney leaned forward and rested her forehead against his.

"Thank you for being so supportive, Ike. I know you still have big reservations, and that you worry..."

"I'm always going to worry, Sid. But I'm also always going to be in your corner. Always going to be right behind you. Keeping you safe, propping you up, doing whatever you need me to do. I am right here. No matter what."

"I love you."

"I love you."

His lips were soft and firm when they pressed against hers, and Sidney melted into his embrace. Their tongues caressed in a kiss so slow and deep she felt it in every part of her body. They were both breathless when they came up for air.

"Are you hungry? I'm sorry there's no dinner."

"It's okay."

"If you give me a few minutes to get comfortable, I'll order us some takeout."

"I've got a better idea."

Isaac looked at her with a twinkle of mischief in his mysterious light grey eyes, and Sidney couldn't help but smile.

"Oh?"

"Why don't we get our takeout and go back to the beach. We can sit on a bench and watch the waves and the lighthouse. Might give us some more wedding ideas."

Sidney melted again, this time for a wholly different reason.

"I love that idea!"

EPILOGUE

"Where did you find the time to buy all these candles and rose petals, let alone set this dramatically romantic scene?"

Isaac smiled that big, panty-dropping-full-double-dimple smile that always made her insides weak, and glanced around their bedroom assessing his handiwork. Sidney could only giggle at him.

She'd come home from the salon — a reward to herself for the tough two weeks she'd just endured — to find their bedroom set for a seduction, complete with flickering candles, rose petals sprinkled on and around the bed, and chilled sparkling white grape juice at the ready.

Now, they were lying among tangled sheets with the scent of sex and roses still lingering in the air as she softly panted.

"Well, you didn't think I was going to make our first time after our medically induced abstinence a run of the mill occurrence, did you? I mean, not that any time with you is ever run of the mill. But it had to be special. It had to be unforgettable. It had to be romantic."

Sidney caressed his face, and stared up into his mystical eyes.

"Every time with you is special, unforgettable, and romantic, Isaac. You have no idea, do you?"

She could see him searching her eyes as if looking for the truth.

"No idea of what?"

"Of how much you mean to me. Baby, no man has ever loved me the way you do. And I'm not talking about sex. I'm talking about the way you encourage me, and protect me, and lift me up. Your love for me is so pure and true. You worry about me, you fight for me."

Isaac took her hand from his face and kissed her palm.

"And I always will, darlin'. You are my whole world, Sidney. I lived like a hermit or a monk for so many years. In a lot of ways I was afraid of interacting with the world around me. Afraid of being touched or of touching others. Locked inside the prison of my own body. And then you came along and freed me. You freed me, Sidney, and you opened up the world to me. I love you so much."

"I love you back, baby. And I cannot wait to become Mrs. Isaac Taylor."

"Isaac and Sidney Taylor."

"Detective Sgt. and Mrs. Ike Taylor."

"It all has a very nice ring to it, doesn't it?"

"It most certainly does. And it'll be official in less than two months time."

"Can't come soon enough for me."

"No?"

"Hell no. I can't wait to marry you, and raise a family with you, and grow old with you."

"Ooh. Well, that might be a problem."

"What do you mean?"

"Well, I don't plan to grow old. I'm going to grow more fabulous, but I'm not going to get wrinkled and gray."

"Oh, I see. Well that's ok. I'll grow old and gray and wrinkled, and you can be this fabulous, snazzy-dressed, jazzy grandma type with the old geezer of a husband. How's that?"

"Can you imagine being a grandpa someday? Telling our grand-kids all about how we fell in love, and the adventures we had when we first met?"

"I wonder if I'll be teaching one of our grandkids the ins and outs of being a hype, the way my grandad is with me."

"You aren't going to have to go through what Sterling and your dad did. None of our kids are going to be ashamed of your super-powers, baby. I won't allow it. I'll make sure they know how special and important those abilities are."

"Maybe none of our kids will even have the freaky abilities anyway. Then we won't have to worry about it at all."

"Or maybe all of our kids will have your abilities. Did you ever think of that?"

Isaac groaned, and Sidney stared at him.

"Ike, would you really not want to pass your abilities on to our children?"

"Their lives would be much simpler without them, Sidney. You have to realize that."

"Of course I realize that. But simpler isn't always better. Your psychic abilities are what make you unique, baby. And you can do such incredible things. Your abilities saved my life on more than one occasion. I believe that when you've finally mastered them, they will become a source of strength for you, and give you a power like you've never known. Just like what happened with that home invasion guy, and the telekinesis."

"You're startin' to sound like Geneviève now."

Isaac looked into her eyes, and Sidney wondered what he was thinking. He reached out and ran a single finger over her cheek.

"You're so amazing, Sidney."

He changed the subject, and Sidney wasn't going to let him get away with that.

But then his lips touched hers, soft and firm. Their tongues slow danced.

She moaned as his hands roamed her body, caressing her hip, her waist, her breast.

He trailed kisses across her jaw to her earlobe and down her neck.

Sidney touched him everywhere, allowing her hands to travel the taut muscles of his back down to his firm ass, and loving the soft moans of appreciation that move always drew from him.

He'd told her once that feeling her hands on his bare naked flesh was sometimes more orgasmic for him than an actual release, and Sidney loved that her touch had the power to do that to him.

He enveloped her nipple with his mouth, and the warm heat of it seared her skin.

She hissed and arched her back, pressing her breast into his face, silently begging for more.

"I love you, Isaac. I love the way you make love to me."

"Mmm."

It was his only response before he entered her.

Eyes locked together, he filled her completely, and Sidney widened her legs and lifted her hips, adjusting to the sheer size of him.

They stared into each other's eyes for the longest time, never looking away as their bodies moved in concert, writhing together. With every thrust, he pushed her higher, drove her further over the edge.

They went over the cliff of ecstasy as one, moaning out a duet as their bodies sailed through the air.

A single drop of sweat left a strand of his hair and hit her cheek, and Sidney smiled at him.

Isaac lowered his full weight down on top of her, still staring into her eyes. He kissed her lips and grinned.

"I hope we just made a baby."

His sweet words were whispered, and the spark of wonder in his grey eyes twinkled at her. Sidney giggled and ran her fingers through his damp hair.

"So do I."

***

Thank you for reading *Murders & Romance*. If you enjoyed reading the continuing romance between Isaac and Sidney, keep turning the pages to read a fun and sexy passage from book six in the series, *Curses & Vows*, or CLICK HERE to download *Curses & Vows* now!

CURSES & VOWS

Book 6 Sneak Peek

"Isaac?"

"Hey, darlin'. You still up?"

He glanced around the well-appointed guest room and felt nothing but loneliness.

"I'm just crawling into bed now. Not that I'll be able to sleep much. Our bed feels very cold and lonely without you."

"Tell me about it. I feel like a stranger in a strange land over here."

"I'm sure Bree and Adam have done everything they can to make you comfortable in their guest room."

"Oh, they have. And Grandad's just across the hall in the other guest room. But I'm missing your sweet-smelling, soft, warm body. I got nothing to curl up to over here but a pillow, and that is no kind of substitute for you."

Sidney giggled, and sound of it made him smile.

"It's just one night. And think about it... this time tomorrow, you and I will be Mr. and Mrs. You'll be completely stuck with me then."

"I can't wait to be completely and totally stuck with you, forever. But what I'd like to know is who came up with this rule that the bride and groom aren't allowed to see each other the day before the wedding? That's a load of superstitious crap right there."

He could hear the frustration in his own voice, but it couldn't be helped. Sidney laughed at him.

"I've missed you today too, baby. But I think the tradition goes back to when marriages were arranged and the families didn't want the couple to see each other beforehand out of fear they'd back out if they saw who they were marrying. Terrifying prospect if you ask me."

"Aw, hell. And here we are, a hundred years later, still suffering 'cause they weren't allowed to choose for themselves? Forget that, I'm coming home."

"Isaac! You can't."

"Well, why the hell not? It's not like it's actually bad luck or anything."

"How do you know that? And after everything that's already gone wrong with this wedding, and the unwelcome family surprises? I just don't want to tempt fate, or... you know... piss it off."

Isaac's righteous indignation deflated like she'd popped his bubble with a giant spitball.

"It's just one night, baby. And think about how much sweeter tomorrow night will be when we're finally married and alone, and on our way to... wherever our honeymoon is."

Isaac laughed out loud.

"Nice try, darlin', but I'm still not telling you where we're going."

"But I don't even know if I've packed the right things, Ike! You could at least give me a hint."

"I did give you a hint. I told you that all you really need is a bikini and a toothbrush. Mostly just the toothbrush, 'cause I don't expect to let you leave the room too often."

Sidney's sexy giggle connected with his dick, and he stifled a groan.

"So, since you're making me endure this torture of sleeping without you tonight, I was wondering..."

His voice trailed off as he wondered exactly how to ask this question. He had no clue how men actually set these things up.

"Yes?"

"Well, do you remember back when we first got together? Um, back when I was still very awkward about... well, about sex and being intimate, and all that?"

"Yes."

He could hear the curiosity in her voice, and it only made him more nervous. He licked his lips and softly cleared his throat before trying again.

"Well, you said that if there was ever anything that I wanted to try, I should just tell you?"

"Isaac, is there something special you're wanting to try when we're on our honeymoon?"

"Well actually..."

"Maybe a little anal play perhaps?"

Heart stopped.

Thoughts gone.

Words forgotten.

"A... a little what now?"

Had she said those words, or had he imagined them? Was she still talking?

"...I mean, I've never done that before, but I know you're really kind of an ass man, and I think..."

"Sidney, stop. Talking. Please. I-I can't think when you say things like that."

Her soft, sexy laughter only made things worse, and he repositioned the wood between his legs.

"Isaac, you're not being bashful right now, are you?"

"A little. I mean, this isn't exactly a normal conversation. And that's not what I was getting at, although now it's all I can think about."

Sidney laughed even harder.

"So, what were you getting at then?"

"Well, I was hinting at... you know... phone sex."

"Ohhh!"

"Yeah."

"Well, do you want to know what I'm wearing?"

Her voice was suddenly breathy and hyper-sexy, and Isaac just had to laugh. And he was certain that was the wrong response.

"What's funny? I'm trying to start the phone sex conversation here."

"How do you switch gears like that so quickly? Doesn't anything ever faze you, darlin'?"

"Only scary bad things. But stuff like this? Sexy, secret stuff between you and me? That doesn't faze me one bit, Isaac. Why should I be embarrassed or shy with you, baby? You're the man I love, the man I want to share all of me with, body and soul. I want to do everything I can to give you physical pleasure. Especially knowing that you were deprived of it for so long. Tell me what you want, and I'll do my best to give it to you."

Isaac swallowed and wished like hell that they were together.

"God, I wish we were in the same house right now. Are you sure you won't let me come home? Not even for a few hours? No one will even know but you and me."

Sidney laughed at him, and Isaac grinned.

"Baby?"

"Yes, darlin'?"

"What are you wearing?"

JOIN LASHELL'S FACEBOOK READER GROUP

Want to get the scoop (like blurbs, release dates, cover reveals, etc.) on all of Lashell's newest books before anyone else? Want dibs on being the first to read and review her latest releases? Want to hang out and ask her questions about her books, or join a community of other readers to discuss favorite characters and plot points? Then joining her Facebook Reader Group is the way to do it! Click the link below to join.

https://www.facebook.com/groups/853329598037117/

ACKNOWLEDGMENTS

Cover Design by Sonia Freitas of
www.chloebellearts.com

ABOUT THE AUTHOR

Lashell Collins is an American author of romantic suspense, paranormal romance, and rockstar romance. She walks to the beat of her own drum, but that's okay 'cause she's got a pretty good sense of rhythm. Basically, she's a geeky, quirky, laid-back, rocker-loving kinda girl who's married to a retired cop, motorcycle-riding, bad-boy alpha all her own, and she likes to write about sexy werewolves, rockstars or police officers, or some inventive combination of the three. Between her book characters and the ones she knows in real life, her plate stays pretty full. But she loves to hear from readers, so connect with her in the following ways:

Newsletter Sign-up:
http://www.lashellcollins.com/newsletter
Website:
http://lashellcollins.com

ALSO BY LASHELL COLLINS

Jagged Ivory Series **(Rockstar Romance)**

Jagged Hearts

Jagged Dreams

Jagged Addiction

Jagged Secrets

Jagged Surrender

Kelly Family Series **(Romantic Suspense)**

Ethan: A Kelly Family Novella

Storm: A Kelly Family Novella

Frankie: A Kelly Family Novella

Marina: A Kelly Family Novella

Where There's Smoke: A Kelly Family Novel

The Smoking Gun: A Kelly Family Novel

Lunar Falls Trilogy **(Paranormal Romance)**

Secrets of Lunar Falls

Lies of Lunar Falls

Redemption of Lunar Falls

Exiled: A Lunar Falls Novella

Rock Shifter Fairytales **(Paranormal/Rockstar Romance)**

Soul Stealer

Lion Tamer

She Wolf

The Raven

Rogue Moon Series **(Paranormal Romance)**

Rogue Moon

Fated Moon

True Romance Series **(Rockstar Romance)**

True Romance

All Fired Up

Isaac Taylor Mysteries **(Romantic Suspense)**

Voices & Visions

Lovers & Monsters

Freaks & Family Legacies

Lullabies & Dead Bodies

Printed in Great Britain
by Amazon